THE MIRROR OF N'DE

THE MIRROR OF N'DE

L. K. MALONE

Kregel
Publications

The Mirror of N'de: A Novel

© 2011 by L. K. Malone

Published by Kregel Publications, a division of Kregel, Inc., P.O. Box 2607, Grand Rapids, MI 49501.

Cover art and interior map are by Ryan Hill. The map is based on an ancient Babylonian map of the world, circa 600 BC.

Library of Congress Cataloging-in-Publication Data

ISBN 978-0-8254-2667-4

Printed in the United States of America

11 12 13 14 15 / 5 4 3 2 1

To my beloved father,
whose challenging discussions and hard
questions made me think, and whose unyielding
love and support made me feel safe.
I'll always love you, Daddy.

And to my stepdad,
whose values and grace were an inspiration.

I was blessed to have you both in my life.

NAMES

Aa'mash (ah-MAHSH) – *f., Ramash initiate*

Abarak (ah-BAR-ack) – *groundsmaster*

Alila Rakam (ah-LEE-lah RAY-khahm) – *friend of Hadlay, Nomish's sister*

Anak (eh-NAHK) – *Nafalin son of a Nafal prince*

Apoc Sutram (ah-POKE suh-TRAHM) – *Ba'ar's father*

Arba (ehr-BAH) – *Nafalin son of a Nafal prince*

Asb'el (azb-EL) – *Nafal prince*

Asinus (AS-ih-nus, like *asinine*) – *Overlord of the Lawgivers*

Aurum (OUR-oom) – *Overlord of the Treasury*

Avakh (AH-vekh) – *woman in the Mirror of N' de story*

Ayom (ah-YOM) – *Zêr-Shungalli's cupbearer*

Azazel (as-ah-ZAYL) – *Nafal prince*

Ba'ar Sutram (bah-AHR suh-TRAHM) – *f., Oresed initiate*

Blodeuwedd (blod-EYE-wed) – *one of Zêru's creatures*

Bonobos (buh-NO-bows) – *Overlord of Science*

Brecho (BREH-kho) – *master of the plumbing*

Buthotos (boo-THOUGH-toes) – *Overlord of Security*

Citna (kit-NA, as in sad) – *f., Oresed initiate*

Daram Rakam (DAH-rem RAY-khahm) – *Nomish and Alila's father*

Emah (ay-MAH) – *Nafalin prince*

Enheduana (en-hed-oo-AH-na) – *also* Ummi Ekleti

Fa'an (fah-AHN) – *f., Ramash initiate*

Gader'el (GAHD-er-el) – *Nafal prince*

Gibor (gih-BOR) – *Nafalin son of a Nafal prince*

Glenelg (glen-elg) – *Ramash friend of Hadlay's mother*

Hadlay Mivana (HAHD-lay MEE-vah-nah) – *f., Ramash initiate*

Iaras Mivana (YAR-as MEE-vah-nah) – *Hadlay's mother*

Igigi (ee-JEE-jee) – *also "the powers"*

Kasadya (kuh-SOD-yah) – *Nafal prince*

Kayshti (KAYSH-ti) – *m., Ramash initiate at the Tower, twin to Ma'at*

Kera Rakam (KEER-ah RAY-khahm) – *Alila and Nomish's mother*

Khalam (KHAHL-em) – *clever and powerful people ruled by Meshah*

La'ag (lah-AHG) – *old Ramash man*

Lelyeh (LEYL-yeh) – *leader of the Khalam*

Ma'at (mah-AHT) – *f., Ramash initiate*

Mada (MAHD-ah) – *man in the Mirror of N'de story*

Magira (mah-GEER-ah) – *chief cook in the Tower*

Marba Mivana (MAR-ba MEE-vah-nah) – *Hadlay's father*

Meshah (MAY-shah) – *powerful King in story of N'de*

Nabu (nah-BOO) – *Babylonian god of wisdom and writing*

Nafal (nah-FALL) – *giant, terrifying warriors*

Nafalin (nah-fall-EEN) – *mixes of human and Nafal*

N'de (nuh-DAY) – *city built by Meshah for the Shee*

Nemat (neh-MAHT) – *Oresed friend of Ba'ar*

Nomish Rakam (NOE-mish RAY-khahm) – *friend of Hadlay, brother of Alila*

Og (OGE, as in *owe*) – *Nafalin son of a Nafal prince*

Ogret (OGE-ret) – *mistress of the scullery*

Oren Sutram (OWE-ren suh-TRAHM) – *brother of Ba'ar*

Oresed (OWE-re-sed) – *ruling class of people in Turris*

Pinim'e (PEE-nim-eh) – *Nafal prince*

Raimog (RAY-mowg) – *f., Ramash initiate*

Ramash (RAY-mahsh) – *oppressed tribe of peasants*

Rasab (RAH-sahb) – *m., Ramash initiate*

Refa (REH-fah) – *terrifying shades that feed on souls*

Remesh (ray-MESH) – *"dregs"*

Rezen (REH-zen) – *f., Ramash initiate*

Sfika (SFEE-kah) – *Overlord of the Tower*

Shee (SHEE) – *plain people ruled by Meshah*

Shungallu (shoon-GALL-oo) – *emperor of Turris*

Sirach (seh-RAKH) – *also* the Atheling *and* the Being

Tahat (tah-HAHT) – *f., Oresed initiate*

Turran (TOO-ran) – *citizen of Turris*

Turris (TOO-ris) – *city*

Ummi Ekleti (OO-mi EHK-let-EE) – *female occupant of dungeon*

Viridesc (veer-ee-DESK) – *former Overlord of the Treasury*

Yeqon (yeh-CONE) – *Nafal prince*

Zamzom (ZAHM-zohm) – *Overlord of Mysteries*

Zêr-Shungalli (ZEHR shoon-GALL-ee) *or* Zêru (ZEHR-oo) – *son of the emperor*

Ziz (ZEEZ) – *Nafalin son of a Nafal prince*

MAP OF HADLAY'S WORLD

The Being

*H*adlay Mivana opened her eyes, and fought a momentary panic. Where was she? This was not home. She was in a room, the strangest room she'd ever seen, with walls of glowing stone. She turned full circle, but saw no doors, no windows. No way out. She was trapped!

But then, set in the farthest wall, the stones began to shimmer. To change into a mirror unlike any she had seen. Its surface was smooth as standing water, clear as air itself. She walked to it, thinking if she touched it, her hand would go clean through. But when she tried, the mirror hardened.

She could not say how she knew, but she was certain that something she needed, something dearer than her own parents, lay beyond this mirror. And as its surface hardened, she felt a stab of grief. Whatever the mirror hid, her very soul longed to see it. She shoved, but the mirror would not give.

A sob wrenched up from her chest, and she pounded the mirror, trying to break through. She struck it, kicked it, then flung herself against it, to no avail. Exhausted, bruised, she dropped to her knees and wept. As her tears fell, the reflection in the mirror shifted, until the image she saw was no longer her own.

What—or who—he was, she could not say. But his beauty made her tremble. His form was like a very fine horse, but he glowed as if lit from within by a pure white light, and his movements rippled with the colors of a rainbow. He had wings of flame, and when they stroked the air, she could feel their warmth. His forehead bore a marking, like three gold rings intertwined.

Whatever he was, she wanted to look at him forever.

"You have not known me." His voice flowed around her, refreshing as a cool evening breeze. "But I have loved you since the dawn of time."

"Who are you?" she wanted to ask, but her lips could not form the words.

The Being (it seemed wrong to call him a creature) stepped closer, his eyes liquid and warm. "Choose me as I have chosen you, and I will give you all your heart desires."

What did he mean? She wanted desperately to please him, but how? And why would he choose her? No one like this, so beautiful and perfect, would ever wish to know a lowly girl like her.

He seemed to see her doubt, for his eyes turned silvery with tears, and his image began to vanish.

"No!" Hadlay screamed, pressing her face against the mirror. "No, please! Don't leave me!"

His voice now came to her as a whisper. "There is a key that will bring you to me, but you must first take hold of it."

"Key? What key? Where can I find it?"

The voice faded even more. "Listen well, little love: On this day, your laughter will give way to dread. When this takes place, you will begin to grasp the key . . ."

⚘

"Hadlay Mivana!" Her mother shook her shoulder until she stirred. "Out of bed, lazybones! It is the fourth time I have called you. The sky is light!"

Hadlay rolled away from her mother's hand. She did not want to wake. Her eyes, wet with tears, did not want to open. She hugged her pillow, pressing deeper into its softness. She wanted to go back, back to that room, that mirror, back to *him*. Who was he?

"Choose me . . ." he had said. But how could she choose him?

"*Hadlay!*" Her mother's rebuke shattered her reflection. "Did you not agree to begin your apprenticeship at the Rakams' shop this morn? You have looked for this day since you were old enough for sandals, and now you're late!"

Hadlay's heart did a little flip as she remembered. Today she became an initiate, beginning her journey to adulthood. She could try to return to her dream tonight. But this day was important!

She scrambled out of her bed, a wool-filled mat on the floor in a quiet corner of her home, and stretched her arms above her head to loose the knots in her muscles. She had expected to be changed, somehow, upon reaching this day. It was a little disappointing that she felt no different.

Her mother poured water into a wooden washing basin. Slight and favored with a kind face, deep blue eyes, and a thick plait of light brown hair that dropped to her waist, Iaras Mivana was clearly of the Ramash people, a tribe of peasants deemed worthy of only the most servile tasks. But she carried herself with quiet dignity. Only the fine wrinkles carving themselves between her brows spoke of her fears and worries. She cast a reproving eye at yesterday's clothes, which were still on the floor beside Hadlay's bed.

Hadlay hurried to gather them up.

"Your best tunic," Iaras said with no little frustration, holding out her arms to receive them. "I had hoped you would clean and hang it for work today, but now you'll have to wear the other."

For a day as portentious as this, Hadlay wanted to look her best, and the other tunic was not nearly as nice. But she bit back the argument. She cared little if the clothing she wore was a bit dusty and wrinkled, but many arguments had taught her that Iaras Mivana cared a great deal.

"I'll not call you again." Her mother closed the curtain that separated Hadlay's sleeping space from the rest of their tiny home.

Hadlay washed quickly and positioned herself before a bit of polished tin that reflected her image. She could not help comparing it to the mirror in her dream. This was so hazy, so blurry. So imperfect. But then, so was she.

She was often told she resembled her mother, though she herself did not see it. She disliked the liberal dusting of freckles on her nose and cheeks, and her hair was paler than her mother's, marking her even more as Ramash. Oresed children pulled her hair and taunted her, and she often wished she looked more . . . well, like them.

She had mentioned this to her mother once, and regretted it instantly. Her mother's eyes had filled with tears, and she'd drawn Hadlay into a tight hug. "It is no shame to be Ramash. Nor to look it. Never let anyone tell you otherwise."

It may be no shame, Hadlay thought, making a face at her reflection, but it was no honor, either. Not in Turris.

"I don't hear you dressing!" Her mother's reminder brushed aside her reflections like cobwebs.

Eyeing her hair critically in the mirror, Hadlay did her best to imitate her mother's even plait. Despite all her efforts, some curls sprang free, and no amount of spit would smooth them. She bound off the braid with disgust, wondering why she bothered. She hastily donned a frayed, slate-blue tunic with its matching girdle, then pulled open the curtain and entered the main room.

Her family's home was sparsely furnished. A three-legged table sat in the center of the room, with two squat stools beneath. The walls had recently been replastered with fresh mud, and looked less weathered than usual. Hadlay's father had rigged a reed thatch roof that could be raised in the daytime to admit light, so they needed candles only at night. A carved wood chair, their one good piece, sat beside her mother's loom.

Hadlay glanced up to the loft where her parents slept, then at the stable, which took up the south wall of the house, with a half wall to keep the horse from invading the family area. Her father was already gone.

Iaras gave her an apologetic smile. "He said to tell you he would be with you in spirit tonight. He wanted to stay for the ritual, but you know we can't afford even a day's delay. Other traders would pick off the good finds if they arrived at the markets first." The unspoken worry in her mother's blue eyes made Hadlay's stomach tighten.

As a slave who had won his freedom, Marba Mivana had found it difficult to gain employment in the city, and had turned to more dangerous work. Only a very few, hardy men were willing to venture past the outer wall that encircled the fields where the city's crops were grown. The desert beyond was infested with monsters and Refa, terrifying shades that fed upon the soul like leeches, gripping the mind with confusion and fear. Hadlay's father braved these deadly foes to trade with the Nomads, the wild marauders of the desert.

Hadlay put on a brave smile and touched her mother's arm. "He'll be all right."

Iaras sighed and gave a tight smile in return. "I only wish he didn't have to risk it."

But it was that or face the slavers again. As it was they barely had enough to pay the rent.

At least, as of today, Hadlay would finally begin to earn her keep. She would receive little, but perhaps enough to help.

Iaras scraped the last bits of meat from a bone and dropped them into a kettle filled with fat drippings and vegetables from the garden. They had to make do with scraps from the butcher, but Hadlay's father vowed that the meat that clung to the bone was best anyway. "Remind the Rakams they are invited for evening meal."

Hadlay grinned, forgetting her worries for the moment. "And the Final Telling." Oh, she had looked forward to this evening for all her years!

Her mother handed her a piece of cheese and a crust of barley bread, tipping up Hadlay's chin with a finger. "Work hard, now! I don't want to hear you've been slacking."

A Near Miss

Ringed by walls fifty cubits high, the city of Turris boasted a looming tower along its southern boundary. Made of kiln-baked brick and bitumen for mortar, the Tower ascended to the clouds and cast the city in its shadow for much of the day. The position of the shadow told the time of day. She was indeed quite late. Finishing her cheese, Hadlay rucked up the long skirt of her tunic and ran.

As she crossed the river that divided the city, her surroundings changed from the small, clustered mud homes of the cramped Ramash sector to sprawling houses of whitewashed brick and tile that became grander and taller as she went. Here lived the Oresed, enjoying ease and luxury, fed and clothed by Ramash labor.

She dashed round a corner without looking and was nearly bowled down by a running man.

His head was shaved, leaving only a single, pale lock at the top of his head, tied into a knot that distinguished him as a Ramash slave. "Hide— quickly!" he whispered, scrambling away from her.

She barely had time to squeeze into a doorway before a furious Oresed man pounded around the corner. The man wore the gray tunic of the Tower service and carried the seal of lawgiver in his hand. An authority! Hadlay shrank even farther into her niche, wishing she could become invisible.

The man shouted a strange word, and the slave stopped running. Or, more accurately, he continued to run, but it did no good. His feet now paddled uselessly in the air, as if something had grasped him by his collar and lifted him from the ground.

Another Oresed hurried up, breathing hard. "That's him, sire! That's the slave who escaped—and he took my gold shekels!"

Hadlay cringed for the slave's sake. Escaped slaves were usually just returned to their masters for punishment, but thievery was another thing.

The authority spoke again, and the slave was turned upside down and shaken. There was a clink as a gold ring clattered to the street. Hadlay stifled a protest; the ring hardly weighed a shekel. No doubt the Oresed was exaggerating his loss to see that the slave received a greater punishment.

The Oresed snatched up the ring. "This is one of them, sire, but there was another."

Hadlay glanced down and was horrified to see the other ring by her doorway. It must have fallen when the slave had run into her. If they found it there, they would find her too, and there would be no telling them that she was not involved.

"*Turrershu!*" the authority shouted, and the man was shaken again, even harder than before. "Where is it?"

Thinking quickly, Hadlay reached out from her hiding place and picked up the ring, then flung it as hard as she could toward the unfortunate slave. It clinked beneath his head, which swung dangerously near the hard earth. She felt a twinge of guilt at adding to the evidence against him, but the first was enough to convict. Slaves could not even claim to own the clothing on their backs, and certainly no Ramash, free or slave, possessed gold rings of any weight. Her people bartered with goods and services.

"There it is!" The accuser pointed.

Hadlay used the distraction to slip from her hiding place. As she edged around the corner, she cast one final, guilty look at the slave, now lying on the ground, struggling as if pinned by a dreadful weight. He would be taken to the Tower's dungeon to wait for sentencing at next Midweek Gathering. She didn't want to think what punishment he'd face.

A chill swept her at the sudden thought that she might one day be in his sandals. Shivering, she hurried on, more careful now to look before she stepped around each corner.

A Ziggurat with a Head

Most vendors were already open for business by the time Hadlay reached the row of shops and stands that made up the city's marketplace. Forgetting her caution, she raced the last distance to the shop managed by the parents of her best friends, Alila and Nomish Rakam.

The shop was stocked with items both practical and exotic: sturdy crocks and other cookware, beaded headdresses, vibrant bolts of cloth, slippers of the softest kidskin. The slippers had been purchased from Hadlay's father, who had obtained several pairs from a tribe of Nomads that excelled in leatherwork. Shelves lined the thin walls of the shop, and tables sat in neat rows through the center.

"It is good my parents are off trading," Alila chided as Hadlay rushed in. "Or we would have to dock you at least an omer of grain."

"What kept you?" Nomish's eyes brightened as he saw her.

Alila was a quiet girl with bronze-colored hair and moss-green eyes. Nomish was tall, with hands and feet that spoke of growth yet to come, and hair the color of flame. He was nearly ten moons older than his sister. Still, because midsummer had passed before his birth, they were entering initiation at the same time.

Hadlay's friends looked unlike the Ramash, but unlike the Oresed also. When Hadlay had once asked where they had gotten their hair, Nomish had winked and said it was rumored there was Nomad in their blood. Alila had later confided that, in truth, their grandmother was half Oresed, the by-blow of an Oresed noble and a Ramash servant. Of course, no Oresed would own the kinship.

"I had a strange dream." Hadlay took the broom Alila offered her. "It was difficult to wake from it." As she swept, Hadlay told them about it, more to pass the time than anything. But as she spoke, she felt drawn in again. She could still feel the warmth of the Being's flaming wings, see the kindness of his eyes.

"Do you suppose this dream has meaning?" Alila asked.

"Pah!" Nomish said. "Dreams are merely reflections of our thoughts and experiences. They have no meaning."

Alila rolled her eyes. "Pay him no mind, Hadlay. He jibbers like that horrid dung-throwing monkey your father bought on his last journey."

Nomish's face went red as a pomegranate, and he beat a hasty retreat behind a curtain to the rear of the shop.

There had been no formal offer, but everyone assumed that before their initiation was over, Nomish and Hadlay would become betrothed. As a younger girl, Hadlay had hated the idea; Nomish was an irritating older brother, making mischief on Alila and Hadlay. But in recent moons, she had grown to like him well enough. Besides, she knew of no one else who'd want her; she had nothing of value to bring to a new family.

She was sweeping near the door when it opened, and two large feet tracked through the dust she'd carefully piled. Another pair of feet followed and tracked it further.

"I saw you thunder down the street earlier, Hadlay," came an imperious voice she knew only too well. "Has no one ever taught you how to behave among your betters?"

Hadlay gritted her teeth and bowed before her two least-favorite people, Ba'ar Sutram and her friend, Nemat.

Ba'ar was nearly a head taller than Hadlay, and beautiful in the Oresed way, with glossy raven hair loose over her shoulders and glittering obsidian eyes set in a smooth, oval face. Today she wore a white tunic with blue-green embroidery, and a hammered gold headband. Ba'ar's only flaws were hands and feet far outsized for her frame. She wore no rings or bracelets and only black kid slippers to keep attention from these imperfections. Hadlay sometimes stared at them, knowing it annoyed her.

Nemat, though somewhat better dressed, was ill-favored with uneven dark eyes, a pug nose, and a chin that barely interrupted the slope between her mouth and neck. Were she not as unmannerly as Ba'ar, Hadlay might have felt a bit more kindly toward her. She often pitied the way Nemat trailed after her friend like a hungry pup, lapping up any attention that was spared her.

Ba'ar sniffed delicately, wrinkling her nose. "Honestly, you people smell like you live in stables. Oh, wait—you do!"

Nemat gave an obliging titter.

Hadlay gritted back the retort that came to mind. Ba'ar Sutram's parents owned many homes in the Ramash sector, including Hadlay's, and the Mivanas could barely afford the rent as it was.

Alila hurried to them, her eyes downcast as was proper. "Do you require assistance, mistress?"

Ba'ar made a shooing gesture. "We will call if your services are needed." She glanced down and kicked at the dust she had spread about, scattering it even more. "If this is the best you can do with a broom, Hadlay, don't ask for work as a servant at my house."

As if she would ever! Hadlay set to work again, sweeping with such force she sent up little puffs. Her mother had told her many times to pay Ba'ar no mind, but Hadlay did not see how this was possible. Alila gave her a sympathetic grimace and went back to her task. No one knew why Ba'ar loved to single Hadlay out for this harassment, but it had been so since they were small.

The two Oresed girls passed slowly along the tables, picking up various items and casting them down again. It seemed to Hadlay they were intentionally putting them in the wrong spots. She and Alila would have a time of it setting things right again.

A cough caught Hadlay's attention, and she looked up to see Nomish gesturing her to join him behind the counter. She swept the dust outside, brushing it away from the door, then went around the counter.

Nomish made a show of teaching Hadlay how to record a sale, pressing figures on a soft clay tablet. But the words he wrote had nothing to do with sales.

See that bird in the cage beside the entry?

Hadlay glanced up and noticed for the first time a small, stick cage hanging from a chain attached to one of the roof beams. In it was a brilliant green bird, with a hooked beak and red patches on his head and wings.

Father bought it from a Nomad trader, Nomish noted. *It is a most talented creature. It mimics things it hears, and I've taught it something special.* After making a show of pointing out a few features of the sales record, he suggested that Hadlay practice with a fresh tablet, leaving her with a good vantage of the shop. He turned away and set to work stocking a shelf behind the counter.

Soon after, Ba'ar wandered near the cage, and Nomish emitted a little hiss, though he continued to look busy.

The bird gave forth a sharp flatulent noise, like the one Hadlay had once heard slip from her father after he'd eaten cabbage. She fought back a giggle and pretended to be absorbed with her work as Ba'ar whirled, looking for the source of the sound. Nemat, who was some distance away, glanced at her, but seemed to decide that discretion was called for and returned to her shopping.

After a moment, Ba'ar went back to what she was doing. Nomish waited a little while, then made a small wiggling movement with his fingers.

This time, the bird erupted with a noisy, protracted belch. Hadlay had to hide her giggle in a fit of coughing.

Ba'ar turned again, looking about for the source of the noise. When she saw Nemat was staring, she flushed indignantly. "That was not me!"

Nemat quickly averted her face, but Hadlay saw her efforts to conceal a smile.

Just then, Ba'ar's younger brother, Oren, entered the shop. "Pity us, Ba'ar!" he said, loudly enough that even passersby on the street turned to hear him. "That frog-call startled a dog two streets away! What on earth did you eat this morning?"

Hadlay ducked her head, pretending to be absorbed with the receipts. Her eyes stung with tears as she bit her lip to keep from laughing aloud. A muffled noise behind the shelves told her that Nomish was fighting a similar battle.

Ba'ar's face turned nearly as red as Nomish's hair, and, after a moment of searching for an explanation for a noise that clearly came from her area and nowhere else, she huffed and flounced out of the store, her brother trailing close behind. Nemat stood back a moment, struggling to compose herself before she followed.

Hadlay and her friends waited until they were well down the street, then exploded with pent-up laughter.

"Ba'ar scowled so hard I thought her face would shrivel like a fig!" Tears streamed down Nomish's face.

"And poor Nemat! She could not decide whether to laugh or pretend she was deaf!" Hadlay said. "But Oren coming in like that was the best of it!"

Alila opened her mouth to add something, but then she froze. Her face paled and her smile vanished. Hadlay followed Alila's stare, and her stomach knotted.

Asinus, Overlord of the Lawgivers, stood in the entry. Judging by his thunderous scowl, he must have witnessed everything. Of all the authorities to happen upon this prank, Asinus was the one they all feared most.

The overlord waddled between the tables with some difficulty, for his hips were wider than the aisle. He always wore grand black woolen tunics with elaborate, many-fringed mantles and a cylindrical helmet that came to a point. Hadlay's father had once said the man looked like a ziggurat with a head. Asinus's round face might be mistaken for jolly if not for the thick, black brows, which shaded hawkish eyes, and his pouting lips that looked moist as if he had just gnawed off a greasy bite of meat.

The three friends dropped their eyes, for it was never wise to stare at an authority, particularly an overlord. They waited.

Asinus allowed the silence to stretch to the point of breaking before he spoke. "Surely you know it is illegal for the Ramash to make sport of their betters."

Previous encounters with Asinus had persuaded them that any answer would only increase his rage, so Hadlay and her friends kept their silence.

"You have violated the laws of Shungallu! I have repeatedly warned you that our emperor is an all-powerful *wizard*." He said the word with a terrible reverence. "Even though he is far away, nothing escapes his watchful eye. You should *tremble* at the thought of offending him!" He punched the counter for emphasis, and Hadlay flinched. "Even the Nafal fear his wrath, and yet you have the audacity to laugh! You *remesh!*" He spat the word with revulsion. Like many Oresed, Asinus called Hadlay's people *remesh*—a slight variation on the word *Ramash*, but this word meant "dregs," the worthless, bitter gunk left at the bottom of a wine barrel after the good drink was consumed.

"Were it up to me, you would all be cast out to the mercies of the desert. However, His Majesty has seen fit—" He stopped short, as if thinking better of what he had meant to say. A thunderous silence followed as he blotted his sweating forehead with his sash. Then, clearing his throat, he continued. "Since you are minding this shop by yourselves, I must conclude that you are initiates, old enough to pay for your infraction. You will appear at Gathering this midweek to receive a purgation."

Hadlay's stomach did a little flip.

"It was my fault!" Nomish startled them all with his outburst. "Hadlay and Alila did not know what I was doing."

"Laughing at an Oresed's humiliation is crime enough. They are equally guilty."

Hadlay squeezed Nomish's arm, signaling him to speak no more. Another word might bring worse than a purgation.

Asinus turned and stalked away, pausing at the door to spear each of them with an ominous glare. "Do not fail to appear at Midweek Gathering."

BECOMING A BETTER PERSON

The stew was delicious, Iaras," Mrs. Rakam said. "I hope you'll give me your recipe for the bread." She pushed away her empty platter and adjusted her position.

No doubt she was uncomfortable. The Mivanas' table was much too small for company, so the two families sat on straw mats arranged in a circle on the floor, with a lamp to light their conversation.

"Thank you, Kera. I'll teach it to Hadlay and she can share it with you at the shop tomorrow."

As the pleasantries continued, Alila shot Hadlay a meaningful look and directed a small nod at their parents.

Hadlay shook her head slightly and frowned. Why did *she* have to be the one to tell their parents about their encounter with Asinus?

Seeing their silent argument, Nomish scooped up a last mouthful of stew with a piece of flatbread, then launched into the story of the day's mischief. At the description of the belching bird, Hadlay thought she saw her mother's eyes sparkle with repressed humor.

Daram Rakam snorted when Nomish recounted what Asinus had said to them. He was a tall, lean man, and the source of his children's irreverent sense of mischief. "'Violated the laws of Shungallu,' hah! That pompous bullfrog makes up laws to suit himself. This one he made when old man La'ag laughed at him after he tripped over his own staff and sprawled into a pile of compost."

Hadlay and Alila broke into giggles at the image, but were quelled by a fierce look from Mrs. Rakam.

A round-faced woman with an ample figure and flaming hair, Kera Rakam seemed always to be restraining the high spirits of her husband and children. "Hush, Daram. I'll not have our children disrespecting authorities."

Mr. Rakam winked when his wife stopped looking.

"Um . . ." Alila spoke quietly, forcing everyone to be very still to hear her. "What kind of purgation do you think he'll make us do?"

Iaras exchanged a glance with Mrs. Rakam that did nothing to calm Hadlay's fears, then gave them a tight smile. "It won't be so bad. Every one of us here has endured at least one purgation. They are difficult, but you get through them."

"Nothing to be afraid of," Mr. Rakam said. "No Ramash attains adulthood without at least one to his credit."

"What your father means to say"—Mrs. Rakam shot a glare at her husband—"is that everyone makes mistakes. It is the mark of an adult to learn to atone for them."

Hadlay's mother rose to get some oil for the lamp, which was growing dim. It was only for company that the lamp was even used. Oil was expensive, and the Mivanas usually made do with tallow candles. "It is even better to make it right. The three of you should offer Ba'ar your apologies."

Hadlay groaned. "But Mother! Ba'ar is a horrid girl. You've seen how she treats me! And the purgation will be punishment enough."

"An apology is not a punishment, Hadlay." Her mother relit the lamp and returned the remaining oil to its storage place near the stable. "This is an opportunity to become a better person."

Hadlay ground her teeth. "Becoming a better person" usually meant doing something odious, like tending the neighbor boy when he ate a slime mold and got the vomits. Now it meant apologizing to that screech owl Ba'ar. Sometimes growing up sounded perfectly awful.

"Come on, enough gloom." Mr. Rakam gave them an infectious grin. "It will be over before you know it."

"Consider it a valuable lesson," Mrs. Rakam said. "As adults, you'll have to think about the consequences of your actions. Especially as you deal with Oresed."

"What your mother means is it's well and good to have fun, just be careful who sees you have it," Mr. Rakam said, earning another glare from his wife.

Alila shifted and made a little sound that meant she had another question.

"Yes, dear?" Mr. Rakam asked.

"Do . . . do you think it's true what Asinus said about Emperor Shungallu?" Alila's eyes darted between her parents. "Does he truly know everything we do?"

Now that Hadlay thought about it, the idea bothered her too.

Mr. Rakam rolled his eyes. "If he did, he would have struck me dead long ago."

"I wouldn't discount it so easily." Mrs. Rakam gave a little shiver. "Shungallu has been the emperor of Turris for as long as anyone can remember. My grandparents told me he was emperor when they were children, and their grandparents before them. It is said that he can appear and vanish at will and hurl objects without touching them."

"Pah!" Mr. Rakam snapped his fingers. "The authorities can hurl things, and they aren't all-knowing. Besides, no one has seen the emperor in generations. He's dead, long dead by now."

"Some say that the emperor is kin to the Nafal. And it is known that they live longer than we do," Mrs. Rakam said. "The one called Gader'el oversaw the foundation of this city many generations ago, and he is still seen from time to time."

The room went silent for a moment. The Nafal were giant, terrifying warriors, more than twice the height of men. It was said that just two of them could destroy a city overnight. They came to Turris sometimes, and when they did, even the authorities scattered to avoid them. Hadlay had encountered one when she was small, and she could still feel the piercing chill of his gaze.

"Well, if the emperor does exist, where is he?" Mr. Rakam asked. "All we see are the overlords, and I am weary of their claims that they serve a greater power. They serve themselves, more like, and the emperor is just a great scarecrow meant to frighten us so we won't fight back."

Hadlay sensed that he would have liked to say more, but the look he received from Kera stilled his tongue.

"Nomish, would you like more stew?" Hadlay's mother asked, watching him swirl a piece of flatbread in his empty bowl. Second helpings were another rarity in the Mivana household, but no guest ever left their table hungry. Even if it meant the family would not eat again for days.

"Thank you, Mrs. Mivana. This is wonderful." Nomish received an extra portion for his compliment. The way he ate, Hadlay wondered if Nomish had a second stomach, like the great horned beast her father had brought home and butchered for an Oresed customer after his last journey.

Nomish began to say something, but seeing his mother's cocked eyebrow, he dutifully swallowed before he spoke. "Overlord Bonobos says the emperor has been visiting holdings in distant lands for many ages. Bonobos also says he is not a *magical* wizard, but simply an exceedingly wise man who found the scientific ways to harness the elements. Perhaps he found a way to harness age as well."

Bonobos, Overlord of Science, was the only authority Hadlay had heard of who ever had a kind word for a Ramash, and he was something of a hero to Nomish, who had a fascination for learning. Whenever Bonobos came to market, Nomish could be found nearby, hanging on his every word.

"Bonobos is entirely too impressed with his own thoughts," Mrs. Rakam said. "All that nonsense about alchemy . . ."

"What's that?" Hadlay asked.

"Alchemy is a new science." Nomish's words came out in a rush. "For one thing, it's supposed to be a way to turn common metals, like iron or lead, into gold."

"And if there were anything to it, do you suppose Bonobos would be using that rusty iron claw for a hand?" Mrs. Rakam asked.

"I've always wondered how he lost that hand," Iaras said.

Mr. Rakam's eyes twinkled. "I hear he lost it to an angry husband—the man is known to be fond of women."

"*I* hear he blew it off in his laboratory while 'studying the flammable properties of fermented manure.'" Mrs. Rakam mimicked the overlord's pedantic language with a satirical tone.

"Now, dear. We don't want our young ones to disrespect authorities." Mr. Rakam said with feigned innocence, bringing a grin to Nomish's face.

Mrs. Rakam blushed. "I apologize, children. I was carried away."

"Bonobos dreams of a better world," Nomish said. "How could that be wrong?"

"He's not going to find a better world in a pile of manure."

"Well, at least he would never require us to do a purgation just for laughing."

Hadlay sighed. "I dread learning what Asinus has in mind for us."

In the pause that followed, Alila cocked her head. "Wasn't that what your dream said? 'On this day, your laughter will give way to dread'?"

Hadlay had not thought of the dream again since their confrontation with Asinus, but now that Alila brought it up, it did seem strangely predictive.

"What dream was this?" Hadlay's mother asked.

Hadlay related the dream again, aided this time by Alila, who added some details Hadlay had mentioned before but skipped in this telling. When she was finished, she looked up in time to catch a very odd look exchanged between her mother and Mrs. Rakam. "What's wrong?"

The two women smiled—a bit too heartily, it seemed to Hadlay—and shook their heads.

"Nothing, dear," Mrs. Rakam said.

"Nothing at all," her mother agreed. "It's a very interesting dream."

"Do you think it means something?" Alila asked.

"Oh, no, dear. It's just quite an odd coincidence, that's all." Mr. Rakam smiled, but it looked forced.

"Precisely." Nomish didn't seem to notice the strange behavior of their parents. "It was just a dream, for Nabu's sake."

"Nomish is right," Hadlay's mother said. "Such fanciful things are best forgotten."

"Yes, forgotten," Mrs. Rakam echoed.

"In fact, it would probably be wise never to think of it again," Mr. Rakam said. "Or speak of it."

Hadlay had a feeling that the adults were "protecting" them from something. She hated when they did that. She knew from long and aggravating experience that no amount of begging would persuade them to explain themselves.

What could be so troubling about a stupid dream?

THE FINAL TELLING

The meal was long since finished and their platters cleared when darkness finally descended over the city. The two families gathered near the cookfire, whose dying embers would light the ritual that was to be performed this eve.

"Children, sit on the blanket." Hadlay's mother and Mr. Rakam settled on the floor before them. Mrs. Rakam went to the door and took an anxious look outside before she came to sit beside her husband.

Iaras assessed each of the initiates with a sober gaze before she spoke. "You know something of what will take place tonight. But now we shall tell you why you've had to wait so long for this."

She glanced at Mr. Rakam, and he nodded, encouraging her to take the lead in this.

"In ages past, the Final Telling would have taken place during a full gathering of our people, a grand celebration of this day, when all young people who enter their thirteenth summer begin the steps toward adulthood. But now it is forbidden for the Ramash to gather in groups larger than nine, or for our people to speak of our histories and teachings. It is said the emperor himself made this law."

Mr. Rakam's face was unusually serious. "You may be sure that what you hear tonight will be told in many Ramash homes in Turris, but you must never speak of this outside our homes, for we have no way of knowing who, even among our own people, might report us to the authorities."

"If they learn that we still speak of our history," Mrs. Rakam cast another anxious look at the door, "we will be punished quite severely. This is why, until you come of age, the secrets of our people are not told to you. We must know that you are old enough to hold your tongues."

Mr. Rakam looked at his children, first Nomish, then Alila. "Now, think on the story you are about to hear, the ancient bedtime tale passed on from our parents, and their parents before them. Like all Ramash traditions, it is forbidden as well. Have you ever told a soul that you know it?"

Both Nomish and Alila shook their heads, and at her own mother's probing glance, Hadlay did the same.

"Well, then, you've passed the first test. Since you have been faithful in small matters, you can now be trusted with weightier matters." Mr. Rakam smiled. "We begin this evening as we have ended many evenings before, telling you the story of the Mirror of N'de. You are initiates now, no longer children, so this is the last time you will hear this tale until you tell it to your own children."

"But why is a silly bedtime tale forbidden?" Nomish asked. Hadlay sat straighter. She had wondered this as well.

"It is enough that it is Ramash," Mrs. Rakam said, a note of bitterness in her voice. "I believe the authorities would forbid us to exist at all, if only they did not need us to do their slaving."

Hadlay's mother reached out to tease one of Hadlay's unruly curls. "I've always loved telling you this story. It's always been the best part of my nights."

Mrs. Rakam let out a noisy sniffle, and her husband put his hand over hers. He cleared his throat. "Let us begin."

Iaras drew a deep breath, and with a solemn smile, she spoke, "There was once a great and powerful king named Meshah. It is said that he knew all secrets, even the mysteries of the future. It is said that he could ball up the wind and hold it in his hand or command the sun to cease its movement in the sky. But Meshah was no magician. He had no need of secret words or elixirs or powers, as the authorities do. He was, quite simply, King. The very cosmos knew this and obeyed him.

"Meshah ruled over two peoples, the Khalam and the Shee. The Khalam were clever and powerful. They could take any shape they liked, and their skin glowed, reflecting light in all its colors. But where there was no light, then they were simply dark. There may be Khalam all around us in the night, but you would never know unless one *tickled* you."

As Iaras spoke, Daram reached out and tickled Alila and Hadlay, and chuckled at their giggles and squeals. "Are you sure you are not still children?" he teased. "Perhaps we should save this ritual for another year."

"No!" Hadlay cried.

"We are ready—truly, Father," Alila said.

Mrs. Rakam gazed at her pensively. "You are barely of age, Alila. Perhaps you should wait until next year."

Alila's mouth dropped open at her mother's words, but Daram squeezed his wife's hand. "Our children are both initiates, Kera. It is difficult, but we must let them grow." He smiled at his daughter, then turned his attention back to Hadlay's mother.

Iaras continued, though her own eyes shimmered suspiciously. "The Shee were not so different from us. They were neither powerful nor wise. Rather plain, in fact, though Meshah thought they had a beauty of their own. Perhaps it was because the Shee had more need of him, but Meshah was especially fond of them, particularly their leader, Mada, who was his dearest friend. Meshah even built a home for them, a city called N'de.

"Every home in N'de was a palace, and every street was paved with gems that sparkled in the night like stars. And at the center of the city was a maze made of stones, each one glowing with its own inner light. Each turn in the maze brought you to a new chamber, full of fresh wonders. One chamber contained a table set for a feast, with golden platters filled with every delicacy. The only vegetables to be found were the kinds you liked, and if you didn't like any, then the sweets for dessert would be just as good for you.

"In another chamber, your feet would release their hold on the ground, and you would fly up, up, up until the sky was no longer blue, but black. There, you would see great balls of flame with smaller orbs spinning like tops around them. You could paint shapes in many-colored clouds, and spiral into black whirlpools, where your body turned to rubber and time stretched, and then be shot out like a marble, bouncing through floating bits of stone, before gently setting down again. There were more rooms with even greater marvels, things no one who had seen them could describe, and no one who had not could imagine.

"The greatest wonder of N'de, though, was Meshah himself. Have you ever made a baby giggle? Held a kitten and heard it purr? The greatest joy you've ever known is only a glimpse of what it was like to be with Meshah. And no matter how much you loved him, he loved you even more."

Iaras paused here, taking a long drink from her goblet, and Mr. Rakam took over the telling of the tale.

"But in a chamber at the center of the maze, there lurked a danger far more terrible than anything we fear today. That particular chamber contained a mirror, the only mirror in N'de. You see, Meshah knew that mirrors had a way of corrupting people. Some would look at themselves and become vain, taking pride in silly things like the color of their eyes. Others would hate what they saw, and feel great shame. Either way, what a mirror always did was make a person focus on himself, and self-focused thinking is the source of every kind of misery.

"Meshah knew, too, that if one person looked into that mirror, it would only be a matter of time before others did the same, until all N'de was governed by that mirror, and by the pride and shame and jealousy it inspired. He did not want this, for he loved the Shee and wanted them to be happy.

"Many have asked why Meshah did not simply destroy the mirror and eliminate the problem or use his power as King to command all living in N'de to obey him without question. But Meshah wanted the Shee to have the most precious gift any king can give—freedom. Without free will, one is merely a puppet, and how can a puppet be happy? How can a puppet love? Both true love and true happiness are not emotions, after all, but choices, and choices require the ability to choose.

"So Meshah gathered all the Shee together and explained the dangers of that mirror. Then he decreed that any Shee who looked into the mirror would have to leave N'de. This freed the Shee, for they could choose the mirror and leave N'de and Meshah, if they wished. But it protected those who chose to trust him and remain with him.

"The Khalam were wiser than the Shee, and should have needed no warning to avoid the mirror. But Lelyeh, their leader, sneaked a peek one day, and he very much liked what he saw. The more he thought a bout how beautiful he was, the more certain things troubled him. First, it bothered him that Meshah favored the Shee—especially that stupid Mada. If

Meshah had made a place as grand as N'de for Mada and his people, then surely he ought to give something even better to Lelyeh!

"After a time, it even began to bother him that everyone loved Meshah most of all. 'Why, look at me!' He preened before his own reflection. 'With just a little work, I could be more glorious than Meshah!' These thoughts festered in Lelyeh's mind until he could bear it no more. He devised a plan to avenge himself against his rivals.

"Now, among the Shee there was a female named Avakh. She was beautiful, but very simple, even for a Shee. Avakh loved to spend time in the chamber of the animals, for she had a friend there, a cheetah that purred loudly when his ears were scratched.

"One morning, Lelyeh went early to the chamber of animals, and he trapped the cheetah and tied him up. Then he took the cheetah's form. When Avakh came for her daily visit, he bounded up to greet her. 'Perhaps we could take a walk today. Would you like to visit other chambers?' Now, you and I might be surprised to hear an animal talk, but in N'de, it happened all the time. And so they wandered through the maze, with Lelyeh in the guise of the cheetah guiding Avakh slowly to the chamber with the mirror.

"When they reached it, Avakh stopped. 'I cannot go in there!'

"'Why not?' Lelyeh asked, as if he did not know.

"'King Meshah says this chamber is forbidden to us. If we even pass through the door, we will change in terrible ways and be exiled from N'de forever.'

"You may have noticed that Avakh didn't understand the decree correctly. Meshah decreed that no one should look in the mirror. It was quite all right to go through the door, though there was little reason to do so.

"Lelyeh realized that this gave him an advantage. 'Are you sure? I go in here all the time, and I have not changed.' Lelyeh stepped up beside Avakh and rubbed against her, pushing her nearer to the door. 'Why don't you give it a try?' Before she knew it, Avakh stumbled into the chamber.

"'Do you feel any different?' Lelyeh asked.

"'Not in the least! But why are we forbidden to enter?'

"'Meshah doesn't want you to look in the mirror because, if you did, you'd be able to make yourself as beautiful as he is.'

"This sounded good to Avakh—who wouldn't want to be so beautiful? And nothing had changed when she entered the room, so why not go on? With Lelyeh encouraging her, she walked up to the mirror and saw her own face for the first time.

"At first she was a little disappointed. She didn't look nearly as good as Meshah. But after a time, she decided she did look very nice compared to other Shee. All she needed was a few adjustments and she could outshine most of her friends. She spent many hours before the mirror that day, arranging her hair this way and that. Lelyeh even conjured up cosmetics for her to try. When she thought she looked her best, Avakh went looking for Mada.

"As she had hoped, Mada was impressed. 'Avakh, you look so different!'

"Avakh turned so he could see her from all angles. 'What do you think? Do I look fat in this tunic?'"

"Mada hesitated, sensing that the wrong answer would mean trouble. 'You look fine. Why did you do your hair that way?'

"'Well, once I took a good look at myself in the mirror—'

"'You looked in the mirror?' Mada asked, horrified. 'When Meshah learns, you will be banished!'

"'Why should he banish me? I'm the same as before, only better looking. You thought so too, a moment ago.' She thrust out her lip in a carefully practiced pout. 'Come and see for yourself. Why shouldn't we know what we look like?'

"No one knows why Mada relented; we only know he did. And the instant he saw himself, Meshah's voice echoed through the passages of the maze.

"'Mada? Where are you?'

"At the sound of that voice, all Mada's courage left him. He raced from the chamber, seeking a place to hide, hoping Meshah would never find him.

"But of course it was no use. A troop of Khalam found them, catching both him and Avakh by the shoulders. The Khalam took flight, gliding through the maze with their prisoners. Their outstretched wings flashed like lightning, and they sang with voices full of glory. Their words were unknowable, but Mada would remember the song for all his days.

THE MIRROR OF N'DE

"Meshah waited in the chamber of the mirror. He wore robes of pure light, so bright Mada had to shade his eyes. Dropping the prisoners at his feet, the Khalam surrounded their king, carefully keeping their backs to the mirror, their wings shielding their faces from its reflection.

"'What have you done?' Meshah's voice cracked with grief. 'I warned you about the mirror. Why did you not believe me?'

"Avakh fell to her knees, trembling, and Mada prostrated himself beside her. 'Have mercy, oh King!'

"'How I wish that I could!' Meshah said. 'If only you could see what that mirror has done to you! Your corruption will spread to everyone you know, just as it has already spread from Avakh to you. If you remain in N'de, you will destroy it.'

"'But I did not understand!' Avakh cried. 'I was deceived by the cheetah!'

"Now, the cheetah who had been Avakh's friend had been brought to Meshah by another flight of Khalam. Mada rushed to him, furious. 'Why did you deceive Avakh?'

"'I did not,' the cheetah said. 'I was attacked and bound by another, who took my form.' He lifted a paw to show the sores where the ropes had torn his flesh.

"'Who did this thing?'

"The cheetah turned, searching the faces of the Khalam. He glimpsed the one who stood behind Meshah, trying to hide, and his lips curled into a fierce snarl.

"Mada followed his gaze and saw his foe. 'Lelyeh!'

"Lelyeh sneered at them. 'Do I not rival the king in my beauty? Yet Meshah preferred you! But now he sees your unworthiness!' He turned to Meshah. 'The Shee do not deserve your favor!'

"'Silence!' Meshah thundered.

"Lelyeh's eyes flashed even as his voice failed him.

"Terrible in his rage, Meshah pronounced judgment on his former servant. He spoke in rhyme, for he wanted his words to be remembered:

> The victory you have won this day is fleeting as a breeze.
> You chose to turn away from me and act just as you please.
> I send you off to have your way, but you'll never be at ease,

> For the weapon you've used to wound my heart
>> will bring you to your knees.

"At a wave of Meshah's hand, a light came from the mirror, burning brighter and whiter until it swallowed Lelyeh, leaving a plume of pitch-black smoke and a scream that echoed through the chamber.

"Then Meshah turned to Mada and Avakh. They trembled under his fearsome gaze.

> You've already changed and cannot remain.
>> I wish it were not so.
> You'll live out your years in sorrow and fear,
>> but I would give you hope:
> There is a way to return to N'de and end your years of woe.
> You must trust me—this is the key—become like me,
>> or as you used to be, before you had to go.
> I have decreed that when you succeed,
>> you'll find the way back home.

"When Meshah finished speaking, the mirror lit again, and Mada felt its heat sear his flesh. The next thing he knew, he and Avakh were lying at the foot of the mirror. For a moment, he thought that perhaps he had not been banished after all. But nothing was the same. The maze remained, but its chambers were empty now and its stones were dark. And everything outside—N'de itself—was gone.

"Mada and Avakh built their home outside the maze, and spent their lives seeking the way back to N'de. But try as they might, though they re-entered the maze many times, they never again found the chamber with the mirror. They died without seeing Meshah's face again, and were buried by their children. Generations came and went, and the maze itself—if it ever existed—disappeared beneath the sands of time. Somewhere, the children of Mada and Avakh are waiting still to find their way home."

THE SECRET

Iaras smiled as Daram finished. "So it ends, this ancient tale, told by Ramash parents to their children long before the Oresed came and conquered. We tell it still because, to us, it represents our people's dearest hope. Just as Mada and Avakh were deprived of their homes and heritage, so our people have been denied as well. As they and their children lived and died hoping they would one day regain what they had lost, we Ramash hold that same hope."

"And now you will learn the first of our people's secrets," Mr. Rakam spoke so quietly that Hadlay had to lean in to hear. "You see, the Ramash were once the keepers of this land, before it became the city Turris. In those days, our ancestors protected an ancient monument, and with it a riddle that would one day reveal its mysteries. Then the Oresed came and conquered, took our homes and freedom, and both the monument and riddle were lost to us as well. But the augurs, who led our people in the times before the Oppression, promised that the day would come when the riddle would yet be solved.

"The augurs foretold that, in that day, a shattering truth will go forth from the monument into all the lands, and with it a great leader who will guide us with goodness and justice, setting all things right again. Every Ramash, when he comes of age, is charged with the duty of finding and solving the ancient riddle in order to bring forth that day."

Mr. Rakam sat forward, his intent gaze taking in each of the children in turn. "And so this night, the night each Ramash child begins his journey to adulthood, we give you this charge: Seek the riddle and its solution with all your heart, through all your days. For we all long for the Oppression to end."

Mrs. Rakam pushed to her feet. "And now it's time we took our leave. Even if you are initiates, it is well past time you found your beds."

Hadlay frowned, staring at her mother and Mr. Rakam. Was this it, the first of the secrets she had waited the whole of her life to hear?

Nomish seemed to be very much of the same mind. "So that is what we came to hear tonight? That we must solve some mythical riddle, without even the smallest clue what it is?"

"I don't believe it is a myth," Hadlay's mother said. "I believe with all my heart that it is real."

"But . . ." Nomish gazed at her as if befuddled. "But it makes no sense! Even if there were a riddle, and even if we could solve it without knowing it, how would doing so set us free?"

His father tousled his hair. "Some of us believe that the riddle is simply a metaphor for the challenge of winning freedom for our people. What matters is that we never give up. Even in the darkest times, we must always cling to our dreams and seek out ways to bring an end to the Oppression."

"Our dreams . . ." Alila murmured. She glanced at Hadlay. "In your dream, there was a mirror too, and you wanted very much to pass through. Do you suppose your dream had something to do with the bedtime story?"

For a moment, the theory made sense to Hadlay. After all, she had heard the story so many times she could easily recite it herself. Perhaps in her dream, she had envisioned herself as Avakh, staring at the mirror, wanting desperately to pass through again, to return to the wonders of Meshah and N'de. But what about the Being? The story never mentioned him.

As she thought these things, Hadlay nearly missed the tense look that passed between their parents.

Mr. Rakam drew his thumb under Hadlay's chin in an affectionate gesture. "Alila is right, exactly right. You just relived the story in your dream. Nothing to worry about."

"Not in the least," Mrs. Rakam said. "Best forgotten. Now, children, let's be off." She put an arm around Alila and steered her toward the door. "We have a long walk before we rest tonight."

Hadlay's mother saw them to the door and stood and watched until the Rakams had vanished in the gloom. When she turned back, she gave Hadlay a troubled look, then came and smoothed a hand over her daughter's unruly hair. "It was merely a dream, Hadlay. You mustn't worry about it—or the purgation. Now, go to bed. Morning will come early, now that you must earn your living."

FROM UNEXPECTED PLACES

Bonobos says it will be a light penalty," Nomish said as the two families made their way to the public square, "since it is our first offense, and only a small one. Perhaps it will simply be the masks." The masks were iron contraptions in the shape of donkeys and other beasts, that were fastened to the penitent's head for days or sometimes weeks. Embarrassing, but not too painful.

"Ba'ar's mother came in the shop the other day. She has asked Asinus to give us the lash so we learn to leave her 'poor dove' alone." Alila's eyes watered as if she could already feel the sting of the whip.

"I knew that confessing to Ba'ar was a bad idea." Hadlay shot a resentful glance at her mother. "Had we not done so, Ba'ar and her mother would not have known what we did until after Asinus had already decreed our punishment."

It had gone badly. Far from receiving their apology, Ba'ar had become angry and vengeful. Hadlay had no doubt that, whatever purgation they would have to endure, Ba'ar would make it her goal to see they suffered.

"Well, better the lash than the manacles," Nomish said. "At least a whipping would be over quickly."

The manacles were iron cuffs that affixed the victim to the city wall, often in contorted positions, until the following Midweek Gathering. Bound hand and foot, the victims were unable to defend themselves when gangs of Oresed youth made sport of beating them with rods and pelting them with manure and rotten fruit. When they were finally released, they often had to be carried away, cramped and broken, smelling like an open sewer.

"The three of you are suffering far worse than the purgation itself by giving this so much thought," Hadlay's mother said, to a nod from Mrs. Rakam.

"Just a short while now," Mr. Rakam ruffled his son's hair and tweaked Alila's cheek, "and you'll have it behind you."

Hadlay wished her father were with them as well, but he was still on his journey and not expected for another day. She would have felt braver with his arm around her.

They passed through the grand, arched gateway to the Square of Meeting. At the far end of this courtyard stood the great Hall of Justice, where the judges of Turris weighed matters of law each day. The Hall stood on a stone platform, raised to the height of two men, with steep stone stairs leading to its entry. At the top of the stairs, there was a wide ledge that formed a raised stage from which the judges rendered their rulings. Two stone columns framed the stage, and between them a thick pole supported a giant copper disc, which bathed the stage in glowing amber light, reflected from the sun.

Asinus stood imposingly in this light, flanked by large, leather-clad guards. A contingent of Tower servants stood nearby, waving dampened palm fronds to cool him.

Attendance at Midweek Gathering was required of every able adult in Turris, so the square was always overcrowded. Everyone stood silently, growing ever more miserable as the day's heat increased, and Asinus showed no sign of running out of things to say.

". . . for his laws are just, and we are fortunate to be governed by them." Asinus finally paused, and he seemed to expect a response, so the crowd applauded politely.

A narrow-lipped authority stepped up, looking flushed from the late-morning heat. He cleared his throat and raised a clay tablet. "The Tower will receive applications for apprenticeships beginning at next Midweek Gathering. Candidates must be Oresed initiates of high moral character, fastidious hygiene, superior . . ." He droned on.

Hadlay rubbed her neck, which had cramped from looking skyward for so long. Why couldn't they get on with the purgations? It was agony, standing in this heat and wondering what awful thing Asinus would contrive for them.

A hand slipped into hers. Alila's eyes were ringed from nights of sleepless worry. Hadlay gave her what she hoped was an encouraging smile, and was pleased to see Nomish move in close on her other side.

It did not help at all to remember that she'd dreamed again last eve. Once again she had found herself in the doorless room gazing at the mirror, the glowing Being gazing back at her. This time he had come right up to the mirror, so close that she could hear his great heart beating. She would have given anything to touch him.

But his words had still been confusing: *On this day you will hear words you long to hear, a promise as good as the one who makes it. But what you fear most this morning will seem trifling by midday; you will face a trial you did not expect. Recall my words and you will not see its end. By this you will begin to grasp the key . . .*

She pushed the memory aside as the authority stepped back, giving the platform to Asinus once more. Alila's hand began to tremble.

Asinus called the names of the accused, and, at a guard's command, they were raised, sometimes struggling, to the platform beside him, as if lifted by invisible hands. The city's inebriates were called up first and given the usual dowse in the river. It would do nothing to stop their drinking, but at least they would smell better.

Then the slave Hadlay had encountered on her way to the Rakams' shop was dragged forth in shackles. Hadlay was stunned at the change in his appearance. It had been no more than three days, yet he looked pale and gaunt, as if he had not eaten in weeks. His clothes were tattered and bloody, his body covered with vicious sores, and, most frightening of all, his eyes were vacant, like a home whose occupants had perished long ago.

"You were accused of thieving by the good word of an Oresed and found in possession of the stolen gold shekels. Have you anything to say?"

The slave sagged, too weak even to speak.

Asinus glowered at him. "You are hereby sentenced to pulling."

Hadlay shuddered. Pulling was a penalty reserved for more serious offenses. She watched as the poor slave was shoved to the front of the platform. The guards held his hands outstretched, and one of them spoke a mysterious word.

Several sets of manacles hung by long chains on each of the columns, and one set, a chain from each side, drifted toward the slave and clamped noisily around his wrists. The guards moved away, and he tumbled from the platform as if pushed, the full weight of his body jerking against the chains. He cried out as his shoulders wrenched in their sockets, and Hadlay could see the strain across his chest as the chains stretched his arms to their limits. In time, his shoulders would dislocate, and if they left him long enough, he would slowly suffocate.

Guilt gnawed at Hadlay's belly as she recalled that she had thrown the shekel that had helped convict him. She had chosen to spare herself at this poor man's expense. Perhaps she deserved the punishment she was about to face.

Asinus had stepped up to call the next name when the disc above the platform began to glow more brightly. Asinus shot a furious look at it, then his jaw dropped.

The disc blazed brighter, and a face appeared in it, as if amidst flames. It was a narrow face with a neatly curled white mustache and beard. A golden turban crowned his hair.

Hadlay could hear whispers through the crowd.

"Who is that?"

"How could this be?"

Asinus gathered his wits and stepped forward, though his haughty over-confidence was badly shaken. "Most Sovereign Majesty! We did not expect the honor of your presence among us. How may we serve you?"

The man in the disc did not acknowledge him.

"Citizens of Turris, I am pleased to announce that I am returning to your city with my son, Zêr-Shungalli, who has just entered his thirteenth summer."

The image's voice was briefly drowned out by the mutterings of the crowd.

"Returning? I thought he was dead!"

"A son? The emperor is many generations old, is he not?"

"*Silence!*" Asinus thundered.

The image had continued speaking throughout the outburst. ". . . to celebrate his initiation and mark the beginning of his apprenticeship to my throne, I have given my son the authority to issue one command. Zêru was greatly displeased to learn of the oppression of the Ramash people during our long absence from this city. Therefore, by command of Prince Zêr-Shungalli, all the laws of Turris that oppress the Ramash are now repealed."

"Your Majesty." Asinus raised a hand. "Perhaps—"

The emperor continued without seeming to notice. "Henceforth, the Ramash are full citizens of Turris, with all the rights and obligations that entails. They may now own land and property, and they are equal to the Oresed in every way. This day shall be known as the Day of Parity."

The emperor's face disappeared as abruptly as it had appeared, and the disc's glow dimmed to its normal intensity. It was like watching an ember lose its heat.

It took a moment for the gathered Turrans to find their voices. Then the crowd exploded with chatter.

"He has been gone for long ages, and the prince has never lived here! What do they know of this city?" came the voice of an outraged Oresed.

"How do we even know that was the emperor?"

The Ramash voices were far more excited. "What does it cost to purchase a home?"

"Fair wages for a day's labor!"

A scuffle nearly broke out before Asinus was able to command their attention again. "Let us proceed with the day's business." He gazed at his ledger. "Nomish and Alila Rakam and Hadlay Mivana!"

One of the guards gave a command, and Hadlay's sash and collar tightened, as though they had been gripped by rough hands, and she felt herself rising from the ground. Nomish and Alila rose as well. Alila was kicking her feet and crying.

"Wait!" Nomish shouted as the three were dropped onto the stage. He stood and squared himself before Asinus. "We need not suffer a purgation today!"

Asinus stared at him in disbelief.

"There can be no punishment when there was no crime, and the law you say we broke is repealed today, by order of the prince himself!"

Hadlay almost laughed with relief as she realized Nomish was correct. Scrambling to her feet, she helped Alila rise to stand beside her brother.

Asinus stepped toward them, his face crimson with anger. "You dare to challenge me? The law was not repealed when you broke it." His thunderous expression slowly gave way to a greasy smile, which Hadlay found somehow more ominous. "Indeed, your insolence is all the more offensive, given our great emperor's generosity. Perhaps your punishment should be increased." Asinus turned to the crowd, raising his hands for silence. "I myself bear witness to the crime. These three *remesh* initiates are guilty of making sport of Mistress Ba'ar Sutram, an Oresed girl of excellent family." He paused, allowing the Oresed to grasp the insult.

Hadlay's eye caught on Ba'ar, who had moved to the fore of the crowd below. The girl's dark eyes shone with spiteful glee.

Asinus continued. "These *remesh* took great pleasure in humiliating one of our own dear Oresed children!"

An angry murmur rose, growing loud and threatening.

Asinus allowed it to swell for a moment, then raised a hand. "I had planned to sentence them to the masks of fools, humiliation for humiliation, but in light of the emperor's great mercy, I believe a more lasting lesson is required to chasten them, and indeed all Ramash who may be tempted to abuse our great ruler's kindness."

Asinus gave a weighty pause, appearing to consider his options, though Hadlay felt sure he had already reached a decision. "I hereby sentence each of these offenders to be pulled, beside this thief."

Hadlay was uncertain that she had heard correctly until she saw the horror on her mother's face. How could this be just punishment for a simple joke?

Asinus turned to the guards. "Take them."

There was a brief scuffle below as Mr. Rakam tried to run up to the platform to protect his children. He was overcome quickly, and Asinus ordered that he be lashed for interfering with justice. A troop of guards moved in to prevent further difficulty.

Hadlay felt a sharp push between her shoulder blades, and she stumbled to the edge of the platform, with Nomish sprawling near her feet. Alila fainted in terror and had to be slapped awake by a cruel guard. Another guard caught Hadlay's arm and moved her to position. She resisted, but the guard overpowered her, sneering at her effort. Shooting him a defiant glare, she thrust her hands upward, permitting her wrists to be shackled by the manacles. If she could not avoid this, then by the emperor's beard, she would face this Oresed mob and show them what it meant to be Ramash!

Hadlay heard a grunt from Nomish as he was flung from the platform, and then he was hanging, his arms outstretched tightly, just above the heads of the crowd below. She felt a vicious blow between her shoulder blades, and then she too plunged to the length of the chains.

The manacles ripped into her wrists, tearing her skin at the first jolt, and then all of the muscles of her arms were aflame, and she could feel her joints grinding.

After a few moments, Hadlay heard Alila scream, then saw her swinging beside them. She sobbed, writhing as though she hoped to twist free.

Hadlay heard a shout of laughter. "Suffer, Ramash scum!"

"Filthy *remesh!*" another cried.

Through her dizzying pain, Hadlay realized with horror that the Oreseds' anger at the emperor's announcement was coming to focus on her and her friends. The shouts turned into terrifying threats. Someone said he would burn the Rakams' home while they slept. Then an Oresed boy slipped under the crossed spears of the guards and hurled a stone at Nomish. Within moments they were all being pelted by rocks.

"Death to the Ramash!"

Hadlay might have screamed, but could not draw breath to do so. She felt blow after bruising blow strike her body, her arms, even her face, and she was helpless to defend herself. Blood spattered on her clothing as a stone connected with her chin, and another, heavier one smashed into her eye.

She was going to die. Her arms screamed in agony, and her lungs expanded only with effort, straining against the pull of the chains to capture tiny whiffs of air, just enough to keep her conscious as daylight began to dim. Or was it dimming? Everything seemed to be swimming through some kind of haze.

She remembered the voice from her dream: *Recall my words and you will not see its end. By this you will begin to grasp the key.*

And then she saw no more.

Painful Awakening

Hadlay struggled awake, thrashing her way free of sleep as if it were a tightly wrapped shroud. She felt as though she had died and been buried, and was now coming up, half-rotted, from the grave.

Had it all been a nightmare? An attempt to move her arm told her no—her shoulder felt as though it had been wrenched from its socket. Every part of her ached so badly that she longed for oblivion again.

Something cool and damp touched her jaw.

She opened her eyes—or the one eye that would open—and found her mother sitting beside her, a damp cloth in her hand. "Marba," her mother called.

A moment later, her father appeared in the doorway. A slight man and rail-thin, Marba was all sinews and tendons and leathery skin. Though he was naturally pale, as most Ramash were, the desert sun of the wastelands had bronzed him so that, were it not for his light hair and gray eyes, he might have passed for Oresed.

For a moment, Hadlay thought he was angry with her for getting in trouble. Then his face softened and a tear traced the sun-baked crinkles around his eyes.

Her mother soaked the cloth and applied it again. "We were not certain you would come back to us."

"How long—" Hadlay's voice came out in a dry rasp.

Her mother gave her a sip of water to soothe her throat. "Two days."

"You've been in and out," her father said, then forced a smile. "More out than in." He dropped to one knee beside Hadlay's bed. He started to take her hand, then seemed to think better of it, satisfying himself with a gentle touch to her cheek. "I wish I had not been away. I would've—"

"You'd have got yourself lashed like poor Daram Rakam," Iaras finished for him. "And I'd have two of you to nurse. Poor Kera likely has not had a moment's rest since Midweek."

"Alila and Nomish?" Hadlay asked.

"Your father has been to see them."

"Last eve." He gave what was probably meant to be a reassuring smile, though it wobbled with strain. "Alila fared the best. Some bruises and sore arms, but she is well. She asked after you, but her parents are unwilling to let her out until the city is calmer. As for Nomish . . ."

A hard stare from Hadlay's mother silenced him.

Hadlay gripped her father's hand, ignoring the pain in her arm. "Tell me!"

He wouldn't meet her eyes. "He woke yesterday."

"And?" Hadlay demanded.

"He took a stone to the head. He is unable to see or speak."

Hadlay tried to sit up, but the pain, as well as her mother, pushed her back to the bed.

"There is nothing you can do," Iaras said. "Nomish will heal in time."

"How do you know?" Hadlay asked.

"If your mother says he will heal, Nomish would not dare to do otherwise." Marba smiled fondly at his wife.

More of the purgation returned to Hadlay's mind. "How did we survive?"

"You may thank Overlord Bonobos." Iaras smoothed Hadlay's hair, tears welling in her eyes. "He learned what was happening and summoned guards from the Tower to disperse the crowd and release you."

"What of the slave who was pulled beside us?"

"The guards took him down along with you three. He was still conscious, and he had the presence of mind to slip away in the melee."

"I don't remember any of that."

"You fainted before the ordeal was finished, and we feared the worst. But it is probably as well that you did not see its end."

The dream words that had echoed through Hadlay's mind as she lost consciousness returned to her now: *Recall my words and you will not see its end. By this you will begin to grasp the key.*

"What is the matter?" Hadlay's mother asked, her knowing eyes fixed on Hadlay's face.

Part of Hadlay wanted to say, "Nothing." Her first dream had clearly worried her mother and the Rakams. But it was disturbing to be having these dreams, which foretold unpleasant happenings. She wanted to understand, and her mother seemed to know something.

Her parents listened as she related the dream, and what the Being had told her this time.

When she finished, her father rose, a strange look upon his face. "You say 'another' dream? There have been more?"

"One other," Hadlay's mother said. "Hadlay mentioned it at the evening meal when the Rakams were here."

"The Rakams know, then?"

Her mother nodded.

Marba paced for a moment, then shrugged. "Well, I believe they will hold their peace about it."

"As do I," her mother said.

"And we will not speak of it either, outside our home," he said, directing his gaze at Hadlay.

Her father rarely gave orders, but it was clear this one was not to be questioned.

"What is this about?" Hadlay tried to sit up again, but the pain made her stomach lurch. She sank back, feeling helpless and frustrated.

Her father's smile was sympathetic. "The things we are not telling you are dangerous. It's best you not know."

"I can keep a secret."

"Of course you can, my darling girl. And in time you will know. But let us keep you safe a while longer." Her mother grimaced. "As safe as we can."

Hadlay could see by the firm set of her father's face that there would be no persuading him this day. She closed her eyes and felt his kiss upon her forehead.

"Rest, Hadlay. All will be well."

Her mother stayed with her, bathing her face with the soothing cool water as sleep settled over her once more.

When she woke again the room was dark, and she was alone.

CHANGES AFOOT

Hadlay stayed in bed another day, then her mother insisted that she rise.

"Your muscles are set up like mortar," she said, helping Hadlay to stand. "The more you move, the better it will be."

Every movement hurt at first, but, as her mother promised, each step was a little easier.

As Hadlay changed her nightrobe, she saw for the first time the extent of the harm that had been done to her. She gasped to see at least a dozen black and yellow bruises across her ribs, on her legs, and a fist-sized one on her hipbone. Her wrists were ringed with crimson, scabbing welts. And when she looked in the polished tin that reflected her face, there was a brief, startled moment when she thought some strange half-beast was leering back at her. Her left eye was swollen nearly shut, and an awful-looking bruise with a thumbnail-sized scab at its center covered the whole of her right jaw. With the swelling, her face was twisted and grotesque.

But for all the damage done her, at least she would heal with time. She could see and speak. She thought of Nomish, and her heart raged. The Oresed had tried to kill them over a silly prank! The injustice of it burned inside her. What she wouldn't give to make them pay!

Her mind was troubled by other things as well. What were her parents keeping from her about these dreams? Why wouldn't they tell her?

Never before last week had she had so strange a dream, certainly never a dream that told of things to come. What was causing her to have them now? And what was this key that seemed to be at the core of it all?

That morning, she ate with her parents at the table but then had to return to bed. By the next midweek, she was up the better part of the day, though mostly sitting. She was not able to attend Midweek Gathering, however, nor would she have gone if she had been.

That evening, Asinus came knocking.

Hadlay's father was out at the market. A good thing, as he'd vowed more than once that the next time he glimpsed Asinus, he would do him harm.

Hadlay's mother kept the overlord and his guard standing at the door; Hadlay knew Iaras would die before allowing Asinus to enter her home. Sitting at the table with some foul-smelling poultices on her wrists, Hadlay could hear the discussion.

"What do you want?" Iaras asked.

"The emperor has ordered that all initiates of Turris must report to an overlord."

"Why?" Hadlay could hear the alarm in her mother's voice.

"The Tower is in need of new servants."

"The Tower appoints only Oresed servants."

"Since our sovereign has seen fit to make the Ramash equal in all things, we are told that even *rem*— Ramash initiates are to be considered."

Hadlay could hardly believe what she was hearing, but the choked-back outrage in Asinus's tone told her it must be true.

"My daughter is hardly able to serve anywhere," came her mother's clipped reply. "You well know why."

"The emperor did not leave allowances for infirmity. By his order, all Turran initiates will submit to a series of tests designed to determine suitability for apprenticeship in the Tower. I have come to take some preliminary information."

"I'll answer for my daughter."

His voice boomed into the room. "Do not interfere, woman! I'll speak to her myself!"

"You'll do no such—"

Hadlay cleared her throat before her mother could give the beast another opportunity to torture a Ramash. "It is all right, Mother. I'll answer."

Reluctantly, her mother opened the door a bit wider so that Asinus could see Hadlay as she struggled to her feet, gathering up the skirt of her tunic so that she could limp to the door.

Asinus's two guards, who stood at his bloated flanks, blanched at the sight of her injuries, then quickly looked away. Asinus, too, seemed momentarily affected, but he recovered quickly.

"You can walk." He fixed her with a steely glower. "You should have attended Gathering this morn."

"She cannot stand for as long as *you* can talk!"

Hadlay gasped. Her mother would surely be lashed for that!

But Asinus surprised her by restraining his temper, though his thunderous expression made clear he was doing so with difficulty. He drew a clay tablet and stylus from a fold in his robe and addressed himself to Hadlay. "Your full name?"

"Hadlay Mivana."

He grimaced as he wrote, as if even writing a Ramash name disgusted him. "Age?"

"Thirteen summers."

"Can you read?"

Even from her vantage, she could see that he had already written *no*. "You will have to change that."

Asinus gave her a startled look, then rubbed out his answer, shaking his head and muttering something about giving sapphires to toads. Most Ramash were not literate, but her father's former master had employed him as a personal scribe. Marba had taught the skill to Hadlay and her mother, and the Rakams had asked to be taught as well. It benefited them to be able to keep their own ledgers, so the Oresed who traded with them—not to mention the owners of the shop—were unable to cheat them.

Glowering, he made the necessary revision. "Write?"

"Well enough." She smiled because she knew it would annoy him, though she imagined that her bruises made it more of a grimace.

He marked the tablet again with a disgusted snort. "Any maladies or ailments?"

"None but what *you* inflicted."

Hadlay caught her mother's arm, silently begging her to be still, but Iaras continued to glare at Asinus, her eyes blue fire.

"None," he wrote, then handed his ledger to a guard. "The testing will be next Midweek following Gathering."

"She won't be equal to any physical challenge," her mother said.

"Then she'll fail. I doubt any Ramash will pass anyway, competing against good Oresed youth." Asinus turned and waddled away, his two guards trailing him.

Her mother closed the door, muttering, "Someone ought to catch that man alone by night . . ."

Hadlay was of no mind to argue.

Hadlay's father arrived home shortly after. When Hadlay and her mother apprised him of Asinus's visit, he nodded, his eyes bright with anger. "He came to the Rakams' while I was there. Had I not been occupied holding Daram back, I'd likely have laid on him myself. He had the nerve to command Nomish to stand and walk! The boy managed a few steps before we made him sit again."

"A wonderful sign!" Her mother stirred the thin soup she had made from the leavings of last night's meal, relief smoothing the tension in her brow.

"Overlord Bonobos paid them a call just after. He told about the emperor's meeting with his council. Bonobos said he had intended to speak of the purgation, but the emperor somehow knew already. He was quite angry with Asinus for ignoring his order repealing the law you had broken. Asinus likely paid these calls personally so that he could tell the emperor he had seen for himself that the children were recovered."

That explained why Asinus had not spewed his usual bile, Hadlay thought. "How are Alila and Nomish?"

Her father smiled. "There is good news. Nomish has regained his sight and hearing."

Hadlay swallowed a relieved sob. She hadn't realized how worried she'd been.

"Alila is recovered, though even more timid. She hid in the loft when Asinus came and refused to come down until he left." He chuckled. "You would have enjoyed seeing Asinus shouting his questions up to her when she would not obey his order to descend. His face was red as a drunkard's."

"When can I see them?"

"I'll take you tomorrow."

"You will not!" Her mother wagged a dripping spoon in his face. "It's not safe for a Ramash to walk the street."

"Daram opened the shop again two days ago, and he says everything appears to have returned to normal. Some Oresed have even apologized for what happened to Nomish and Alila." He sat at the table beside Hadlay. "You know I would never take her if I did not believe it was safe."

"Please, Mother!"

Iaras returned to her cooking, her lips pursed. "You and Daram Rakam are far too opt imistic. If the Oresed are being kind, there is evil coming, I say."

They did not have to wait long before they learned what it was. That evening, the Sutrams' slave came to collect the rent. Only it wasn't the same rent he had collected last moon; the figure was more than doubled.

"What is this?" Her father frowned at the bill.

"Emperor's orders. The Ramash are to be treated equally, so you'll pay equal rents to what Oresed tenants pay."

"If we lived in equal homes, that would be fair, but this shelter is hardly equal to an Oresed's privy."

The man shrugged. "Pay or be out by week's end. That's all I know."

"Why is Master Sutram doing this to us?" Iaras asked. "Is it because of what Hadlay did to Ba'ar? She has apologized and more than paid a price for it!"

"It is not only you," the slave said. "Almost all the landlords are boosting their rents. And there is worse. The word is that the price for everything—including foodstuffs—will be raised, at least double."

Iaras gasped. "How will we manage? Oh, Marba—"

"We'll find a way." But Marba's face was pale as he turned to the slave. "Will you return at week's end? We'll try to have the rent by then."

"Fair enough." The man turned to leave. "I've only collected one rent the entire day. Most Ramash will be sleeping out of doors this time next week."

THE WARNING

In the end, there was nothing to be done. No Oresed would buy her father's goods. A few of the shops managed by Ramash made small purchases, but even they were less free with their bartering. After all, they had higher rents to pay, as well. The Mivanas packed their belongings and moved in with the Rakams. Together, they now paid a bit more for the one home than they had previously paid for two.

"Can't we petition the emperor?" Hadlay asked.

"No one speaks to the emperor except the overlords," came her father's clipped reply, "and they're all Oresed."

"B-Bonobos is different." Nomish had recovered his sight and speech, but he was left with a stutter. "He will surely b-broach the matter at the next council."

"Bonobos has been kind, but he is Oresed, and a privileged one at that. He will not concern himself with our troubles," Mrs. Rakam said.

The families settled in, though there were many difficulties with making one home of two families. With Nomish and his father injured, it was impossible for them to climb the ladder to the loft. Instead, Nomish had the bed that had once been Alila's, and their parents had the floor near the hearth, softened with a good straw-filled mat. Hadlay's parents took the narrow ledge that formed the loft.

But after trying to share it with them one night, Hadlay and Alila reluctantly conceded that the only place for them was in the stable, which was separated by a half wall from the rest of the house. It wasn't so bad once they got the Rakams' ancient donkey and the Mivanas' horse to understand that they would henceforth pass the nights outside. Some diligent cleaning made it almost another bedroom, though there were some lingering smells Hadlay didn't like to think about.

It was in this stable that Hadlay had yet another dream. At first the Being was tender, his colors soft pastels like the sky at dusk. "You have suffered much, little love, but your fortunes will soon change." Then he began to shift, dawning to amber as if lit by burning flame, and his eyes pierced to her soul. His voice darkened to a tone of warning. "Beware false friends. Seek the key, little love, for if you refuse it, you will know only destruction. On this day, you will fail in the task that you set yourself to accomplish. When you see that my words are true, you will begin to grasp the key."

Hadlay woke with a start and struggled to sit. Why was this Being troubling her? And what was this key he kept speaking about?

She wondered if the things her parents were keeping from her would answer these questions. Why wouldn't they tell her?

Alila stirred beside her and awakened. She rubbed her eyes. "Are you all right?"

"I'm well enough. Go back to sleep."

"Another nightmare?" Both girls had been plagued with them since the pulling.

"No," Hadlay whispered. "Another dream."

Alila sat up sleepily. "Like the one you told us about in the shop?"

Hadlay nodded.

"My parents were most disturbed by that."

"Mine as well. Do you know why?"

Alila shook her head. "But I heard them arguing long into the night. Mother wanted to order Nomish and me to stay away from you."

Hadlay was stunned by this news. "Why?"

Alila shrugged. "Father would not allow it. He said that true friends stand together, protect each other. The next morning at table, he said we must swear never to speak of your dream again, not to anyone."

"Mine said the same." Hadlay flung up her hands in frustration, then winced. It still hurt to raise her arms. "Why are they so anxious?"

Nomish was up and walking, though with a pronounced dragging of his left foot, so they heard his approach long before his face appeared over the stable half-wall. "What are you w-whispering about?"

"Hadlay had another of her dreams."

Nomish glanced back at the hearth to make certain that his parents were still sleeping. "May I enter?"

Hadlay nodded, and Alila gestured to the foot of their bed. He lowered himself with a pained grunt, and Alila scooted down to sit beside him. "What was this dream about?"

Hadlay settled as comfortably as she could, very close to her friends so that there was no chance their conversation could be overheard. She told them first about the dream she'd had the day of the pulling, and then about the latest.

Alila's wide eyes shone in the dim light. "What does it mean?"

"I don't know," Hadlay said. "I don't believe I want to know. All these dreams are of evil things. Perhaps I should not leave this house today."

"You have no ch-choice," Nomish said. "And there is a t-task set before you today—the emperor's testing."

"That must be it," Alila said. "And since the Being said that you will fail the task, then you will not be chosen."

Hadlay hadn't given the test much thought, and indeed had assumed that she would not pass, since no Oresed judge would ever award a Ramash a position of status. But she still found that she was disappointed with this assessment of her dream. In the depth of her heart, she had hoped at least to put in a good showing in this test, whatever it might be. At the very least she'd hoped to match the performance of the Oresed initiates, show them just once that she could be their equal.

"I wouldn't like it if you excelled anyway," Alila said. "Our lives have been planned for us since we were children. You are apprenticed at the shop, and one day you and Nomish will marry, and you will be my sister."

Nomish flushed at the mention of marriage, but he nodded. "If any of us were chosen, it would change everything."

There was a brief lapse in the conversation, as Nomish's words hung in the air.

"It would, wouldn't it?" Hadlay mused. "Change everything, I mean."

"What are you talking about?" Nomish asked.

"What if one of our people did pass the test today and gain entry to the Tower? Could you imagine: a Ramash serving the emperor and his son? Living in the Tower? Becoming an authority?"

Nomish chuckled. "That's far-fetched, even for you."

Alila giggled. "What I wouldn't give to see Asinus's face if it came to pass, though."

"Oh, he'd be beside himself, wouldn't he?" Hadlay said, imagining the overlord's reaction.

"Just don't get your hopes up," Nomish said. "It's about as likely as a pig sprouting wings."

THE EMPEROR'S TESTS

It was the first Midweek Gathering they had attended since the pulling. Hadlay and Nomish each had to put an arm around Alila to keep her standing during Asinus's lecture, this time on the powers of Emperor Shungallu. People shuffled miserably in the heat of the day before he finally began to deplete himself of words.

"Do not provoke the emperor to anger, for his wrath is terrible and does not turn aside easily."

Hadlay recalled Bonobos's report of the latest council meeting. It pleased her to know that Asinus had experienced the emperor's wrath personally.

Finally, the overlord stepped back and glanced expectantly at the disc above him. As if on cue, it began to glow as it had before. This time, however, the light took shape and drifted down to the platform, and the emperor himself emerged. Many in the crowd cried out and scrambled back, putting distance between themselves and the platform. The authorities could work magic, but nothing such as this!

There was an awkward silence, then a few people seemed to gather their wits. A weak cheer began and shortly the whole crowd joined in. Hadlay cheered as well; the emperor's decree had done her people no good as yet, but at least he had meant to help.

The emperor allowed the cheers to continue for a time before raising a hand for silence. "Good people of Turris, it is usual for the Tower to recruit six new servants each year. This year, since my son and I have returned, we will need five times that number." He raised his hand again to quiet the excited whispers of Oresed parents.

"I myself shall preside over the testing of your children, for this season's recruitment has a special purpose. Zêr-Shungalli shall one day rule Turris in my name, and he is apprenticed to this role now that he has entered his initiation. When the time comes for him to reign, he will need his own authorities and overlords."

More eager murmurs swept through the Oresed as they realized the implication.

The emperor's gaze trailed over the assembly. "Among the initiates chosen this day, certain few who excel in the Tower will be chosen for more important duties. Six of them will be apprenticed to my overlords."

Hadlay studied the emperor as the Oresed cheered this announcement. He towered far above the others on the platform, and his severely slender build made him an odd pairing with Asinus. His skin glowed in the sunlight; Hadlay thought that he might well light a darkened room simply by entering. His hair was silvery-white, but Hadlay was uncertain this was an indication of age. She wished she were close enough to see his eyes, which appeared to be an amber color. His voice was deep and musical, his movements so graceful he seemed to be dancing. His robes shone many colors in the sun, much like seashells. Jeweled rings flashed and dazzled her as he gestured. Hadlay had never seen anyone quite so beautiful.

It occurred to her that she had never heard anyone mention if the emperor had a wife. Who was Zêr-Shungalli's mother? Perhaps a Nomad the emperor had encountered during his extended travels? Or perhaps Nafal— though Hadlay didn't believe she had ever heard of a female of their kind. She wondered what his son looked like.

As the cheering died, the emperor raised his hand. "The tests we are about to administer will determine each candidate's patience, obedience, loyalty, and discretion, for these are the first qualities that a good servant must possess. I assure you that the selection will be without bias or falsity." He made a beckoning gesture. "Step forth, initiates. The time of your testing has come."

Even though Hadlay understood from her dream that she would fail the test, she felt determination stiffen her spine as she moved into place. She would do everything she could to impress the emperor.

Alila tugged on her hand, trying to keep to the rear of the group, her eyes darting anxiously at Asinus. But Nomish pressed forward, his jaw set. Hadlay guessed that he had thoughts similar to her own.

The emperor surveyed the initiates, taking his time. There were nearly two thousand youths before him. "Please remain quiet, where you are, while I confer with the overlords regarding some important details." He gathered his council and spoke with them, too quietly to be heard, for a considerable time.

As the moments drew long, some of the initiates began to cluster in small groups and converse among themselves. Alila tried to engage Hadlay with questions about what might be coming, but Hadlay's mind was too focused on the task ahead to respond. Nomish seemed similarly absorbed, much to his sister's frustration.

It took an awfully long time before the emperor returned to the front of the platform. He spoke a word Hadlay did not understand, and then Hadlay felt an odd, cold feeling in her hands. She raised them, and was stunned to see that both of them were a vivid red, from the fingertips to a sharp line at the wrists. They looked as if she had dipped them in blood. She rubbed at them, but the color seemed to be embedded in her skin.

Nomish had red hands too, but Alila's were blue.

"How did he do that?" Alila rubbed at her fingers with a corner of her tunic.

Hadlay looked around. It appeared that about half of the group had blue hands, while the rest had red.

The emperor waved a hand to silence anxious murmurs from the crowd. "Do not be concerned. The colors are to divide you for the testing. Now, kindly form five lines, each before one of the overlords. There is one additional question we must ask before the selection can begin."

Hadlay and her friends fell in with the nearest of the Ramash groupings. The Oresed initiates hurried off to form their own groups, apart from the Ramash.

The overlords descended from the platform, each heading for one of the groups. Hadlay had hoped that Bonobos would preside over her group, but although he started in their direction, Asinus stepped in front of him with obvious determination.

Hadlay and her friends exchanged angry glances. None of them wanted to speak to the man, and they well knew Asinus would do his best to assure that all Ramash in this grouping were disqualified.

The overlords kept the lines at some distance so they could speak with each initiate privately. One by one, each initiate stepped up before an overlord, listened to the question, said a few words, and was directed into one of two groups.

Then it was Hadlay's turn. She walked up to Asinus, determined to meet him with a steady gaze. He might try to kill her again, but he would never again see her tremble, not for him.

The question was not what she expected: "The selected initiates will be taken to live in the Tower, only permitted to return home for a short visit every third moon. Would you object to this arrangement?"

All desire to excel in this test departed. However she might enjoy proving herself equal to the Oresed, the idea of leaving her parents, and possibly her two best friends, easily overshadowed her pride. She had to disqualify herself.

She lowered her eyes, not wanting to see the triumph on Asinus's face. "Yes."

Asinus directed her to the group on the left.

Nomish and Alila arrived a moment later. As she had expected, most Ramash children were directed to the same group. Hadlay could see the smug satisfaction on Asinus's face as he disqualified initiate after initiate.

When all of the initiates had been sorted, Hadlay reckoned that there were perhaps two hundred disqualified. The rest had gone to the other, larger group, and looked extremely pleased with themselves.

Ba'ar was one of the last initiates to answer the question, and Hadlay was surprised to see her directed to join the disqualified group. It was difficult to believe someone so self-absorbed and haughty would choose her family over the honor of becoming the servant of Zêr-Shungalli. Though her friend Nemat had already been sent to the other group, Ba'ar looked strangely pleased with her answer.

When the overlords returned to the platform, the emperor waved his hand over the initiates, speaking again in his strange language. Hadlay saw that, while some of the initiates in her group still had red or blue hands, the hands of the initiates in the other group had changed to green or yellow.

The emperor waited for the crowd to quiet. "Before the testing is done, I would like to thank all the people of Turris for allowing their children to come here today. I am certain each one of these young people has many fine qualities, and I regret I can only choose a small number for this honor."

As the emperor spoke, Hadlay noticed that Asinus, who stood to his right side, had begun to shuffle his feet uncomfortably. She saw a bright red pimple on his nose, right at the tip, and she wondered how she had missed it when she spoke to him earlier. It seemed to be growing before her eyes, and becoming increasingly luminous.

She wasn't the only person who noticed. Several people in her group began to titter and elbow one another. A girl nearby caught her friend's eye and meaningfully touched her nose. The friend giggled.

Hadlay and her friends did not laugh. They had already suffered a painful lesson about laughing at an Oresed. If they could be pulled for laughing at Ba'ar, they did not even want to think about laughing at Asinus.

The pimple grew until it was the size of a thumb, then, horribly, it did what pimples do—it burst, sending whitish fluid flying in all directions. Asinus uttered a strangled sound and used the sleeve of his robe to wipe the matter from his face. He looked as though he wished to disappear.

Even then, Hadlay dared not laugh. She could see Nomish's cheeks stiffen in a determined effort not to even smile. To her dismay, though, Alila's restraint shattered and she doubled over, giggling shrilly. Hadlay feared for her, even as Nomish gestured for her to hush.

The emperor waved his hand again. Hearing a gasp, Hadlay glanced around, and noticed that most of the initiates in her group were now staring at normal-colored hands. The other group's hands were plain as well. Her own hands, however, as well as Nomish's, were still a brilliant shade of red.

The emperor looked down upon the initiates, once more taking all of them in with his eyes. "I thank you for your attention. You may all now return to your homes."

Had the emperor changed his mind? Weren't they going to be tested? Hadlay glanced at Nomish, but he seemed as confounded as she was.

The emperor continued. "Following the next Midweek Gathering, those initiates whose hands are red shall gather here for transport to the Tower.

Each of you may bring one small personal item. All of your other needs will be met in your new home. I congratulate you for being chosen."

With that, the emperor vanished, leaving a square full of very confused Turrans.

Caught Red-Handed

How could you have passed the tests when there were no tests?" Alila fretted at the seam of her tunic, clearly distressed that Hadlay and Nomish would be leaving her, though Hadlay knew that she was also relieved not to have been chosen with them.

The two families worked together to prepare the evening meal as they tried to come to grips with the day's surprises. Hadlay's father moved the table near the hearth so the embers from the fire could light their meal. Oil and candles were both things of the past now, as the prices of every necessity had increased. They were fortunate to have the mule and the horse to provide manure to be dried and burned in the cookfire.

"What qualities did the emp-emperor say were most important for s-servants?" Nomish asked as he dipped water from a clay crock into their cups, and set them on a tray. "Patience, obedience, loyalty, and di-discretion."

"So I remember." Mrs. Rakam served up small helpings of soup into seven bowls. Since most Ramash could no longer afford to buy meat, the population of rats and pigeons in Turris was quickly diminishing. Hadlay noticed that she served herself a bit less so she could give more to Nomish. Even so, he would go to bed hungry this night. "But I do not understand how you were tested for these qualities."

"Immediately after he s-said that, he told us to remain quietly where we were while he s-spoke with the overlords."

"So?" Hadlay carried the tray of filled cups to the table. She still hoped they had misunderstood and she and Nomish had in fact been disqualified.

"Ha-Hadlay and I stood quietly and did not move or talk, even though it t-took a very long time. Patience and obedience." He ticked off two of the qualities on his fingers. "Alila talked, and she was elimina-nated."

Alila's lips tightened, though she seemed to think better of whatever she'd considered saying.

"What about loyalty?" Mrs. Rakam asked.

Nomish eased himself to his stool, sighing as he flexed his sore leg. "When Asinus asked if we would object to leaving our homes and families, Hadlay and I both answered in the affirmative."

"As did I," Alila said.

"Yes, but you had already been disqualified in the first test."

"What did your answers prove?" Hadlay's father sat beside Nomish, though Hadlay knew that he would be on his feet again before long. Her father always paced when he was upset.

"That we pre-preferred those we love over the honor the emperor was offering. Loyalty." He ticked the third item from his fingers.

"But how will loyalty to your family serve Zêr-Shungalli?" Hadlay's mother asked, taking her own seat beside her husband.

"The test showed that we p-possessed the quality," Nomish said. "The emperor m-must believe that in time we will have the same allegiance for him and his son."

"I see now. And you exercised discretion when you did not laugh at that monstrous furuncle on Asinus's nose, even when it exploded all over his face." Iaras's lips twitched at the memory.

"Yes. After all we have suffered, we knew better than t-to laugh at an overlord."

"Ironically, that is thanks to Asinus," Hadlay's father said. "I am certain he would slash his own throat if he realized he had taught you the lesson that allowed you to pass the final test."

"We could inform him and hope." Daram winked at the stern look from his wife and squeezed in beside Alila. The Rakams' table was larger than Hadlay's family's had been, but even so, it was difficult to eat without bumping elbows.

"But why would the emperor trick us like that?" Hadlay nibbled on her bread, but she really wasn't hungry. "I did not want to be chosen, once I knew the cost."

"I had hoped to fail also," Nomish said. "Though I did w-want to excel against the Oresed."

"That is exactly why he tricked you." Understanding dawned on Marba's face. "He said the test would be without bias or falsity. How could you falsify your answers if you did not understand the test?"

"The emperor is very wise," Hadlay's mother said. "By testing in this manner, he was able to select those initiates who actually possessed the qualities he desired, rather than those who would have said or done anything to gain the honor he was offering."

"But we don't want to go!" Hadlay heard the shrillness of her own voice. "That ought to count for something!"

"Whether or not we want it," Mrs. Rakam said, "we have been accorded quite an honor."

"I hardly care for this honor." Iaras's eyes shone with tears. "I have heard—" She glanced at the children and stopped herself.

"Let them hear. They should know what they face."

Hadlay wanted to kiss her father. For once, an adult was taking them seriously.

When her mother spoke again, her voice was soft, betraying her reluctance. "I have heard that some of those taken into Tower service are never seen again." She glanced at Kera. "Do you remember Viridesc, Overlord of the Treasury? My friend Glenelg works in her family's home, and she tells me no one has heard from her in moons."

Hadlay's father rose and began pacing, as she had expected he would do. When Nomish cast eyes at Marba's neglected meal, Marba gestured for the boy to take it.

"I'm sure she is merely busy." Mrs. Rakam swirled a bit of bread in her bowl to soak up what remained of her soup. "Overseeing the emperor's treasury must be a heavy responsibility. If something had befallen her, the news would travel."

"Perhaps." Hadlay's mother said, frowning. "Still, I dislike sending our children to the Tower with all those Oresed, and worse—the overlords."

Marba's pacing slowed. "What if there were an alternative?"

The question caught the full attention of everyone at the table.

Marba spoke slowly, measuring his words. "I have many friends among the Nomads. I believe some of them would be willing to shelter us."

There was a brief silence as everyone considered his suggestion. Then Mrs. Rakam pushed her bowl away and stood. "Unthinkable! I will not have my children facing the dangers of the desert!"

"You do not think they are in danger here in Turris, with Asinus and the Oresed? And in the Tower they will be without our protection!" It was the first time Hadlay had heard her mother raise her voice to Mrs. Rakam.

"Not even Asinus would dare to harm our children now that the emperor has chosen them," Kera said. "Those savages in the desert don't care who they kill!"

"Marba has traded in the desert for years. He always returns home safely."

"Excuse me, Iaras, for saying this, but your family is accustomed to hard living. My children are not."

"Our children were fortunate to survive that purgation, Kera. If Asinus had had his way—"

"But things have changed!" Mrs. Rakam said. "Don't you see? The emperor has returned, and he has seen fit to raise our children to positions of prestige. Think of it—my Nomish has been accepted into Tower service! The emperor is offering him an opportunity that no Ramash could ever have hoped for in his wildest dreams. When Nomish is a Tower servant, even the Oresed will fear him." Then she paused, as if having a second thought. "Still . . . perhaps it would be better if *you* left the city."

"You just finished saying what a fine opportunity this would be, Kera," Daram said, frowning at his wife's apparent turnabout.

"For Nomish, yes. But Hadlay has been hav—" She cut herself short and pressed her lips together.

In the ensuing silence, the glances the adults exchanged made clear they had all taken her meaning well enough.

"You are speaking of my dreams!" Hadlay could endure the frustration no longer. She gazed first at her mother, then her father, seeking some affirmation. When they did not speak, her anger flared. She pounded the table, startling everyone. "What is wrong? You all are behaving as if I have some awful sickness."

Mrs. Rakam patted her hand. "It's nothing you need to be concerned with, dear. I'm sorry I brought it up."

Hadlay's mother nodded and opened her mouth to speak, but Marba put his hand on her arm. "The only way she will understand the need for silence is if she knows the danger."

There was a momentary battle of wills in the look they exchanged, then Hadlay's mother acquiesced.

Kera Rakam began to shoo her own children from the room, but Daram stopped her with a raised hand. "They should all hear."

She glared at her husband, but relented with a hard sigh. "You must never speak of this outside our home. Never, do you understand?"

"It is usually at the ascension ceremony, when an initiate is recognized as an adult, that a Ramash learns these things. The knowledge is held until one is mature enough to mind his tongue." Iaras said this with a sharp look at Hadlay.

Marba drew his stool close to the table and kept his voice low, so that everyone had to strain to hear. "At the Final Telling, you learned that our people once protected a sacred monument, and a riddle that would one day solve its mysteries. In those ancient times our leaders, the augurs, studied the riddle, parsing it carefully for clues to its solution. They received their call to leadership through dreams, special dreams that spoke about the riddle. All the Ramash revered and protected the augurs, and the augurs made their homes inside the monument so they could study it."

Daram took up the story now. "Our people were not warriors, and when the Oresed army came, led by Nafal generals, we were easily conquered. They buried the monument, and though our people tried to hide the augurs, the authorities eventually found them all and killed them, every one."

"But not before torturing them in terrible ways." Mrs. Rakam cast her eyes about the room with a shudder. "It was meant as an example to terrorize our people. We were forbidden by order of the emperor to speak again of the augurs, the monument, the riddle, even our history."

Marba spoke again. "Just before the final augur was killed, he gave a prophecy. He swore that no matter what the Oresed did, the monument could never be destroyed, nor could the riddle be taken from our people. In each generation, he said, there would always be dreamers, people who would continue the line of the augurs—though we must never call them that—and through them our connection with the monument would be preserved until the time came for the riddle to be solved. Since that day, there have always been some among our people who have these dreams, which speak unerringly of things to come. We pin our best hopes on the dreamers, to one day solve the riddle and set us free."

Hadlay felt the stares of her friends as the import of all this reached them. Did this mean she was an augur, or whatever they were called in these times? The very thought seemed ridiculous. She was no one special. What could she have to do with such things as monuments and riddles? What could *she* do to set her people free?

Mr. Rakam gave her a kind smile. "There is much debate among our elders, Hadlay, whether any of this is true, or whether it is just a fable meant to give us hope. These dreams, though they have been uncannily predictive, may only be strange coincidences or some sort of unknown magic."

Her mother caught her hand and pressed it between her own. "Even so, these people, these dreamers, are always in terrible danger, Hadlay. The authorities know about the final augur's prophecy, and they seek to keep it from coming to pass."

"If they find dreamers, they kill them." Mrs. Rakam cast an anxious glance at her children. "And everyone who knows them. When I was a girl, nine Ramash were flayed alive because they knew a dreamer. The authorities sought to silence any who might have heard her speak of her dreams. The youngest of the nine was my friend and . . ."

Alila was staring at Hadlay, her eyes round as pigeon eggs. Hadlay realized that her friend was afraid of her.

Daram saw his daughter's face and held up his hand. "Enough, Kera. It is sufficient that our children understand why these dreams must not be spoken of outside this home."

Kera pulled Alila into a tight, one-armed hug. "As you say, Daram."

There was a long, uncomfortable silence round the table. Hadlay suddenly feared for her parents—and her friends. What if it somehow got out that she had dreamed? Maybe her father's idea of leaving the city was best for all of them.

Then Nomish broke into a wide smile. "But Hadlay's dr-reams are not predictive!" Turning his gaze to Hadlay, he asked, "Remem-member the discussion we had this morning about your latest one?"

Hadlay's mind was too full of confusion to follow his line of thinking.

"Did you dream again?" Her mother chewed the inside of her lip. "What did this one say?"

Hadlay hesitated. If simply hearing of her dreams could get her parents and friends killed, she did not want to speak of them.

But Nomish had no such concerns. "The Be-Being told her that she would fail in the task set before her this day. But she was chosen, so she did not fail—the dream was wrong!"

It took a long moment for his meaning to reach everyone. Then relieved smiles began to appear.

"Well, then!" Daram Rakam grinned. "Nothing to worry about!"

Hadlay's mother gave her a hug. "There. We knew it was nothing."

"Nothing at all," Mrs. Rakam said. "Still, dear, given the danger, it's best not to mention dreams again. Not to anyone."

Hadlay wanted to join in the celebration, but something was not quite right. Nomish's pronouncement made sense—certainly she had not failed the emperor's test. And yet somehow she felt they were missing something.

She glanced up, and caught her father's troubled gaze. He, too, clearly sensed there was more to this.

THE PROCESSIONAL WAY

"Hurry!" Mrs. Rakam set a brisk pace to the public square. "We must not be late!"

Hadlay and the others trudged silently behind her. Every step required a force of will. How could they walk so calmly to a place where she and Nomish would be taken from their families?

Her father's idea of leaving the city had been eliminated earlier in the week, when Daram had returned from the shop to inform them that a series of Nomad raids in the outer fields had prompted the overlords to seal the city's gates. No one would be entering or leaving Turris for at least a full moon.

Hadlay had suggested hiding, but Nomish had rejected the idea, reminding her that their parents could not afford to hide. They had to work, and the authorities would surely punish them if their children failed to appear as commanded.

A clattering sound behind them caused them to squeeze against a wall at the side of the narrow street to allow an ox-drawn cart to pass. The Oresed driver gave them a disdainful look as he passed, then did a furious double take at the sight of Hadlay's red hands. Hadlay had tried all week to scrub the red away, but the more she tried, the worse they looked.

She glanced up at her father. His eyes were hollow from sleepless nights, probably spent worrying about her.

Her mother broke the silence, her voice strained with an effort to sound cheerful. "I have a good relationship with Magira, the chief cook in the Tower. I occasionally work for her daughter's household, and she visits often when I am there. She has agreed to carry messages for us when she can."

"She also comes by our shop now and again, as does Overlord Bonobos," Mrs. Rakam said. "We will be able to communicate."

Mr. Rakam spoke for the first time all morn. "If ever you need us, get a message out, and we will find a way to help."

They had forgotten until this morning that the emperor had said they could bring a personal item when they moved into the Tower. Hadlay had rushed about, tossing through all her belongings, trying to find something that would remind her of home. She'd settled on a small etching that Alila had done of both their families, in fine, baked clay. Her father had constructed a frame for it, to protect it from damage. Nomish had brought a game that he had often played with his family, involving colored pawns, pyramidal dice, and a board with twenty squares.

For the first time in Hadlay's memory, Asinus's sermon went by too quickly. She stood between her parents, holding their hands and willing time to stop. But too soon, the red-handed initiates were told to say goodbye to their families, and Hadlay saw that her father's effort not to cry would not last through their final hug.

A commotion near the platform startled Hadlay, and she looked back to see several carriages arriving. The animals that drew them were not horses, but something Hadlay had never seen before. They looked almost like the small rodents the neighbor boy kept as pets, but they had long, shaggy hair, horns, and stood at least a head taller than Nomish. Instead of yokes, they ran inside large, spherical cages that rolled upon the street like wheels.

"Board quickly, initiates." One of the drivers gestured. He wore good leather sandals whose brightly painted straps wove around his ankles and calves, a gray wool kilt with red fringe along its hem, and a belt inlaid with silver at his waist. A narrow drape of embroidered wool, matching his kilt, hung over his left shoulder and trailed down his back, and his polished helmet gleamed in the day's light. "The emperor wants you in the Tower for midday meal."

A swell lodged in Hadlay's throat. She had never been away from her parents for even a night. How could she bear leaving them for moons on end, communicating only by messages?

"See that you stay out of trouble, Hadlay. No matter how things are, be respectful." Her father's eyes filled, and he hugged her tight. "And speak no more of your dreams!" he whispered. "Not even to Nomish—not in the Tower." He set her back, watching her face to see that she understood.

"Don't forget to get me a message as soon as you are settled." Iaras tucked a stray lock of winding hair behind Hadlay's ear.

A sob escaped Hadlay before she could prevent it, and her parents caught her up in their arms. She opened her eyes again and peered over their shoulders to see the Rakams crying as well.

"Move along!" the driver called, this time a bit impatient.

Marba's jaw set, and he put an arm around Hadlay and propelled her to a carriage.

Nomish and another Ramash girl were already seated, looking more than a little awed. It was the first time Hadlay had ridden in a carriage, and this one was much more opulent than any she had ever glimpsed in passing. The frame and seats were covered with white quilted satin, fastened at regular intervals with gold studs. Hadlay sat facing the rear, wanting to see her parents for as long as she could.

The carriage was just about to leave when a peremptory voice stopped it. "Hold! My daughter has yet to board."

Hadlay heard Nomish groan, and turned to see the Sutrams hurrying toward them. For once Ba'ar wore no gloves, and kept her bright red hands raised before her, making certain everyone saw them.

Ba'ar stopped cold when she saw who already occupied the carriage. "Father, this one is all Ramash. Let me take another."

"The others have already left." Apoc Sutram was a burly, much-overdressed man with the Oresed dark hair and thick, bushy beard. With irregular, coarse features and small, swinish eyes, he was the homeliest man Hadlay had ever met. Ba'ar was fortunate to be favored with her mother's beauty; only her large hands and feet told of her paternity. "You will have to make do."

Ba'ar huffed. "Then at least make them ride up with the driver, Father. I have no desire to smell their stench the whole way to the Tower."

Mr. Sutram stuck his large, unhandsome head inside the carriage. "You three will have to go to the fore. My daughter wishes to ride back here."

"No one is riding with me," the driver snapped. "Board, and be quick about it."

Mr. Sutram puffed up, preparing to argue, but the driver simply whistled to the creatures pulling the carriage, and it began to move.

"Hold!" Mr. Sutram ordered, but the coachman continued moving.

All right," Mr. Sutram shouted, and the carriage stopped. "Ba'ar, get in."

"But Father—" Ba'ar hadn't moved, and she now stood far behind the carriage.

Mr. Sutram opened the carriage door. "Get in. You've looked forward to this all week. Do you want to be left behind?"

Hadlay wondered how Ba'ar could have passed the second test. If she had been looking forward to this all week, she could not be too troubled by the thought of leaving her family. Why, then, had she given an answer that seemed to disqualify her?

"Oh, all right!" Ba'ar stalked to the carriage and allowed herself to be helped in. Hadlay scrambled to the seat occupied by Nomish and the other Ramash girl, so that she wouldn't have to sit with Ba'ar. Mr. Sutram shut the door. A heavy silence descended; no one wanted to start a conversation that would end unpleasantly.

The carriage began to roll, and Hadlay strained her neck around to get one final glimpse of her parents. They waved, and then the carriage was off, weaving heavily through the crowd and out of the courtyard, then turning to proceed down the Processional Way, the widest street in Turris.

&

It seemed no time at all before they pulled up to the enclosure that separated the Tower and its grounds from the rest of Turris. The enclosure was made of stone, a thick wall that stood as high as two men. One of the drivers spoke a strange word, and an iron gate appeared, opening with a rusty bellow.

Nomish's eyes widened. "H-h-how d-did—"

"I had heard you'd developed a stutter, Nomish Rakam," Ba'ar said. "The moment the emperor hears you speak, you'll be sent packing. He won't want a defective serving his son."

"He's taking *you*," Hadlay blurted. "He can't be too selective."

Ba'ar's gaze whipped around to Hadlay and darkened. "Don't you *dare* speak to me, *remesh* brat!"

Hadlay half rose from her seat, but Nomish yanked her down and pinched her arm hard, cautioning against further outbursts.

The driver drew the carriage to a halt. "All right, everyone out."

The Tower loomed above them now, so tall Hadlay could not even see its top. It was dizzying, staring up at it. It was broader at the base than she had thought, taking up most of the south wall of the city, and becoming progressively narrow as it stretched into the sky. A staircase spiraled around it, looping ever upward toward the pinnacle, and Hadlay saw workmen on it. The ones high up seemed no larger than ants.

"They are still building," the driver said, following her gaze. "It is not yet high enough to suit the emperor."

Ba'ar flounced out of the carriage and demanded to know who was in charge so she could report Hadlay's offense.

Hadlay climbed down next, feeling small and insignificant. She had lived her life in a home with two rooms and a stable. This place—this home of the emperor—made her feel like a speck of dust in her old doorway. What must it be like to live in such a place? It jolted her to realize she would soon know.

Two uniformed servants greeted them, bidding them to follow.

There were a good many stairs leading up to the entrance, and Nomish had some difficulty traversing them with his dragging leg. Hadlay offered her arm, but he waved her away. She moved to flank him, in case he lost his balance. By the time they reached the top of the stairs they had fallen well behind the other initiates.

"What's c-come into you, speaking to Ba'ar like that?" Nomish asked as they hurried to catch up. "You'll be in t-t-trouble again, and we do not know what pun-punishments they hand out here!"

"I'm sick of her insults."

"It's not worth another p-pulling, is it?"

One of the servants waited for them at the Tower door, cutting off further discussion. "Hurry—the other initiates are already in the dining hall." He gestured them into a huge foyer, guarded by a statue of a snarling cheetah impaled by a spear. The statue gleamed in a light that appeared to come out of several jars stationed along the walkway, steady and unflickering, brighter than any lantern Hadlay had seen.

A woman was pouring something into the jars, or rather she was keeping watch as a pitcher, rising on its own, poured something. Nomish goggled at this, and Hadlay knew that a thousand questions were leapfrogging through his mind. How was the woman doing this? What was the liquid? How did the jars work? Before he could ask any of them, however, their guide hustled them onward.

Something furry ambled toward them. It looked somewhat like a little dog, but it had a broad flat head; a long body; curved, lizard-like front legs; and a snaking tail. It blinked at them with bubble eyes, then made as if to yap at them, but no sound came out. The way it gazed at them was a bit unnerving, as if it had almost human intelligence.

"It's a nuppy," their guide told them, following their stares. "Or a pewt—I forget which. Zêr-Shungalli is fond of mixing different kinds of animals. This one is a cross between a puppy and a newt."

Nomish could contain himself no more. "B-but how did he get a dog to b-b-breed with a newt?"

"No one knows quite how he does it, but he brought hundreds of mixed creatures with him from his journeys, though this one's new since he came here. You'll find them everywhere in the Tower." The servant set a hard pace through an endless, winding hall, casting impatient glances at Nomish's halting gait. "You must hurry. It is not good to keep the emperor waiting."

Finally, they reached another archway. The man spoke a word and the doors swung open. A cavernous dining hall stretched before them, with open windows along the front wall, great oak tables lined in neat rows, and stone floors that were polished to a gleam. Hadlay's mouth gaped open; she had never before been inside a structure larger than the Rakams' shop. The thirty initiates took up only a tiny part of it, clustered near a great dais where Hadlay guessed the emperor and his overlords would sit.

"Find your seats," the servant said. "The emperor will arrive shortly."

Hadlay and Nomish went to the table occupied by the other Ramash initiates, to the rear of the Oresed group. Their table was almost as full as the Oreseds'. It pleased Hadlay that the Ramash had fared so well in the testing. She only wished she were not among them.

Ba'ar had found someone to hear her complaint and was standing to the side of the group, voicing it loudly. "That *remesh* girl insulted me on our way here in the carriage. She and her friend just suffered a purgation for making sport of me, but it appears she has not learned."

She was speaking to a woman in a pleated black tunic with several rows of yellow fringe at the hem. The woman's bust and hips were plump, but her waist was unusually tiny, as if it had been cinched. She had graying hair and a grandmotherly face, but at the moment she wore a very stern expression.

Hadlay's heart sank, expecting that the woman would immediately call her over and issue a punishment. The idea of suffering another purgation, though it had seemed distant in the carriage, now loomed ominously.

But the woman did not even glance at her, though Ba'ar was pointing with vigor. Instead, she flicked her hand, much as one might swat an annoying insect. Ba'ar jumped back, putting a hand to her face as though she had been slapped.

"Do not trouble me with your childish spats, girl."

Ba'ar stared at her with obvious confusion. "But—but I'm Oresed!" When that didn't get the response she expected, she continued. "And *she* is Ramash!"

"I've no time for your bigotry."

"But-but . . ." Ba'ar was near tears, rubbing her cheek, which clearly stung. "But I'm *Oresed!*"

"The prince has decreed that Ramash and Oresed are equal. Go away, or I'll smite you again." The woman raised her hand to punctuate the threat.

Flushing, Ba'ar stumbled away, finding a seat at the Oresed table.

For the first time since the pulling, Nomish had the old impish gleam in his eye. "I th-think I may like it here."

A noise up on the dais caught their attention. The overlords of Turris entered and took their seats at the head table. Hadlay noticed that Bonobos and Asinus made a point of sitting on opposite ends, staring darkly at each other.

As soon as they were seated, a mighty wind hurtled through the room, so strong it picked up Hadlay's braid and whipped it against her cheek. Dust and crumbs flew in all directions, stinging her eyes, and she threw up her hands to protect her face.

Then the room was silent. Blinking away tears, Hadlay saw that the emperor now stood at the center of the master table. The overlords rose, Asinus upending his chair in the process. The initiates quickly followed their lead.

A boy stood next to the emperor, about the same age as the initiates. There was little doubt that he was Zêr-Shungalli. He was like his father in many ways, from the narrow features and slender frame to the iridescent robes and dance-like movements. But he was also different—his eyes and hair were black as night and his complexion dimmer than his father's glowing skin. Hadlay wondered again about the boy's mother—what was she like, and why was she not here?

The emperor made a broad gesture of greeting, and his son followed. "My son, Zêr-Shungalli, and I welcome you to this Tower." His deep voice echoed in the cavernous room. He gestured for everyone to take a seat. "You have been chosen from all the initiates of Turris because you possess certain qualities I value. I imagine some of you are still confused about the way you were chosen. Who has understood?"

There was a pause, as the initiates glanced around at each other. Ba'ar's hand shot up, a smug expression on her face. No doubt this explained Ba'ar's answer to the question determining loyalty. She had understood it was a test, and had given the answer that would bring her to the Tower. Hadlay wondered what the emperor would say if he knew that she had falsified her answer in order to come.

Nomish raised his hand more hesitantly, and Hadlay followed, though she felt it was somewhat untruthful to do so, since Nomish had been the one to solve the puzzle, and she had only understood after he explained.

"You, boy"—the emperor gestured to Nomish—"explain to the rest."

Looking as though he wished the floor would open up and devour him, Nomish rose. "Th-the f-f-fir-first t-t-t-est was for p-pa-patience." He flushed as his anxiety aggravated his stutter.

Some of the Oresed initiates began to snigger and whisper among themselves. Furious, Hadlay lashed at them with her eyes.

Zêr-Shungalli held up his hand, stopping Nomish from speaking further. "You are the boy who was nearly killed in a purgation last moon, in defiance of my son's order." He glared at Asinus.

Nomish flushed even redder as he nodded.

"I'm told you have a limp as well?"

Nomish nodded again, and Hadlay feared Ba'ar's warning would come true, and Nomish would be evicted. She caught his hand, squeezing it tight.

The emperor regarded Nomish with a solemn gaze. "I won't have a cripple serving my son." He waved his hand in a gesture that Hadlay took as a dismissal.

Nomish must've taken it that way too, for he slumped in abject humiliation and turned to leave. But after a few steps, he hesitated. He lifted his leg, bending it slowly. "The stiffness is diminishing!" His eyes widened and he raised his hands to his mouth. "I cannot believe it! I am speaking as I once did!"

"Is there any further pain?" the emperor asked.

Nomish shook his head, grinning. "Hardly any!"

"You are to say, 'No, Your Most High Majesty,'" Asinus barked.

The emperor flicked his hand, and Asinus toppled off his chair. He rolled about the floor like an overturned beetle, unable to rise until servants rushed to assist him. It took three strong men to right him.

The emperor's gaze turned to Hadlay. "You, girl, rise also."

She obeyed, though her knees wobbled beneath her.

He regarded her, no doubt noting the faded bruises on her wrists and face. "Have you any lingering effects from the pulling?"

Hadlay shook her head, then hastened to add, "None, Your Majesty." She did not want to tell him that her arms still stiffened each night when she slept, or that she still hung between the columns in her nightmares.

"That is not quite true, is it?" He waved a hand, and a strange warmth descended over her body. Her arms grew light. She raised them, but felt not even a twinge of pain. The scars and bruises at her wrists were still visible, but no matter, so long as the ache was gone.

"I was most displeased when I learned that this purgation was carried out despite Prince Zêru's clear command. I shall reiterate my son's order: you who are Ramash may consider yourselves the full equals of the Oresed, and none here"—he cast a hard look at Asinus—"may treat you otherwise."

The Oresed initiates seemed to find something on the floor that kept their attention, but some of them had sullen expressions.

"Thank you, Your Majesty," Nomish said, his voice still pitched with excitement. "Thank you very much!"

The emperor nodded. "Now, continue your explanation of the test."

Hadlay sensed that she was dismissed, and quietly took her seat again as Nomish explained each of the tests. The other initiates wore expressions of dawning understanding as they heard him. All but Ba'ar, who sulked, arms crossed.

When Nomish finished, the emperor smiled. "Very good, boy. I am impressed with your intellect." He turned to the others. "Do any of you have questions?"

One Oresed boy raised his hand. "Sir—Your Most High Majesty—why were we not informed that these things were part of the test?"

"I elected to test you secretly, so that no one would falsify the results." He raised his eyes and spoke to the other initiates. "Which of you might have done things differently, had you known you were being tested?"

Hadlay started to raise her hand, then realized that she would be admitting that she had not wanted to come here. Afraid she might offend the emperor, she quickly dropped her hand to the table.

Unfortunately, he had seen. He gave her an empathetic smile. "It would be understandable, given what you have suffered, that you would fear coming here. I take it you did not wish to pass the test?"

Hadlay swallowed. "Once I knew it meant leaving my family, Your Majesty . . ." She hesitated, but the emperor gestured for her to continue. "I hoped to fail the test."

The emperor nodded. "I knew that many of those who had the qualities I wished for would feel as you did, young lady. I regret that I must part you from your family, but I believe you will one day be glad that you failed to disqualify yourself."

The emperor continued speaking, but Hadlay did not hear him. Her ears buzzed as a sudden realization bore down on her, almost crushing her with its weight. The Being in her dream had not said that she would fail in the task the emperor had set for her. He had said that she would fail in the task she set *herself* to accomplish. And she had been trying, by the end, to disqualify herself.

Her mouth felt dry, and she reached for a goblet of water, but spilled more than she managed to drink. She glanced at Nomish, but he was absorbed in the emperor's speech.

She wished there was a way to speak to her father, but she dared not send him a message about this. Nor, she realized, could she tell Nomish, not if it put him in danger. She was alone with this.

What could she do?

She had no choice. She would ignore the dreams, pretend that they were not happening. She would speak of them to no one, and go on about her business. Perhaps the Being would grow tired of bothering her and go to someone else. Someone better, wiser, more capable of solving riddles.

The idea calmed her somewhat, and, taking another sip of her water, she returned her attention to the emperor.

". . . no doubt you all wonder what the coming days will bring. These people sharing my table are my overlords, who will be overseeing your instruction." He gestured to each in turn. "To my far right is Asinus, Overlord of the Lawgivers. Beside him is Aurum, Overlord of the Treasury, and Buthotos, Overlord of Security. To my left are Bonobos, Overlord of Science, and Sfika, Overlord of the Tower." At the introduction, Bonobos airily waved his hook. Sfika was the grandmotherly woman Ba'ar had approached. "There is a sixth, Zamzom, Overlord of Mysteries, whom a few select initiates shall meet at another time."

The emperor continued. "Soon, you will be divided into five groups of six initiates. Each group will rotate through two-week sessions with each of the overlords, performing assigned chores and lessons. The overlords will assess you for abilities suitable to his or her field of authority. At the end of five cycles, you will each be assigned an apprenticeship.

Nomish grinned at Hadlay. He had long wished he could apprentice himself to Bonobos. Now his wish might come to pass. Hadlay did not know which of the overlords she would have mentor her. Other than, of course, she would rather lick the feet of a chicken than spend her days with Asinus.

The emperor went on. "No doubt many of you tried to wash the red from your hands, am I correct?"

There were nods around the room, and Hadlay noticed that a few had hands even more raw than her own.

He whispered a word into the air, and then he smiled. "Look again."

Exclamations of wonder rippled through the room as the initiates discovered that their hands were plain again. The emperor spoke another word, and a number of the initiates gasped as they rose up from their seats, floating in the air above their tables. Likely it was the first time they had experienced it. Hadlay had been lifted before. Remembering the last time, just before the pulling, her lungs froze—she couldn't breathe! It struck her as she hung there, paralyzed, that if the emperor ever wanted to harm her, there would be nothing she could do.

He gestured and they drifted to their seats again. The moment she was released, Hadlay scooted over to Nomish and clutched his arm.

"In the days and weeks to come, many of you will learn to perform wonders such as these. Your fellows in Turris call it magic and speak of it fearfully. But it is quite common here in the Tower. Those who show the strongest command of the powers will receive further instruction from Zamzom, learning the deeper mysteries."

Hadlay and Nomish exchanged glances. They had seen magic performed by the authorities, of course, but it had never occurred to them that *they* might work it. Would they be able to appear and disappear as the emperor had done? Or cause people to lift into the air? The thought of being able to swat Ba'ar without touching her, as Sfika had done, made Hadlay want to giggle—until it occurred to her that Ba'ar might be able to return the favor.

The emperor spoke again, breaking into the tangle of Hadlay's thoughts. "From time to time in the performance of your duties, you may be privy to conversations between myself and my son, or confidential matters of government. *You will speak of these things to no one.*" A thousand whispered echoes filled the chamber as he paused, and the hairs on Hadlay's neck prickled. "Take this counsel to heart, as you will not be warned again, and violation of this first rule will bring immediate and, I'm afraid, quite severe punishment. The remaining rules you will learn as you participate in your instruction. Take your duties seriously, and you will do well."

Having finished his welcoming speech, the emperor waved a hand, and suddenly a stream of platters—with no one to carry them—entered through the doorway and floated toward them. A few of the initiates leaped from their seats.

"It's quite all right," the emperor said. "Remain seated."

The initiates returned to their benches, though most of them continued to stare warily at the platters as they settled upon the tables.

Well past his astonishment at the magic, Nomish was gaping at the food. There were platters heaped with meat and fowl; fresh fruits; and all manner of vegetables, soft breads, and cheeses; and there were pitchers of sweet juices to wash everything down.

The aromas were unlike anything Hadlay had ever smelled, though even as she thought this, she found herself longing for the plain fare at her mother's table.

"Have you ever seen such a feast?" One of the boys mumbled over a mouth full of bread. "I feel I've died and gone to N'de!"

Another boy kicked him hard, silently reminding him that the bedtime story of N'de was forbidden. It would not do to speak of such things here. Hadlay glanced over her shoulder to see if anyone at the Oresed table had noticed, and she was relieved that no one seemed to be listening.

Perhaps it had been a good thing that Ramash had never before been accepted into the Tower. Unguarded moments such as this could put them all in great danger.

Rules and More Rules

"Step lively, initiates." Sfika's sandals beat a rapid rhythm up a narrow, winding corridor.

Hadlay was becoming confused by all the turns and bends. She could swear they had doubled back several times.

Nomish groaned, rubbing his stomach. "I may never eat again."

She laughed. "You didn't have to try to eat everything on the table."

He gave her a puzzled look as if she'd spoken in a foreign tongue. "And let good food go to waste?"

Another boy, whose name was Rasab, came to join them. He was small of stature, shorter even than Hadlay, and severely thin. His head was bare, sprouting patches of stubble that spoke of a recently shorn slave-lock. "Even with all we ate, the platters were still half-full when we left the table. I wish I could send some of it to my father. Our master leaves us to scavenge for our meals, and scraps have been harder to come by lately."

Sfika stopped abruptly when they reached two heavy wooden doors, no different from any number they had passed. "Here we are. Boys, your dormitory is to the left. Girls, to the right. Rule Number Two: There is to be no crossing this hallway to enter the other dormitory." At a gesture from Sfika, the doors swung open as if pushed, though no hand had touched them.

The girls' dormitory consisted of a rectangular room the size of ten Ramash homes. Its walls were a jade-colored tile, with a sole, narrow window at the end. Comfortable-looking beds lined the walls—shallow wooden boxes with thick mattresses made up with ivory linens and plum-colored blankets. Beside each bed was a wooden side table with a good-sized drawer, and a narrow clothing rack in which hung several pale gray tunics with white trim, sashes, and belts. Matching slippers sat on the floor beneath. Even from a distance, Hadlay could tell that, despite the uninspiring color, the clothing was far finer than any she'd owned.

"Your beds have been assigned, and there will be no switching," Sfika said. "Girls, settle in while I speak to the boys."

Hadlay looked more closely and saw that each bed had a girl's name engraved at the foot. She walked down the row and found hers all the way at the end by the window. She was dismayed to realize that Oresed and Ramash were mingled. Ba'ar's bed was directly across from hers, and another Oresed girl, whose name was Citna, was to her right. She heard groans as others made the discovery as well.

"I see I shall have to become accustomed to the stink of Ramash," Ba'ar muttered as she claimed her bed.

"Did you hear that?" Hadlay asked the Ramash girl whose bed was across from Citna's. "I'll vow I heard a fly."

Citna sniffed. "No wonder, with the stench coming from your direction. At first, I thought it was something I had stepped in."

Hadlay saw her exchange a wink with Ba'ar. No doubt the two would soon be fast friends.

Just then, something flew in through the doorway and soared around the room, dropping feathers and nuts everywhere as it banged into walls.

Several of the girls screamed and dived under their blankets as the frantic creature flew about seeking an exit. A few others seized whatever they could find to use as weapons.

Snatching up a hamper that was evidently meant for laundry, Hadlay stepped up on a bed, swiping at the animal as it passed by. She missed once, twice, leaping from bed to bed after the beast, until finally she felt a satisfying *whump* in the hamper. She grabbed a pillow and covered the top so it could not escape.

Sfika appeared in the doorway. "What is all this ruckus?" she asked through clenched teeth. "Has no one acquainted you girls with the fact that this is the emperor's home? If you have disturbed him, you will be dreadfully sorry! Rule Number Three: Everything must be done as quietly as possible."

"Something just flew in from the corridor." Hadlay held up the hamper. "I've caught it, whatever it is."

The girls who were hiding under their blankets peered up at her, then they came out, looking a little sheepish.

Sfika came over and peeked at the creature, which appeared to be stunned. "It is one of Prince Zêru's squinches, escaped from the bestiary again." Before someone could ask the obvious question, she enlightened them. "A squinch is a mix between something called a squirrel and a finch. I'm afraid there are many such monstrosities around the Tower these days."

The hamper jumped in Hadlay's hand. "It's awake!"

Sfika spoke a strange word into the air. "Some kennelgrooms will be coming up the corridor. Go out and meet them with the hamper and they'll take this creature back to the bestiary before it escapes again. Squinches can chew through almost anything."

Hadlay went out into the hall, where she was relieved to see a number of men running toward her. Wondering how Sfika had known they were coming, she handed the hamper over with an explanation. They thanked her and departed, and she returned to the dormitory. She waved at Nomish, who, along with several other boys, had gathered around the door to the girl's dormitory to see what the noise was about.

Sfika was giving instructions. "Personal items belong in your nightstand drawers, which have been charmed to open only for the girl whose name is on the nearest bed. You'll place your old clothing in your laundry baskets tonight, and they will be disposed of."

"But this is my favorite tunic!" Ba'ar protested.

"My best as well." Hadlay didn't add that her mother had made her clothing. She looked at the careful stitching along the hem and wanted to cry.

"Small loss for you," Citna said with a smirk.

"When you receive an instruction, there will be no argument. Rule Number Four." Sfika braced her hands on her hips. "Each of you has been provided seven good tunics for everyday use, and one formal tunic for use at special occasions. From now on, you will wear the clothing provided for you. Try not to stain or tear anything, as you will be punished if your garments need replacement before year's end. Each evening, you will place dirty tunics in the hampers, and each morning, put on new ones. Now, follow me."

The initiates—both girls and boys—filed after her, again winding around bends until they were thoroughly confused. Sfika reached a door and it swung open. "Here is the boys' privy. The girls' is a little further down the corridor. You will each be expected to bathe at least thrice weekly."

Several of the Oresed boys groaned. The Ramash youth looked at one another with blank stares. *Bathe?*

"Toad's nostrils, no wonder you stink!" Citna exclaimed. "Have you never heard of a bath?"

"Of course they haven't," Ba'ar said. "It's the way *civilized* people cleanse themselves."

Hadlay felt heat rise to her cheeks, but Sfika spoke before she could retort. "Ramash homes don't have baths. They cannot afford them."

This silenced Citna, who seemed stunned by the idea that someone might not be able to afford something she clearly viewed as mundane.

But Ba'ar was not impressed. "They are paid little because their labor is worth little. They are ignorant and bestial, living in stables with their animals. Who would employ them, except for the most menial work?"

Sfika gave her a withering look. "Evidently the emperor is prepared to do so. I advise you to mind your tongue, for you sound as though you are ridiculing his decision. Rule Number Five: Never criticize the emperor, even by implication. He has little tolerance for insult. And you'll find he has ways of knowing the things we say and do."

The initiates exchanged worried looks.

"Follow me," Sfika ordered, walking into the washroom.

The room was tiled with a mosaic depicting the sea and all its creatures, and there were wood stools with holes lining the walls, and small and large bronze basins with spouts and drains that kept water cycling through them. Sfika explained the uses for each of these and described the method for taking a bath. Hadlay didn't see the point, but she was curious enough to try one.

"All right, back to your dormitories." Sfika spoke loudly to be heard above the noise of rushing water. "You'll spend the afternoon becoming acquainted, and then come to the kitchen when summoned for evening meal."

The initiates followed her out of the washroom and partway down the corridor before Sfika looked back and saw that they were behind her. "I said, 'back to your dormitories.' Rule Number Six: Always follow instructions."

"Yes, ma'am," Nomish spoke up. "But we—"

"Don't know how to get back!" Sfika tapped her forehead. "I knew I was forgetting something—the guiding tiles!" She gestured for them to turn about. "Now, all of you think about your dormitories. Good. Look down at the tiles on the floor. Do you notice that some of them are lighter than the others?" The initiates nodded. "Just think about where you want to go, and the lighter tiles will guide you there. Do take care what you are thinking, though—random thoughts can lead you far astray. Now, good afternoon, initiates. I shall see you after the evening meal."

As promised, the tiles guided them back to the dormitories, though not without some confusion when one of the boys realized he had urgent need of the facilities back in the privy, and the guiding tiles began to retrace their steps.

The girls divided into two groups, the Oresed by the door, and the Ramash around Hadlay's bed. Hadlay's group introduced themselves and began an animated discussion of the things they had seen thus far.

"Did you see those beasts that drew the carriages?" asked Rezen, a tall girl with thick, sand-colored curls that looked even more unmanageable than Hadlay's.

"They're called yamsters. I was told they are part hamster and part yak, whatever that is," Fa'an said. Hadlay had met Fa'an before—she sometimes spent time with Alila. She seemed nice enough, though being with her made Hadlay long for her friend instead.

"What other creatures have you seen?" Hadlay asked.

"I haven't seen others," a girl named Aa'mash said, "but one of the servants warned that if we see a fly that has white stripes along its wings, we mustn't startle it. They're called flunks; some sort of cross between fly and skunk. The servant said that several escaped their case last week. Someone tried to swat one in the dining hall a few days ago, and they only just got the stink out of the tapestries."

"Good to know," Fa'an said.

"Also, there were furmites—hairy, crawling things that chewed holes in everything, even stone. The emperor ordered those creatures exterminated, but not before they had bored tunnel holes all over the Tower."

Another girl, called Raimog, cleared her throat. "Has anyone learned whether any servants here are married?"

"No," said Ma'at, a shy girl who clutched a small rag hare. "Why?"

Raimog's eyes filled with tears. "I was going to announce my betrothal next moon. I was hoping perhaps we could still do so. My intended was not chosen, but he would be pleased to do any work they might give him, if he could remain with me."

The question caused Hadlay to look at the faces of her newfound friends and wonder what kind of future any of them could hope for.

As they chattered, Hadlay occasionally caught drifts of the conversations among the Oresed girls. They seemed to be having more difficulty getting on.

"He is Nafal!" she heard Citna say.

"No, he isn't!" said another girl, whose dark eyes burned with anger.

More of the Oresed girls joined, taking one side or the other, and everyone spoke at once. The quarrel broke off abruptly when Rezen spoke up from the Ramash group and reminded the Oresed girls of Rule Number Three. Before they could return to their conversations, a servant came to summon them.

This time the initiates were taken to the kitchen, a large, overwarm room with a brick oven and a blazing hearth. Hadlay would have expected the room to be filled with servants, cutting, mixing, carving, and stirring. All this work was going on, but without human hands to guide it. Floating knives sliced a roasted side of meat. The slices drifted to a large platter already garnished with cucumbers and onions. In the hearth, a kettle boiled merrily, while a wooden spoon stirred. Hadlay jumped as an oven beside her burst open, and several loaves of bread floated over to a basket on the counter.

The person who seemed to be directing all of this was Magira, the chief cook Hadlay's mother had befriended. Magira was pale for an Oresed, though she had the dark eyes and hair. Her face was round and kind, and she was plump, just as Hadlay thought a cook should be. She wore the gray Tower tunic with yellow fringes at the hem. When she noticed that the initiates had entered, she smiled broadly.

"Greetings!" As she spoke, there was a clatter all throughout the kitchen. Hadlay glanced around to see knives, spoons, and platters dropping everywhere. One hunk of meat slithered from its platter and plopped to the floor.

"Oh, dear!" Magira spoke a few words, and everything resumed. The meat on the floor rose and lobbed itself into a chute cut through one of the walls. After ensuring that everything was working once again, Magira turned back to the initiates. "The powers are quite helpful. Unfortunately, they are also easily distracted. I trust you are settling in well?"

The scents that hung in this room caused Hadlay's stomach to rumble, even though she had vowed just a few hours earlier that she would not be able to eat another bite that day.

"Well enough, ma'am," one of the boys said.

"Good!" she said. "Well, help yourselves to the platters stacked on the counter, and then fill them from the kettles at the hearth. From now on, you'll report here at mealtime, and though you may find the servants' food a bit plainer than the emperor's banquet, I promise you'll not go hungry."

True to Magira's word, the food was not quite as rich as what they'd eaten earlier, but it looked tasty enough. The initiates filled their platters and sat at several wooden tables to the rear of the kitchen. Soon they were engaged in lively discussion. The Oresed girls returned to their dispute, which got quite out of hand until Magira came and broke it up.

"How do you suppose the t-tiles know where we want to go?" Nomish wondered.

"Did you just stutter?" Hadlay asked.

"I don't believe so. I've been speaking normally since the emperor healed me."

"I heard it too," Fa'an said.

"Well, if I did, it was probably habit." Nomish rose to refill his platter.

Another boy, who had introduced himself as Kayshti, turned to join them. "I've not eaten this well in all my life."

"I wonder how our parents are faring," Ma'at said, her voice nearly a whisper. The mention of family brought them all to a gloomy silence.

Sfika bustled into the kitchen. "All right, initiates, finish up!" She glanced at a couple of the Oresed boys. "Start clearing the tables."

"No need," Magira said. "It's really quite simple—" She started to say something, evidently intending to do the work by magic, when Sfika caught her arm.

"Let them do it," Sfika said. "They must learn to follow instructions."

One of the Oresed boys protested and received an invisible swat similar to the one Ba'ar had gotten and a stern lecture about Rules Four and Six. Without being asked, Hadlay rose and set to work, and, after shoveling a last bite into his mouth, Nomish followed suit. Rezen set to wiping the tables with a clean cloth, humming a beautiful song Hadlay had never heard before.

With all of them working, the tables were cleared in short order, the plates rinsed clean, and everything back in order.

While all this was going on, Hadlay found an opportunity to speak privately with Magira. Nomish was sweeping nearby, where he could hear what was said.

"I'm Hadlay Mivana." She kept her voice low, not wanting to draw attention to the conversation in case it might be against one of Sfika's rules. "My mother is Iaras."

Magira nodded. "Of course, dear. I saw the resemblance right off. I expect you would like me to pass a message to your families?" She nodded toward Nomish, drawing him into their conversation.

"Just . . ." Hadlay's eyes welled with tears as she thought of home. "Tell them Nomish and I are well. And that we . . ." She choked, unable to finish the sentence. The last thing she needed was Ba'ar to see her crying.

"We miss them," Nomish finished for her.

Magira's eyes were damp as well as she scooped both Hadlay and Nomish to her sides, one under each arm.

Nomish grinned. "And tell my parents that my injuries from the pulling trouble me no more—the emperor has healed me!"

"I'll be sure to tell them, dears. They'll be pleased to know you're faring so well."

Rasab had overheard. "If you are willing, mistress, would you speak also to my father? He is a tentmaker, and his master's shop is near the meat market." His lower lip wobbled as he spoke. "Our master was most displeased when I was chosen by the emperor, as he meant to sell me in the fall—I fear he will deal with my father harshly."

Magira regarded him with a kind smile. "I'll look in on him, my boy, and tell him you are well. And I'll do what I can to persuade his master to treat him kindly. The man would be a fool to make an enemy of you, now that you serve the emperor."

A tear gleamed in Rasab's eye as he bowed to her. "Thank you, mistress."

"Everyone in the Tower calls me by name, boy. I am Magira to my friends."

Flustered, Rasab bowed again and returned to his cleaning.

When the work was finished, Sfika inspected the kitchen, walking between the tables and instructing one of the boys to come brush up some stray crumbs. Finally, she nodded. "Good enough. Now, go to your dormitories and get some sleep. Rule Number Seven: Always get plenty of rest. Mornings here come very early, and you have much to learn!"

THE BESTIARY

The key is nearly in your hand," the Being's voice rippled through Hadlay's dream. "You came close to rejecting it, but now you have returned. Accept my calling, dearest one. Receive the key while you can, for time is growing short."

Hadlay wanted to ask about the key, but the Being's color changed from opaline white, traced with all the colors of the rainbow, to glaring reds and oranges. "Be heedful now, for darkness and confusion are all around. You will find friends among those you now consider foes, but there also will be enemies among those you believe to be your friends. The things you desire seem good to you now, but the cost is greater than you know. Leave aside these things and seek only the key . . ."

Hadlay jolted awake, her heart slamming against her ribs. Another dream! How had she come close to rejecting the key? She did not even remember seeing one. And all this talk of enemies and friends—what did it mean?

She squeezed her eyes shut, remembering her decision yesterday to give these dreams no mind. They were dangerous. She could not speak of them. She would not think of them.

She rolled over and opened her eyes, allowing them to adjust to the darkened room. A slip of moonlight came through the one window, illuminating the shapes of the other beds. A horrible pang of loneliness washed over her. She would not see her father's smile today, nor hear her mother's voice scolding her to hurry and dress.

She rose and walked to the narrow window near her bed. She tried to put her head out the window, but she bumped her forehead against something hard. On closer inspection, she realized that there was a strange, clear stone of some kind set within the window frame, keeping the cool night air at bay. There were wavy-looking distortions; it was like looking through water. She touched it delicately. It was hard as flint, and cool. When she took her hand away, a smudge from her finger remained on the surface. She used her sleeve to dab at it, and the smudge was wiped away.

She was surprised to discover she was very high up, nearly at the top of the wall that ringed the city. Below her, the city's rooftops were bathed in moonlight.

The other girls were breathing deeply and evenly, except the shy one, Ma'at, who appeared to be having a fitful dream. It would be some time before they woke.

Last night, Hadlay had made her bed in a stable with her dearest friend, whispering long into the darkness and finally dozing off to the sound of her father's snore. Tonight, she was alone, even among so many girls. She did not want to lie down again. In the silence she would torment herself with longings for home. Better to be busy.

She took a tunic from the rack beside her bed and donned some slippers, then made her way between the rows of sleeping girls. Sfika had said that they had to take baths; this seemed a good time to try one.

The corridor was faintly lit by the strange tiles that guided her, taking her round one bend, then another, until she was certain she'd been misled. Finally, though, she reached the girls' washroom.

The room was dark when she entered, but then the jars of light began to glow, dimly at first, but steadily increasing, until the room was brightly lit. It unnerved her that the jars seemed to know that she was here. She wished Alila were with her as she warily regarded the large basins full of warm water. Alila's timidity always made her feel brave. She took a deep breath, then hurried to the first of the basins, pulling off her nightrobe and stepping into the water.

She sat and allowed herself to sink down until the water came to her chin. As the warmth soaked into her body, she began to understand the benefit of bathing. The emperor might have healed her yesterday, but through the night, the stiffness and aches had settled in again. In the warmth of the water, her discomfort eased once more. This was wonderful, an experience she would not mind repeating thrice weekly—daily if it was allowed.

A tiny whirlpool rotated above the drain, where old water ran out as the opening above poured new water in. She brushed it with her foot, felt it tickle her toes. After playing with it a little, she poured some of the fluid Sfika had shown them into her palm and rubbed it on her skin. It didn't seem to do anything other than make her feel slippery, and that quickly dissipated in the warm water. She unbraided her hair and took the other gooey liquid and rubbed it through, then ducked under the water to rinse it out as Sfika had instructed. Suds bubbled around her, and she caught them in her hands and blew them into the air.

After a time, she noticed that her fingers were pruning. There seemed to be nothing more to do, so she rose out of the basin and put on the fresh tunic. She had never felt such soft fabric. It looked like wool but had the silky feel of cat's fur.

Along the far wall, there were several small cupboards, each bearing an initiate's name. She located hers and opened it, finding a hair comb, a soft cloth, and a small bottle of fluid, the use of which she did not know. She dabbed a little of it on her finger. It smelled of flowers. It felt like oil, though it looked more like milk.

Then she noticed it: On the inside of the cupboard door hung a round, flat piece of clear stone, similar to what she had seen earlier in the window. When she moved to look at it, she was startled by her own reflection. It was a mirror! It reminded her of her dreams, though the mirror in her dreams was much brighter and perfectly clear. This one had a greenish tinge and wavy distortions that first made her nose grow large, and then her forehead, as if she were making faces at herself. Looking closer, she could also see tiny bubbles and little flecks of what looked like dirt. Still, the similarity was so great that it seemed important. What did it mean? Had her dreams been leading her here to the Tower?

Hadlay's head ached with all the unanswered questions. She thought of her father, wishing she could ask him what to do, but of course she could not. Once more she settled on her course. She would ignore these dreams. She would refuse to think of them.

Feeling terribly alone, she used the cloth to soak up the wetness of her hair as best she could, then combed and braided it. When she finished, she thought of returning to the dormitory, but she saw no profit in sitting there watching the others sleep. She preferred to explore a bit.

The tiles were no help, since she had no idea where she might want to go. Racking her mind for things she'd heard about that sounded interesting, she thought of the bestiary. Immediately the tiles lit up, showing her the way.

As she made her way down endless corridors, Hadlay became aware that the strange, greenish mirrors were everywhere. When they were coupled with the lighted jars, they seemed to amplify the light. She knew Nomish would find the mirrors and their uses endlessly fascinating. She only found them troubling.

After rounding what felt like the hundredth turn, Hadlay came to a huge door, behind which she could hear all manner of animal sounds. The smell that came to her also confirmed she had found her destination. She opened the door slowly, praying she would not release any of the beasts inside.

The sight that greeted her was truly astonishing. The dimly lit room was enormous, nearly the size of the entire marketplace of Turris. Untidy rows of cages formed jagged aisles. One wall was enclosed with some type of mesh, and Hadlay could see birds—or birdlike creatures—perched inside it.

She glanced around, but saw no one to object to her presence. Cautiously, she moved toward the cages, wondering how close she might go without disturbing the animals.

"What are you doing here?" A loud voice made Hadlay jump.

A shadow near the wall shifted, and then Zêr-Shungalli emerged into the dim light. The emperor's son! How had she not seen him when she entered?

His fierce black eyes and thundering expression filled her with terror. She froze for a moment, heart in her throat, uncertain what to do. Should she bow? Run? She found her voice. "Excuse me, Prince Zêru. I did not know you were here, or I would not have entered."

"Did you come to harm my creatures?"

"No!" The denial sprang from her mouth. "Only to look at them. I encountered some of them yesterday, and they were so interesting, I . . ."

"Interesting, you say?" His scowl evaporated. "Which creatures did you see?"

Taken aback by his abrupt change of mood, it took Hadlay a second to focus on his question. "Well, there were yamsters drawing our carriage—what exactly is a yak?" She wondered belatedly if it was allowed to ask him questions.

He smiled, so apparently he didn't mind. "They are something like an ox, but with long, shaggy hair. We found them in our travels abroad."

"Well, yamsters are certainly strange," Hadlay said.

"They don't make very interesting pets, though. All they want to do is sleep all day and plod on their wheels all night." He pointed to a huge cage near the far wall, with a giant wheel spinning as the yamsters took turns in it.

Hadlay studied him from the corner of her eye. She was short, but she had never known anyone who could rest his elbow on the top of her head without raising his arm. Looking closer at his skin, Hadlay saw that it was covered with tiny, shimmering flecks, almost like the scales of a fish in the way they caught and reflected light. His features were even and pleasant, and his dark hair had a blue-green sheen that almost glowed.

Zêr-Shungalli was handsome, she decided, but in a strange sort of way. She wondered again if he and his father were kin to the Nafal.

"What other creatures have you seen?" he asked.

"A nuppy—but it rambled off before I could get a very good look. And then a squinch flew into our dormitory, and I caught it in a basket . . ."

"You were the one who caught it?" He smiled, revealing teeth as white as pearls. "I am pleased with you, then. I was afraid it might get out of the Tower. A snowl got away during the half moon, and father was very angry with me. He doesn't want my beasts getting loose and frightening the citizens."

"What is a snowl?"

"A mix of snail and owl. I had named him Blodeuwedd. He trailed slime all over one of the guardsmen on the wall before he flew away."

The creature sounded perfectly disgusting, but the prince looked sad, so Hadlay said, "I'm sorry. But surely he'll find his way home. Owls are very smart."

The prince shook his head. "He's dead by now, I expect."

"How do you know?"

"Because we"—he hesitated, glancing at her sharply—"*they* have a special diet. They cannot live long on normal foods." His eyes seemed to focus on something distant. Something that grieved him deeply.

Hoping to cheer him up, she asked, "How many creatures have you mixed? Can you show me more?"

"We brought many back with us from our travels, and the servants here are already finding uses for them. Here's a new project I'm working on." Prince Zêru pointed her to a cage, in which paced a small, doglike animal with reddish fur.

"That's a fox!" Hadlay exclaimed, surprised to see a normal creature in this room.

"I'm thinking of mixing him with a swan."

"Making a swox?" Hadlay chuckled at the thought. "How do you get these creatures to mix?" Nomish would strangle her if he knew she'd met the prince and had failed to ask.

The prince laughed, and for a moment it seemed as if many other voices laughed with him. "Perhaps I'll show you one day." He directed her over to the mesh cage that lined the wall. "My oldest mix is Alphonse—he's a mix between an eagle and serpent. He hides when strangers come in, but if you look, you'll see him behind the birdhouse."

Sure enough, trembling behind a wooden birdhouse was an eagle-ish creature—feathered and winged, with talons—but its body was long and narrow like a snake, and two mean-looking fangs protruded from its beak.

"A feathered serpent! I shouldn't think he'd be so shy," Hadlay said. "He looks very frightening."

When she looked at the prince again, she found him studying her.

"You're Ramash, aren't you? I have never seen one up close before." He walked around her, looking her over in a way that made her feel like one of his creatures. "Not so different from the Oresed, except the gold hair, which is actually quite nice." He came around and looked at her face. "Those spots on your nose—what are they?"

"Freckles." Hadlay was unnerved by this scrutiny. She wanted to lower her eyes, but somehow she could not. "They . . . come from the sun . . ."

He absorbed the information, then turned back to his creatures. "Asinus says that the Ramash are ugly, but I guess you look all right."

Before Hadlay could decide how to respond, a horn sounded, echoing throughout the room. The creatures in the aviary flapped their wings, scattering feathers and what looked like bits of raw meat everywhere.

"It's morning," the prince said. "Father will be waiting for me."

Before she could thank him or bid farewell, Prince Zêru vanished, leaving Hadlay staring into the empty space where he had stood. She blinked, turning full circle to see where he had gone, but only the creatures remained. With a lingering look at the fox, she hastened out, heading for the dormitories.

As she walked, she replayed the encounter in her mind, trying to clarify what it was about Prince Zêru that had left her with so many conflicting feelings. Other than being a little blunt, she decided, he had actually been pleasant to talk to, though he seemed unhappy somehow. Like his father, he had a music and grace about him that made him beautiful to watch. And yet something about him both fascinated and alarmed her.

As she rounded a corner, she nearly collided with Nomish, who was muttering to himself and following the tiles. He looked quite nice in a fresh knee-length kilt, with belt and sandals all similar in color and texture to the clothing Hadlay wore. At the moment, though, he seemed confused. "I had planned to go to the washroom, but the tiles keep taking me up to the kitchen." Just then, his stomach growled loudly.

Hadlay laughed. "Follow me. I'll get you there."

"Where have you been?" Nomish demanded, plucking a feather off Hadlay's robe as they walked.

"The bestiary. Zêr-Shungalli was there."

"Really? Did you meet him? What's he like?"

She was considering what to tell him about the meeting when Sfika appeared, with a few sleepy-eyed initiates trailing behind her, evidently headed toward the privy.

"There you are!" she exclaimed. "I had feared you might have tried to leave during the night. The Tower's outer portals have been instructed not to open for unaccompanied initiates, so you would have wandered until someone tracked you down. Rule Number Eight: No one is going home."

As vast as the Tower was, Hadlay suddenly felt very like the fox that had been pacing in its cage.

FLUNKED!

"Today, Overlord Asinus will begin with your instruction in protocol." Sfika gathered the initiates after the morning meal and led them to the dining hall, where Asinus sat waiting. He smiled, revealing pitted yellow teeth that reminded Hadlay of her father's aging horse.

Before Sfika even left the hall, Asinus had launched into one of his lengthy oratories, made worse by the fact that he refused to permit the initiates to sit. It seemed that sitting in the presence of one's betters was one of the first violations of protocol. Hadlay wondered why the emperor had invited them to sit at the banquet yesterday, but she knew better than to ask.

"If you encounter the emperor or his son, you must avert your eyes and prostrate yourself instantly. If you fail to do so, you will be hanged by your feet off the high flagpole for a day."

Hadlay hoped that Asinus would not hear of her meeting with the prince, since she had failed to do this. She wondered why the prince had not seemed to care.

"You must always have a pleasant smell when you are near the emperor or his son. If you smell otherwise, you will be required to shovel the stables for a month."

Well, at least she'd had a bath this morn. Though given the strong smells in the bestiary, she could not imagine that the prince would have noticed if she hadn't.

There were at least one hundred fifty titles by which one might address the emperor and his son, mostly variations on "Your Royal Majesty," or

"Your Regal Highness." Asinus listed every one, and the context in which it was to be used.

He droned on through the day, continuing even as he ate his midday meal. The initiates stood, undismissed and miserable, watching him wolf his food and trying not to flinch as his words hurled half-chewed bits of food an impressive distance from where he sat. It was only when one of the Oresed girls, who had been shuffling from foot to foot with increasing desperation, finally flung up a hand and begged to use the privy that they had any break at all. And they were ordered back right away, to stand the rest of the day until Asinus's voice grew ragged.

Before dismissing them, Asinus rose and paced ponderously before the assembled initiates. He shook his head at the Ramash as if he still could not believe they had been accepted. Then he paused before Ba'ar.

"Ba'ar Sutram, I have not had an opportunity to see you at work, but I know your family. At the end of your evaluation, I shall request that you be apprenticed with me."

Ba'ar beamed at him. "Of course, Overlord Asinus! It will be a pleasure to learn from you!" She turned a prideful gaze at the other Oresed.

Hadlay grimaced. Ba'ar an overlord! No doubt she would gleefully continue Asinus's ill dealings among the Ramash. Hadlay wondered if there was a way to prevent him from choosing her.

"You are dismissed," Asinus said, casting a hard look at the Ramash initiates.

"Don't worry, Citna," Ba'ar said as the initiates made their way to the evening meal. "I'll ask that Asinus apprentice you to one of his lawgivers or scribes. We cannot all become overlords."

"You are too kind, Ba'ar," Citna replied, though Hadlay thought she could see a flare of anger in her eyes.

The meal was a silent affair, with most of the initiates too mentally exhausted to converse. And then it was time for sleep again. As the girls changed into their nightrobes, Hadlay went to her nightstand to look at the picture Alila had etched for her. The drawer stuck when she tried to open it, so she kneeled by her bed and pulled the stand nearer to inspect it more closely. When she tried it again, the drawer opened smoothly, as if nothing were wrong. Except—

Hadlay yelped and nearly fell over as the drawer released a fly, which she quickly realized must be a flunk. It buzzed around the room, trailing stink behind it. One of the girls tried to shoo it away, startling it and making things worse.

"Why, Hadlay," said Citna with a wicked grin, "it seems you did hear a fly earlier."

Summoned by the commotion, Sfika appeared in the door, looking even angrier than she had yesterday. "Silence! Did I not warn you that sounds travel in this Tower? The emperor and his son have long since retired, and if you've disturbed their rest—" She stopped short, her upper lip curling in disgust. "What is that horrid smell?"

Citna gestured toward the flunk, which was climbing up a wall near the doorway. "That . . . whatever it is . . . just escaped from Hadlay's nightstand. I must say her taste in pets is quite appalling."

"It's not mine!" Hadlay protested. "I never saw it before this eve."

"Then how did it come to be in your nightstand?" Citna asked. "The drawers open only for their owners."

"Was it in her nightstand?" Sfika asked the other girls.

"It was!" Ba'ar spoke up with gleeful outrage. "I saw it emerge from her drawer myself."

Sfika glared at Hadlay. "I heard about your visit to the bestiary this morn. Prince Zêru believed you were just there to look, and he instructed me not to punish you. But I see now that you had mischief in mind."

She pointed at the flunk, which dropped from the wall, dead. "Pick it up and dispose of it. And when you are finished with that, you will carry every robe, blanket, and pillow from this room to the laundry, where you will work through the night ridding them of the stench that has no doubt permeated the fibers. The rest of you, follow me to the privy, where you may bathe and change into new nightrobes while the chambermaid makes up your beds with fresh linens." Her eye caught Hadlay, who had not moved. She flicked her hand, and, across the room, Hadlay felt the slap. "Be busy, girl, or you'll learn a harder lesson."

A GLIMPSE OF THINGS TO COME

Hadlay decided that the only way to dispose of the flunk and its stink was to drop it down one of the stools in the privy. As she entered, the other girls glared at her.

"You nearly got us all in trouble," Fa'an chided as she helped Rezen wash her wild hair. "If we had disturbed the emperor . . ."

"I didn't do it!"

"Then how did it get into your nightstand?" Rezen asked.

"I don't know, but I didn't put it there." Hadlay stormed from the room before an argument could break out. It stung that even the Ramash doubted her.

She found the robes and bedding piled outside the dormitory when she returned.

A servant had already stripped the beds and was magically remaking them, blankets tucking and folding themselves, fresh pillows fluffing themselves. She cast a hard look at Hadlay. "I don't suppose you care that your prank brought me out of my bed tonight."

Fighting back tears, Hadlay gathered up an armful of bedding and clothing and set off for the laundry.

The chief laundress was waiting for her, also cross at having her night's rest disturbed. "There is no magic here. Every item must be washed by hand." She showed Hadlay how to wash the laundry in large vats, some milky with lye soap. Then she headed for her quarters, which were off the main room. "Wake me when you're finished, not before. I'll inspect your work before you leave."

It took several more trips for Hadlay to collect the rest of the laundry. It seemed she was to receive no assistance in any part of the chore. Then she set to work. One by one, she washed and rinsed twelve blankets and hung them to dry over cables that stretched across the room. Then she did the same with the dozens of tunics, sashes, slippers, and nightrobes, and beat the stink out of all the pillows. By the time she was finished, her hands were sore and red from the harsh soap and scrubbing, and she could see dawn's light tracing the west windows.

Heaving a sigh, she wandered to a window and looked out. She was far above the southern wall of Turris. Guards, looking as small as mice, patrolled the walkway below. The width of the wall surprised her; she had assumed it was only as thick as most stone walls, but from this height, she saw that it was wide enough to accommodate two chariots abreast.

To her left, she could see a thick growth of palm trees along the river, and the fields where the city's crops were grown. And, in the distance, another wall snaked along the landscape, dividing the fields from the wastelands. But what caught her attention was what lay beyond those walls.

The sun was just beginning to peer above the sands on the western horizon, edging everything with golden light. A thin scattering of clouds turned a brilliant rose, then fiery orange, as the sun ascended. The beauty of it made Hadlay shiver. Was it like this every morning outside the walls? No wonder the Nomads preferred to live away from Turris and its walls within walls, and no wonder her father enjoyed his journeys! She thought she would endure much hardship and danger to see this glory every morn.

The morning horn startled her from her thoughts, and she turned to see the chief laundress emerge from her quarters. "Did it take you all night, then?" Her eyes widened as she took in the number of freshly washed garments that were hanging about the room. "I did not realize you had to wash the entire wardrobe." She shook her head. "I would have helped."

"No matter," Hadlay said.

"Well, you'd best remove your own clothing and have a bath—I'm afraid you still smell of flunk. You can use my privy. Toss your clothes out and I'll take care of them. Hurry, or you'll miss the morning meal."

"I'm too weary to care about food," Hadlay said. "I just want to find my bed."

"There will be no rest for you today," came Sfika's stern voice from the doorway. "You're to attend lessons along with the others. And if you are late to the morning meal, you will not eat. Busy yourself—you've less than two spans."

Hadlay groaned as Sfika turned and left. Backbreaking work all night, then another full day? How would she remain standing?

She was surprised to receive a cheering smile from the laundress. "You did a wonderful job on all that laundry, dear. And you are quite young. With a little food, you'll have strength enough to face the day."

HOG WILD

They spent the morning with Buthotos, Overlord of Security. He was a powerfully built man whose tunic and mantle were fringed with brilliant red, offsetting the dusky color of his skin. He wore a long cloak that stood out at the rear, perhaps concealing a curved scimitar. His face was fierce, almost inhuman, with bulging eyes and a mouth rowed with many sharpened teeth. He held his arms out to his sides, almost like the pincers of a crab. Hadlay's flesh prickled when he looked at her.

"The Tower is heavily defended at all times, by both physical and magical means. Take note of these defenses, as they can be quite dangerous to anyone who is not careful." To demonstrate, Buthotos shoved aside the heavy bolt that held the doors, jumping back just in time to avoid a nasty-looking blade that dropped through a slit in the door frame with a *schwack*.

"Wondrous!" Kayshti exclaimed, and several of the boys, even Oresed, nodded agreement. "That would surely slice a man in two!"

The boys pelted Buthotos with hundreds of questions as he guided them through the armory, the guard towers, and the high walls surrounding the Tower grounds. Hadlay wanted to groan each time a hand was raised. Her feet and back ached from the long night's labor, and she wanted nothing more than to find a place to sit. When they were finally released for midday meal, she nearly fell asleep at the table.

"But I saw him!" Kayshti nearly shouted at his companions as he sat at the table. "There was a man in the moat, I swear!"

"Buthotos said it was just a fish," Nomish said, tearing off his third hunk of bread and slathering it with soft cheese.

"I looked where you pointed," Fa'an said, "and I saw a fish tail slap the water."

"If you cannot tell the difference between a fish and a man, boy," Ba'ar said in a scathing tone, "you had best not apprentice with Magira." She smiled as her companions snickered.

"I saw a man's face in the water—I did," Kayshti said with a stubborn scowl. "What harm would it have done to check? He could have been drowning!"

"Perhaps it was a reflection," Nomish suggested. "We were all looking down into the water. Maybe what you saw was one of us."

"Maybe . . ." But Kayshti didn't seem persuaded. Ma'at, who turned out to be his twin sister, gave him a consoling pat.

Hadlay sighed and pushed her platter away. She was too tired to eat.

"Are you all right?" Nomish asked. "You look as though you slept poorly."

Fa'an huffed. "Serves her right. I still haven't gotten the smell of flunk out of my nostrils."

Hadlay explained to Nomish what had happened.

He frowned. "But how did the flunk get into your nightstand?"

"So you don't believe me either." She wanted to scream. It was so unfair!

"I believe you." Nomish took her hand beneath the table. "I only wondered how it came to be there."

"Someone must have put it there." Hadlay stole a glare at Ba'ar. "And when I find a way to prove it . . ." In truth, she had no idea what she would do. But she promised herself that she would do *something*.

They spent the afternoon with Abarak, the groundsmaster. He was a balding man whose leathery skin spoke of many years working in the open sun. He acquainted them with some of Prince Zêru's mixes that had been put to work in the outer fields. There were burroles, a combination of burro and mole whose natural desire to tunnel broke up the soil with ease. "We are still looking for a way to get them to burrow in straight rows," the groundsmaster told them. "They are, unfortunately, nearly blind and dreadfully stubborn."

In the shearing barn, they encountered a flock of shabbits—a mix of sheep and long-haired rabbits whose silken wool made their clothing. Next came the grainery, where yamsters rolled their wheels to grind wheat into flour. Then there was the slaughterhouse, where the sights and smells made Hadlay briefly reconsider eating meat.

Their final stop took them into a tunnel beneath the Tower and stables, where workers known as gong farmers maintained the flow of the waste-water channels by clearing the filters daily and hauling the wastes out to the fields to be used as fertilizer.

"Why is this job not done by the powers?" Nomish asked.

Abarak shrugged. "We have tried, but the powers will not work here or in the slaughterhouse."

Or the laundry, Hadlay thought, and wondered if there was a connection.

"The labor is done by debtors to the Crown," Abarak said, "and servants who have displeased the emperor or his son."

"Now, there is a duty suitable for the Ramash," Ba'ar quipped, turning up her nose at the sludge-like mess that was being shoveled into a filthy cart for transport.

Her comment was overheard by a nearby gong farmer, who happened to be Oresed, and from the look on his face he considered the comment insulting. He glared at Ba'ar's back as she continued along the wooden catwalk that rose over the pits of waste, then he waded purposefully toward a lever that jutted from the far wall. Catching Nomish's arm, Hadlay drew back, putting distance between them and Ba'ar. Just as Ba'ar passed, a chute opened above her, drenching her with foul-smelling waste.

Citna, who had held back as well, doubled over with noisy laughter, while Nomish and Hadlay, remembering the purgation, gripped the railings of the catwalk and struggled to keep their faces sober.

Even the groundsmaster found humor in it. "I see you are already immersing yourself in the essence of Tower maintenance."

The remark brought renewed guffaws from Citna, who was leaning against the railing when it gave. She pitched backward off the catwalk, directly into a pool of kitchen waste—rotting fish, overripe tomatoes, and rancid meats being among the more identifiable matter.

Hadlay was in agony. Her entire body ached from her efforts to restrain the laughter that threatened to break loose from her throat. A chortle escaped Nomish and she pinched him hard, giving him a warning look.

Their forbearance preserved them. Citna struggled to her feet and began slinging rotten fruit at those who were laughing at her. A moldy peach struck Ba'ar in the forehead, and to everyone's great astonishment, she flung herself off the catwalk and set after Citna, hurling sludge and garbage as she went. The two of them rolled around in the mess, pulling hair and shouting curses.

After a moment, the groundsmaster jumped in, but before he could reach them, a rancid slab of meat struck him across the face, and he fell. When he rose again, a slimy leaf of lettuce clung to his balding head like a badly-made wig. With a foul curse, he caught Citna by the shoulders and ducked her into a greenish pool of slime. And then it was all-out war. Even roaches scattered from the pit to escape the fracas.

"Hurry!" Nomish grabbed Hadlay's arm, and they rushed for the exit, hastening along the catwalk and into fresh, open air. A number of Ramash and a few Oresed initiates followed. The last one out reported that those left behind had been dragged into the pits, and a pitched battle was now underway.

They were just debating what to do when Sfika flew up to them, looking irritated. "Have I understood correctly? Is there a free-for-all in the gong farm?"

"How did you know?" Nomish asked, but he was drowned out by several other initiates, who were stumbling over one another to offer more information.

Sfika held up a hand to silence them, then gave Hadlay a narrow look. "I see last evening's punishment has at least persuaded you to behave yourself. Remain here." She charged into the tunnel. When she emerged again, she was splattered with foul-smelling matter of a kind Hadlay did not care to identify, and her face was the color of a plum. A chagrined groundsmaster and over a dozen filth-encrusted initiates emerged behind her.

Sfika sputtered for a long moment before she collected herself. "You will not enter the Tower in this condition," she said to the initiates, her voice quivering with rage. "In fact, you will not enter the Tower at all this eve. Since you have seen fit to comport yourselves like hogs, it seems right that you bed down with them tonight."

"I'll do no such thing!" Ba'ar's eyes flashed.

"You will." Sfika squared off and stared her down. "And if you argue again, you will sleep a week in the sties."

"You—I—I shall tell my father!" Ba'ar's shoe made a squishing noise as she stamped her foot.

"And he will do what?" Sfika mocked. "Your father might be important in Turris, girl, but he is no one inside these walls. One more argument from you, and you shall be sharing the hogs' meals as well as their beds."

As the filthy initiates shuffled off toward the pens, the clean ones lingered, uncertain whether the penalty applied to them. Sfika noticed them and huffed. "What are you still doing here? Off to the kitchen or there'll be no food for you."

As they hurried off, Hadlay saw Sfika turn to the groundsmaster, who looked quite terrified. "Now, as for you . . ."

BURNING ANGER

As exhausted as she had been all day, Hadlay slept fitfully, and was awakened long before morning by dreams of Alila and her mother being attacked by Prince Zêru's pets, tearing at them with fangs and claws.

It had been only three nights, yet it seemed an eternity since she had hugged her mother or listened to her father's stories. She stared at the ceiling, hoping that her weariness would overcome her, but it soon became plain that she would not rest. She decided to rise, enjoy another of those baths, and go visit the kitchen to see if Magira was at work. Perhaps the cook already had word from home.

Hadlay had just stepped from the bath and slipped on her fresh tunic when a flash in the mirror startled her. She whirled to find Zêr-Shungalli glaring at her.

"Where have you been?"

She stared at him, uncertain what he was asking and feeling rather vulnerable, considering she had only just pulled on her clothing. What if he had appeared a moment earlier? Did he not know this was the girls' privy?

He glowered at her, and again his eyes fixed her so she could not pull away. "I have waited for you in the bestiary these past two morns."

Hadlay's mind raced. Why would he have expected her to return? "Pardon me, Your Highness. I did not realize . . ." She hesitated. "Did . . . did you instruct me to come?"

He made an impatient noise. "You came the first day. It was quite reasonable to assume you would make a habit of it."

Hadlay did not think it was reasonable at all, but she was afraid to argue.

"I wish to punish you," he announced.

"Pun-punish me?" Hadlay stammered. "Whatever for?"

His eyes darkened and an invisible fierceness assailed her as he raged. "You stole a flunk! And now it's *dead!*" The words echoed around Hadlay, battering at her like unseen hands.

"No, Your Highness! I did not steal any of your creatures!" What would he do to her? Hadlay wanted to run, but she found she could not move. "I swear it by . . . by my own right hand!"

"Your hand, then?" he asked scornfully. "*Qâssa qulâ!*"

Hadlay's hand began to burn as if being held in a fire. She jerked it back but the pain remained with her like a glove she could not remove. Tears burned her eyes as she flung her hand about, unable to keep still, unable to avoid the pain. She rushed to a basin, plunging her hand into the water, but the burn continued. "Please, Your Highness! I swear I did not do this thing!"

"The flunk was in your nightstand drawer, was it not?" he asked, and the heat intensified.

"Y-yes it was." Hadlay choked out the words. She could feel her skin shriveling from the heat. "But please, I did not put it there!"

"Who did, then, if not you?"

"I don't know!" The pain was searing her forearm now. Even if she did persuade him to stop, she would surely lose her limb. Sobbing, she dropped to her knees. "I beg you—have mercy!"

"*Amâtîsha kinnâni!*" His eyes, still fierce, became unfocused, as though he was listening to a voice Hadlay could not hear. A moment later, he gave a satisfied smile and stepped back. "I believe you." He waved his hand, and instantly the pain in her hand ceased.

Trembling, Hadlay raised her hand and stared at it. It looked exactly as it had before. It was difficult to believe that, with all that pain, there was no mark, no evidence of the burning heat. She was drenched in sweat and did not trust her legs to hold her.

The morning horn sounded. The prince smiled at her as though nothing ill had taken place. "I will see you in the bestiary tomorrow morning."

Before Hadlay could reply, he vanished, leaving her alone once more.

Hadlay struggled to her feet, her knees still shaking from the pain. She stumbled to a basin and plunged her hands into the water, savoring the coolness. Then, feeling as though she might still be watched, she knotted her sash and plaited her hair.

She did not want to go to the bestiary tomorrow. Not in the least. But how could she avoid it?

THE POWERS THAT BE

"Don't be a fool, girl! Of course you'll go!" Magira dismissed Hadlay's worries with a gesture. "Prince Zêru has said it, and you must obey."

"But . . ." Hadlay wanted to tell her how afraid she was, but the warnings against speaking ill of the emperor or his son still rang in her ears.

"He is a sweet boy, dear. He simply has not had many companions. He has spent most of his time in the Lands Beyond with those awful beasts of his. Poor Zêru just has not learned how to behave. But look at his care for that tiny, dead flunk, stinking though it was. He was only angry because he thought you'd harmed it."

The kettle in the hearth began to boil, and the scent of porridge sweetened with ground dates and cardamom filled the kitchen. Hadlay took a spoon and stirred it to keep the mixture from burning at the bottom.

"You needn't do that, girl," Magira said. "It'll stir itself." To the spoon she said, "*Bu'ish!*"

Hadlay stepped away, watching the spoon swish around the kettle. "How do you do this? Where does this magic come from?"

"The powers are all around you. You need only learn to command them. *Butuq!*" With the word, Magira set a large knife to work slicing almonds.

Hadlay sighed. "I would give anything to be able to do that one day."

"You'll go far here with that attitude!" Magira gave her a broad smile and a pat on the shoulder.

Hadlay felt a little encouraged, though she still had her doubts. If a Ramash could command the powers, surely it would have happened before.

"Zêru needs a friend his age, Hadlay. And it seems he has chosen you for that honor. This is a great opportunity. Consider what good you might do for the Ramash if you have the prince's ear."

"Why do you care whether this does good for the Ramash?" The question escaped Hadlay before she realized it was rude.

But Magira only smiled. "I care for fair dealing; always have. *Tabalshû-ma rihis!*" She sent the knife off to a basin with running water for a quick rinse, then put it to work on a wheel of cheese. "*Butuq!* It is quite unjust the way your people are treated, and the best way to end it is to make the emperor's son your ally. So go to the bestiary each morning, as the prince expects. You would not want to disappoint him."

"No, I wouldn't." The words dragged from Hadlay's lips. "I'll go."

Magira patted her hand. "Now, before you ask, I did have an opportunity to speak with your mother yesterevening, and she was pleased to hear you are settling in. She asked me to tell you that she and your father are well, though they miss you dreadfully."

Hadlay turned toward the fire to hide the tears that came to her eyes. "Was there news of the Rakams?"

"They are well also. There was a message from Alila to both you and Nomish, telling you to hug one another for her."

Just then Nomish wandered in. He looked exhausted, Hadlay thought, and his leg was dragging a bit.

Magira gave him a one-armed hug. "Speak of the devil, and there he is! I can see this boy and I will become dear friends, as often as he comes begging for food."

Nomish grinned, accepting a slice of fig. He joined Hadlay by the fire. "I did not sleep well last night. Too many strange noises."

"Magira has spoken to my mother. All is well at your home."

"Tell him what Alila said," Magira urged with a wink.

Hadlay related Alila's wish, then gave him a quick hug, which he returned with a hesitant pat on her back. She didn't have to see his face to know that it was red.

"Well, now!" Magira said. "Hadlay, why don't you pull the kettle from the fire while Nomish sets up bowls and spoons? The others will arrive any time now."

Hadlay approached the kettle, then hesitated. It seemed a good idea to give the porridge a final, good stir. Trying to remember the word that Magira had spoken a few moments ago, she said, "*Pu'is!*" The spoon jumped from the kettle and came after her, dripping hot porridge and smacking her backside. "No!" Hadlay shouted, trying to get away. "Stop!" But the spoon just kept chasing her. "Go away! Help!"

"*Naparki!*" At Magira's command, the spoon stopped chasing Hadlay and clattered to the floor. "*Misâ!*" The spoon went off to the basin for a rinse, while several clean cloths damped themselves and set to cleaning up the mess. One of them even wiped the porridge from Hadlay's bottom, and others flew to Nomish and scrubbed behind his ears, impervious to his struggles to get them off.

"Why didn't it do what I told it?" Hadlay asked.

Magira chuckled. "It did. In fact, I'm impressed. I could barely get a spoon to wriggle first time I tried. The only problem was that you gave the command to 'smite' rather than to 'stir.' Be patient—you'll be taught the proper ways."

"But Ramash don't perform magic," Nomish said. "I've never known any of our people to do so."

"The powers obey those who serve the emperor. And until now, only Oresed were chosen to serve. But things are changing in Turris now that the emperor and Zêru have returned."

Sighing with regret at the need to do her work manually, Hadlay used a hook to pivot the rack on which the kettle hung so that it was no longer over the fire. Nomish left for the scullery to collect the bowls and spoons. Hadlay was watching the spoon return to the kettle when Asinus barged into the room. He snatched the spoon out of the air and used it to taste the porridge. With a dissatisfied grunt, he tossed the spoon back in.

Magira looked him up and down appraisingly as she approached. "You seem in a sour mood this morning. What could have put you in such a state so early in the day?"

"It is none of your concern, woman!" Asinus snapped.

"Then what are you doing in my kitchen?" Magira retorted. "Surely you do not need feeding." She poked a finger at his round belly.

"Do not take that tone with me, cook!" Asinus bellowed, looming toward her.

Magira drew herself up. "In my kitchen, I'll take any tone I please, you swag-bellied mud gerbil!" As she spoke, the paring knives ceased their work and drifted toward Asinus, as if reading her sentiments.

Nomish limped in, balancing a tall stack of bowls, his pockets rattling with spoons.

"You, boy!" Asinus lashed out, startling Nomish so badly he almost dropped his burden. "How dare you limp when the emperor has declared you healed?"

Nomish stared at him, speechless.

"If I see you limp again, you'll labor in the gong farm for a week." With that, Asinus whirled and stormed from the kitchen, snatching up a loaf of bread as he passed the cooling rack.

"You put that back, you rapacious boar-pig!" Magira shouted after him. She turned to the two wide-eyed initiates and chortled. "By the looks on your faces, you'd think I had just insulted Shungallu himself! Old Asinus is not nearly as important as he makes out. The emperor barely tolerates the man."

Nomish stared at her. "Then why did he make him an overlord?"

"Oh, the emperor has his reasons, I'm sure." Magira glanced at Nomish, who was still balancing his load of bowls. "Set those down before you drop them, boy!" She turned back to her work. "Mangy, swine-bottomed sow bug," she muttered under her breath. "I should think someone that unsightly ought to at least be good-hearted."

Hadlay looked at Nomish, whose mouth was still hanging open, and suppressed a giggle. As many things as there were to dislike about this place, there were a few she quite liked.

OCTOKITTY

B a'ar and the other initiates who had spent the night in the hog pen arrived for the morning meal—freshly bathed but looking a little worse for wear. Hadlay could not hear their conversation, but words like "stink" and "dung" kept drifting to her table. She couldn't resist allowing Ba'ar to see her give a gloating smirk.

Nomish scraped her shin with his sandal. "She'll find a way to get even, Hadlay."

"Yes, but she'll cause me trouble anyway. I might as well savor the moment while I can."

After they ate, Sfika arrived and called the group together. "Come along, initiates. This will take the better part of the day."

She led them down endless corridors, turning and turning again until Hadlay was certain they were hopelessly lost. Finally, they reached the great entry hall she'd first seen on entering the Tower. Sfika led them outside, to the great walkway that ringed the Tower and spiraled up to its pinnacle. "Up we go!"

Hadlay had never seen—let alone climbed—so many stairs. The initiates were soon gasping with the effort, as Sfika led them at a pace that allowed no respite. As they rose above the rooftops of the city, they began to form a thin line, each initiate clinging to the wall of the Tower, afraid to step too near the edge of the stairs and the terrible drop to the ground below.

Aa'mash was the first to stumble, and a couple of the Ramash girls squealed as she nearly took them down the stairs with her. Wheezing, the three collapsed in a pile, unable to continue.

Seeing their distress, Sfika stopped. "Oh, all right! I thought you might appreciate some exercise. But . . . *Elish bilshunuti!*"

Hadlay uttered a strangled scream as something took hold of her collar and her belt and lifted her. Several of the other initiates shrieked too, as they all found themselves swinging in the air. Sfika's feet lifted from the stairs as well, though she was carried in a more dignified manner, as though she were standing on a platform.

The pace of their ascent quickened dramatically now that they were no longer walking on their own, nor following the staircase. Hadlay gasped as a flock of birds swooshed past, fanning them with their wings and piercing the air with their calls. It was terrifying to be hanging from nothing, so far above the hard earth.

The other initiates calmed slowly as the ascent continued without mishap.

"Oh! Look at the houses!" one of the Oresed girls called out.

"Mine is just there." Ba'ar pointed pridefully. "The one that towers over the others. It is one of the largest mansions in the city. Hadlay, can you see your little hovel, or is it too tiny to be visible from this height?"

Hadlay ignored her, keeping her eyes on Sfika. Looking down made her insides lurch, and her last meal was too fresh in her stomach. And for some reason her ears felt funny—like they were full of wax or something. She used her small finger to try to clear one, but it did no good.

After they had continued to climb for some time, one of the Oresed girls spoke up. "Overlord Sfika?"

"Yes, girl." Sfika did not seem impatient. She yawned once, then again. Perhaps the long ascent was boring her.

The sight of her yawning, combined with three sleepless nights, made Hadlay yawn too, and she was surprised to feel her ears pop.

"When will we learn magic?" the girl asked.

Sfika turned to face them, continuing the ascent with her back to the stairs. "Some of you never will. The powers choose whom they heed. But there are plenty of duties for those who cannot command them, so never fear."

Citna gave Sfika a confident smile. "And for those of us who can command the powers? When will we learn?"

"Each duty has its own commands. You will learn them as you need them. Some of you may only master a few commands. Others will be more adept."

"And of course, those of us with the most ability will become authorities or even overlords one day," Ba'ar said.

"Not necessarily. Magic is not the only ability that serves the emperor. There are overlords who have no command of the powers at all. Always put the emperor's interests first, and you will go far. Rule Number Fifteen."

Hadlay groaned. How many rules were they expected to learn? Was there an actual list, or did Sfika, like Asinus, just make rules up as it suited her?

Finally, they reached the top of the Tower. Hadlay was surprised to find a huge vat of water there, which seemed to be filled constantly by a chain of giant buckets drawn up magically from the river surrounding the walls of Turris.

Workers labored along the rim of the Tower, apparently building up the outer walls. Nomish watched them, frowning. "How do you suppose they raise these vats as they build the Tower higher?"

A chubby, balding man stepped up and sketched a bow. "Greetings, initiates!"

"This is Brecho," Sfika said. "He is master of the plumbing. It is his job to direct the filling of this vat, which drains through chutes that are distributed throughout the Tower. This is what provides the water for all the baths, the kitchen, and waste disposal for the Tower."

"I'm having a bit of trouble today," Brecho said, frowning at the water. "Some of the main chutes have been developing blockages, and I can't find a way to unplug them." He gestured for the initiates to move closer to the edge of the vat. "See? The worst is that large one at the center."

A series of dark holes could be seen beneath the water in the vat, most of them with big whirlpools dancing over them, similar to the one Hadlay had seen in the bathing basin. But the large hole Brecho spoke of had only a very lazy, spindly eddy.

Hadlay leaned forward for a better look, and she felt something strike her between the shoulders. Before she could catch her balance, she went tumbling into the vat. The splash wetted several of the Oresed girls, who shrieked with indignity.

"Quick! Grab the pole!" Brecho shouted, pointing at a long staff braced against the far wall.

Nomish was first to react, snatching up the pole, but even as he stretched it out to her, Hadlay felt herself begin to spin, slowly at first, then more quickly as she began to sink. Caught in one of the whirlpools, she was sucked into a chute.

She couldn't see—there was no light at all, and rough stone walls scraped her hands and knees. She tried to catch herself, but her scrabbling hands found no purchase. The water dragged her in one direction, then abruptly changed course, shooting down another channel, hurling her round and round in a dizzying spiral.

Was this how she would die? Hadlay wondered how it would feel to drown. She jolted almost to a stop when she hit something soft, but it gave way and on she went, now racing down the twisting chute headfirst. She opened her mouth to scream, but water surged in and choked her.

Then she landed, with a massive splash, in a large basin full of hot, soapy water.

A huge woman with a great, bulbous nose was leaning over the basin, and she caught most of the splash with her face. She gave forth a shriek that rattled the walls and didn't stop screaming until Magira rushed in to find the cause of the commotion.

"Great galloping Gilgamesh, girl, how did you land yourself there?"

Before Hadlay could answer Magira, Brecho appeared, breathless and looking anxious. "Thank the powers! I feared you might be swimming in the moat!"

The woman whom Hadlay had splashed seemed to come to herself, wiping suds from her eye—she had only one great, angry eye beneath her one, bushy brow. "What is the meaning of this?"

"Now, Ogret," Magira patted her hand soothingly, "I am certain the girl meant no harm." She turned to Hadlay. "This is Ogret, mistress of the scullery."

Hadlay nodded a greeting and climbed out of the basin just as Sfika rushed in. Taking in the splattered walls and soaked scullion, Sfika's eyes narrowed as they fell upon Hadlay. "You again . . ."

Before Sfika could voice her outrage, Brecho flung himself into the basin, staring up into the great spout through which Hadlay had emerged. "Brilliant, just brilliant!" he exclaimed, inspecting the flow of water from the spout. "Young mistress, the powers must have sent you to me!" He splashed the water joyously. "See, Ogret? You have a full flow of water again!"

In a trice, Ogret was standing over him, cupping her hands beneath the spout. "Oh! How wonderful!"

"Let me see!" Magira inserted herself between the two. "Quite so! Good girl, Hadlay!"

"What did I do?" Hadlay was still dizzy from the chute and terribly confused by this point.

"You've solved the plague of my career!" Brecho said. "How did you think of it?"

"Explain!" Sfika stepped to the edge of the basin. The others sobered abruptly.

Brecho splashed his hands under the spout again. "I had only just mentioned the problem to your initiates, do you recall? Some of the chutes were clogged, and I couldn't find a way to unplug them. Well, one of the chutes led to this basin."

Ogret nodded. "It had slowed to a trickle in the last week."

"I was at a loss as to how to clear it, and here this young initiate has solved the problem right off!"

With the full flow of water, the now-crowded basin had filled to the brim, and sudsy water began to spill over the sides. "Quick! The drain!" Ogret plunged her hands into the water, emerging in a moment with a great wad of cloth. "We had been using this to keep the basin from draining itself dry. But no need any longer." Then she plunged in again, splashing about wildly. "And here's your clog!" With Brecho's aid, she was able to wrestle what looked like a large cat, though instead of legs, it had long, winding tentacles with suction discs. It hissed and wrenched itself from their grip and launched itself down the drain.

"Zêru's octokitty!" Magira clapped her hands. "He was so unhappy when she disappeared. She was pregnant, you know, due for kits any time when she vanished. She must have had them by now."

"She must have made her nest in the chute. And this girl," Brecho gestured at Hadlay, "seems to have dislodged it. They'll all find their way to the moat, I'm certain."

"The best place for them. As for you," Sfika turned to Hadlay, her eyes narrowing. "The next time you have one of your ideas, you report to me before trying it."

"But—"

"She'll do that," Magira said, giving Hadlay a shushing gesture.

"Now, out of that basin, the three of you. Mop up that water, Ogret. Hadlay, Brecho, follow me. We have a great deal yet to see, and you've already delayed us far too long!" Sfika whirled and left, her rapid footsteps clattering from the scullery.

As they trailed along behind Sfika, Brecho caught Hadlay's arm. "Do you suppose you can do it again for the south chute? There's blockage there as well. And the chute for the maids' privy . . ."

THE TOWER

The first two levels below the vats contain the emperor's private apartments," Sfika said, leading them past a closed and guarded iron door. "There is no reason any of you will need to enter here, but the next level includes the prince's suite." She kept up her typical rapid pace down a narrow, winding corridor. As they approached the next door, a guard stepped up and opened it for them. "Memorize these corridors. This is the only place in the Tower where the guiding tiles will not lead you. Probably some sort of security measure."

"Do you mean to say we've descended three levels of the Tower?" one of the Oresed girls asked. "How did we do so, without the use of stairs?"

"There are no stairs within the Tower," Sfika told them, as if that answered the question. She stood aside and gestured them into the chamber. "Some of you will serve here during your instruction," Sfika said. "Do your gawking now, so you can be efficient when you come to work."

The first thing that drew Hadlay's eyes were the wide windows, finished with that strange clear material. "It's called *glass*," Ba'ar said when one of the Oresed boys reached out to touch it. "All the better homes have it." She moved on behind Sfika, missing the foul look the boy sent her.

Zêr-Shungalli's suite included a large private sitting area, a small table, a desk, and cushioned chairs set in a group near the window. The chamber was populated by some of his beasts, including the nuppy Hadlay and Nomish had seen before, which poked its odd little tongue at them and wriggled under the couch.

Rezen took it all in with her mouth agape. "This place, with all its wondrous chambers—it reminds me of that bedtime story—"

She received a stiff elbow from Raimog, and she flushed.

Hadlay watched the Oresed initiates, but none of them showed interest in Rezen's comment.

Heavily armed guards manned every chamber doorway here, and some used long tubes to gaze through portals in the outer walls. Hadlay wondered at the need for this precaution but had no chance to ask about it before Sfika rushed them onward.

The next level contained the emperor's treasuries. Vault after vault—each guarded by armed sentinels and staffed by a clerk—contained mountains of gold talents, piles of minas and shekels, stacks of cases containing precious stones, exotic fabrics, myrrh, and sundry other items of particular rarity or value.

"I wonder what the emperor does with all this treasure," Ba'ar said, her eyes gleaming.

"Just a few talents could probably put all our parents back in their own homes," Kayshti murmured.

"You mustn't speak like that again!" Sfika said. "The last treasurer, Viridesc, took a shekel to repay a debt, and she paid more dearly than you could imagine. Rule Number Twenty: never even *think* of stealing *anything* within this Tower."

Hadlay caught a worried look from Nomish and remembered her mother's comment about Viridesc's disappearance. As confusing as the rules were, it was clear that they would have to be careful to follow them.

Below the treasury, they found themselves in the kitchen, where Magira oversaw a small staff of servants who maintained and stocked a larder, a special room that was quite cold so that food could be kept fresh much longer. Nomish wanted to know how the room was chilled, but Sfika pretended not to hear his question.

Magira guided them to the scullery, where Ogret beamed at Hadlay. "The water is still flowing freely!" she exclaimed as she scrubbed a large, greasy platter. "Thank you so much, Mistress Hadlay!"

"What are you thanking her for?" Ba'ar asked. She scowled when she learned the answer.

"Why is this work not done with magic?" Citna asked.

"The powers will not work on the most unpleasant drudgery," Sfika said. "Just as in the gong farm."

Ba'ar gave Hadlay a smirking smile. "There! I knew the emperor had his reasons for letting the Ramash come!"

Hadlay balled her fists, but she did not want to have more trouble with Sfika, so she kept her mouth closed.

"Bonobos says—" Nomish began.

"Pah, Bonobos!" Sfika waved a hand in contempt. "Learned he may be, but he blinds himself to the obvious." She refused to discuss it further, much to Nomish's frustration.

Sfika led them on through levels dedicated to the work of various royal craftsmen, who labored to keep the Tower in repair; to the laundry and wardrobe, where clothing was made and cleaned; to levels used for various functions of government.

"And this is Overlord Bonobos's laboratory." Sfika cracked the door. They caught only a glimpse of the room before a small explosion sounded, and a noxious green vapor rolled toward them. Sfika quickly closed the door again.

Hadlay could see the frustrated frown on Nomish's face. "But—"

"You'll have plenty of opportunity to explore this area when you train with Bonobos." Sfika would brook no argument.

From there, they passed the dormitories, and then more work areas. The bestiary was near the base of the Tower. It had its own point of access from the outside. Hadlay noticed that most of the initiates seemed hesitant to enter, and Sfika herself allowed them only a brief look before leading them on with a shudder, muttering beneath her breath.

The tour took them well past time for the evening meal, so Sfika told them they would skip the final levels. "The next level down is Overlord Zamzom's workshop, which some of you will see in due time. And following that, there is the dungeon. We shall hope you never have occasion to go there."

Sfika had one last piece of business for them before they retired. It was time for the initiates to be divided into their groups of six. Sfika permitted them each to select one person they wished to work with. Naturally, Hadlay and Nomish chose each other. Sfika then chose three pairs for each of the five groups, seeming intent upon mixing Ramash with Oresed. When she reached Ba'ar, who had teamed with Citna, she paused and asked, "Which Ramash girl were you complaining of at the banquet?"

Ba'ar hesitated, then a calculating expression stole upon her face, and she pointed to Ma'at. Ma'at, not knowing what any of it was about, did her best to disappear among the other girls.

Sfika gave Ba'ar a shrewd look. "Do you think you can fool me?"

Unnerved, Ba'ar's eyes stole toward Hadlay.

Following her gaze, Sfika smiled. "Now I see the truth of it. Well, just as you feared, you and your partner will be teamed with these Ramash." She ushered them over beside Hadlay and Nomish. "The sooner you make peace, the more pleasant your work will be." She added Ma'at and her twin brother, Kayshti, to the team.

Hadlay stared at the floor. No matter where she turned, she couldn't escape Ba'ar. No doubt Ba'ar would find many more opportunities to make trouble for her.

STRANGE FRIENDS

Sleep failed Hadlay again that night, even though she was beyond exhaustion. The abrupt snorts coming from Ba'ar's bed were nothing like the languid rhythms of Hadlay's father's snores. And a few beds down, Ma'at seemed to be having fretful dreams again. There were other noises as well—strange bumps and squeaks that sometimes convinced Hadlay that someone was prowling the room, though the moonlight streaming through the window showed that all were in their beds.

She had only begun to drowse when she felt herself moving. When she opened her eyes, it seemed her bed was traveling down a long, dark tunnel. Was she dreaming? She rolled to one side and pushed herself up. No. She was no longer in the dormitory. She was floating—bed and all—down a narrow hallway.

She considered jumping off, but the bed was high off the floor. Hadlay hung her head over the side, trying to see who was carrying her, but there was no one there.

For an anxious moment, she was torn. She wanted to shout for help, but she was afraid to get in trouble with Sfika for causing a commotion. It wasn't until the smells of the bestiary drifted to her that she began to realize what was happening.

The door to the bestiary swung open, and her bed drifted through, coming to rest on the floor.

Zêr-Shungalli stood in the center of the room. "You're late."

At least he didn't seem angry. Hadlay struggled to untangle her legs from her blankets and rise. "My apology, Your Highness."

131

The prince caught her arm and tugged her down the rows of cages. "Come see the swox."

Hadlay had to run to keep up with his long strides. They rounded a corner, and she was faced with what had to be the oddest creature in the bestiary. The back half of the creature was all fox, with paws and a lovely, bushy red tail. But the front was more swan, with webbed flippers for feet and great, red-feathered wings tucked neatly at its sides. It was still pacing, just as the fox had done, only now, when it panted, its tongue lolled out from the bill of a swan. When it saw them, it let out a yappy honk and waddled up to the bars of the cage to tug at Hadlay's sleeve.

"Look! He likes you already!" Prince Zêru exclaimed. "He must understand that I mixed him for you."

"For me?" The prince had been so angry with her yestermorn. Now he was giving her a gift?

A furrow creased his brow at her hesitation. "Don't you like him?"

"Of course I do!" Hadlay assured him, bending to examine the swox more closely. She had always wanted a pet, but her mother had told her that they could not afford to keep any beasts other than the horse, which her father needed for his trading. Of course, it would never have occurred to her to want a swox, even had she known that such creatures might exist. She stroked its neck, careful to avoid the fangs that protruded from its beak. She must have hit a good spot, because the creature arched its long neck against her hand, and one of its webbed feet began to thump, trying to help her scratch its ear. Abruptly, it stretched out his neck and, before Hadlay could move away, gave her a wet tongue across the face.

"You can name him, if you want."

"What would be a good name for a swox, do you think?"

"Well, if he has the best of both beasts, he will be clever and graceful. But if he has the worst, he will be devious and ill-tempered."

Just then, the flash of the prince's jeweled sandal caught the creature's eye, and he snatched the shoe from his master's foot, dashing off to hide it in his nest.

The prince grinned down at Hadlay. "Devious it is, then. *Tûra!*"

At his word, the sandal flew back to its owner, with the swox chasing and snapping at it. Prince Zêru laughed, and the whole room seemed to laugh with him.

"I think I'll name him Filch," Hadlay said, "because he's a thief."

"When he's older, you can take him with you. Just be certain he returns to the bestiary to be fed each morn."

Hadlay didn't know what to say. No one had ever given her a gift such as this. And she had never received anything from someone so important. "Thank you, Your Highness." She made a deep bow.

"This means we will be friends, does it not?"

Hadlay was surprised to hear loneliness in the question. She remembered Magira's words, that this boy had few friends his own age. She smiled. "If you wish it, Your Highness."

"Call me Zêru. Are all Ramash eyes the color of sky?"

"Not all. My friend Nomish has green eyes. Though he is not all Ramash."

"Nomish—he's a mix too, then?"

Hadlay thought about it. "I suppose . . . in a way. But I don't think the same way your creatures are mixed."

"Will he be my friend as well?"

"I'm certain we shall all be great friends." Suddenly, she was reminded of the Being's words her first morning here. "You will find friends among those you now consider foes . . ." It was true that once, she had considered all who governed Turris to be her enemies. The Being was trustworthy yet again.

The morning horn sounded just then, and Zêru vanished, leaving Hadlay to wonder how she would get her bed back to the dormitory.

A FINE KETTLE OF FISH

Hadlay had managed to find a servant who took her bed back for her, using the magical word *bil*. She made a mental note of it, in case Zêru did that again. Now she hastened to the kitchen, eager for the morning meal.

Her friends were already eating when she entered. She served herself a basted egret egg and a hard roll with sesame butter, longing once more for her mother's plainer fare.

Magira finished gutting a large fish for the evening meal and washed her hands, then brought a pitcher of iced chai to Hadlay's table. She leaned down and spoke quietly. "I meant to ask you last night, how did you come to be in Ogret's washing basin yesterday?"

"She fell into the vat at the top of the Tower." Nomish said.

"Someone *pushed* me into the vat," Hadlay muttered.

"Are you sure?" Magira glanced over her shoulder. "I don't suppose I need to ask who did it. I've seen the way you and Ba'ar glare daggers at each other."

Nomish swallowed a mouthful of cheese. "Likely she put the flunk in your nightstand as well. You need to stop provoking her, Hadlay, before she gets you in more trouble."

Magira frowned. "I find it difficult to believe that Ba'ar did that. It would take some powerful magic to ward off the charms on those nightstands, and none of you have learned enough to manage it. Sfika commanded the powers herself, binding them to the nightstands so that they only open for the person whose bed is . . ." She paused, apparently considering something.

"Well, whoever is doing this, I wish that kettle of fish guts would empty itself on them!" No sooner had Hadlay spoken than the kettle levitated and drifted to some initiates who had gone to the oven for more fresh rolls. It upended itself, dumping its foul-smelling contents on them. Mayhem erupted as the initiates scattered, distancing themselves from the stench and goo.

"By the yamsters of Zêru, girl," Magira whispered, "you are favored by the powers. You don't even know their language, and they already do your bidding!"

"Who—who is responsible for this outrage?" Ba'ar sputtered, snatching a cloth from the counter to wipe at the splashes on her tunic. Hadlay almost howled with glee.

Magira quelled Hadlay and Nomish with a warning glance and rose. "I apologize, my dears. I must have gotten distracted, and the kettle took a mind of its own. *Misâ!*" Several rags and a bucket of clean water hastened to clean up the mess. She turned to the girls who had taken the worst of it—Ba'ar, Citna, Fa'an, Raimog, and Rezen. "You five had best hurry off for a quick bath and fresh clothes before the day's work starts."

As order was restored, Magira returned to the Ramash table. Assuring herself that no one was listening, she leaned in and spoke rapidly. "You mustn't let on what you just did, my girl. If Sfika knew you'd worked more mischief . . ."

"But I didn't mean to!"

"And you'd best watch your tongue henceforth, or you'll be in more trouble than you can manage!" She glanced around again. "For whatever reason, the powers heed you, Hadlay Mivana. But I'll warn you, take care how you use them. I've seen people use them to harm others, only to have their curses rained on their own heads when the emperor grew displeased with them. Do nothing to another that you would not have done to you one day." She gave Hadlay a searching stare to ensure her words had reached home. "Now, finish up, and lend a hand clearing the dishes."

Putting Asinus Behind Us

As the initiates cleaned the tables, Sfika informed the groups of their assignments. To Hadlay's great dismay, her group was sent to Asinus.

"At least we're putting Asinus behind us early," Nomish said as they made their way to the Hall of Oration and Governance.

Grandly named, the Hall was just a large room with walls of shelves on which stacks upon stacks of clay tablets were stored. At the fore of the room stood a raised rostrum and a lectern, which was Asinus's place of honor, flanked by several raised desks where harried scribes worked to record his words. The initiates stood just inside the doorway, uncertain what to do.

Ba'ar and Citna rushed in, freshly dressed and damp from bathing.

Asinus glowered at them. "In future days, be on time. I have no patience for tardiness."

"Near as I can see, the old boar has no patience for anything," Citna murmured.

"What was that?" Asinus asked. "Did someone speak?"

Citna turned to face him with a honeyed smile. "I said that I was equally impatient, as I am so looking forward to learning from you." The lie elicited a titter from Ba'ar.

Asinus gave her one of his rancid yellow smiles. "Well, my dear, I shall look forward to instructing you on the great culture of Turris, which is the true cradle of human civilization. The nuances of governance are delicate and exacting, and only those of fine intellect will grasp it." His eyes wandered over the group, lingering balefully on the Ramash. "I see I shall be wasting my breath on most of you."

Hadlay heard a deep sigh from Kayshti, but thankfully he spoke no word.

"I shall begin with a brief history of our land and peoples. Perhaps this will give you some grasp of why things are ordered as they are." Asinus cleared his throat, and Hadlay sighed, trying to steel herself for one of his lengthy orations.

"In the times before the Oresed came and civilized this land, this whole area was a great desert. There was only sand—no creatures, no plants, and certainly no people. But Emperor Shungallu saw potential in it. He conjured the river which now divides our city, and then he called up the trees and grasses and fields that thrive along the water's edge. When the trees were tall, he conjured the creatures, the birds and the beasts, even down to the crawling insects. He raised up this Tower we now dwell in, so that he could live in comfort among his creatures. Then one day, he called forth the greatest of his creations, the Oresed, taking from all his other creatures the qualities he liked best, and mixing in a few things from himself."

"And what of the Ramash?" Ba'ar asked, though her smug expression told Hadlay that she already knew the answer.

Asinus gave her a gratified smile. "Ah, yes! Thank you for the question, Mistress Sutram. When the Oresed multiplied and filled the city, they pleased the emperor so well that he thought they should have servants of their own. And so he turned back to the creatures of the bogs, and he selected the common lemming and mixed it with the Oresed, much as Prince Zêru blends his creatures, to create the Ramash. Like lemmings, they are simple, doing what they see others doing, following rather than leading. They are inferior in every way, qualified only for the most menial labor. But their service frees us for greater endeavors."

"Why, then, did the emperor honor the Ramash with the Oresed, bringing us all here to serve his son?" Nomish asked. His expression was innocent. Only Hadlay knew him well enough to recognize the anger in his eyes.

Asinus speared him with a stare so ferocious that Hadlay feared Nomish would suffer even worse than a purgation. But to her surprise, Asinus held his temper in check. He drew a long, hard breath, then simply turned back to his Oresed favorites.

"Here you see at work the very principles of which I've been speaking. While some, such as yourselves, are intelligent enough to respect the authorities designated by Emperor Shungallu, these offspring of lemmings," he nodded at Nomish, "can only be commanded by more primitive considerations. I've found that only pain and fear can truly master them." He turned an evil smile on the Ramash initiates. "You are no doubt aware that the emperor has ordered us to treat you well. However if any of you dares to question me again, I do have the authority to punish infractions. Have you any further questions?"

They responded with glum silence. Asinus gave them a gratified smile as the city's lawgivers and judges filed into the room, gathering before the lectern.

The servants who were selected to work here served initially as scribes. Each day, the judges of Turris came to this hall with cases they had heard. The council of lawgivers would discuss the merits of all sides and enact laws by which such cases would be governed in the future, while patient scribes recorded every word. Given Asinus's fondness for lengthy oratory, Hadlay could not imagine a more detestable duty.

"The laws of the emperor are unchanging," Asinus intoned, "but the laws of men, being imperfect, are ever in need of adjustment as new circumstances come to bear. We must also be consistent, ensuring that the laws made once are used always. Thus, it is essential that we codify our laws in writing." He leaned in close to Ba'ar and Citna. "Here is the word that invokes the powers to write our laws." And, smiling greasily at them, he whispered it.

"What's that?" Kayshti spoke up. "I did not hear you, sir."

Asinus sneered at him. "It would be lost on you at any rate. No *remesh* could possibly command the powers."

Hadlay wished she could inform him that she already had, but she remembered Magira's warning and kept her peace.

For the rest of that day, the Ramash initiates did their best to overhear the magical word of invocation. But the Oresed girls were equally determined to see that they did not. When Ba'ar spoke it, Citna would cough loudly, and when Citna spoke, Ba'ar would drop a tablet on the floor.

Despite her frustration about this, Hadlay was gratified to see that it took three tries for Citna to be able to get the stylus to begin impressing itself on the damp clay tablets. Ba'ar struggled for much longer.

"Perhaps for now you should do the writing yourself, Mistress Sutram," Asinus suggested. "There are times the powers must be shown what we wish by example."

Ba'ar glanced about, as if hoping no one was near enough to hear her, then ducked her head. "I cannot read or write."

Hadlay's expression must have betrayed her astonishment at this revelation, because Ba'ar shot her a foul look, then turned back to Asinus. "My family has always had *slaves* to handle such things."

Asinus gave Ba'ar a reassuring smile. "As well you should. But fear not. A magical scribe needs only to give the command. The powers themselves are quite literate."

As the day wore on, Hadlay began to hold out hope that Ba'ar would be among those who could not command the powers, but eventually she was able to persuade the stylus to write. The result looked very much like the tracks of chickens in damp sand, but Asinus seemed pleased with it.

"There!" He held up Ba'ar's tablet for all in the room to see. "As you see, both Oresed are already commanding the powers, while the Ramash cannot."

Nomish opened his mouth to protest, but Hadlay caught his hand and squeezed, begging him to keep his peace.

The laws themselves were hardly as grand as Asinus made them out to be. That day's work dealt with additions to the regulations concerning ox carts on the streets of Turris. It seemed that someone had complained about the width of the merchants' ox carts, which nearly filled the narrower streets of the city and made it difficult for other traffic to pass. Thus, a law was passed requiring that the width of an ox cart could be no more than half the width of a lesser street of Turris.

Then one of the lawgivers noted that the smaller carts might not be adequate to accommodate some merchants' wares. So an addition was made, allowing the carts to become twice as long.

And then another lawgiver spoke up. "Won't the long carts have difficulty navigating the sharp turns of the city streets?"

This incited a lengthy debate. Some of the lawgivers advocated setting up a network of cart routes so that the long carts only moved either north to south or east to west, and Asinus agreed, so a law was passed to this effect. But then another lawgiver noted that this would require additional labor to transfer loads from cart to cart, and no one could come up with a suitable way to organize this.

Through all this, the scribes' styluses were busy, marking tablet after tablet, and as each was filled, the scribe would direct it to float across the room where it was placed on a rack to dry. Each time an old version of a law was stricken, the scribe would speak a word, and the tablet containing that version would be dashed on the floor, so that late in the day, there was quite a pile of rubble.

By the day's end, they were back to the original double-wide ox carts, which were now required to pull off each few streets to allow others to pass.

"Why didn't they just pass this law to begin with?" Ma'at whispered.

Unfortunately, she had been overheard.

"Overlord Asinus, young Ma'at here has a question for you." Citna gave Ba'ar a sly wink.

Asinus turned from his lectern to glare at Ma'at, who trembled visibly. "Well?"

"It was nothing important," Ma'at mumbled.

"Speak up!" he roared.

Ma'at looked as though she might faint. Hadlay was momentarily reminded of Alila, and a pang of longing surged through her.

"She asked why you didn't pass that law to begin with," Citna answered for her.

Asinus stepped down from the lectern with such force that the entire rostrum shook. "You dare to question the wisdom of the lawgivers of Turris?"

"No! I . . . I just wondered! I didn't mean . . ." Ma'at cast a desperate look at her brother.

"I did warn you against questioning me. *Qulu!*" Asinus thundered.

Hadlay recognized the command as similar to the one Zêru had given that had caused her hand to burn. She looked at Ma'at, expecting to see the girl writhing in agony. But she merely looked afraid.

"*Remesh qulu!*" Asinus shouted again, growing red in the face. Ma'at only looked at him, shaking as though she expected something terrible. Then, slowly, a look of wide-eyed relief dawned on her face.

Hadlay didn't know whether to laugh or be angry. On the one hand, Asinus intended to hurt another innocent Ramash. On the other, she was overjoyed to see his impotence. For whatever reason, the powers were not heeding him.

"*Qulu! Qulânni!*" Asinus sprayed them all liberally with flecks of spittle as he shouted. Suddenly, he began to stagger, his black eyes wide, his face contorted with surprise. He slapped at himself, as if trying to put out a fire. "*Kussânni! Napar—napar—*" He sobbed, reeling around the rostrum. The initiates scurried out of his way.

One of the lawgivers hurried forward. "*Naparki!*"

Asinus staggered, panting, for a moment longer, then relaxed. He wobbled to one of the benches and sat. The bench creaked dangerously, but held.

"That . . . That was a demonstration of what can happen to those who question!" He wheezed, then glared at Ma'at. "Be grateful that I did not curse you, girl!"

Ma'at blinked at him. "Yes . . . sir . . ."

Asinus blotted his face with the hem of his tunic. "You are all dismissed for the day."

The Beginning of a Canyon

The next morning, Hadlay hurried to the bestiary, eager to talk with Zêru about the events of the previous day.

He chuckled when she got to the part about the kettle of fish guts. "Of course the powers favor you! You are my friend, are you not?"

Hadlay was glad that he seemed pleased about it. "Can you teach me to command them?"

"Won't you learn this as you train in your duties?" He drew a piece of meaty-looking food from a container and tossed it to Alphonse, the eagle-serpent mix.

"Asinus refuses to teach the Ramash anything. And with the others, I'll learn how to chop carrots and haul water and tedious things like that. I want to learn real magic—the kind that makes people tremble when authorities come near." It occurred to Hadlay she might be revealing too much, but she continued. "I want to know how to make people rise in the air and feel the sting of a slap. I want to appear and vanish the way you and your father do."

Zêru shook his head. "I cannot teach you to appear and vanish."

"Why not?" She blurted the question, then wondered whether it was wise to question him.

He didn't seem to mind. "Only Nafal and sons of Nafal are able to vanish in one place and materialize in another. Humans are incapable."

Hadlay made note of this, for Zêru had unwittingly answered one of her questions about the emperor. He was indeed Nafal. "Will you teach me things I can do?"

"Why do you want me to do this?"

Hadlay hesitated. Should she tell the emperor's son about her personal disputes with others? It was probably a violation of one of Asinus's rules of protocol, but she had long since forgotten most of them.

"Tell me." Zêru seemed genuinely curious.

She decided to be honest. "People like Ba'ar and Asinus have lorded it over me all my life. If I had real power, I could repay the harm they've done."

"Asinus! That toad violated my command before the whole of Turris when he punished you and your friends!" His face darkened with anger. "Let me do it. I'll fix him for you!"

Hadlay wanted to protest, but was afraid to vex him. She sighed. "As you wish."

Zêru studied her expression. "You'd like to do it yourself, is that it?"

Hadlay nodded, hoping he would not be offended.

Zêru considered, then shrugged. "All right, then. But the powers will only obey you if you agree to my terms."

"Anything you ask!"

He laughed, and the laughter echoed through the chamber. "You have given the perfect answer. But you will need to be patient. My father will not object to small pranks and little humiliations, but if you were actually to use the powers to disrupt order or to harm one of his overlords, he would be most angry."

Hadlay tried not to frown. Patience! Her mother was always telling her to be patient whenever it came to something she wanted badly. She hated being patient!

Zêru seemed to read her mood, for he squeezed her shoulder. "The Bitter River did not carve its canyon in a day. Small things, done over time, will serve your purpose. My father tells me that subtlety can be far more effective than an obvious weapon."

Hadlay nodded again, trying harder not to show her disappointment. She had imagined herself doing wonderful, frightening, and painful things to her enemies, just as they had done to her. Still, even knowing that she could play small pranks was better than feeling powerless.

"And you must pretend that you are unable to command the powers.

Otherwise, they'll suspect you instantly, and you'll be in more trouble with Sfika."

Hadlay struggled to keep her frustration from making her tone too sharp. "But Zêru, what good is power if no one knows I have it?"

He dismissed the argument with a shrug. "If you are caught using the powers to harass my father's chosen servants and authorities, Hadlay, even I will not be able to protect you. We must be careful, subtle, or this will not work."

Hadlay saw the wisdom in what Zêru was saying, but this was not going to be as much fun as she had anticipated. After being told all her life that she could never hope to be more than a menial, she had finally found a way she could excel. And she had to keep it secret. Grinding her teeth, she nodded.

Zêru's broad grin flashed in the dim lighting. "All right, then. Now, when a human invokes the powers, he must be in the room while they are operating. His authority only continues while he is personally directing them. If things happen to Asinus only when you are with him, even if you pretend you cannot command the powers, and even as stupid as he is, he will eventually realize. However, I can command the powers from anywhere. I will see that things happen to him when you are far from him and cannot be blamed."

Hadlay thought for a moment. "Can you be certain that no Ramash can be blamed? I would not like to see one of my friends in trouble."

Zêru nodded. "When he is alone, then. Asinus will assume that my father is angry with him. It would not be the first time." He tossed the last of the food to his beasts and turned to Hadlay, smiling. "Tell me what Asinus is teaching you, and I will teach you things you can do."

TROUBLE IN TURRIS

Shutur!" Hadlay kept repeating the word that was meant to command the powers to record Asinus's orations, but the stylus refused to budge.

Ba'ar gave Hadlay a superior smile as she presented a stack of finished tablets to Asinus. Since she could not read, she had no way of knowing that all of them simply repeated the phrase, "Asinus is a pompous son of a flatulent yak."

Asinus barely glanced at them before handing them off for filing. "Your penmanship is improving, Mistress Sutram." A couple of clerks, taking the tablets to the shelves, broke into uncontrolled giggles. Asinus glared at them and resumed his oration.

Hadlay let him ramble awhile before she whispered, *"Kubussu leqâ!"*

Asinus's cap, a black, fitted thing that covered his bald head when he was in the Tower, pulled itself off and floated above him. He snatched at it, but it jerked just out of reach of his fingers. *"Tûra!"* he shouted, but the cap flung itself across the room, dancing there as if to laugh at him. After several more attempts, he whirled, red-faced, to glare at the initiates. "Which of you did that?"

Citna, who had already been blamed more than once, threw up her hands in dismay. "Not I!"

"I can vouch for her this time," Ba'ar put in. "I was standing right next to her, and I would have heard if she gave a command."

To Hadlay's surprise, Asinus never even considered suspecting the Ramash. Though Ma'at, Nomish, and Kayshti had surprised him by eventually commanding the powers, the overlord remained convinced that they were capable of only the most menial works of magic. He glared again at Citna, but her look of desperate innocence seemed to convince him. Turning, he crossed the room to collect his cap, which hopped away from him several more times before finally allowing him to catch it.

Hiding a smile, Hadlay turned away.

Nomish glanced at Asinus to affirm that his attention was elsewhere, then leaned toward Hadlay. "I've seen you command the powers, Hadlay. And now I see why you pretend that you cannot." He gave her a solemn look and whispered, "Remember Magira's warning."

Hadlay had come to look forward to the evening meal each night. She enjoyed hearing her new Ramash friends tell of their days' lessons, and she always found time for a word with Magira. Whenever she went out for supplies, Magira made a point to call on either the Rakams or Mivanas, and when she returned, Hadlay hung on every word of her reports.

This evening, though, Hadlay sensed that Magira was concealing something. "Is anything wrong at home?"

"No—no, dear, they are all quite healthy. It's only . . ." Magira glanced at Nomish, who was busy taking platters to the scullery. "It appears to me the Rakams' shop is not as fully stocked as usual. I hear that the Oresed traders have made it difficult for the Ramash to afford their wares. And there is worse. The emperor is instituting a new tax, sixty shekels for every man and woman, due by summer's end. Overlord Aurum was speaking with the collectors yesterday when I served her midday meal."

Hadlay's stomach tightened. With all that had been going on, she had all but forgotten her fears for her family. "My parents are barely fending off the slavers as it is. They'll never be able to pay a tax!"

Magira pursed her lips, regarding Hadlay. "You are the prince's friend now, are you not? Perhaps you should ask him to intercede."

Remembering the way Zêru had burned her hand, Hadlay hesitated. "He might be angry if I presume on our friendship."

"If he truly wants to champion your people, he should appreciate your telling him about the problem," Magira said. "You'll never know unless you try."

&

The next morning in the bestiary, Hadlay gathered her courage. "Zêru, are you truly concerned about the Ramash people?"

"What?" He blinked at her. "Oh, yes, of course. Father says I am, does he not?" He squinted at his eaglent. "Does Alphonse look sickly this morn?"

Hadlay glanced at the creature. He was sitting on his perch as usual, but his feathers looked fluffed and his head wound down behind his wing. One foot was pulled up into his feathers, and he seemed to be sleeping. "Perhaps he's only tired." She absently scratched Filch's ear. "Are you aware that the Oresed have doubled the Ramash rents, though they pay them no more than before for their labor?"

"No, I hadn't heard," Zêru replied, tapping his knuckles against the bars of the cage. "Alphonse? Are you all right, boy?"

The creature lifted his head and peered blearily at Zêru, then fluffed his feathers and resumed his sleeping posture.

Filch tugged at Hadlay's sleeve, begging for a treat. She used a bit of food to coax him to sit up. "The Ramash are poorer now than they were before your edict granting them equality. And now I hear there is a tax coming."

Zêru didn't spare her a glance, but his jaw tightened. Was he impatient with her?

Hadlay swallowed her uneasiness. She had to ask. "Zêru, is there anything you can do to help?"

"I'll see what Father says." He rapped against the bars again. "Alphonse?"

Hadlay mustered a smile. At least now the emperor would hear about her people's troubles. "Thank you, Zêru. This means a great deal to me."

The eaglent roused again and this time realized there was food to be had. Shaking his feathers into place, he stretched out his wings and glided to the bars, where he snapped the bits of meat from Zêru's fingers.

"That's right! Just sleepy, then, were you? Good boy!"

Jealous for attention, Filch gave a yappy honk and nipped at Zêru's hand.

Zêru laughed, giving him a pat. "I think Filch is old enough to leave the bestiary now, Hadlay. Why don't you take him with you? Just see he comes here with you each morning for his meals."

THE WISDOM OF IGNORANCE

Hurry! We don't want to be late!" Nomish broke into a trot, leading the group to the laboratory. With their long two weeks with Asinus behind them, the group had learned this morning that their next assignment was with Bonobos.

Hadlay, Filch, Ma'at, and Kayshti hastened to keep up, while Ba'ar and Citna trailed behind, grumbling.

Nomish burst through the door, casting an eager gaze around the room as if he couldn't decide what to inspect first. Hadlay and the others entered with more caution, remembering the explosion they'd heard when Sfika had shown them the laboratory.

The room was filled with tables. The longest was aligned with the far wall, and the others were arranged against it like the jagged teeth of an ill-used comb. Jars, bottles, tablets, lamps, and utensils were scattered haphazardly, used and forgotten. On one table, an urn full of some kind of liquid had spilled, leaving a sizzling hole in the wood. It smelled of rotten eggs.

Filch took one suspicious sniff and squawked, tucking his tail between his legs. He scooted over to Hadlay and sat so that his body pressed against her leg.

"You really should send the beast away." Citna eyed Filch warily. "He has followed us all morning, and I don't wish to get in trouble."

"Prince Zêru will be most angry if he learns you've made a pet of one of his creations," Ba'ar said.

Hadlay ignored them. She had not told anyone except Nomish that Filch was hers. Zêru had said that they should keep their friendship secret.

"Welcome, initiates!" a voice sounded from the head of the room.

The initiates looked around but saw no one.

"Wondrous!" Kayshti clapped his hands. "Has Bonobos become invisible?"

There was a loud thump, and the head table jumped. Filch yipped, then honked angrily at the table until Hadlay got him to hush.

A hairy hand clutched the table and Bonobos pulled himself up from the floor, rubbing his head. "Sorry! I dropped an instrument. It went somewhere under the table, but I can't find it."

Nomish dived under the table and emerged with an evil-looking set of pincers. "Here you are!"

"Good boy!" Bonobos accepted the pincers and used them to retrieve a blob of something from a jar. He dropped this into a second jar, where it splashed. A moment later, several noisy pops came from the jar, and an acrid orange steam began to rise.

Hadlay had never met Bonobos before, though she had seen him several times from a distance. His body and legs were thin, but he had a belly that bulged so that he looked like a length of rope with a knot at the middle. His dark hair parted at the center, arranged so that it flared out over his ears at each side, and his face was shaved, though he had missed a spot or two along his jaw and beneath his pug nose. He had a soft round cap tucked under his belt, which more or less matched his brown-fringed tunic.

His right hand bore several ugly scars, and the left was gone altogether, replaced by a metal hook. A ragged scar was visible on his jaw; Nomish had once told Hadlay that the scientist had absent-mindedly tried to scratch an itch with the hook rather than his good hand.

"Well!" Bonobos said. "Pull up some stools and let's get to work!"

The initiates hesitated, casting wary looks at each other.

Bonobos chuckled. "I take it Overlord Asinus has impressed on you the many Tower protocols?"

The question elicited unhappy nods from the initiates. The list of rules had expanded during the past two weeks to well over a thousand.

He waved his hook cheerily. "Well, you may safely ignore most of them. The only person who insists on such formalities is Asinus; the rest of us get on quite well without them. And, between us," he added with a wink, "both the emperor and Zêr-Shungalli prefer more casual treatment."

Sighing with relief, the initiates arranged stools so that they could see and hear him, though all but Nomish put some distance between themselves and the jar, which continued to pop and hiss suspiciously.

Bonobos hopped up on the table so that he was sitting on it. "I was born Thoth, but the emperor renamed me Bonobos, Overlord of Science. You may call me Bonobos."

Nomish raised his hand. "The emperor renamed you?"

Bonobos smiled. "From time to time, when the emperor calls someone to a special duty, he will give them new names in keeping with their position. All of the overlords have received this honor—and some of you may as well, one day."

Hadlay pondered this. It seemed enough that the emperor had taken her from her home and family. She did not particularly like the idea of him changing her name.

"It will be my duty at this time to teach you the function of various more technical features of the Tower and its grounds, as I have invented a number of them," he said. "I trust you have already discovered the guiding tiles?"

The initiates nodded in unison.

Nomish raised his hand.

"Yes?"

"How do they work?"

Bonobos favored him with an enthusiastic grin. "Marvelous question, dear boy. I have been asking it myself."

"But you said—"

"What? Oh, yes. I did say I had invented some of the things here, didn't I? But I cannot take credit for the tiles. The emperor tells me they have always been here. No matter how much we build on the Tower, no matter how many levels are added to its height, with every new floor we lay, some of the tiles become guiding tiles. They're everywhere except in the corridors leading to the royal chambers, for some reason. I have been trying for some time to ascertain their mechanics."

Nomish's hand shot up again. "From what I have seen, a person who wants to command the powers must voice a command or make some sort of gesture. But the tiles know where we want to go before we say a word. Does this mean that the tiles are not operated by the powers?"

"Very astute, boy! It does seem that the powers need to be told or shown what we want them to do. The tiles are the only things I am aware of that know our thoughts before we speak them. What makes them different? And then there are places—like the gong farm—where the powers do not seem to work at all and yet the guiding tiles do go there. Could it be that the vapors there interfere with the powers? I have more questions than answers, I'm afraid." He gave an oddly blissful smile.

"What about the lights?" Nomish asked.

"I've always thought you had a wonderful curiosity, Nomish Rakam, and that is a sure sign of superior intellect." Bonobos's remark drew a sullen glare from Ba'ar. "Now, where were we? Oh, yes, the lights. I can give you something of an answer there." He strode to one of the jars that was lighting the laboratory and pulled it down from its niche in the wall, placing it on the table. Cautiously, he pulled off the ball-shaped clear top, which Hadlay suspected was composed of glass, to reveal two thin strips of copper, between which arced a tiny, brilliant bolt of lightning.

"No doubt some of you will have to learn this for yourselves, but for those who are willing to take my word for it, you do not want to touch this lightning." Ignoring his own advice, Bonobos touched a finger to it. A loud zapping sound was heard, and he jerked back his hand, putting the injured finger in his mouth.

"At this rate, he's going to lose the other hand," Citna muttered.

If Bonobos heard, he ignored her. Sliding his hand down to the neck of the jar, he pulled out the stopper, and with it what appeared to be two metal rods. As he did so, the arc flickered, then disappeared. "It is now safe to touch." He passed the stopper around. It was made of a thick, black, tarry material, punctured through by two iron rods, with thin metal strips extending from its top. Below the cork, the rods were surrounded by copper cylinders, wet with reddish liquid.

Nomish touched the liquid and sniffed his fingers. "It smells like wine or vinegar."

Bonobos clapped his hand against his hook, apparently attempting to applaud, then winced as if he'd hurt himself. "You are quite right, boy."

"But how does it work?"

Bonobos gave a cheerful shrug. "I am uncertain. I only constructed the jars and rods. The addition of wine was suggested by the emperor himself, and I do not know why it works. Wine must have a kind of energy—perhaps this is the reason it intoxicates as well. I have been looking for a satisfactory way to test this theory."

"Thus far, you have failed to explain the tiles, and now the workings of a simple light?" Ba'ar rolled her ebony eyes.

Bonobos gave her an impish grin. "Well, Mistress Sutram, if it is so simple, I would be pleased if you would explain it to us all."

Ba'ar sputtered. "I never said I—You . . . Oh, never mind!"

"May I take it that you admit you do not know?"

Giving him a blistering glare, Ba'ar nodded.

"Wonderful!" he exclaimed. "Young Ba'ar here has just shown us the first and most necessary step toward knowledge. In fact, in my opinion, the wisest words ever said were, 'I don't know.' Once you admit you are ignorant, you will almost always try to remedy the situation."

Ba'ar appeared uncertain about how to receive these comments. She stiffened at being called ignorant, but then Bonobos also seemed to be saying that she was wise. With a sniff, she remained silent, probably fearing that any further comment would only bring additional embarrassment.

Bonobos continued. "A great many of the wonders you will see here at the Tower are currently inexplicable, though I do not believe that the inexplicable is necessarily supernatural. Overlord Asinus will tell you that our emperor is not a natural man, that he is a great wizard. With all respect to the good overlord, I consider this an unfounded assumption."

The initiates greeted this announcement with a stunned silence.

Bonobos grinned. "There! I've shocked you. I hope to do so many times over the coming days. A good mind never accepts a thing simply because it is said, or even because it seems a logical conclusion. You must always question, always study. This is the essence of advancement. It is true, as you will see when you get near them, that the emperor and his son are not ordinary men. Certainly they are larger and stronger. Intellectually, they are far more advanced. It is my belief that what Overlord Asinus calls wizardry is simply very superior knowledge at work, so superior that it has even affected the emperor's form. It is my belief that Emperor Shungallu and Prince Zêru represent what we ourselves may one day aspire to become."

Ba'ar snorted. "It would seem to me the answers to all these mysteries could be obtained by asking the emperor himself, rather than this useless speculation."

"You would think so, wouldn't you?" Bonobos said. "But our emperor enjoys his mysteries. When asked about his nature, his powers, or his inventions, for that matter, he will only state that some things are best left to interpretation. I believe he wishes us to study and learn things for ourselves."

He studied each of the initiates' faces, then gave them a wide smile. "It appears from your expressions that I've managed to pique your curiosity. I hope you will find our further studies of equal interest. I will do my best to endow you with a basic knowledge of the sciences, including medicine and alchemy."

Citna hesitantly raised a hand. "What is alchemy?"

Bonobos smiled. "Ah, more wonderful curiosity! Alchemy is an exciting new discipline which I believe may be the very core of the emperor's secret and perhaps even the key to the advancement of all humankind."

Hadlay stilled at the mention of the word "key." Was this, then, the thing she was supposed to seek? Was she somehow supposed to learn the mysteries of alchemy? It seemed an overwhelming task. Why would the Being bother with her, when Nomish was so much quicker to learn such things?

Then she remembered her decision to ignore the dreams and refocused her attention on Bonobos.

". . . since you have all learned to master the stylus by now, I suggest you come to our sessions prepared to take notes."

Ba'ar and Citna smirked at Hadlay, who stifled a small groan.

THE DUMBWAITER

When Hadlay arrived at the bestiary the next morning, Zêru was waiting for her.

"Let's have some fun!" he suggested, drawing her to a small cupboard that was cut into the interior wall of the chamber. He flung open the door, revealing a wooden box. "Do you think you can fit in here?"

Hadlay hesitated. "Is it safe?"

"Why not?" He stepped to one side, giving her access. "Go on, try to get in!"

Hadlay had to curl into a tight ball to fit. It made her nervous that the box wobbled with her weight, as if it was not firmly affixed to the wall. "Zêru . . ."

"You'll be fine," he assured her. *"Ana bît nuhatimmi shûlîshi!"*

"Hey! What—" The box jolted, then shot up through a narrow black shaft. Terrified, Hadlay braced herself against the walls of the box. "Zêru, help!"

"Don't worry!" His voice came from far below. "You're probably almost there!"

"Where?" And then she felt a shudder, and the box came to a bone-jarring halt, then descended again, as if it had missed its mark.

"Did you make it?" Zêru's dim voice echoed up to her.

"Make what? How do I get out?" Hadlay reached out to the front of the box, where the cabinet door had been, but she felt only cold stone. As she touched the walls, she could feel something sticky and thready attaching to her fingers. Spider webs! She hated spiders! "Zêru! Get me out!"

The cabinet dropped a little, and suddenly the doors to the cabinet flew open. She tumbled into a small alcove off the kitchen.

Magira, who had been working nearby at the oven, gave a little shriek and stumbled back, landing on her ample bottom. Clatters resounded all through the kitchen as the utensils she had been directing dropped to the floor. "Marduk's mustache, girl! What are you doing in there?"

A rush of wind signaled Zêru's arrival. "It worked!" he exclaimed. "You may not be able to appear and vanish as I can, but this is nearly as good."

Hadlay struggled to rise, then hurried to help Magira. "What is that thing?"

Zêru cocked his head. "Didn't you know about the dumbwaiters?"

"Dumb—whats?"

"Bonobos installed them after hearing the emperor speak of something like them in the Lands Beyond," Magira said. "Using shafts at the core of the Tower and a system of cables and pulleys, we can transport items through the Tower. It's faster—and much easier—than carrying them through all those corridors."

Zêru grinned. "And they can carry you as well. Of course you won't have the guiding tiles to help you. But if you say where you want to go, the dumbwaiter should take you there."

FLAPDOODLE!

"Flapdoodle! Galimatias monkey jabber!" Bonobos was fond of making such exclamations several times each day, often for no cause whatever.

This time, however, he had his reason. This day's lesson was to be an explanation of the origins of Turris. Bonobos had begun by saying there was once a great desert, when Ba'ar interrupted.

"We already know all that," she said. "The emperor created the forest, and then he made the Oresed—"

Which was what had prompted Bonobos's explosion.

Ignoring Ba'ar's baleful glance, he continued. "With all respect to Oresed mythology, scientific study tells us that there was no creation. It is plain from every evidence of nature that everything that exists has always existed. If the cosmos had to be created by the emperor, then what or who created him? That which is created is necessarily inferior to its creator. Therefore, to say the emperor was created suggests that there is something or someone greater than he. Can anyone tell me of anything that is greater than our emperor?"

No one wished to speak, and the silence lengthened.

"No?" Bonobos asked. "Well, I have investigated, and I tell you that I find no hint of any being greater than the emperor. And as we all know, absence of evidence is evidence of absence."

Hadlay had no idea what he had just said, but Nomish nodded his agreement.

"Then what *does* the evidence indicate?" Kayshti asked.

Bonobos gave the boy a broad grin, as he always did when he was asked a question. "The evidence indicates that there was always a desert. There is nothing but sand beneath our feet. I myself have dug holes as deep as ten or fifteen men, and seen this for myself. And there is evidence too that all living creatures change as time goes by. Have you ever examined a lizard? Have you noticed that its skin has scales like a fish? And it has feet like a bird's, and a body not unlike a cat's, and a winding tail like a serpent. I believe that once, a very, *very* long time ago, there were only lizards.

"And then, just as we breed dogs, carefully purifying a line of unwanted traits, and enforcing qualities we want, so the forces of nature have selectively purified all creatures. In other words, even we humans are simply much-advanced, greatly purified lizards. And you have heard me say already that the process will continue—until one day humanity may be very like the emperor!"

The lesson was interrupted by a yap from Filch, who had cornered one of the laboratory rodents behind a table.

Bonobos pointed to him. "And you see, here is another evidence for the development of which I speak. Prince Zêru has taken an interest in this procession of life, and through his experiments he seeks to advance other creatures as humans have advanced."

The rodent slipped into a crack between the stones, and Filch dived in after him, getting his head stuck. He squawked, flapping his wings and sending feathers flying. Hadlay jumped up and freed him. She returned to her table, and Filch curled himself around her feet.

Citna smirked. "That creature is quite an advancement."

"Aren't you speaking about creation?" Ba'ar gave Bonobos a challenging glare. "How do you know that the emperor has not done the same with us?"

Bonobos shook his head. "The prince's work is not actual creation, my dear, because nothing new is produced. Zêr-Shungalli takes animals that already exist, such as a cheetah and an eagle, and the result is Anzu, the fierce creature that guards his privy."

"Are you saying that the emperor does not have the power to create? Or," Ba'ar's voice took an ominous tone, "that His Majesty himself was once a lizard?"

"He does have tremendous power, dear girl," Bonobos said, cheerfully ignoring the more dangerous question. "But his is the power of a vastly superior mind. Our emperor has not created the elements. He has simply understood them. He has learned to control them. And once one can harness the elements, he wields the power to mold all things to his liking."

"Is that what you hope to do with the principles of alchemy?" Nomish asked.

"Exactly!" Bonobos tapped his head. "Of course, alchemy is at best a very rudimentary version of what the emperor can do."

Ma'at raised her hand. "I still don't understand. What is this *alchemy*?"

"It is simply the pursuit of perfection!"

Ba'ar snorted. "The pursuit of gold, more like."

"Well, yes, Mistress Sutram, there is that," Bonobos said. "But don't you see, gold is the perfection of all metals. Gold is what lead aspires to be—and it is the work of the alchemist to help lead reach that perfect, purified state. We seek to remove the impurities until only the gold remains."

"And it is this same process through which we humans might one day aspire to be like the emperor?"

"Well said!" Bonobos thumped Nomish on the back with his hook. Nomish's eyes bulged, and Hadlay stifled a giggle. "I believe that is why the emperor supports my studies. He has dispatched Zamzom to the farthest reaches of his empire, seeking an elusive element—carmot—that we hope will enable us to achieve his lofty goals."

"And what are these goals?" Ba'ar asked.

"Well, for one thing, longevity—that appears to be a special concern of the emperor's. Think of it! Emperor Shungallu has been living and governing Turris since long before any of our grandparents or their grandparents lived here! If we could learn the secrets of alchemy, perhaps we too could enjoy this longevity."

Hadlay could not help but wonder why, if the emperor already knew the secret of longevity, he needed to send someone off to search for this carmot. But Sfika had warned against questioning the emperor, so she kept her peace.

Unguarded Thoughts

What are you pondering?" Hadlay asked. All through the evening meal, Nomish had been unusually quiet.

He scooped a hearty bite of stew into his mouth with a bit of flatbread, forgetting the spoon that sat beside him. The Ramash initiates were still unaccustomed to using utensils to eat; at home, they had not been able to afford such things. "It seems odd that two overlords of the emperor have such different thoughts on the matters of his nature and our origins."

"I am certain that the legend Asinus favors is untrue," Rezen stroked her unruly hair. "My parents assure me that our people were here long before the emperor or the Oresed. Back in the days of the riddle and the monument—" She broke off, blanching as she realized what she had been saying.

Hadlay stole a look over her shoulder at the Oresed table and was relieved to see it was noisy with quarrels and laughter. A few boys had begun a duel, magically using their spoons and knives.

"Perhaps we should discuss this when we have more privacy," Rezen suggested.

Privacy. The word evoked a longing in Hadlay. Other than the night in the laundry and a few brief moments each morning in the privy when she bathed, she'd not had any time alone since she'd entered the Tower. And more than all, she missed feeling free to talk with Nomish.

That night, Hadlay was awakened from a deep sleep by Sfika's urgent whisper.

"Up, girl!" She was speaking to Rezen. "There is news from home!"

Several of the other girls stirred. A few sat up to see what was happening.

"What's wrong?" Hadlay asked, trying to keep her voice quiet to avoid waking those who still slept.

"This does not concern you." Sfika shook Rezen's arm again, then half-dragged her from her bed.

"What is it?" Rezen was awake now and clearly frightened. "Is it my father?" A half-moon before the initiates had been selected, Rezen's father had been injured, and Hadlay knew that Rezen feared that his inability to work would send the family to the slave market.

"All I know is that your presence at home is required," Sfika answered. "No need to pack, dear—we'll send your things along tomorrow." She bustled from the dormitory with Rezen close behind.

Hadlay lay back in her bed. She was concerned for her new friend and her family and hoped she would hear more details soon. But in a strange way, she was also reassured. At least if something were to go terribly wrong with their families, she now knew that she and Nomish would be allowed to return home to help.

She turned on her side, hoping sleep would come again.

WHAT'S THE PASSWORD?

For the next two weeks, Hadlay's group was to learn from Sfika, taking chores in various areas of Tower maintenance. They gathered in Sfika's office to receive assignments.

"There is no reason for you to learn as a group during these two weeks," Sfika told them. "Each of you will receive your own chores, and I will hear reports as to your ability and behavior, so pay attention and do as you're told. Citna, you're off to the wardrobe. Ba'ar, since you have already spent a good deal of time with the livestock, you will be working with the groundsmaster."

Hadlay bit back a smile at Ba'ar's outraged look. She made a mental note to ask Zêru to see that Ba'ar made the acquaintance of fleas while she worked with the animals.

Sfika continued with the assignments. Kayshti went to the master plumber, who was already putting his young assistants to work, sending them for fast and terrifying rides down all the chutes to keep them clear. Kayshti looked thrilled with the prospect. Nomish was sent to work with the glaziers. And Ma'at went to the kitchen to work with Magira. Each filed out once they had received their assignments, leaving Hadlay alone with Sfika.

Sfika gave Hadlay an appraising look. "You are to serve in the royal chambers." She came around her desk and stood over Hadlay. "It is clear that you have gained young Zêr-Shungalli's favor, girl." She shot a glare at Filch, who cowered behind Hadlay, stretching his long neck to peer over her shoulder. Sfika made him nervous. "But you have yet to show me that you are worthy of that honor."

Hadlay wanted to tell Sfika that she was not guilty of any of the trouble she was accused of causing, but she knew it would do no good.

Sfika turned and, taking a large brass key from her desk drawer, she moved off to a cupboard, which she unlocked. As she rummaged in the cupboard for whatever it was she sought, Hadlay's eyes remained on the key. Was this the key the Being in her dreams wanted her to seek? Once again, she reminded herself that she had decided to pay no attention to the dreams.

Sfika turned back to Hadlay, pocketing the key. "You will follow Prince Zêru's personal aides, making note of the things they do. Stay quietly in the background, as most of the prince's days are spent in lessons with his father. And whatever you hear, you must never speak of it. The consequences for betrayal of his trust are much worse than you could imagine."

Sobered by the warning, Hadlay left Sfika. In the corridor outside Sfika's office, she set her mind on the prince's chamber, and was surprised when the guiding tiles failed to light up and lead the way. Then she remembered what Sfika and Bonobos had said, that the tiles would not lead to the royal chambers, and, after pondering the problem for a moment, she set her mind on the treasury, which she knew from the tour of the Tower was on the level below the royal chambers. The tiles immediately lit, and Hadlay, pleased with her own cleverness, set out to follow them.

They seemed to go on forever, winding this way, then that. At last they led her past the kitchen, and to the treasury, before they once more ceased to light her way. Without the guiding tiles to help her, she took a few wrong turns after that, but eventually found her way to the prince's chambers.

"Hold!" Zêru's door was flanked by several giant guards—the special ones, like Buthotos, whose uniforms had the long cloaks with the strange, lifted tails. The tallest of them, whose cloak had an additional red fringe along its hem, squinted down at her fiercely, his arms held out to each side almost like the pincers of a crab. He was unarmed, as far as Hadlay could see, but she had no doubt he could kill her in the blink of an eye. Cowering behind Hadlay, Filch poked his head under her arm and hissed.

The giant circled them with a menacing air. "Your names?"

"H-Hadlay Mivana."

"And the beast?"

"What? Oh—his name is Filch."

Instantly, the door to the chambers sprang open, crashing against the wall and narrowly missing the nearest guards, who turned toward it, ready for battle.

The chief guard nodded. "That is the word that opens this door."

"What? Filch?" Just as quickly, the door slammed closed. Hadlay jumped away. Filch squawked at her when she stepped on one of his webbed feet. "Sorry, Filch!" The door slammed open again.

This time, the guard turned to glare at Hadlay. "That's the password. Now, stop saying it!"

Summoning her courage, Hadlay slipped between the guards and through the door as quickly as she could.

Hadlay had not fully appreciated the grandeur of these chambers during Sfika's tour. The antechamber, Zêru's sitting room, was as large as several shops in the marketplace, its walls higher than the tallest Oresed home, worked with images of fantastic creatures and grand royal processions in jewel-toned tile. The wide windows along the outer walls displayed a brilliant blue sky scattered with wisps of cloud far off in the distance. Several cushioned ivory benches, carved in the shape of cheetahs with glittering jeweled eyes, sat near the window. A magnificent desk stood in a corner, surrounded by lamps and cluttered with clay tablets.

Filch yapped, and Hadlay turned just in time to see him disappear through another door, chasing Zêru's nuppy.

"Filch!" At the sound of his name, the door to the chamber slammed shut, making her jump. "You come back here!"

"There you are!" A voice behind Hadlay made her turn again. The person speaking was not Zêru, but another boy who looked a bit like him. He was very tall, slim, and had the same shining skin. But he was dressed more humbly, wearing an ivory tunic with silver sash and silver fringe around the hem. "I am Ayom, Zêr-Shungalli's cupbearer. You are expected in the royal dining hall."

"Should I bring Filch?" Hadlay asked, starting as the door to the chamber slammed open once more. The guards outside swung around, snarling.

Ayom grimaced. "His Highness will have to change the password. That will become annoying very quickly." To Hadlay, he said, "Leave the beast and follow me."

Hadlay had to run to keep up with Ayom, whose legs were nearly as long as her whole body.

The royal dining hall was even grander than Zêru's chambers. A long, gleaming table dominated the room, and crimson draperies graced the window on the outer wall, with clusters of potted palms and figs framing each side. Each chair—and there were at least thirty—was emblazoned with a different image, and two, on either end of the table, were inlaid with gold and ivory, with great curled ram's horns framing the crest rail. Their cushions were embroidered with twelve-pointed stars.

Zêru stood near the window, his skin glowing with reflected sunlight. He grinned when he saw Hadlay. "There you are! We are going to have fun these two weeks! Where's Filch?"

Hadlay heard the door in the next chamber slam again, followed by a loud curse.

"Why are there so many guards outside?" Hadlay asked. "Aren't the Tower defenses sufficient to keep trouble out?"

Zêru shrugged. "Father says sometimes the danger comes from within."

A creak near the far wall of the room drew Ayom's attention to an ornate tapestry. He hurried over and pulled it back to reveal the cupboard that housed the dumbwaiter. "Your meal is ready, sire."

Remembering that her job was to assist Zêru's servants, Hadlay trotted over to Ayom. "What would you like me to carry?" She reached for one of the platters.

The servant pushed Hadlay's hand aside. "I am the only one permitted to touch His Highness's food. I am his taster." Taking a tray from a nearby shelf, he drew out all of the silver platters and a shining goblet.

"Another necessary precaution," Zêru told her, though Hadlay could not see the sense in it. Did Zêru fear being poisoned? Who in this Tower would dare to do such a thing? The overlords warned constantly that the emperor knew everything that took place here. Surely no one would risk his wrath by trying to harm his son.

At Ayom's command, the platters floated to the table. Hadlay remained beside the dumbwaiter and closed the cupboard doors.

Zêru came over to her and patted the doors. "I had not considered it, but this would be a way for you to come here without having to pass the guard."

Hadlay winced. She had not enjoyed her previous voyage in the dumbwaiter and was not eager to repeat the experience. But it would save her a very long walk each morning while she served here. "How do I tell it to come here?"

"Ana urush malki shûlânni!"

Hadlay repeated the words several times to be sure she had them. A new thought occurred to her as Zêru led her to the table. "If the dumbwaiters are unguarded, what would prevent assassins from using them to come here?"

Ayom chuckled, and Zêru grinned. "Anyone small enough to fit in there would hardly be much of a threat." He looked down at her and brushed the top of her head. "No offense."

Ayom uncovered Zêru's food, which appeared to be an array of sparrow eggs, some sort of meat, and honeyed breads. He gestured to a position behind Zêru, evidently intending that Hadlay should stand there.

As Hadlay obeyed, she saw Ayom sprinkle the food—all of it, from the sweet pastries to the meat—with fluid from a small vial. The reddish liquid glistened as it soaked into the food, giving it a ruddy appearance.

"His Highness enjoys this flavoring," Ayom explained.

Hadlay couldn't imagine liking anything enough to want its taste on every kind of food. But she didn't say so. It might be taken as a criticism.

Ayom twisted the top of the container to seal it and tucked it into a pouch at his waist, then portioned a small bite of each item onto a side plate, from which he ate. Swallowing, he stepped away from the table. "Your meal is ready, Your Highness."

Hadlay had left the morning's table feeling full, but the sight of Zêru wolfing such a fine meal made her hungry again. She hoped her stomach would not growl—she vaguely remembered a warning from Asinus that bodily noises were not tolerated in the royal presence. She had come to feel comfortable around Zêru in the noise and stink of the bestiary, but in these grand surroundings, she was once again intimidated.

Her eyes wandered toward the nearby window, and she was struck again by the extreme height of this tower. The outer walls of Turris, though she knew them to be many houses high and quite wide, looked rather like a newly hatched snake winding around the city. The rooftops were mere dots the size of bugs. And in the distance, past the outer wall that protected the emperor's fields from Nomads, she could see a golden horizon shimmering in the light of the morning.

A hard elbow to her ear brought her attention back to Ayom, who shook his head severely. Evidently she was supposed to watch the prince eat.

When Zêru finally pushed away from the table, Ayom stepped forward again. "*Espâ!*" At his word, the platters began stacking themselves, then rose and drifted toward the dumbwaiter. "*Naptî!*" The cupboard door swung open. Once the platters had settled inside, Ayom said, "*Ana hurshi shûrissunûti!*" and the device dropped from view again.

Feeling a bit useless, Hadlay turned to Zêru. "Sfika says I am to assist your servants—" She was interrupted by the sound of horns from the next chamber.

Zêru rose. "Father is coming."

The emperor! The nearest she had ever been to him was in the dining hall that first day, and she had been one among many initiates. The idea of being nearly alone with him was overwhelming. "Zêru, should I leave? What—"

The great door to the chamber swung open, and several servants, some Nafal, some more like Zêru and Ayom, filed in. With no answer from Zêru, Hadlay quickly found a place among these. She felt terribly conspicuous, a mouse among so many giants. She tried to tuck herself behind one of the larger potted trees by the window. But the emperor saw her immediately as he strode into the room.

"Ah! You must be the Ramash girl my son has spoken of."

"This is Hadlay, Father," Zêru said.

"Step forward, child!"

Hadlay didn't have much choice. At the sound of the emperor's voice, she had begun to move, as if unseen hands propelled her forward.

The emperor circled, bending nearly double to inspect her. "Very small, even for a Ramash. But yes, the yellow hair is nice—almost the color of gold, would you say, Zêru? Yes, very pleasant. Raise your eyes, girl."

Hadlay had been careful to keep her gaze to the floor, mindful of

Asinus's warning not to meet the eyes of the emperor. Now, reluctantly, she looked up at him.

His face dazzled her, glowing so brightly in the light from the window that it almost hurt her eyes. His white hair and beard caught the light of the sun and reflected many colors as he moved. His crown, made of polished gold, looked dull compared to his complexion. Hadlay was reminded of the many colors of the Being, and she wondered if there were some connection.

His hand, sparkling with many jeweled rings, caught her chin, sending shivers through Hadlay's body. "Eyes the color of sky, just as you said. I can see why she interests you. You may keep her, if you wish." The emperor released her and turned back to the table. "Now, let us begin your lesson . . ."

Feeling as though she had been dropped from a height, Hadlay stumbled back to a place in line with the other servants.

The Emperor's Secret

Hadlay had just finished cleaning Zêru's privy after some of his creatures fouled it. Unfortunately, this was one of those tasks that could not be done magically, and it fell to her, as the only human servant, to take care of it. She heard Zêru and his father enter the dining hall.

"But Father, why permit so many conflicting theories?" Hadlay realized he was asking the emperor the questions she had posed to him only that morning. "Won't that make the people curious?"

The emperor's voice sounded a little impatient. "So long as they argue over competing falsehoods, they will never guess the truth. It would not be wise to reveal who I am until the people are prepared." The emperor looked up and saw Hadlay watching through the open door. With a gesture, he slammed the door between them.

Hadlay fought the urge to rush to the door and press her ear against it. What was he saying?

&

Who was he? Hadlay was still pondering the question as she ate the evening meal.

"Brecho sent me down the chutes today, and I took a wrong turn and ended in the gong farm." Though Kayshti was still damp from bathing, the other initiates had noticed a smell about him, and he now sat alone on one side of the Ramash table.

"And I learned what causes those distortions in glass," Nomish said.

"Fine particles of dust thicken the material. The glazier says that Bonobos is working on a way to remove the impurities." Hadlay knew that Nomish was impatient to return to the laboratory. He could hardly pass an hour without making some mention of Bonobos and what must be going on with his work.

"I learned the word to chop the ends off carrots," Ma'at said. "*Bittaq!*" A huge cleaver lifted itself from Magira's cutting board, and whacked a corner off the table. The initiates scattered, leaving stools overturned and goblets toppled.

Magira hurried over to the table and caught the cleaver as it dropped. "The word you need is *butuq*, dear." She summoned cloths to tend to the mess.

"Sorry." Ma'at flushed as her friends returned to their seats.

"What did you learn, Hadlay?" Fa'an asked. "Have you managed any magic at all yet?"

Something about the way Fa'an asked made her want to defend herself, but Hadlay forced herself to feign dejection.

Nomish gave her a dubious look. "What do you do up there all day, then?"

The question caught the attention of the Oresed table, and the room went silent.

She ached to tell her friends what she had overheard, but didn't dare. She cast her mind about for a safe topic, one that would be interesting without breaching the emperor's confidence. "Well, yesterday the emperor and prince sent dispatches to the governors of the Lands Beyond." She had, along with several other servants, actually helped scribe the missives. With so many there to listen in, it seemed unlikely the messages were confidential.

"You remain during the prince's lessons?" one of the Oresed girls, who had served in the royal chambers in the previous session, asked.

"Sometimes."

The girl sniffed. "I never had to do that. I always spent my days with the chamber servants. Making the beds, cleaning. All done with magic, of course. But since you cannot command the powers, I suppose they have no use for you." This brought snickers from her companions.

"What are the Lands Beyond?" Rasab asked.

"They are the many lands the emperor sojourned in during his time away from us," Ba'ar said, absently scratching her ear. "Everyone knows that."

"Why are you always trying to be so superior?" One of the Oresed boys glowered at her. "Not everyone knows." The Oresed table was quickly embroiled in a heated dispute.

"Where are these lands?" Rasab asked over the din. "I thought everything beyond the outer wall was inhabited by Nomads and Refa."

"There is a large map in the counsel chamber." Hadley thought it should be safe to speak of this, since Tower servants cleaned this chamber daily, and the map was openly displayed. "There are seven lands beyond the seas—one is called Avalon, another is Heorot. And I think there's Nineveh . . ." She shrugged. "I don't recall them all. Nafal princes govern them on the emperor's behalf."

"Pah! Geography!" the Oresed girl interrupted, breaking from the debate at her table. "I overheard something much more interesting when *I* served Zêr-Shungalli. He was speaking with his father about his marriage, and he asked whether he could father children with a human bride."

The statement brought the argument at the Oresed table to a halt.

"A human bride?" Nomish asked. "Wouldn't he want a female of his own kind?"

"Have you ever seen a female of his kind?" Ba'ar asked. "From what I have heard, Zêr-Shungalli and the others like him are sons of Nafal who were married to human women. They always have boy children. Never girls."

The Oresed girl smiled. "It sounded as though he means to choose a bride from Turris."

That got everyone's attention.

"Did he say who?" Citna asked.

Aa'mash frowned. "He doesn't know any initiates from Turris, except—"

"Of course!" Ba'ar surged to her feet. "My father wondered why the emperor had involved himself in the selection of mere servants. They intend to choose one of us!"

"Not necessarily." Nomish's brows drew together. "Why would the son of an emperor marry a servant, even one as honored as those who serve the Tower? The emperor would more likely want to marry the prince to the daughter of a king in one of the distant lands. That would help to forge a strong alliance."

The Oresed girl shrugged. "All I know is what I overheard."

"He's so handsome!" another Oresed girl gushed. "What do you think, Tahat, has Zêr-Shungalli shown favor to any of us?"

"Well, he did say I had an interesting smile!" She gave a broad grin, revealing pearly teeth so crooked they stuck out like the tusks of a boar.

"I hope I get a chance to serve in the royal chambers!" the other girl said.

Nomish worried at his lower lip. "Did you know about this, Hadlay?"

"Zêru never mentioned it."

He glanced at Filch, who was sneaking a silver ladle from Magira's basket, then frowned again. "What will you do if . . ."

Hadlay realized what he was thinking. She leaned in, whispering so no one else could hear. "Nomish, Zêru wouldn't choose me. I'm just his friend—more of a pet, really," she added, remembering the emperor's words: *You may keep her.* She smiled at Nomish and spoke more loudly. "I'm sure he will prefer a wealthy Oresed girl. Someone from an important family, as you suggested."

"Someone like Ba'ar," Ma'at murmured.

"By the gong farm, anyone but her!" Kayshti grimaced. "Could you imagine her as the royal princess?"

The idea soured Hadlay's mood. It was bad enough for Ba'ar to be Asinus's apprentice. Ba'ar as princess would be disaster for the Ramash.

She would have to help Zêru choose someone else.

That evening, as the girls were preparing for slumber, a servant entered and magically commanded two of the beds to leave the dormitory. The first bed was Rezen's, and the second belonged to one of the Oresed girls.

"Why are those being removed?" Ba'ar asked.

The servant glanced at her and shrugged. "I was told that both girls have been dismissed from the emperor's service and sent home."

Ma'at came to stand beside Hadlay as the servants departed. "Do you suppose Rezen's family is all right?"

Hadlay shrugged. "I hope they are. Have you ever met them?"

"I think my parents know them slightly. The other girl—the Oresed— which one was she?"

Hadlay had to think a moment. Other than Ba'ar and Citna, she had never paid much attention to any of them, and she knew none of them by name. "I think she is the one who argued with Nomish earlier this eve."

"Tahat—the one who talked about Prince Zêru choosing a bride?"

Hadlay nodded. Perhaps that was why she had been dismissed. Hadn't Sfika warned that disclosing things discussed in the emperor's chambers would be cause for punishment? She resolved to be even more cautious of what left her lips in the future.

FRIENDS IN HIGH PLACES

Even though Hadlay had reassured Nomish, the idea that Zêru might choose her refused to leave her mind. Each day as she reported to his chambers for service, she found herself wondering what it would be like to eat at his table instead of standing behind it. What would it be like to wear those gold-fringed, gossamer robes, rather than her plain, gray tunic? To have jeweled rings and a crown to wear—and talents upon talents of gold to send to her family?

What would it be like to help Zêru command the city? To have such power and wield it openly? Oh, the Oresed would tremble then!

She couldn't say she hated the idea.

And their afternoons were, as Zêru had promised, great fun. One day, they raced the entire circuit of Turris, each aboard a gold-trimmed chariot drawn by gold-spotted horses that had been mixed with cheetahs. The next, Zêru taught Hadlay how to command the powers to lift her, and she soared through the great throne room, doing flips and whirls. She once again thought of the old Ramash bedtime story. This place had so many wonders—just like the maze in N'de!

Today, they stood atop the highest pinnacle of the Tower. Now that Hadlay could invoke the powers to keep her up, she was no longer so terrified of heights. She looked down at the little wisps of clouds and wondered what it would be like to soar through them like the birds.

"Zêru, could we—"

Zêru grinned. "Why not? Only stay outside the city wall. Father would not like it if we were seen flying over Turris." He flung himself from the Tower, and then glided as though he had sprouted wings.

For an instant, Hadlay hesitated. But then she felt the familiar sensation of something like hands lifting her, and she too was flying. Following on Zêru's heels, she dived steeply over the farmlands, where she saw workers pulling up a dead tree with the help of a giant white elephant. As they flew over, the creature lifted its face toward them, and for a moment, Hadlay thought its eyes and ears seemed almost human. But it had the elephant's long trunk and gleaming white tusks, which jutted out crookedly like those of a boar. For some reason, the sight troubled her, but she pushed the thought from her mind, determined not to spoil the fun.

They flew low over a herd of shabbits, scattering them over the shallow hillside. Then up, up, they flew, until she thought she might actually touch the sun.

"This way!" Zêru shouted over the winds that blew around them. And he zipped off, with Hadlay in hot pursuit.

Then she saw it, looming up ahead: the outer wall. The wall that ringed the outmost limits of Turris, meant to keep the Nomads at bay.

Zêru zoomed up and over the wall and out above the open desert.

Hadlay followed him—truthfully, she did not know if she could have stopped herself, since she did not seem to be directing the powers. Beyond the farms, the land became more barren, vast expanses of golden sand interrupted by tufts of vegetation. As they descended nearer the earth, she saw a small group of brown tents in the distance. "What are those?"

"Nomad traders!" Zêru shouted. "They'll try to shoot us down if they see us! Let's go in the other direction."

They veered off, though Hadlay stared back over her shoulder. These were the people her father traded with. She would have liked a closer look at them. But Zêru was right. Her father said he was safe among the Nomads only because they knew he was poorer than they. Hadlay shuddered to think what they might do if they managed to capture the royal prince.

They raced along, skimming over dune after dune, until Hadlay wondered how far Zêru meant to go. Then, even in the heat that drifted up from the sand, she felt a terrible chill, and an unspeakable terror gripped her, as if she sensed death reaching up to devour her. These were the wastelands, full of monsters and—

"Zêru! Stop! There are Refa here! We are in danger!"

"Refa!" Zêru laughed that echoing laugh of his, as though a million voices joined him. "They would never harm me! Or you, so long as you are my friend." He looked over his shoulder, and seeing the fear on Hadlay's face, he circled back. "All right, then. Back to the Tower!" Turning, he zoomed off.

As they passed over the outer wall again, Hadlay felt as if an icy fist had been pried loose from her heart.

A few moments later, Zêru touched down lightly on the highest terrace of the Tower and caught Hadlay as she dropped beside him, nearly falling over the edge. "Was that fun?"

She nodded, wondering if this was all a dream. It seemed so long since she had gone hungry and slept in a stable. Since she had seen her parents. Perhaps her father had been among the Nomads in those tents. A sudden, aching homesickness overwhelmed her.

"Are you all right?" Zêru asked.

She brushed at her eyes and forced a smile. "Yes. Just a little winded."

He grinned. "Maybe tomorrow we'll swim in the moat! I just added a new creature there—she has lovely, long hair and sings beautifully!"

Hadlay only half listened to Zêru's animated chatter as they made their way back to his chamber. The thoughts of her father had reawakened her concerns about her parents. Magira hadn't reported about them for several days. Were they all right?

"Zêru . . . did you ever speak with your father about the Ramash?"

She had interrupted without thinking, and for a moment, Zêru's eyes went black and fierce. The realization struck her with some force that he was still the royal prince, and she a lowly servant.

Hadlay dropped her eyes. "I'm sorry, Your Highness. You were saying?"

He paused, then shook his head. "No, it's all right. What was it you asked me?"

Hadlay repeated her question. He stared at her blankly for a moment, then appeared to recall their discussion. "Yes, yes. I did bring it up. Father was most troubled when I told him what you had said. He is working with the overlords on a solution. It is a vexing problem, but I have no doubt they will solve it."

Hadlay could not help wondering why it should be difficult. The treasury was full of gold talents, enough to ease the burdens of every poor citizen of Turris. But Sfika's warning about asking such questions still rang in her mind, so she kept her peace. There must be something she did not understand yet. But if the emperor truly cared as Zêru said he did, surely he would find a way to help.

Iron Mixed with Clay

You are farther from me now than when you began." The Being's colors ranged from deep blues to violets, the colors of longing and of sadness.

As always, Hadlay did not understand what he was saying, and yet his words filled her with a sense of loss. How had she moved away from him? How could she return? She thought again of Sfika's key and wondered if she was supposed to steal it. What would happen if she did?

"You have taken something that is mine alone," he warned, his voice like cracks of thunder. "Until now, no real harm has come of it, but soon you will learn the danger, for what you do to another will prey upon you. When you see the truth of this, you will begin to grasp the key."

"What did I take that is yours?"

"I alone will keep accounts. I alone decide who pays and who is paid."

Hadlay still did not know what he meant, but she had come to believe this Being, even though she never understood him until his prophecies came to pass.

His voice turned soft and sweet. "And now you are turning toward the key again. In days to come, you will hear strange counsel. Listen and reflect on it."

Hadlay was curious about his warning, but other things were on her mind as well. "Why have I come here, to the Tower? Am I here to help my people?"

"You are. Though not in the way you imagine."

Hadlay thought she understood. "Then I must marry Zêru. But what of Nomish?"

The Being's wings stroked the air, warming her with their flame. "You are meant for a much greater union. If you will receive it."

"What does that mean?"

"A choice is coming, two ways to help your people. One will seem a blessing but be a curse. And one will seem to bring great danger, but there is no loss you could suffer that could surpass the reward. Seek what I offer you, beloved. Do not keep grasping at what is mine alone. Seek the key. Only the key . . ."

Someone was shaking her shoulder. "Hadlay!"

Ma'at stood over her. "You've overslept. It's our last day with Sfika—and you know how she is when we are late."

Hadlay glanced at the window. Ma'at was right—they were very late. Probably too late for the morning meal. Wondering why Zêru had not summoned her to the bestiary, she rose and grabbed a fresh tunic.

Filch had taken to sleeping on the floor by her bed. Hadlay had made a nest for him using a spare blanket. This morning he lay sprawled on his back, his paws and webbed feet in the air, tail stretched one direction and long neck stretched the other. Hadlay bent and gave his belly a scratch. "Wake up, Filch! You need to go to the bestiary for your meal!"

As if he understood her, Filch wriggled free of his nest. Giving her a farewell honk, he waddled off.

"Should that creature be sleeping here?" Ma'at asked, as Hadlay pulled on her tunic. "He's getting far too attached to you. What if his master misses him?"

Hadlay considered telling her that Filch was a gift from the prince, but decided against it. She had known Ma'at only a short while and did not know whether she could keep a confidence. Hadlay shrugged. "Filch goes where he pleases. If I chase him off, he just comes back again."

"Come on! You know how long it takes to get up to the kitchen."

"Don't worry—just follow me." Taking Ma'at's hand, Hadlay led her down the hall to a dumbwaiter cupboard near the servants' chambers. "Now, you'll have to trust me. Get in here."

"But . . ."

"Do you want to be late?" Hadlay gently prodded her toward the opening.

As soon as Ma'at was inside, Hadlay gave the rope a tug, as if she intended to raise the dumbwaiter by hand, since Ma'at still did not know Hadlay could command the powers. But as soon as the box rose out of view, she whispered, "*Ana bît nuhatimmi shûlîshi!*" She poked her head into the shaft. "When you come to a stop, push with your feet. You'll find yourself in the kitchen!"

Ma'at's squeals echoed down to her for a short time. When they stopped, Hadlay gave her a moment to collect herself and climb out. Then she summoned the box again, and climbed in herself. She had just made her way from the hidden alcove to the tables when Sfika arrived.

"Gather round." Sfika stood at the center of the kitchen and waited until the initiates had joined her. "Before you go, I have reports that a number of things have gone missing. A brass candlestick from the dining hall, a silver spoon from the kitchen, and a glass hand mirror from the servants' quarters. If any of you happen to see these as you go about your duties, please report to me."

Once they were dismissed, Hadlay ducked back into the dumbwaiter and raised herself to the royal dining hall. She rapped three times on the cupboard door before letting herself out.

Zêru was sitting at his table, his head down on his arms as though he had been crying.

"What's the matter?" Hadlay hurried to his side.

"Alphonse died last night." Zêru sniffled into the sleeve of his robe.

Hadlay knelt beside him. "I'm sorry, Zêru." She was tempted to pat his arm, but didn't know if it was allowed. Instead, she took a napkin from the table and offered it to him. She knew how much he'd loved his pet.

Horns sounded from the next room, and Hadlay moved to her place behind Zêru's chair just as the emperor and his servants arrived.

"I heard, son," the emperor said, bending over Zêru and squeezing his shoulder. "We will find a solution. I promise."

Hadlay heard a quiet noise by the door. She turned to find Ayom giving her a meaningful look. He nodded toward Zêru's chambers. She drew away and followed him through the door.

He closed it behind them. "Let us allow them some privacy."

"What are they trying to solve?" Hadlay asked. "Alphonse is already dead."

"It is the same with all mixed kinds." Ayom spoke distractedly, as if he, too, were grieving. "We are like iron mixed with clay. Eventually, the clay crumbles, and we fall apart."

"We?" Hadlay asked. "You speak of yourself?"

Ayom nodded. "I speak of Nafal-human mixes as well, yes."

The import of his statement reached her. "So Zêru will . . ."

Ayom nodded, staring at the door. "So will we all."

CITNA'S ANTIC

Hadlay was still pondering the problem as she got ready for bed that night. Zêru was going to die? How soon? The idea of losing her new friend troubled her. She had come to enjoy his company almost as much as Nomish's.

She longed to discuss the problem with Nomish, but she realized this was probably another topic that the emperor preferred to keep private. She had so many secrets now, she hardly risked talking with anyone for fear of letting something slip.

As she kicked off her slippers, she accidentally bumped the edge of her laundry basket. Something shiny peered out from among the discarded tunics.

Leaning in to look more closely, she saw what it was—a brass candlestick! Hadlay knelt down beside the basket and rummaged through the things inside. A hand mirror. A spoon. Here were the missing items Sfika had spoken of! Additionally, tucked deeper in the basket, she found Sfika's key.

Glancing over her shoulder to be sure no one had seen, she quickly reburied everything under her soiled tunics.

Tomorrow was laundry day. The launderers would discover these items, and she would be accused of stealing them!

Her first thought was to hide them somewhere else in the Tower. But the other girls were getting into bed, chatting about their day. If she walked out now, someone was sure to question her. Reluctantly, she climbed into her bed and closed her eyes. There was nothing she could do until everyone was asleep.

The lights went down. Hadlay lay in the darkness waiting—a very long time—for the last of the whispers to die away.

As she waited, she wondered who was so set on making mischief for her. Who had hidden those things in her laundry? Who had pushed her into Brecho's vat? Who had put the flunk in her nightstand?

She remembered that she had wished that the kettle of fish guts would dump itself on the person responsible for it all, and it had dumped itself on Ba'ar and those closest to her. She had assumed Ba'ar was the target. But it didn't fit, somehow. As much as Ba'ar hated Hadlay, she also wanted to advance herself here. Hadlay doubted she would risk stealing from the Tower.

Who else had been drenched in fish guts that morn? Rezen, Hadlay remembered, but instantly discounted the girl. She was Ramash—and a friend. Besides, she was no longer in the Tower. And Fa'an . . . She had never seemed to like Hadlay, come to think of it. But why would she do something so mean?

And how could Fa'an have gotten a flunk into her nightstand? From all accounts, Fa'an was still struggling to command the powers. How could she overcome the charms that kept the nightstands closed to all but the owner?

Then Hadlay remembered that Magira had started to say something, just as the kettle had unloaded its contents: . . . *they only open for the person whose bed is* . . . Yes! That's what Sfika had said as well, that the drawers were charmed to open only for the girl whose name was on the nearest bed.

When Hadlay found the flunk in her nightstand, hadn't she originally had trouble getting it open? She'd pulled it over to her bedside so that she could try again—and then it had slid open easily!

Before she'd moved it, the nightstand had been nearer *Citna's* bed!

Hadlay had never done any harm to Citna, nothing to deserve being the target of such spite. Other than be Ramash.

Well, enough was enough. She was done being a victim of the Oresed and their bigotry. Tonight, she would see this wrong righted.

When the breathing in the room became regular and deep and a few soft snores began to rumble in the darkness, Hadlay sat up. She looked at each bed in the moonlight from the window. Everyone appeared to be asleep.

She rose, crept quietly to her basket, and pulled out the tunic that wrapped the stolen items. If Citna would go to this extreme to cause her trouble, she would certainly continue trying. She had to be taught a lesson.

So Hadlay tiptoed around her bed, unwrapped each item and slipped it into Citna's basket, then covered them all with another tunic. All but the key. Holding it in her hand, Hadlay felt she had to keep it. If this was the key the Being in her dream spoke of, she needed to learn what he wanted with it.

Quietly, she opened her nightstand drawer. While she now understood how these nightstands worked and knew that Citna could open the drawer as well, she did not believe Citna would bother with Alila's picture. Carefully pulling the baked clay from its frame, she tucked the key inside, then secured it once again.

Then she returned to her bed, smiling.

The initiates were just clearing the platters from the table the next morning when Sfika arrived, flanked by two muscular guards. "You, girl!" she stabbed a bony finger at Citna.

Hadlay saw Citna go pale, and ducked her head to mask her smile.

"Follow me!" Sfika marched out of the kitchen, with Citna and the guards trailing.

It was the last time they saw Citna for several days.

SETTLING ACCOUNTS

Their next session was in the treasury. The treasurer's name was Aurum. Hadlay was tempted to ask what had become of Viridesc, the one her mother had spoken of, but Overlord Aurum was an irritable, fishy-looking woman with little patience for initiates. They soon discovered that she liked it best if they stayed out of her way. So they learned the commands for money counting from the lower clerks and accountants.

"*Nikkassî epush,*" Nomish murmured, and a stack of silver minas shifted, one at a time, from one pile to another, while a stylus, commanded to write, kept count on a clay tablet. Nomish rested his chin on his hand and watched, not bothering to conceal his boredom. It didn't take any special insight to discern that he'd rather be in Bonobos's laboratory.

Hadlay was still pretending that she couldn't command the powers, so she had to do her work by hand. She, too, found it tedious, especially after her two weeks with Zêru. Their mornings in the bestiary were hardly long enough for her now that she knew her friend might not have much more time.

She had broached the subject yesterday. Zêru had seemed surprised that she knew his problem, but once Hadlay expressed her concern for him, he spoke openly, apparently relieved to have someone to talk to. "We don't know why we die. One of my father's Nafal rulers, Azazel, found a supplement for the diet that keeps us alive longer. But even with it, we will only live a fourth of the life of the weakest creature we are mixed from."

"So you will only live . . ."

"One-fourth of the human lifespan," Zêru said. "Perhaps twenty years."

"Unless someone finds a solution," Hadlay reminded him. "What of Bonobos? Has he been working on this?"

"Why do you think Father has him studying alchemy?"

Bonobos had said that one of the goals of alchemy was longevity. But if the emperor already knew the secret of longevity, then he would not need Bonobos. So the long lives of the Nafal must come naturally, then, and Bonobos was wrong in his belief that the emperor had harnessed age. And the emperor needed Bonobos to find a way to save his son's life.

Indeed, hadn't Bonobos said that alchemy was the key? Maybe *this* was the key the Being had spoken of. Maybe she was meant to help Bonobos save the prince's life!

After a slight hesitation as she pondered the wisdom of touching the prince, she put a comforting hand on Zêru's arm. "My friend Nomish is very smart, and he wants more than anything to apprentice under Bonobos. I will tell him that it is most urgent that Bonobos succeed with this alchemy. If anyone can help him, Nomish can."

Even as she'd said it, Hadlay had struggled with her own doubts. Nomish was smarter than anyone she knew, but if the emperor himself did not have a solution to Zêru's problem, how would any human find it? But the Being had charged her with finding the key, and if that meant helping Bonobos, then she and Nomish would have to find a way.

Now, Hadlay calculated the years Zêru might have remaining. "Twenty . . . thirteen . . . seven . . ."

"You're going backwards." Ba'ar's caustic voice cut through Hadlay's thoughts. She was still scratching flea bites, even days after she'd left her duties in the stables. "I don't know what the Rakams were thinking, apprenticing you in their shop. You'd have had them bankrupt within a week!"

Hadlay was tempted to retort, but her mind was too preoccupied to think of a good comeback. She sighed and started counting again.

Filch roused from napping at her feet and padded over to a mound of silver shekels. Something—perhaps a reflection—caught his eye, and suddenly, he plunged his head into the pile. When he came out, one of the rings had wrapped itself around his beak. Filch shook his head, scattering silver everywhere, then dashed around the room, smacking into walls, trying to get away from his captor. Spreading his great, red wings, he flew, brushing heads with his bushy tail.

"Filch!" Laughing, Hadlay caught his neck and helped him wriggle free.

"You should have left the muzzle on," Kayshti said. "All his yapping makes me lose count!"

The room grew suddenly silent. Hadlay turned to see Citna standing in the doorway like a ghost. Her back was pressed against the wall, and she was trembling. "Keep that . . . *thing* away from me!"

Citna looked like a shade, so pale her lips were almost white, and she wore a formal tunic with long sleeves and a gauzy veil draped round her neck. But it was her eyes that startled Hadlay. They were haunted, as if they had seen things too terrible to speak of. The smell of strong herbs trailed after her as she entered.

"Citna! Where have you been?" Ba'ar asked. "I have been alone all week with these Ramash!"

Citna didn't meet her eyes. With a wary eye toward Filch, she shambled to a distant corner and sat. "The . . . dungeon. Awful . . ." Her voice was so quiet they had to strain to hear.

"What were you doing in the dungeon?" Ba'ar rose and went to stand over her.

Citna cowered, swallowing hard. "Can't . . . talk about it."

The initiates exchanged anxious looks. Citna was usually so brash—what had happened to her? Even Ba'ar, seeming to sense her fragility, gave up and returned to her counting.

Filch shot Hadlay an accusing look.

She had meant only to teach Citna a lesson. But she felt as though she had done something much more terrible. She remembered the Being's words in her dream: *you will learn the danger, for what you do to another will prey upon you.* The room seemed to chill as a sense of foreboding settled over her.

The Thief Is Named

The day was not yet out when Aurum swept into the room. "All right, which of you took them?" She glared at each of the initiates in turn, her black-fire eyes boring into them.

"Took what, ma'am?" Kayshti asked.

"Three gold minas have gone missing from the accounts!" She held up a tablet and shook it at them. "Which of you took them?"

"Are you certain there is no mistake?" Nomish asked.

"We do not make mistakes in the treasury!" Aurum snapped. "Someone stole them!"

Citna shuddered and curled into a shaking ball in her corner. "I only just arrived! I have not touched . . ."

"Sfika *shisâ!*" Aurum shouted, and moments later, Sfika arrived out of breath and clearly irritated.

After hearing the accusation, Sfika turned to the initiates. "Empty your pockets!"

Everyone did so at once, except Citna, who seemed paralyzed with fright. Ba'ar hurried over and emptied Citna's pocket for her. No one had any gold.

"All right, to the dormitories!" Sfika strode off, and with uncertain faces the initiates followed.

On the way, Sfika summoned guards, who met them at the dormitories.

One by one, starting with the boys, each initiate's belongings were inspected. Citna, who had managed to trail along, stood quaking by her bed, opening her nightstand with a trembling hand when ordered to do so.

"Nothing!" Sfika said.

Hadlay's things were the last searched. And in the bottom of her laundry basket, there were three gold minas. And the hand mirror that had gone missing before.

Hadlay stared at them. "But I didn't—I never—" She turned to glare at Citna. "How did you—"

Ba'ar stepped between them. "Don't you dare blame Citna! The girl is barely back from the dungeon, and she never touched any gold!"

"I didn't steal these things!" Hadlay said.

Sfika poked her with a finger. "Open your nightstand!"

Shaking with fear and anger, Hadlay complied, then stepped back to allow a guard to search.

Finding only Alila's picture, the guard moved to close the drawer again, but Sfika stopped him.

"No—the girl looks far too relieved. Hand me that picture." Sfika looked it over carefully, then pulled the baked clay from its frame. The key dropped into her hand.

With a poisonous glare at Hadlay, Sfika turned to the guards. "Take this thief to Asinus!"

Hadlay felt magical bonds enclose her so that she could not move, and, at a command from a guard, she was floated from the room. Sfika and Aurum followed, and, after exchanging confused glances, the remaining initiates brought up the rear.

"Ah, Hadlay Mivana!" Asinus gave a malevolent grin as the guards deposited her at the foot of his lectern. He turned to Sfika and Aurum. "What did she do? It must be serious if you brought her to me."

"I did not do anything!" Hadlay shouted. She felt the guards' magical bonds release her and she struggled to her feet. "I have no idea how those—"

"She stole three gold minas from the emperor's treasury!" Aurum interrupted as if Hadlay had not spoken.

"And a mirror—the same one stolen last week." Sfika held the items out as evidence.

"Well, well, well." Asinus turned his gleaming, black eyes to Hadlay and clucked his tongue. "It seems you *remesh* never learn. This will be your last time, you can be certain of that!" Smiling, he folded his hands and paused to think. "How shall we punish you? Hmm . . . Well, when Viridesc—"

"Asinus!" Sfika broke into his ruminations, stepping up beside Hadlay. "We must not speak of that!"

Asinus stared at her for a second, then seemed to take her meaning. "Yes, yes. Quite right. It just seemed the obvious solution. Same crime, same punishment. And I'm certain the young prince would be only too happy—"

"That was the emperor's decision. But I have no stomach for it."

Asinus's full lips pouted. "All right, then. But that still leaves the dungeon. It certainly seems to have done the trick with young Citna."

Citna paled, and, seeing the horror in her eyes, Hadlay was desperate to be heard. Turning, she pointed to the mirror in Sfika's hand. "*Nâmara idna!*" The mirror yanked itself from Sfika's grip and came to Hadlay.

One of the guards stepped up to interfere, but Hadlay threw up a hand. "*Sikpâshu!*" The guard flew back as if pushed.

"*Sha itbû kullimâniâti!*" The mirror began to glow. Hadlay held it up so that everyone could see. "Watch! This is what happened."

Shapes formed in the glass. Servants coming and going, and then . . . something else. A creature . . . Filch. He was carrying something to Hadlay's wardrobe. The minas! The key!

"Trickery!" Asinus brayed. "Chicanery! This girl cannot conjure the powers! I myself have seen her fail!" He turned to the other initiates. "Which of you—"

"*Kubussu leqâ!*" Hadlay said, and his cap yanked itself from his head, dancing just out of his reach. It felt glorious, finally, to show these people what she could do.

"Give that back," he grunted, making a swipe for it and missing.

Sfika took the mirror from Hadlay's hand. "That's quite enough. *Tûra!*"

At her command, the cap flew to her hand, and she passed it to its owner.

Asinus pulled the cap back on, so hard that its sides caught on his ears. Then he returned to his lectern. "You . . . you have been pretending to be powerless!" His eyes widened as he realized why. "So you could make mischief on me!"

"On all of us!" Ba'ar said.

"She must be *doubly* punished!" Asinus thundered.

Belatedly remembering Zêru's caution about taking care not to be caught in her mischief, Hadlay froze. "I . . . I . . . I'm sorry. I didn't—"

"Take her to the dungeon! Call the torturer!" Asinus shouted. The guards exchanged an anxious glance, but they stepped forward, reaching for her arms.

"*Stop!*"

Everyone stilled.

Sfika stepped up to the lectern. "Asinus, think for a moment. It would be foolish to torture this girl."

"Why?" Aurum demanded. "It was she who trained that beast to steal the minas!"

"I never—" Hadlay started.

Asinus cut her off. "It was her magic that tormented me these several weeks!"

"And no doubt it was she who planted the evidence against Citna," Ba'ar added.

"Yes, and even if Filch is the one who stole my key, Hadlay clearly meant to keep it," Sfika said. "But who gave her that beast? Who do you think taught her to command the powers, since she has not been learning from us? She just used very advanced magic to resist a royal guard! Where did she receive such authority?" She paused, allowing her reasoning to strike home.

"Prince Zêru!" Asinus whispered. "But why would he favor a—a *remesh*?"

Sfika gave him an impatient glare. "She has been with him in the bestiary nearly every morning since she arrived—at his command, I might add. Clearly he does favor her. Do you wish to risk offending him by harming his friend?"

"But—but she must be punished!" Asinus sputtered.

"And she will be," Sfika said. "There are many duties in this Tower that cannot be performed by magic. One of the most vile, I am told, is cleaning the bestiary." She turned to Hadlay. "Since you are so fond of your royal friend's beasts, you will report to the master kennelgroom each evening and each morning before your regular duties, and you will clean every single cage!"

Hadlay knew well the filth that crusted the cages in the bestiary, and there were so many of them she could hardly imagine the work she would have to do. Even so, she almost sobbed with relief. "Yes, ma'am."

"I believe the matter is resolved." Sfika turned to step down from the lectern.

"Wait!"

Sfika stilled, and all turned their attention to Asinus. Seeing the evil look in his eyes, Hadlay knew at once that her problems were not over.

The overlord smiled, revealing those horrid yellow teeth. "This girl is far too pleased with this punishment of yours, Overlord Sfika. We must do more."

"I've already pointed out—"

"Yes, yes, you've explained quite well why we cannot send young Hadlay to the dungeon. But I doubt Zêr-Shungalli would mind if we sent her friends."

Sfika stiffened. "The dungeon has become worse than torture since the emperor returned, Asinus. I cannot see the good in sending servants who have done no wrong."

Aurum spoke up. "I agree with Overlord Asinus. You know well, Sfika, that the emperor does not take thieving lightly. If we cannot punish this girl directly, then let her bear the guilt of knowing that her friends will suffer for her."

"No, please!" Hadlay found her tongue with effort. It had been bad enough to see the haunted look in Citna's eyes. How could she bear seeing it in the eyes of her friends, knowing she was the cause? "If anyone must go to the dungeon, let it be me. I am responsible for all the mischief."

Asinus's satisfaction was evident. "You see? My punishment will more surely accomplish our ends. As the emperor has said, the suffering of the innocent may achieve what the penance of the guilty cannot."

Sfika considered his remark, then gave a brusque nod. "Very well, then. But three days, no more."

"Seize them!" Asinus gestured to Nomish, Ma'at, and Kayshti.

"No!" Hadlay shouted again as the guards stepped in to take her friends. *"Naparki!"*

"Lêssa mahsâ!" Sfika said, and Hadlay felt as if a dozen hands had

slapped her face. "Be *silent*, girl, and do not interfere, or it will go worse for your friends." She turned to the guards. "Take them!"

Hadlay watched, helpless, as the guards closed in. Ma'at screamed as the magical bindings immobilized her. She was lifted by invisible hands and floated out of the room. Kayshti followed, struggling mightily. But Nomish was the worst. He stood very still, staring at Hadlay, as the bonds wrapped him. His eyes accused Hadlay as he followed his friends.

He had warned her. And now he was going to pay for her crimes. Hadlay tried to choke back a sob, knowing it would only gratify Asinus, but the tears came against her will.

"I hope you are satisfied, young lady," Sfika said and left the chamber.

"Do not bring that beast to the treasury again!" Aurum snapped, then followed Sfika out.

Ba'ar stepped up and stood over her, fixing her with a venomous glare. "Just wait," she hissed. "My father will be most interested to learn that you have made sport of me again. I'm sure your parents will feel his wrath." She turned to leave, catching Citna by the arm. "Come along, Citna."

Citna was staring at Hadlay, her face pale as death, her eyes unnervingly hollow. "You cannot imagine . . ."

Hadlay covered her face, sobbing, as Citna shambled off behind Ba'ar. What had she done?

AN ORDER OF PROTECTION

"Won't you help them?" Hadlay had lost no time using the dumbwaiter to get to Zêru's chambers.

Zêru shrugged. "Father does not permit me to interfere in the overlords' business. And I did warn you that if Asinus and the others ever realized you were behind all that mischief they would seek revenge."

"Against *me!* I could understand that. But my friends are innocent!"

"Father says that sometimes the suffering of the innocent—"

"But it's still not right!"

"Take care, Hadlay." Zêru's tone grew ominous. "It is unwise to criticize my father. If you make *him* angry, Asinus's punishment will seem trifling."

Hadlay slumped. "I'm sorry, Zêru. I'm just worried for my friends. Isn't there any way to protect them?"

Zêru thought for a moment. "*Igigi! Ibrî Hadlay hitnâ!*"

"What did you do?"

He sat on his couch, and patted the cushion beside him. "I commanded the powers to keep them from harm."

Hadlay released a breath she hadn't realized she'd held. "Did you call the powers 'Igigi'?"

He nodded. "They are called by many names, here and in the other worlds."

"They can protect my friends?"

"Physically. But I am told that the people who enter the dungeon are never the same, though I myself cannot understand what is so terrible."

"Have you seen the dungeon?"

"Certainly. I go there all the time."

"Why?"

He turned away. "It is a private matter."

The Dungeon

With no further help from Zêru, Hadlay made her way to the kitchen for the evening meal. Not that she was hungry. She just needed to see a sympathetic face. And maybe Magira would know some way she could help her friends.

She entered the kitchen and had begun to fill a platter with fresh fruits and white cheese when she realized the room had gone silent. She turned to find the other initiates staring at her.

Dropping her eyes to the floor, she shuffled over to the Ramash table. But Fa'an and the others spread themselves out so she had no place to sit.

"Sorry," Rasab muttered. "There doesn't seem to be any room for you here."

Blinking back tears, Hadlay set her platter on the counter and headed toward the exit.

"Hold there, girl." Magira bustled up beside her. "Dirty platters go to the scullery."

Hadlay took a long, shuddering breath. Magira had always been so kind to her. If even she was angry, there was nowhere to turn. Bowing her head, she pointed to the platter. "*Espâ!*" The platter started to float off the counter.

"*Naparki!*" Magira spoke sharply. "There'll be none of that. Carry the dish and wash it yourself."

Hadlay had just finished rinsing her platter when Magira appeared in the doorway. She glanced over her shoulder to be certain no one overheard. "I have an errand for you, girl."

The grim set to her jaw made Hadlay nervous. "What is it?"

"It seems to me that you should have a small idea what your friends will be experiencing the next few days." She handed Hadlay a kettle filled with choice meats and cheeses. "Perhaps Asinus cannot send you to the dungeon as a prisoner, but I can send you as a servant." She led Hadlay to the alcove and opened the small door to the dumbwaiter. "Climb in. Your friends will need their evening meal, and I'll be burned before I'll leave them to the slop the guards will give them."

Hadlay was eager for the chance to bring some comfort to her friends, but after what everyone had said about the dungeon, she was a little fearful too. Nevertheless she climbed in the dumbwaiter and rested the kettle on her knees.

"I think there's room enough for this," Magira stuffed a fresh loaf of bread in beside her knees. "Now, off you go! *Ana bît kîli shukshissi!*" As if the ropes holding it had broken, the dumbwaiter plunged into the darkness.

"Watch what you say down there!" Magira's voice followed her down the shaft.

Though Hadlay was by now accustomed to riding in the tiny box, it seemed to her that the walls grew closer and more confining, the cavern darker, as she descended. On and on the dumbwaiter went, until Hadlay's limbs began to cramp. She began to wonder whether she had sunk below the Tower's base, screaming down to a pit of darkness, a void below the earth itself. The smell of something rotting came to her, and she gagged.

Then came the fear.

Hadlay had known fear before, when she was hanging before the crowds, taking stones to her face. This was different. It was as though an iron fist had gripped her, cold and hard and smothering. She felt sure she was plummeting to her death. She imagined sharp steel spikes below, waiting to tear through her insides. She imagined something . . . horrible . . . ready to devour her.

The dumbwaiter jarred to a halt as though it had struck something solid, thrusting the breath from her lungs.

In the blackness of the shaft, Hadlay could see nothing. It took her a moment to gather her wits. She wanted desperately to command the powers to lift her back to the kitchen. But she couldn't go back, not without seeing her friends. She stretched her feet out, expecting to meet a cupboard door like the ones in Zêru's chambers and the kitchen. But there was no door. There was only darkness. And a silence more terrifying than screams.

Taking deep gulps of air, she summoned her courage and slid partway out of the box, feeling with her feet until she found the floor. Something soft and slimy squished, and her slipper became wet. Clasping the kettle and bread against her chest with one arm, she used her free hand to feel for the wall behind her, then braced her back against it.

How was she to find her friends? She had never experienced such darkness. Even in the deepest night, there was always the light of stars and moon, of candles and torches in the distance. She could always make out dim outlines. Hadlay waved her hand before her face, and jumped when she accidentally touched her nose. The stench in this place was overwhelming, but it was nothing compared to the terror of being alone in this blackness.

And yet not alone. There was a presence here, evil, deadly as a snake. It reached for her . . .

Something brushed her leg. It felt like a tongue! Whimpering, she tried to move away, but something else touched her on the other side. She was surrounded—trapped!

"Nomish?" she whispered.

As though her voice brought the place to life, she was surrounded by noises. Groans and cries, and the sounds of many voices weeping. And then growling, yelping, more like animals. People and creatures suffering untold agonies. She felt something tug at the kettle.

"No!" She wrenched away. "This is for my friends. Magira sent it!"

"Magira!" The name echoed through the darkness, repeated by many voices.

Fighting panic, she reached behind her, feeling for the wall at her back—but it was gone! She was lost now, with no way to get back to the dumbwaiter. No way to retreat from the terror of this place.

"Who comes here?" a voice whispered, almost in her ear. "Have you come to feed us?"

"I am a friend of Zêr-Shungalli!" Hadlay spoke the prince's name, hoping it would somehow protect her.

"Zêr-Shhhhhungalliiiiiii!" the voices repeated, echoing through the chamber.

A dim light came toward her. It was a lamp, but the darkness was so thick that it swallowed the glow as soon as it emerged from the flame. A man's face became visible. He had oddly cast eyes, slanted almost like a cat's, and a thick mane of tawny hair. "What would a friend of Zêru be doing here?"

Hadlay squinted at him. In the dim light, he looked almost like an animal. As he drew closer, she realized that, from the neck down, he *was* an animal. A lion.

Hadlay swallowed and backed away. Then she felt something hard against her back. She turned and in the dim light saw a man very like the frightening sentinels outside Zêru's chambers. But this one had no cloak. For the first time, Hadlay saw why their cloaks hung so strangely as if covering a scimitar: he had a tail. A long, curved, segmented tail that arced up behind him, with a stinger at its tip. A scorpion's tail.

The lion-man sniffed at Hadlay, his whiskers tracing her cheek. "Did the prince send you to feed us?"

"Yes—did he?" the scorpion guard asked.

"Ma-Magira asked me to bring this food to the initiates who were sent here."

The two seemed disappointed at her answer.

"Your friends, are they?" The lion-man growled. "And you a friend of the emperor's son. That would explain it. We hoped they came to feed us too, but the Igigi would not let us touch them."

"Perhaps we can touch you, though." A voice came from behind the lamp. A third creature appeared in the circle of light, this one man and goat. With one hand, he held the lamp. With the other, he reached out with slender fingers and caught a lock of her hair. "Ah, yes, it seems we can."

Cringing as the others closed in on her, Hadlay struggled to reconstruct the words Zêru had used earlier that day to protect her friends. *"Igigi, Hadlay hitnâ!"*

Hissing, the creatures backed away.

Taking a deep breath, Hadlay held up her kettle. "Now, where are my friends?"

"Command us, will you?" The goat-man sniffed. "Friend of Zêru, you may be, but he has not told us we must obey you." He turned away, taking the light with him.

"No, wait!" Hadlay scurried after him. Whatever else, she could not bear to be without light. "I am not commanding. I am asking. Begging. Whatever you like to call it. I will even share this bread with you!"

"Bread, hah!" the lion-man growled. "What use have we for bread?"

"Meat, then—or cheese," Hadlay suggested. "All I have, I'll share with you!"

"You will agree to feed us?"

"Will you?" The scorpion guard spoke behind her.

"All of us?" asked the goat-man.

"Swear?" It seemed a hundred other voices whispered from the black depths beyond the light.

"Yes—yes, I swear!" Hadlay agreed, holding the kettle out. "Take it all!"

The goat-man turned, shining his light on her again.

"We care not for Magira's food, little one," the lion-man said. "It is blood we crave." He smiled, revealing gleaming, razor-sharp fangs.

"No! I only meant the food I brought!" Hadlay tried to draw away.

"It doesn't matter what you meant," the scorpion guard hissed. "You agreed to feed us. All of us."

"Yes, see?" the goat-man said. He reached out and grasped her arm. "We can touch you again. You have given your word. All you have, you'll share with us."

Hadlay froze. "You want all my blood?"

"Not all," answered the goat-man, slipping up beside her and trailing a narrow finger along her arm. "Not yet. If you die, you'll be no further use to us. We will keep you alive—at least until you abandon hope and let the Refa take you."

Hadlay whimpered as his sharp fingernail dug into her skin.

"Don't worry," he whispered, bringing his bloodied finger to his lips. "It will only hurt a little while."

The lion-man's rough tongue rasped her cheek. "Only until you lose consciousness," he rumbled. She felt his teeth graze her shoulder.

"*Igigi, Hadlay hitnâ!*" she shouted again, but the creatures only laughed.

"Not this time," purred the lion-man. "You have promised."

And then the light went out.

Hadlay screamed, trying to turn away from the things that were clutching her in the blackness. "Help! Please help!" But hands, cold and hard as iron, plucked the kettle from her grasp, then caught her limbs, keeping her still. She felt the lion's tongue again, and she tried to wrench away.

A stabbing pain pierced her back, and she knew that the scorpion guard had stung her. Her body went limp, paralyzed by the poison that burned through her veins, and the creatures pulled her to the floor. She was helpless, unable to move, as sharp fangs sank into her skin.

UMMI EKLETI

The horror continued for what seemed an eternity. Hadlay could feel her skin being pierced in a hundred places, feel the beasts drawing on her blood. Her pulse weakened, and she wondered if she would die after all.

Then a voice broke through the nightmare.

"You've had enough. Now leave her!" It was a woman's voice, unfamiliar to Hadlay. She felt a hand on her shoulder and flinched. Was this a new creature, come to finish what the others had begun?

"*Igigi, bilâshi!*" the voice said, and Hadlay felt herself being lifted from the floor. A short while later, she was deposited onto the soft cushions of a couch.

Then a candle flickered. Hadlay stared at it, wondering where she was.

The candle came toward her, and in the light it cast, she saw a woman's face. Her hair was wild and streaked with gray, and a strange, mad look burned in her eyes.

"Drink." The woman pressed a cup into her hand. It smelled of herbs— strong herbs, like what Hadlay had smelled on Citna.

"Foolish girl! You have not blood enough for all of them. What were you thinking?" The woman set the candle down and pushed the cup toward her lips. "Drink—you must replace what they took."

Hadlay turned her face away. "I can't drink blood!"

"It isn't blood," a familiar voice spoke from the shadows.

"Nomish!" Hadlay squinted, trying to find him.

He knelt next to the bed beside her. "What are you doing here?"

"Make her drink," the woman insisted.

"This woman is Ummi Ekleti." Nomish took the cup and pressed it to Hadlay's lips. "She gets a little strange sometimes, but she knows how things work down here. You'd better drink it."

Hadlay sipped with caution. It was thick and coated her tongue with a bitter, herbal taste. She tried to stop, but the woman's hand flashed out and tipped the cup fully into her mouth.

"All or nothing," the woman said, grinning crazily.

Hadlay coughed, sputtering some of the stuff down her front, but she swallowed most of it.

"Puts hair on your chest!" the woman said, taking the cup and moving off into the darkness. Nomish shrugged.

Hadlay pushed herself upright with effort, wincing as the movement pulled her wounds. But she was already beginning to feel stronger. She looked around. Ma'at and Kayshti sat just at the edge of the light, Ma'at clinging to her brother's arm.

"Why are you here?" Nomish asked.

"Magira wanted me to bring you food, but . . . I had to see you. To know you're . . ." Hadlay gulped. She had meant to say "well," but who could be well in this place? She grabbed Nomish's hand. "I am so sorry you're in this horrible place because of me!"

Nomish pulled his hand away. "Why did you do all those things, after Magira warned you against it?"

"I never would have if I thought it would bring harm to my friends!"

"You should have listened!" Ma'at cried from her place by her brother. Kayshti squeezed her tightly.

"I never wanted to hurt you, Ma'at. Nor you, Kayshti." Hadlay hung her head. She had hoped to make it right. But, after seeing this place, she knew she never could. She gasped, catching sight of a jagged wound on her own arm, and two farther down. She squinted at her friends through the darkness. "Have the creatures harmed you?"

Nomish shook his head. "For some reason, they cannot touch us."

"I asked Zêru for help, and he ordered the powers to protect you." Hadlay shivered. Even if the creatures couldn't touch them, she could not imagine how her friends could last three days in this place.

Nomish nodded. "Ummi Ekleti thought as much."

"The candle will not last much longer," the woman's voice came out of the darkness. "The girl must leave now."

Hadlay shook her head. "I cannot go back through those monsters!"

"Ummi Ekleti will take you," Nomish said. "She can command them."

Hadlay wasn't certain she believed him. As the woman moved nearer, Hadlay could see a terrible, jagged wound at her neck. It was rimmed with old scars.

"All but one," the woman corrected, touching the scars. "The plum cannot deny the stone." She reached for Hadlay, lifting the candle. "We must go now, before the darkness comes."

Hadlay pulled away. "I can't leave my friends. Not like this."

"It is courageous of you to want to remain, friend of Zêru. But the creatures will return to claim you if you do. Nothing can protect you. In this place, rash promises come back to bite you."

Nomish squeezed her shoulder. "You have to go, Hadlay."

Hadlay hesitated. She could not imagine staying here, having those *things* attack her at will. But how could she leave her friends to this awful darkness?

"We will endure, Hadlay," Nomish assured her.

"Come with me! You can go up the dumbwaiter, just as I came down!"

Ummi Ekleti gave a bark of laughter, shaking her wild gray hair. "The Igigi will never carry a prisoner from here." She caught Hadlay's hand roughly. "You go now—or never go, friend of Zêru."

Nomish took her arms and pulled her to her feet. "I won't let you stay here. I promised your father I would look after you."

Hadlay sobbed. She had betrayed her best friend, and he was still trying to protect her. She flung her arms around him. "How can I ever make this up to you?"

For a moment, he let her hold him. Then he pulled her arms away. "You can start by leaving."

Hadlay paused to clasp the hands of Kayshti and Ma'at, pressing them to her wet cheeks. "I am so sorry. I wish I could take your place."

"The darkness comes!" Ummi Ekleti whispered, snatching Hadlay's hair and half-dragging her away. "You must come now, or I will be unable to lead."

Hadlay staggered after her, trying to unwind the woman's fingers from her hair.

"Here!" The woman's candle lit the entrance to the dumbwaiter. "You go now, friend of Zêru." Then her eyes grew tender, and she stroked Hadlay's cheek. "You would not like to be my daughter. Do not agree to be."

A glitter caught Hadlay's eye. The woman wore a jeweled pendant. Hadlay could not make out details in the dim light, but it was quite large and encrusted with sparkling stones. She must have been rich once. Hadlay wondered why her jewels had not been taken from her when she came to this place.

She looked at the woman more closely. She did not look Oresed. "Who are you?"

The woman gave a mad grin. "You heard your friend. I am Ummi Ekleti." Then her eyes grew distant. "There was someone else once. But she is gone, I think."

She caught Hadlay's chin in her hand, staring at her with those eerie, vacant eyes. "Seek the key, and when you find it, never let go! Let the Refa take the rest."

Hadlay clasped her hand. "What do you know about the key?"

Ummi Ekleti looked away. "She dreamed once, as you do. But she chose badly."

"How do you know that I dream?" Hadlay held tight to her hand, though she tried to pull away. "Did Nomish tell you? Where is the key? Is it Sfika's key?"

The woman turned, catching Hadlay with her eyes again. "The key is not in this Tower, not until you bring it forth." She pushed Hadlay toward the dumbwaiter. "The darkness is coming. He will not be pleased that I have warned you."

THE EMPEROR'S EYEBROWS

By the emperor's eyebrows!" Magira exclaimed, rushing to help Hadlay out of the dumbwaiter. "Why were you gone so long? I was beside myself!" She turned a ghastly shade of white when she saw Hadlay's wounds. "My dear, what happened? Never mind—I know what happened." She clasped Hadlay against her chest. "You agreed to feed them, didn't you?"

Hadlay nodded. "I didn't realize what I was agreeing to."

"Oh, my dear child!" Magira's hug tightened, nearly smothering Hadlay. "In all my years, I have never known anyone to go down there and stay willingly. I never thought you would leave the dumbwaiter. I expected that, when the terrors gripped you, you would be so frightened you would toss the food to the prisoners and return instantly! I thought Zêru's friendship would protect you. If I had guessed you might stay, I would have fully explained the danger."

Keeping an arm around Hadlay, she drew her to a table and sat her down. The kitchen was empty now. Hadlay supposed the other initiates had gone down to the dormitories for the night.

"Let's get you cleaned up," Magira said, summoning a clean, wet cloth from the basin. "*Mis*— no, I'll do it myself. The powers are seldom gentle." Taking the cloth, she carefully dabbed at Hadlay's wounds, wiping away the blood and dirt. It hurt, but Hadlay bit her lip and welcomed the cleansing.

Magira tugged at the skirt of Hadlay's tunic, exposing a great rip. "Well, this is ruined. There's nothing for it." She tipped Hadlay's chin, examining the wounds at her neck. "But if you gave yourself to those creatures, how did you manage to escape?"

"There's a woman down there—she rescued me."

Magira's eyebrows lifted. "Did she tell you who she was?"

"They called her Ummi Ekleti."

"She's still alive, then. I wondered. She was half-mad when they brought her here, and with those creatures in the dungeon, most prisoners give themselves to the Refa before a week is gone. Perhaps in her case, the Refa won't take her."

"Who is she?"

"The emperor forbids us to speak of her. I will only say that she tried to kill Zêru." With a command, Magira sent the cloth off to the hamper and summoned a vial of salve. "This is useful with wounds. I keep it near, as the powers are sometimes careless with knives." She dabbed a small bit on each of Hadlay's wounds, and though the initial contact stung, the pain lifted quickly. "Did you find your friends? Have the creatures . . ."

Hadlay shuddered and shook her head. "No, thanks to Zêru. He commanded the powers to protect them. And Ummi Ekleti is looking after them as well." She glanced sharply at Magira. "Are they safe with her? If she tried to kill Zêru . . ."

Magira shrugged, grim-faced. "She is quite mad, but she is far less a threat than the other prisoners. Your friends are better off with her."

Hadlay swallowed hard. "They will never be the same, will they?"

Magira smoothed her hair away from her face. "I won't lie and say they will. But perhaps they will be all right, with time."

A sob burst from Hadlay's chest, and Magira pulled her close.

BLOODLINES

Hadlay did not return to the dormitories that night. She could not bear to face the anger of the other initiates—or Ba'ar's gloating—and Magira gave her leave to sleep by the fire in the kitchen. But she could not rest. Every time she closed her eyes, the terrors gripped her, and she felt sharp teeth piercing her limbs. She wondered if she would ever sleep again in this Tower, knowing that such horrors lurked below.

Hoping to distract herself, she wrestled with the question of the key. The Being had said she would hear strange counsel, and she should listen to it. He must have meant Ummi Ekleti. But what had that madwoman meant when she said the key was not in the Tower until she brought it forth? Hadlay was nearly a prisoner here—how could she leave to go look for it elsewhere? Was it somewhere on the grounds? And what good would it do her anyway? Every dream she'd had brought nothing but harm—if not to her, then to the ones she loved. She wanted to be done with the Being and his dreams! And yet she knew that in her heart, she was clinging to her dreams. If she ever did stop dreaming, she would feel a great loss.

Before dawn, she made her way to the privy and bathed, then she summoned a fresh tunic from her wardrobe and changed, sending the torn one to her hamper in hopes it could be repaired after all. She was just braiding her hair when she felt herself being drawn to the bestiary.

Zêru was waiting for her near the door, looking a bit impatient. "Where have you been? Filch has been looking everywhere for you!" The beast punctuated his exclamation with a playful nip at Hadlay's hand.

At the feel of his teeth, Hadlay let out a scream that startled her pet and sent him flapping to the far corner of the room.

"What's the—" Zêru's mouth fell open as he saw her arm. "You went to the dungeon! Why in *Irkalla* would you go there?"

Hadlay shrugged. Zêru sounded irritated, and she didn't want to get Magira in trouble. "I . . . wanted to help my friends."

Zêru caught her arm and examined the wounds on it. "You permitted the creatures to feed on you?"

Hadlay couldn't meet his eyes. "I didn't mean to. They tricked me. When they asked if I would feed them, I thought I would be giving them a kettle of food."

Zêru gave a shout of laughter. "A kettle of food? They are devious, aren't they?" Then his eyes grew dark again. He took Hadlay's shoulders and stared at her. "You mustn't go there again. It is not safe for you now."

"It is not safe for my friends, either," Hadlay retorted. "I'm afraid for them."

He waved her concerns away. "I have protected them, remember? The creatures will not touch them."

"But they suffer, even though they are not harmed in body."

"So I have been told." He frowned, as if trying to solve a puzzle. "What exactly is so fearsome about the dungeon?"

Hadlay stared at him for a moment. Could he really not see? "For one thing, there is that horrible darkness. It almost feels like a physical presence."

"Yes, the Refa," he said. "Where they gather, there is darkness."

Hadlay staggered, bracing herself against a cage. "Refa? There are Refa in the Tower?"

He nodded. "They are everywhere. They like it best in the dungeon, though. They feed on the souls of the condemned."

Hadlay stood immobile, trying to fathom what he was saying. "Then they are feeding on my friends!"

He waved a hand. "They are protecting them, as I have commanded."

"You command the Refa?"

Zêru laughed again. "My father commands this world, and I am his son. What did you think?" He gestured toward a bucket of feed. "Come, my pets are hungry."

Hadlay began tossing bits of reddish food into the nearest cage. "The creatures down there . . . they are also your creatures?"

"Yes. They are my mixtures."

"But . . . they are human!"

He shrugged. "Part. It seemed to me that certain animals had qualities that might make for better servants. Who better to guard my chambers than a man with a scorpion's sting? Who more able to carry a burden than a man with the strength of an ant?" He stopped tossing food for a moment and looked at Hadlay. "Would you like me to mix you with a bird? Then you could fly and sing beautiful songs for me."

Hadlay shuddered. "No, thank you, Your Highness. I can fly already, with the powers, and sing as well as I'd want to."

"I am a mix too, you know. It's not so bad."

Hadlay nodded. "Perhaps, but I'm content as I am."

He returned to feeding his creatures. "Anyway, the idea has found favor with my father—he is eager to build a militia of these creatures. Imagine legions of warriors, half man, half lion! Archers, half-eagle, able to rain arrows from above—and chariots pulled by horses with the minds of men!" He grinned. "With Nafal and sons of Nafal to lead, and the Refa to strike terror among the enemy, who could stand against such an army?"

Hadlay imagined these warriors . . . and what they would do to those they vaquished. Shoving the thought from her mind, she continued her work. Then she paused, staring at a piece of the food she was pouring into the yamsters' trough. "Zêru . . . do all mixed creatures need to eat blood?"

Zêru went still for a moment, then turned to look at her. She wished she hadn't spoken when she saw the black intensity of his eyes. "You will not speak of this outside this room?" His voice had that echoing force that sometimes unnerved her.

She nodded, though she had a sense that she might not want to hear his answer.

"Then, yes," he studied her as he spoke. "Do you remember I told you that Azazel had discovered a special supplement that extends the lives of mixes? These creatures here take their feed mingled with animal blood brought from the slaughterhouse each day. Each beast must have blood, preferably from one of the creatures he was mixed from."

Hadlay stared at him, feeling a numbness settle over her. "Then the human mixes in the dungeon . . ."

He nodded. "Prefer human blood."

The feedbag slipped from her hands. "Then you and Ayom . . ."

"A small amount. But we only take from those who give it willingly." He paused, giving her a strange, piercing look. "As you did."

Hadlay's hand rose unbidden to her throat.

Zêru laughed, as if he knew her thoughts. "Don't worry. I have an adequate supply, for now." He pitched a bit of the food at her. "And you have never agreed to feed *me*."

A TAXING PROBLEM

Hadlay had almost forgotten Sfika's order to clean the bestiary cages, and it had taken much longer than she'd expected. She'd missed the morning meal—not that she'd wanted to eat—in order to finish the chore. Then she stopped for a second bath before going to the treasury.

Even soaking in the soapy water failed to relax her nerves, nor did it make her feel quite clean. She dressed hastily and hurried into the counting room, settling by a large pile of minas, as far as possible from Ba'ar and Citna. After all she'd experienced, she almost welcomed the tedium of counting.

"*Lêssa mahsâ!*"

Hadlay flinched as a stinging slap struck her cheek.

Aurum stood in the doorway, her lips puckered in irritation. "You are late!"

Hadlay dropped her head. "I'm sorry."

Another command from Aurum, and she felt a sharp pinch on her arm. "Make yourself busy!"

Hadlay sighed. At least she could finally use magic to do this work. "*Nikkassî epush!* One . . . two . . ."

Aurum's desk floated into the room, guided by two servants.

"Set it there!" Aurum pointed to a bare space of floor near Hadlay. "I intend to keep my eyes on you every moment until your two weeks end."

Ba'ar snickered from her pile across the room. "I take it Prince Zêru's creatures don't like you cleaning their cages, Hadlay. You seem to have been bitten."

Citna's minas clinked to the floor as she stared at Hadlay. "Did you go to . . ."—she spoke in almost a whisper—". . . see your friends?"

Hadlay nodded.

Citna bit her lip, her eyes filling with tears. "Now you know." Her fingers tugged at the long sleeve of her formal tunic.

Hadlay realized suddenly why she wore that tunic. It covered her wounds. The Being's words returned to her. *What you do to another will prey upon you . . .*

An appalling thought occurred to Hadlay. In her heart, she had blamed Sfika for not trying harder to find the truth before punishing her after the flunk incident. But Hadlay had done the same to Citna. She glanced at Citna, seeing again the girl's unnatural pallor and the anxiety haunting her eyes, and she wanted to be sick.

"*Kizrassa shuddâ!*" Hadlay felt a sharp yank on her braid. Aurum was glaring at her again. "Back to work!"

Hadlay started counting again, but her mind was numb.

She was nearly three-quarters through her pile of shekels when a harried clerk arrived. "Overlord Aurum!" He sounded breathless.

"What is it, boy?" The overlord clicked her fingernails on the desk, rapping out a brisk rhythm.

The clerk hesitated, hunching his shoulders. "The collectors, ma'am. They sent me to tell you that they are having some difficulty collecting the new tax."

The new tax? Hadlay gave up all pretense that she wasn't listening.

The boy glanced up to see how Aurum was receiving his news. "Fully a third of the people the collectors have approached thus far say that they cannot pay."

"Cannot?" Aurum's voice rose to a painful pitch. "Or will not?"

The clerk shrugged, looking as if he would be glad to be anywhere but here. Hadlay guessed that he had been sent here by his superiors so that they would not have to risk Aurum's wrath.

"*Lêt kalîshunu mahsâ!*" the woman shouted, and everyone in the room flinched as slaps were delivered all around.

Ba'ar glared at her. "I did nothing to deserve—*What?*" She turned to Citna, who was pulling on her sleeve. Citna pressed her finger to her lips with an urgent stare. Ba'ar cast another foul look at Aurum before she turned back to her counting.

Aurum scowled at the hapless clerk, who now trembled before her desk. "Very well. Have the assessors go out and value the homes of those who cannot pay. We will take their property if they have no gold."

The clerk started to turn away, then hesitated and turned back. "Overlord Aurum?"

"Yes, boy?" Aurum's expression made clear that his question had best be a good one.

"Well, most of the people who cannot pay are Ramash, ma'am. They do not own property."

Aurum cut him off with a wave of her hand. "Well, then, they will have to plead their case before Overlord Asinus. Perhaps he will be generous and simply make them slaves. Though the torturer has been complaining lately that he has too little to do."

The clerk bowed and sped away.

Hadlay's mind whirled. Hadn't Zêru promised to help? Her parents— and the Rakams too—would be among those who could not pay. And if she knew Asinus, he would enjoy the opportunity to do his worst. Her father would choose torture before he would be a slave again. He might even think that he would rather face the dungeon!

She fingered a gold mina resentfully. Just one of these would solve her parent's problems. And there were rooms full of them! Why did the emperor need even more?

THE EMPEROR'S TABLE

Aurum kept Hadlay long after Ba'ar and Citna were released for the evening meal. She checked and rechecked every ledger before she permitted Hadlay to leave. When the woman was finally satisfied, Hadlay dashed from the room, eager to be away from the oppressive disapproval.

But her pace slackened after a few turns in the corridors. Where should she go? Her stomach rumbled. She had not eaten since yesterday morning. But the other initiates would be in the kitchen, and she did not think she could bear being shunned again. She turned toward the bestiary. At least she could get an early start on her cage-cleaning duties, and, when she finished, maybe she could persuade Magira to give her something. And perhaps the work would exhaust her to the point where she could sleep without nightmares of the dungeon.

"Hadlay Mivana?" A voice behind her made her jump.

Hadlay whirled to find one of the Tower messengers behind her.

The messenger gave a little bow, then teetered, trying to regain his balance. With a cry, he toppled, so that he seemed to be hanging by his feet. Then Hadlay noticed that his feet had wings. A mix! She took a step back.

The messenger righted himself with effort. "His Majesty the emperor desires your presence in the royal dining room. You are advised to come at once."

Hadlay was uncertain she had heard correctly. "The emperor? Wants me?"

"At once." The winged feet threatened to slip from under him again, and he flailed his arms to regain his balance.

Hadlay stared at him. "What does he want?"

The messenger rolled his eyes. "Do I look as though I can explain the emperor's whims?"

"I am on my way." Hadlay turned and headed down the corridor. When she glanced back, the messenger was going in the other direction, keeling into walls like a drunkard as he struggled to balance himself.

What could the emperor want with her? Was she in trouble again? She wanted to run away, but she knew that sooner or later someone would find her. By then, the emperor would be angrier still.

By habit, she started toward the dumbwaiter, but as she reached the cupboard, she stopped short. The idea of climbing into it terrified her. What if, instead of taking her to the royal chambers, the box took a mind of its own? What if it carried her back to that awful dungeon?

Just knowing that within that shaft, there would be nothing but air between her and that horrid darkness, those fearsome creatures, was more than she could bear. It would take much longer by foot, and she worried that the emperor would be angry if she kept him waiting. But there was no choice. She raced up the endless passageways, turning this way and that, following the guiding tiles until they vanished at the treasury, then following her memory after that.

She had forgotten the scorpion guards.

Racing around the last corner, she nearly crashed into one of them. He spun, hissing. Hadlay stumbled away, bracing herself against the wall, as the other three approached her.

"Who comes to the royal chambers?" the leader demanded.

Hadlay could not keep her eyes from the tails of their cloaks, which rose up menacingly, arcing toward her. "F-filch!" she shouted.

"That is not the password!" The leader hissed. "Take her!"

Hadlay gave a little scream as one of the guards gripped her arm. "I have been summoned by the emperor!"

"Silence!" the guard snarled. His stinger slipped free of his cloak, and came toward Hadlay's face.

"There you are!" Zêru appeared in the doorway. With a gesture of his hand, he commanded the guards to back away. "Why did you come this way?"

Hadlay stayed against the wall. She did not trust her legs to hold her.

"Well, no surprise it took you so long, if you came the hard way!" Zêru said, catching her arm. "Come in! I am nearly starved."

Hadlay's legs felt leaden as she allowed him to guide her inside. Zêru was hungry. What if he wanted to feed on her? He had said that she must agree to it. But he was the prince—how could she refuse him?

The emperor was inside, seated on one of the grand chairs. He smiled as she entered. "Come forward, child."

Hadlay hesitated, but Zêru gave her a nudge. "He only wants to talk."

Hadlay inched toward him. Even though he was seated, he still towered over her.

He was wearing gold this eve. His robe was ivory gossamer trimmed with gold. His sash and crown and the rings on his hands were gold. Even his eyes seemed gold. And his teeth, when he smiled.

Hadlay dropped to her knees, prostrating herself before him. "How may I serve, Your Majesty?"

The emperor laughed. "I see Asinus has instructed you in Tower protocol. Stand up, child. I wish to see your face."

Hadlay pushed to her feet, but it took a force of will to meet his eyes. There was something unnerving about the emperor's gaze—it almost felt like a physical touch, cold and burning at the same time, invading her mind.

"My son tells me that you have learned many of his secrets. I thought it would be good to know you better, to determine if you are worthy of them."

Hadlay swallowed hard. What if he decided she wasn't?

His eyes did not leave hers as he straightened and gestured to the royal table. "You will dine with us this eve."

Hadlay glanced at the table, seeing for the first time that Ayom was laying three places.

"Sit," the emperor commanded, and before Hadlay could think to heed him, she found herself in a chair.

The platter before her was made of gold. Hadlay stared at it as Zêru took his seat across from her and the emperor took his place at the head of the table. She was reminded of the Mirror of N'de story again, and the chamber where people ate from platters of gold. She had often thought this part of the story was too fantastical. Outside the emperor's treasury, she had never seen more than a ring or chain, never enough gold to make a whole platter!

Ayom began serving—breast of t'rru bird; roast boar; and light, fluffy rolls dripping with butter. Hadlay looked away as Ayom sprinkled Zêru's food with the red liquid.

"My son's diet troubles you," the emperor observed.

Hadlay wasn't certain how to respond, so she remained quiet.

"Why?" Zêru tilted his head. "We are friends, are we not?"

"Y-yes, Your Highness," Hadlay mumbled. In truth, she was not so certain of that, either. A week ago, she would have been pleased to call him friend. Now, she was quite afraid of him.

"Tell me," the emperor said casually, slicing his meat, "does anything else at this table trouble you?"

Hadlay had to fight down a hysterical giggle. What about this table was *not* troubling? She, a servant—a Ramash—was dining with the emperor! Her eyes sought Ayom for some hint of how to answer, but his face was blank. "N-no, Your Majesty . . ."

The emperor raised his knife, laden with a cut of boar. "Would you feed what is on your plate to your family, then?"

Unsure what he wanted from her, Hadlay nodded.

"We are dining on the flesh of animals. How is that so different from what my son must have?"

Hadlay shrugged. How could she explain?

"It is only blood. Willingly given. And only a small amount." He spoke in a low, soothing tone. "Azazel learned by reading an ancient book that the life of all flesh is in the blood. Zêru must have it to live more than a few years. Do you understand?"

Hadlay had a feeling that she must answer these questions with care. She nodded, trying to read his face.

"Do you grudge him what he needs to live?" He watched her, even as he attended to his meal. She did not wish to think about the consequence of giving the wrong answer.

Zêru gave her an encouraging smile.

She shook her head. "I guess not."

"Excellent!" The emperor took a bite, savoring his food. "You can see, though, why we do not want this widely known?"

"I have promised not to speak of it."

The emperor smiled. "Well said, child." He gestured to Hadlay's platter. "Please, eat! It is not often my son and I share our table."

She took up her knife and set in. The t'rru bird was so tender it was barely necessary to cut it, and its flavor was unlike anything she had ever tasted. She had to keep herself from hunching over her platter, shoveling the food into her mouth.

The emperor's eyes crinkled with amusement as he watched her eat. "I was most impressed when I learned that you braved the dungeon to try to help your friends. Few humans would enter that dark place willingly."

Hadlay paused, remembering what Zêru had said about the darkness. "Zêru tells me there are Refa there—and all around the Tower. And that you command them."

The emperor nodded, his eyes never leaving hers. "I am the emperor, am I not? Ruler of this world and of all its powers?"

His words reminded Hadlay of Meshah, the ruler in the old bedtime story. All things obeyed him—even the cosmos—simply because he was King.

Another thought occurred to her. "If you command the Refa, then perhaps we need not fear them."

The comment seemed to take the emperor by surprise. He laughed, and the sound echoed through the chamber as though many voices laughed as well. "Not fear the Refa, the devourers of souls?" Then he paused, and a smile softened his features. "It would be foolish, child, not to fear that which can destroy you. You may command them, if I will it. But nothing can protect you if you give yourself to them."

Hadlay frowned. She had so many questions—and each of the emperor's answers only confused her further.

"As I was saying, child. I was impressed by your loyalty to your friends, that you would face the terrors of the dungeon—even agree to feed the creatures, hoping to help them." He nodded toward his son. "Zêru will need such friends as you when his time comes to reign." He snapped his fingers. "*Ibrîsha mushsherâ!*"

Hadlay jumped, looking around to see what his magic had accomplished. She half-expected the scorpion guards to race in and arrest her for having the audacity to sit here and eat before him.

"I have lifted your friends' punishment. They'll be in the dormitories when you return this eve."

Hadlay's mouth dropped open. What had she done to merit such kindness? Remembering Asinus's rules, she pushed away from the table and knelt before him, kissing one of his rings. "Thank you, Your Majesty."

"Yes, thank you, Father," Zêru said. "Hadlay has been much afflicted by guilt since her friends were sent there."

"Then Asinus's punishment has achieved its goal." The emperor leaned confidentially toward Hadlay. "I cannot have servants tormenting my overlords, even if I do it myself from time to time."

Hadlay bowed her head. "Yes, Your Majesty."

"Finish your meal." The emperor gestured to her platter. "Are your friends very angry with you?"

"They should be." Hadlay returned to her seat. "Nomish warned me not to abuse the powers the way I did. As did Prince Zêru. I was foolish not to heed them."

"Zêru tells me that you consider this Nomish to be quite wise, and I see you are correct," the emperor said. "Overlord Bonobos tells me he believes Nomish will be a worthy apprentice."

Hadlay broke into a smile. "He will be overjoyed to hear that, Your Majesty. This has been his heart's desire since long before we came here."

"He will serve me well, then. And you, child? What is your heart's desire?"

Hadlay paused, considering his question. She had no great affinity for any of the tasks thus far assigned to her. Asinus was horrid, Aurum tedious, and, to be honest, Bonobos confused her. But she had not forgotten her speculation that she was meant to help Bonobos save the prince's life. Should she ask for that? If she did, would she displace Nomish?

"It shouldn't be a difficult question, child," the emperor prodded.

"I . . . had great fun with Zêru when I was assigned to serve him, Your Majesty," she glanced at the prince, who looked pleased with this comment. "But I did little work here. In truth, I do not know what duties I should perform." Anything but Asinus, she thought of adding, but bit her tongue.

"I did not ask how you wished to serve us." He reproached her gently. "That decision is already made. I asked what is your heart's desire."

This time, the question rang in her, probing to the depths of her soul. "To help my people." The answer came from her mouth without fore-thought, but she realized as she said them that they were true. Whatever else her life brought, she could go to her grave content if she could say she had raised up the Ramash from their desperate lot and forced the Oresed to respect them.

The emperor gave his son a look of paternal pride. "You have indeed chosen well, Zêru." He rose and fixed Hadlay with a gaze so intense that it almost frightened her. "*Qanna sha kaspi ana talbultîsha litukkapû!*"

Hadlay felt a strong tug at her tunic. When she looked to see what had happened, she saw that a silver fringe was affixing itself to the hem of her garment. She looked back at the emperor, wondering what it meant.

"You have pleased me, child. Tell me what reward you would ask of me."

Hadlay stared at him, speechless. Reward?

"Go ahead, Hadlay," Zêru said. "My father and I wish to give you some-thing in recognition of your loyalty."

The emperor's offer emboldened her. Still, she spoke with care, fearing what might happen if her request was overly presumptuous. "I have heard Aurum speaking of a new tax." She took a deep breath. "What if I asked that you revoke it?"

Zêru looked shocked at the request. She did not dare look at the em-peror. She rushed on. "My people, Your Majesty—most of them are very poor, and they cannot afford this tax. They have no homes or property for Aurum to confiscate. I fear that, when they fail to pay, Overlord Asinus will have them tortured or made slaves. My father could not bear that."

When she finally summoned the courage to glance at the emperor, she was astonished to find him smiling, as though he had expected this re-quest. With a ringed hand, he reached out and patted her head. At his touch, Hadlay felt her skin prickle, as if his hand were charged with energy not unlike the lightning in Bonobos's lights.

"My son and I share your concern, little one. We have already contrived a plan, another way for the poorest of Turris—both Oresed and Ramash—to satisfy their debt . . . and even enrich themselves, in time."

"A plan, Your Majesty?"

"I will make an announcement before long." He rose, moving gracefully across the room to the great window and looked down over the city. "I have longed for many ages, Hadlay, to come to this city and claim your people. To reveal a great mystery that many generations have waited to hear."

Hadlay stilled. A great mystery. Was he speaking of the riddle?

"I have wondered if your people still speak of the ancient times, Hadlay." He paused and glanced back at her. "Your expression tells me that they do." Before Hadlay could protest, he continued. "Among your legends there is a story, a children's tale—quite charming, as I recall. Have you heard the story of the ancient city called N'de?"

Hadlay dropped her gaze to the table.

He chuckled, as did Zêru. "I thought as much. It may surprise you to learn, little one, that this story is more history than fable. N'de is real."

Real? How could a place so fantastical be real? But then, hadn't she thought more than once that this place reminded her of the story? She raised her eyes to the emperor. "Is it all real? Even Mesh—"

"Silence!" A thousand voices roared around her. Hadlay clapped her hands over her ears and cringed.

For a moment, the emperor scowled. But then his expression shifted once more. "You must not speak of this, dear girl. The time to reveal my secret has not yet come."

Hadlay's eyes drifted from Zêru to his father. A few weeks ago, she had overheard the emperor saying that he could not reveal who he was until the people were prepared. Was he Meshah, then, come to restore the children of Mada and Avakh to N'de?

The emperor gave a musical laugh as he seemed to read her thoughts. "Rest assured, Hadlay, that as the peoples of Turris give their obeisance to me, we will make this city so great, it rivals N'de."

Hadlay frowned. "Forgive me, Your Majesty, but if the story is true, can't we hope to return to N'de itself?"

The emperor's eyes glowed. "We have worlds to conquer before we will be strong enough for that! In the meantime, let us make what we can of Turris."

Then he turned and, in two long strides, moved to the table again. He caught her chin in his golden hand, lifting up her face. "Will you speak for me among your people when you return home next week? Would you reassure them that I mean the best for them, testify that I have their interests at heart?"

Hadlay felt his power prickling along her skin. She shivered as it rippled down her spine. She smiled. "With gladness, Emperor!"

Emperor Shungallu exchanged a long, significant look with his son. Then he nodded, and turned back to his window.

Zêru took hold of Hadlay's hand. "You worry about your family's poverty." He gestured to one of the golden platters. "What would this platter buy for them?"

Hadlay lifted the platter. After counting shekels and minas for several days, she had a sense of their weight. The platter was worth four minas at least. "I do not know what things cost, Zêru, but this is more than my family has ever had."

He grinned. "Then take all three. And there is more—much more—to come!"

FRINGE BENEFITS

Hadlay paused at the door of the dormitory, considering the wisdom of carrying the three gold platters into the room in full view of the other initiates. She wished she could slip them under her tunic, but they were too large and heavy to be easily concealed. She was trying to think of a place to hide them when Nomish stepped out of the boy's dormitory.

"Nomish!" Hadlay hurried toward him. Relief at seeing her friend pushed all other thought from her mind.

Nomish turned and took a couple of steps toward her. He was favoring his leg.

Hadlay halted, watching him move. "You were injured!"

He shook his head. "It's ju-just my leg. I know Asinus insists the emperor healed me fully, but it still pains me when I am weary."

"Did the creatures—" She could not finish.

"The creatures never touched us." His lips tightened. "But I doubt I will ever sleep well again."

He was still angry with her. Hadlay's eyes welled with tears. "I am so sorry."

Nomish shuffled, looking uncertain as to what he should do. Then, hesitantly, he reached out and squeezed her shoulder. "It's—"

"Where did you get those?" A hard voice came from behind Hadlay. Nomish jerked his hand away, his face bright red. Hadlay turned to find Ba'ar braced in the doorway, staring at the platters.

Hadlay lifted her chin in defiance. "The prince gave them to me."

"Likely as a donkey's egg," Ba'ar retorted. A number of other initiates clustered behind her. "Why would His Highness give anything to a thief?"

"Perhaps because I'm not a mean-spirited old she-camel!" Hadlay said. A few of the girls behind Ba'ar tittered, and she spun, glaring at each of them in turn.

"Hadlay." Nomish's voice rang with warning.

Hadlay winced, remembering that if she got in trouble again, her friends might pay the price. She would be fortunate if they ever forgave her for the harm she had already done.

Then she realized that she had the means to make things right. Turning to Nomish, she pressed one of the platters into his hands. "I want you to have this—for your family." She searched the gathering crowd of initiates, and found Ma'at and held out another of the platters. "And this is for you and Kayshti, and your parents."

She felt guilty at giving away something of such value, but one platter was already more than her family had ever owned, and she felt she owed at least this much to her friends after all they had endured. It occurred to her that Citna probably deserved one too, but she had only three, and she could not ignore her own family's need.

"I wouldn't touch them. They're probably stolen," Ba'ar intoned. Ma'at shrank away from the platter, wide-eyed.

"What is the problem here?" Sfika's voice rang down the corridor. They turned to see her marching toward them.

"Hadlay has stolen these platters!" Ba'ar pointed.

"I did not!"

"Hand them over to me until we sort this out." Sfika took the platter Nomish held, and reached out expectantly toward Hadlay.

Hadlay clung to them, her jaw jutting stubbornly. "Command the powers to show you. Or summon Ayom—he will tell you these were a gift."

Sfika lifted her hand as if to strike. Then suddenly she went quite still, frowning at Hadlay's tunic.

Hadlay glanced down to see what she was looking at, and she remembered the silver fringe the emperor had added to her hem.

Sfika shook her head, apparently stunned at the sight. "I believe you, girl. But I will take the platters anyway—to my office for safekeeping. You

may have them when you return home to visit your family next week."
With a command, she floated all three platters away.

"But—" Ba'ar sputtered.

"That fringe entitles you to punishment rights, by the way," Sfika told
Hadlay, flicking her hand to send a slap to Ba'ar's cheek. With a curt nod,
Sfika spun on her heel and marched off after the platters.

♌

The next morning, Hadlay arose early, as usual, and hurried to her
wardrobe. She was reaching for a fresh tunic when her eye caught on her
laundry basket. Something glittered there.

"Filch . . ." she muttered. He was stretched out beside her bed. With his
long neck, he almost spanned the full length of the mattress now.

She reached into her laundry and pulled out the tunic she had worn in
the dungeon. It was different somehow. It was still ripped, still stained, but
it was oddly changed. It took her a moment to realize that it—and indeed
all of her tunics—now had the silver fringe at the hems.

What did this mean? And what had Sfika meant when she spoke of
punishment rights? Shrugging, Hadlay returned the damaged tunic to the
basket, donned a fresh one, and headed off to the bestiary.

She was raking manure from the floor of the first cage when a kennelgroom entered. She recognized him as one of the men Zêru had charged
with exercising some of his larger creatures. He saw her, then stopped and
stared. Hadlay nodded a greeting and returned to work.

"Would you like me to finish cleaning for you?"

Hadlay hesitated, uncertain she had heard him right. "I'll be finished
with this one in a moment, but you can take the creature for exercise if
you'd like."

"No, mistress." The groom bowed low. "I asked if you would like me to
finish cleaning the cages for you."

Hadlay turned around, looking to see if someone else was in the room.
Then she glanced back at the servant, who watched her, waiting for an answer. He was Oresed, and calling her *mistress*? Maybe he was shortsighted
and had mistaken her for someone else. "Thank you for offering," she said,

"but Sfika has assigned me to this work, and I should finish it, or she will be angry."

The servant seemed dismayed. "But mistress, this is menial labor. Why—"

Just then, Zêru arrived. "Hadlay! Come and see my newest mix!"

Hadlay sighed. She had hoped to be further along in her work before he arrived. Now she would be lucky if she got to eat before she had to begin her duties in the treasury. She set down her rake and hurried out to join Zêru.

Zêru kept her occupied feeding and petting his animals and greeting the newest arrival, a strange-looking mix of duck and a new creature from the Lands Beyond—something called a beaver. Zêru's mixture had a duck's bill and webbed feet, but a rounded, furry body and a fat, flattened tail. It seemed to like water, so Zêru was keeping it in a large basin. It was certainly the strangest creature Hadlay had met thus far.

When the horn sounded, Zêru vanished, and Hadlay turned back to finish her work. But the cages were already clean. The servant who had offered to help was just finishing the last one. He saw her looking and bowed again.

She gave him a tentative smile, torn between relief at seeing the work finished and worry that she would get in trouble—or worse, get her friends in trouble—for not completing the task herself. But there was nothing left for her to do. Bewildered, she left the bestiary. At least she would have time to bathe before the morning meal.

Everywhere she went it was the same, as if she had gone to bed in one Tower and awakened in another. A hush fell over every group of servants she passed. People bowed to her. Even Ba'ar gave way before her as she entered the privy. Something was very strange, and she worried that a trap might spring on her at any moment.

She was jumping at shadows by the time she approached the kitchen. The smells of Magira's cooking made her stomach rumble. She could hear noisy chatter and laughter from the other initiates already inside.

But when she entered, the room went still. The Oresed stared at everything but her. Even the Ramash initiates looked sheepish, casting their eyes down as if she'd caught them talking about her.

"Hadlay! Why don't you try some fresh bread?" Magira bustled over from the oven with a steaming loaf on a wooden paddle. She slid the loaf off onto a counter next to Hadlay and set two knives to work cutting it. "How are you, dear?"

"What is wrong?" Hadlay whispered as she accepted a slice. "Everyone is staring at me. Are they still angry over what I did?"

"It's the fringe, girl," Magira told her. Hadlay's face apparently reflected her confusion, because Magira chuckled. "Your attention must have wandered during Asinus's lecture on protocol, dear. If you see fringe on a tunic it means that the servant has found favor."

She gestured to her own tunic, which had three rows of yellow fringe. "A servant who has pleased an overlord receives fringe—and with it the right to govern others who have no fringe, or fewer rows. The colors are meaningful as well. Those who answer to Sfika wear yellow. Asinus's favorites wear black—you won't see much fringe among his servants, though, since hardly anyone pleases that old hedgehog. Buthotos's warriors and guards wear red fringe, Bonobos's color is brown—but again, you don't see it much in his laboratory, as he is not overly concerned with status. Aurum's favorites wear green. Zamzom and his—though they are rarely seen—wear purple."

"Then what is silver?" Hadlay wondered.

Magira winked. "Silver and gold are the colors of royalty. Your fringe tells everyone that you have gained the favor of the prince himself!"

Indeed, the fringe seemed to change everything. It surprised Hadlay that even the overlords treated her with more respect. Aurum took one look at Hadlay's tunic and had her desk removed back to her office. At day's end, she approved Hadlay's ledger with barely a glance. Even Asinus, though he could not help being disagreeable, only grimaced at her as he passed in the corridor that evening.

It was disquieting, seeing Oresed servants hurry ahead of her to open doors or step back to allow her to pass. They showed her deference, but their eyes still followed her with barely veiled hate. In some ways, she felt more threatened by this.

⅋

The end of their term with Aurum marked the beginning of the third moon, and the initiates were dismissed to visit their homes.

In the carriage, Ba'ar remained silent the entire ride, never once offering a bitter comment. Nomish seemed to think it was amusing, but the silence unsettled Hadlay. What would she find on the streets of Turris? If the Oresed had spun into a near-murderous riot at the pronouncement that Ramash were to be made equal, what would they do when they learned that a Ramash had been given special status in the Tower?

The carriage dropped Ba'ar off first, as her home was closest to the Tower. Her brother, Oren, shouted a greeting from the rooftop as she stepped out of the carriage.

Then it was a long ride through the irregular streets of Turris. People stopped to stare as they passed, unaccustomed to seeing royal carriages. Kayshti and Ma'at's stop came next. They lived in the nicer part of the Ramash quarter. Hadlay had once envied the homes here, but now she was shocked to see how weathered and plain they seemed.

"Thank you again for the platter, Hadlay!" Ma'at pulled herself from her mother's hugs long enough to wave from their doorway.

The home Hadlay's parents shared with the Rakams looked even smaller than Hadlay remembered. Their parents were waiting for their arrival. Several other Ramash stood with them, no doubt drawn from nearby homes by the uncommon sound of carriage wheels on their street.

Nomish launched himself from the carriage, rushing over to throw his arms around his mother and sister. His mother flushed as he handed her his platter, then glanced around and hurried inside with it.

Alila came over and took Hadlay's platter. "Let me take this for you," she said, casting a strangely wary look at the neighbors as the carriage departed.

"Hadlay! Nomish!" Hadlay's mother rushed up and cupped their cheeks with gentle hands. "You're home!"

Marba came up beside her and pumped Nomish's hand. "I cannot tell you how good it is to see your faces!"

Her parents looked thinner and more careworn than Hadlay remembered. They had dressed in their best tunics, but to Hadlay's eye, the wool looked dull and coarse. Worse, when Marba drew Hadlay into his arms, she realized he smelled. She tried not to recoil from the bitter, unwashed scent, but it was surprisingly strong. She remembered Citna's astonishment when she'd learned the Ramash did not bathe. *"Toad's nostrils, no wonder you stink!"* It mortified her to realize Citna was right.

The neighbors crowded around Nomish, clapping him on the shoulder and greeting him cheerfully. He seemed not to notice the smell, and he grinned as he clasped hand after hand. People stroked the fine fabric of his tunic, making much of the grand carriage that had brought them. The neighbors looked so poor. So wretched.

Her father gazed at her with worried eyes. "Hadlay—is something wrong?" He caught sight of the wounds on her arms. The swelling had diminished, but there were still awful scabs to mark where the creatures had torn her flesh. "You've been injured! What happened?"

Hadlay shrugged. What could she tell him? She didn't want to worry him, and she did not dare to betray the secrets of the Tower.

Then it struck her how much she had missed him. Tears flooded her eyes as she flung herself back into his arms. Her mother folded herself into the embrace, kissing Hadlay's forehead and stroking her hair, and suddenly, she was just Hadlay Mivana again, and everything was right in her world.

A FEW SMALL LIES

The evening meal lingered into the dark of night, with Hadlay and Nomish stumbling over each other to tell of their lives in the Tower. Though they had not discussed it before their arrival, both of them avoided talking about the dungeon.

"So the emperor himself gave you these platters, Hadlay?" Mrs. Rakam ran a hand over one of them, admiring its gleaming surface.

Mr. Rakam did not seem as pleased with them. Hadlay had noticed him exchanging a strained glance with her father earlier that evening. She wondered what was troubling them.

It occurred to her that perhaps he thought she had stolen them. She raised a solemn hand. "I swear it, he and Zêru gave them to me."

Her father lifted one of the platters, inspecting it in the dimming light of the cookfire. There were no candles to light their table, and Hadlay suspected they had spent many nights in the dark to save up enough dried dung for this evening's fire. "What did you do, again, to earn his favor?"

Hadlay shifted uncomfortably. It was the first lie she had told that evening. Since the events leading up to the gift had much to do with her sojourn into the dungeon, she had said only that the emperor was pleased about her friendship with his son.

"And how did you come to be injured?" Hadlay's mother asked. She had been watching Hadlay closely all evening, and Hadlay sensed she knew there were things she and Nomish were avoiding.

Hadlay still had formed no answer for this, but Nomish came to her

230

rescue. "In the laboratory—there was a terrible accident. One of Bonobos's clay jars shattered, and Hadlay was struck by the pieces."

Hadlay sent Nomish a grateful smile. "It was my fault. I should have seen that it was shooting steam around the lid." In truth, a jar had exploded during her time in the laboratory, though no one had been injured.

"Are you certain you want to work so closely with Bonobos?" Mrs. Rakam asked her son. Hadlay had already related what the emperor had said about Nomish's apprenticeship. She knew how much the news would please her friend and could not bear to keep it from him, though she feared she was breaking the emperor's confidence. "I'd hate to see you wind up with a hook for a hand as well."

Nomish shrugged. "It is the most interesting work in the Tower."

"Are you feeling all right, Nomish?" Mrs. Rakam said. "You have barely eaten your meat."

"I am quite well, mother," Nomish assured her. "I simply ate too much before we left the Tower." He exchanged a subtle glance with Hadlay.

She understood his lack of appetite. After two moons of meals from Magira's kitchen, it had taken all her will to chew and swallow this sinewy roast pigeon. Catching a meaningful glare from her mother, Hadlay had managed another mouthful before she had found a way to exchange her full platter for her father's empty one. Now she made a show of scraping the last drops of gravy with her bread and smiled her appreciation.

"Tell us about Zêr-Shungalli, Hadlay," Mrs. Rakam said. "What is he like? And why, Nomish, do you not go with Hadlay to the bestiary each morn?" She cast a hard look at her son.

Hadlay hastened to protect him. "I never invited him. Zêru is deeply concerned with his privacy, and I feared that including others would anger him." She knew this sounded feeble, but it was the best answer she could contrive. Another lie.

In truth, it had never occurred to her to invite Nomish. She resolved to do so when they returned to the Tower. Hadn't Zêru asked if Nomish would be his friend too? It struck her that she had been awfully self-absorbed, not thinking to include her best friend in this curious relationship. She wondered if he had felt neglected or hurt by this.

"What of the emperor?" Hadlay's mother asked.

"Well, he's . . ." Hadlay chewed her lip, wondering what she could say. "He's been kind to us. He healed Nomish on our first day in the Tower, and he released . . ." she stopped herself. She could not tell them of the dungeon.

"He released us from a punishment set by Asinus," Nomish finished for her.

"And?" Iaras asked quietly. Her eyes had not left Hadlay, and Hadlay knew she was probing for the things they held back.

"Tell us, daughter," her father said.

Hadlay could see that he too knew that she was not telling everything.

The weight of all the secrets Hadlay had been keeping pressed heavily. She had longed many times in the Tower to be able to share with Nomish the things she was learning about the emperor and Zêru, and now the people she loved and trusted most knew she was holding back, and they were hurt by it.

And why should she not tell, voices seemed to whisper in her mind. Had he not asked her to speak for him among her people? The best way she knew to reassure them of his good intentions was to share what she had learned.

Her father laid his hand over hers. "We want to know everything."

Taking care to avoid speaking of matters private to the emperor and Zêru, Hadlay related some of the discussion at the emperor's table.

When she had finished, the room was silent for a long moment. Everyone exchanged glances, as if uncertain how to receive what she was saying. Hadlay feared that they thought she had gone mad.

"The Mirror of N'de is only a children's tale, Hadlay," Marba said.

"No, the emperor said N'de is real!" Hadlay looked from face to face, willing them to believe her. "And I believe he is Meshah himself! I overheard him tell Zêru that he would reveal his true identity when the people were ready!"

"He said that N'de is real," her mother murmured, taking one of the gold platters and stroking it with her fingers as she thought. Hadlay realized the platters might go some way to help them believe. They had only heard of such treasures in that story.

Mr. Rakam stared at Hadlay. "Did he say that he is Meshah?"

"Not exactly," she said. "But he didn't deny it when I asked."

His skeptical expression told Hadlay he thought she had imagined much.

"I wish you could see the Tower," Nomish said. "There were many times in these last moons that I saw things that reminded me of N'de in the story. And the emperor healed me of my injuries from the pulling! It never occurred to me that he might be Meshah, but I agree with Hadlay that he is benevolent and that he means to do right by our people."

"Never mind all that stuff of legends," Mrs. Rakam said. "He has a way for us to satisfy the tax, even enrich ourselves?" She leaned over the table.

Hadlay saw the doubt on all their faces. But she saw something else dawning in their eyes as well.

Hope.

THE WAY OF SECRETS

Hadlay had hoped she might sleep better with her family near, but it was no use. Each time her eyes closed, the emptiness of her belly rumbled and the straws that lined her mattress poked her side. The lingering smells of the stable did not help, nor did Alila's restless tossing beside her.

Alila had spoken little since their return this midday. She seemed distant, ill at ease. Hadlay wondered if she had somehow offended her friend.

Quietly, Hadlay rolled from the bed and slipped outside. It had been a long time since she had walked in the moonlight.

She was surprised to find Nomish seated on the fresh mud bricks that had been left to bake in the heat of the sun. Their fathers had been repairing some of the older walls of the home. Lines of worry creased Nomish's brow.

"Something is troubling you." She spoke quietly.

He rested his arms on his knees, twisting a piece of straw between his fingers. "I never realized how poor we were."

"I know." She walked over and sat beside him. "Do you think things were like this when we left, and we were just accustomed to it? Or is it worse?"

"I had thought the gold platters would solve their problems," Nomish murmured. "But did you see their expressions? They were surprised—but I did not see the pleasure I had expected. I thought surely—"

"What did you think we would do with them?" A sharp voice came from behind. Alila strode up to stand before them. "No Ramash can afford to buy anything so fine. And no Oresed will purchase anything from a Ramash. The platters are useless to us. Worse, since it is known you brought them here, no doubt the marauders will come to steal them—and whatever else we have remaining."

Hadlay had never seen Alila angry like this. She was not certain how to respond.

Alila saw her astonishment and scoffed. "Did you think the Oresed would be content to simply drive us into poverty? They want us dead. They send out raiding parties to break down the walls of our homes—those of us who still have homes—and steal whatever we have. And if anyone resists, they are murdered. Your 'gift' has placed this home in even more danger."

"I'm sorry," Hadlay blurted, "I did not know!"

"Don't you blame Hadlay!" Nomish stood to confront his sister.

"Look at you, with your soft clothes and your uncalloused hands. Look at your fat bellies!" Alila stretched herself as tall as she could stand, hands on her hips, shouting at her brother, who still stood at least a head taller. "Do you think of us at all when you are eating your fine meals in the Tower?"

"Of course we do, Alila!" Hadlay stood, moving to insert herself between her friends. "We think of you all the time!"

"Do you really?" Alila's voice dripped with scorn. "What good have you done us as you insinuated yourself in the prince's good graces? Things are worse than ever!"

"She has tried, Alila!" Nomish thundered. "The emperor is trying! Didn't Hadlay say he is going to help us with the tax?"

"Oh, right." She snorted. "I forgot. N'de is real, and the emperor means to make Turris its equal! I forgot that Shungallu is truly Meshah himself!"

Suddenly, the night was very still. Hadlay turned, realizing that their argument had roused half the neighborhood. Heads could be seen in windows and peering down from the rooftops in the moonlight.

The emperor's secret was out. Hadlay wondered what price she would pay for telling.

THE EMPEROR'S NEW CLOTHES

You have forgotten the key, which I asked you to seek."

Hadlay wanted to protest—she *had* taken the only key she'd seen. And it had gotten her in trouble! If that wasn't the right one, did it mean that alchemy was the key?

The Being knew her thoughts, and his eyes flowed with silver tears. "The key is not to be found in the Tower, nor learned. If you listened, you would have it by now!"

She frowned. "Why must everything be a mystery? Just tell me what you want."

"You. I want you." His voice was laced with sadness, which was even worse than anger. "Even though you want everything but me."

"I *do* want you!"

"Perhaps. But there are things you want more. I see the choices you have made. Actions without regard to the consequence to others."

Hadlay hung her head. He was right again. "I am sorry."

The Being's colors softened. His wings beat gently, fanning her with their warmth, though she still viewed him only through a mirror. "You have not disappointed me, beloved. Before you were born, I chose you, knowing your faults and the errors you would make. But the time is very short. You must choose soon, either the way to destruction or the key. Turn from the path you have taken. Choose me as I have chosen you. Choose the key many have touched but no one has held. Choose the path back to N'de . . ."

"N'de? How can I return there?" She asked. But the vision faded from her mind. "Wait! Tell me how to find this key!"

She jolted awake, reaching for something she could not see. She laid back, pressing her palms against her eyes, blotting out the dawning light that sifted through the slats of the stable door.

The Being had spoken of N'de. Since the emperor had said that he planned to return there one day, perhaps the key had something to do with him. She opened her eyes. Maybe she was finally beginning to understand. But what was this key, and how would she find it?

She lay quietly, trying to sort through the rest of the puzzle in her mind. The next she knew, a hand was shaking her shoulder.

"Hadlay!" For a moment, Hadlay thought she was still in the Tower, only dreaming of home. Then the smell of the stable touched her nose, and she opened her eyes.

"Wake up, slackabed!" Her mother spoke in a stern tone, though her eyes were smiling. "Do they let you laze about in the Tower all day?"

Hadlay smiled. "I've missed your waking me."

Her mother laughed, ruffling her hair. "The morning meal is ready. And we must not be late for Midweek Gathering."

Hadlay groaned. It was time already to return to the Tower. Only one night home. It was not enough. There was so much more she wanted to say to her parents, so much more she wished she could do for them.

Her mother sat on the edge of Hadlay's bed. "You have not told us everything."

Hadlay sat up, rubbing her eyes to buy some time. What could she tell her mother that would not betray more secrets? She might already face the emperor's wrath for confiding as much as she had. Finally, she shrugged. "I got in trouble a few times, Mother. That's all."

Her mother frowned. "Hadlay, did we not warn you to be on your best behavior?"

Hadlay nodded. "I guess I have always needed to learn my own lessons."

Iaras chuckled, stroking Hadlay's cheek. "That you have, daughter. You remind me of your father in that way." She rose to her feet. "Well, it can't have been too bad if you have the emperor's favor. But do your best to behave, won't you?"

"I'll try."

Hadlay watched her mother leave, wondering if she should have said more. But it would have only worried her parents—and possibly caused them to take some awful risk to keep her from returning to the Tower. Besides, in truth, though the punishments were terrible, she actually liked the Tower. She enjoyed Zêru's friendship. And now that she was able to command the powers openly, she was going to excel at something for once in her life. She could show the Oresed once and for all that she and her people deserved respect.

She rose, donned a fresh tunic, and rolled the worn one to put into her small bag. She felt uncomfortably dirty, as though she had cleaned the bestiary and then failed to bathe. Her back and legs itched. No doubt there were bugs in that old mattress. But she felt so much more free here than in the Tower.

She made her way into the main room of the home. Nomish was already at the table, stuffing his mouth with bits of bread. The gold platters were stacked on the table.

"Don't worry about those, dear. They were a kind gift," Mrs. Rakam said to Hadlay, sending her daughter a hard look. Alila flushed and looked away. "We will find a way to trade them for something useful."

Hadlay smiled. She had thought of a solution during the night. "Let us take them back with us to the Tower. We will make sure to be seen carrying them today, so no one thinks you still have them. We will give them to Magira and ask her to exchange them for food and things you can use for barter."

"Wonderful idea!" Daram said, seating himself beside his son. Hadlay could see the relief on his face. Her father too smiled as if a weight had been lifted from him.

Mrs. Rakam patted her shoulder. "Thank you, dear. You could not have known about the marauders. We asked Magira not to tell you."

"We didn't want you to worry." Hadlay's mother handed her a slice of bread. It tasted of mold.

The meal passed far too quickly, and the walk to the public square was much too short. Hadlay clung to her father's hand, enjoying the feel of her mother's arm draped across her shoulder as they endured Asinus's lengthy sermon. She had placed her platter on the ground as Asinus droned, and now stood upon it, keeping it safe without having to bear its weight.

She noticed several Oresed staring at it, and she scowled at them. These were people who had stoned her as she'd hung helpless in this place—and now they wanted to steal from her and harm her family! She longed to shout a command and watch them all scream and thrash about, burned by unseen fires. But she dared not use the powers here, not without the emperor's approval.

Somewhere behind her, she heard someone whisper her name. She turned to see a small cluster of Ramash speaking under their breaths. A few of them cast a sidelong glance at her. She sighed. The story of last evening's shouting was making its way among her people. She had no way of knowing how much had been heard. But she was almost certain the last, most damaging, comments had been loud enough for everyone. She wanted to be angry with Alila for betraying her trust, but in truth, it was she who had spoken out of turn.

She was so caught up in her own thoughts that it took a moment to realize that Asinus had finished his sermon. He was preparing to read the list of purgations when someone—a tall, Oresed man—shouted up at him. "Where is my daughter? Why did she not return home last eve?"

Asinus's heavy black brows knit together as he glowered at the man. "This is not the time to discuss your personal concerns!" He returned to his tablets.

The man rushed for the stairs to the platform. Two large guards blocked his way.

"Arrest him for disrupting the order of the public square!" Asinus pointed, and the guards took the man's arms, preparing to drag him from the courtyard.

"You know where she is!" the man screamed. "Why won't you tell us?"

Asinus had turned again to his tablets when he realized that the crowd had gone silent and was looking upward. He followed their gaze, and his mouth dropped open.

A great, golden chariot was circling above them, drawn by huge, winged lions with the heads of men. Hadlay shuddered, squeezing her father's hand. As the chariot descended, Hadlay saw that the emperor and Zêru stood within it, the emperor at the reins. The chariot circled down until it was just above the platform. Asinus and his guards scrambled to make way as it landed, and the lions gave startling shrieks, like eagles, while snatching at the guards with their claws.

Drawing the chariot to a halt with its open back toward the crowd, the emperor and Zêru turned to face the citizens. They waited for the awed murmurs to die down.

The emperor wore a gleaming white robe with jeweled trim, and when the chariot glided into the light that reflected from the disc over the platform, he shone as if he were the sun itself. His crown was crusted with gemstones, and his rings flashed in the light.

Zêru had on a light blue tunic with a cloak draped over one shoulder. His crown was smaller and less ornate, but it was inlaid around its base with brilliant blue lapis lazuli. He, too, glowed in the reflected light, though he looked more like the moon.

At a nod from his father, Zêru stepped forward and raised his hands, commanding silence. "Citizens of Turris, this day begins a new era. We must put behind us the tyrannies and injustices that have for too long spoiled this great city, and look toward a future that is full of opportunity and challenge. As my father told you on our return from the Lands Beyond, we were gravely troubled to learn of the difficulties faced by the poor and the helpless, the lowliest of our citizens. We resolved to raise them up and make them equals in our society."

An angry murmur rose from among the Oresed in the crowd. Zêru gazed at them dispassionately until there was silence again. "We are aware this was not a popular position with some of our citizens, but we will not be deterred."

Hadlay glanced up at her father, wondering if this speech was helping him to see the things she found so endearing about Zêru. But his mouth was tight, his eyes distrustful. She wished her parents could know the prince as she did.

Zêru continued. "And now I see we must do more to bring these people to their rightful place in our empire, as full and equal partners with the Oresed." This time, when angry voices rose, Zêru snapped his fingers. Hadlay saw several Oresed jump as if they had received a shock from one of Bonobos's lamps. The murmuring dwindled into fearful quiet.

Now the emperor spoke, and Zêru took a short step back. "As you may have heard, the Crown is levying a new tax. As with all things, it will apply equally to both Oresed and Ramash."

Some of the Oresed exchanged satisfied glances, and Hadlay knew they believed that the Ramash would be crushed by this new debt.

One of the Ramash men near the platform spoke up, though his voice trembled. "My people cannot be equal in this, Your Majesty. The equality we have thus far experienced has cost us everything we owned! We have no means to pay your tax."

"Silence!" Asinus brayed. "Do you dare to question the emperor's right to tax as he wills?" He signaled his guard to go and arrest the man.

The emperor waved the guards away. "I am aware that there are many poor in Turris—mostly Ramash, but some Oresed also—who cannot pay the tax." He spread his hands outward, toward the people. "My son and I have concluded that there must be another way for those citizens to satisfy this debt."

"Another way? What does this mean?" Hadlay heard a voice nearby whisper, and the question repeated itself through the square.

"Will he renounce the tax for the Ramash, and leave the Oresed to pay the whole debt?"

The emperor smiled and continued, ignoring the distraction. "This will not be charity. Those who have no money will be allowed to work off their debt to the Crown by performing services."

Though no one dared to speak up, Hadlay could see the Ramash exchanging anxious glances. What ways would they be asked to serve? She heard the word "slavery" whispered somewhere behind her. Her father's grip on her hand tightened.

"A great many changes are coming to Turris. This land has long been at peace, but an enemy has risen in the Lands Beyond. We must prepare ourselves to conquer or be conquered. We will need citizens to serve in every capacity as we raise a vast army for the protection and expansion of the Turran Empire."

Another voice rose up in the crowd, this one with an edge of hysteria. "He will force us into servitude!"

Zêru stepped forward again, speaking clearly. "There is no force, and there is no servitude. Who in Turris does not work for his living? This is a way for the poorest Turrans, both Oresed and Ramash, to better their lot in this city."

The emperor raised his hand. "Let the Ramash people hear from one of their own about the lives of those who serve the Crown." At his gesture, Hadlay felt herself begin to rise from the ground.

"Hadlay?" Her mother gripped her shoulders. "What is happening?"

Hadlay realized the emperor meant to bring her up to the platform, to make her speak before all the people.

"Come, Hadlay Mivana," he said. "Come and reassure your people that our intentions are good."

Hadlay clung to her father's hand, hoping there was some way he could anchor her. The thought of speaking before this mob was terrifying—almost as awful as the dungeon. But she did not dare defy the emperor. "It's all right," she managed, glancing down at her mother, who was now holding tightly to her leg. "Zêru summons me this way all the time." With that, she released her father's hand and floated free until her feet were above the tallest heads in the crowd. Then she leaned forward, allowing the powers to carry her to the golden chariot, where she was set down beside Zêru.

"Don't be afraid." He gave her arm a quick squeeze of reassurance. "Once you begin speaking, it is not as awful as you imagine."

The emperor bestowed one of his gleaming smiles on her. "Hello, little one."

Out of the corner of her eye, Hadlay saw Asinus glaring, and she dropped to her knees before the emperor, prostrating herself in obedience to protocol.

"Rise, girl," the emperor said, and Hadlay felt herself coming to her feet. "Speak now. Tell these people what it is to serve the Crown. You will know what to say." He touched Hadlay's head, and suddenly, the right words whispered in her mind. She turned to face the crowd.

"My friends, the Ramash, know me. I am an ordinary girl, unimportant, unschooled. Once I hoped to be a merchant. But when the emperor returned, I was among those chosen to serve in the Tower. I did not wish to go there, but I had no choice. Some might say it was slavery. But tonight I will sleep in a soft bed. I have clean, fine clothes, and good food. The work is not hard, because in the Tower, there is magic." One of her hands rose, almost of its own accord, and Asinus lifted from the platform. With a twitch of her wrist, he turned upside-down, his robes flopping down around his ears, exposing his undergarments. There was laughter from the crowd as she set him, red-faced, back upon his feet.

What had she done? Asinus would surely have her killed! But the emperor gave her a sly wink and gestured for her to continue.

"I can do this, even to an overlord who once had the power to torture me, because the emperor and his son, Zêru, have favored me, a Ramash." Hadlay wondered, even as she heard herself speak the words, whether she believed them. "Those who serve the Crown willingly, faithfully, as I have sought to do, will find the same favor."

No more words came to Hadlay. She looked at the emperor, worried that she had failed him, but he seemed pleased.

The crowd below was rapt now. The hope she had seen dawning in her parents' eyes was shining on the faces of many Ramash below her. The Oresed glowered, but they were silent. They were likely afraid. Afraid of her—and of what her people might become.

And she—Hadlay—had done this!

The emperor turned back to the people. "There was a city, once, so many ages ago that it has disappeared into the mists of myth and legend. Some of you may have heard of this place, although the stories about it were so full of falsehoods that I forbade them. The city was called N'de, and it was real."

Hadlay heard the murmurs from the crowd below, echoing the questions she herself had once asked.

The emperor continued. "N'de is lost to us—at least for now—but we still have hope. If you will willingly give me and my son, Zêru, your allegiance and obedience, we will raise up a new N'de, one even greater than the first, where all our citizens, both Oresed and Ramash, can live in luxury and peace."

A cheer rose from the Ramash, feeble at first, but it gained strength until the whole of the public square vibrated with the noise.

The emperor raised both hands, and the crowd quieted again. "As the collectors come for your taxes, they will also ask for your pledge to serve and obey me and my son in all things. If you cannot pay the tax, only agree to make the pledge, and we will find a way for you to serve. And if you serve well, after your debt is satisfied, you will receive payment. You will be paid in gold and silver. You will soon be able to buy the homes you live in, and in time you will even have the means to buy or build homes that are better. You will clothe your children in fine robes of linen and wool, and you will fill your platters with leavened bread and the fat meat of swine and osprey."

When he paused, Zêru stepped forward again. "On entering my thirteenth summer, like all citizens of Turris, I became an initiate. I have spent my days in apprenticeship, learning the duties I will perform as an adult. I will one day rule this city in my father's name while he leads our armies in the Lands Beyond.

"And like most initiates, during this time, I am expected to select a bride. I have done so." He reached back, catching Hadlay's hand. "To seal this compact between the Crown and the people, I will choose a bride from the initiates of Turris. If she consents, this girl, this Ramash, this Turran, will sit by my side as princess."

Hadlay's mouth dropped open as Zêru drew her forward.

The emperor stepped in behind them, putting a hand on each of their shoulders. "I am pleased with this, but of course, young Mistress Mivana must consent." Hadlay felt a jolt of power surge through her body as he looked down into her eyes. "What do you say, little one? Will you promise now, before all here, to give your allegiance, loyalty, and unquestioning obedience to the Crown, to betroth yourself to my son, and, in the course of time, receive him as your husband?"

Hadlay stared wildly into the crowd, seeking her parents. Her eye caught Nomish instead. He was staring at her, stunned. Betrayed.

She turned back to Zêru. He had never spoken of this. Why had he done this so publicly? What of Nomish? What of their plans? But how could she refuse Zêru in front of all of Turris? What would happen to her—to her family—if she did?

"But what of Nomish?" she had asked the Being once.

You are meant for a much greater union. If you will receive it, he had replied.

A greater union. If she accepted Zêru's proposal, she would help to govern Turris. She would never be poor or frightened again, nor would her parents. She would be in a position to truly help her people.

How could she refuse? "I consent." A cheer rose through the crowd, though when she looked at the Oresed, she saw murderous glares as well.

The emperor's gleaming smile nearly blinded her. "You have answered well, my daughter." He waved a hand, and a cloak of gleaming silver rose up from the floorboard of the carriage and draped itself around Hadlay's shoulders. The emperor himself tied its laces at her throat, then turned to the crowd. "On the day of the marriage, this girl will have a new name— *Mušâtsiat*, which means, 'She who delivers.' And today, in honor of my son's betrothal, I hereby rescind all purgations, both for Oresed and for Ramash."

Asinus stepped forward, his jowls quivering. "But . . . Your Majesty!"

Ignoring him, the emperor took the chariot's reins again, and the two creatures that pulled it reared up, letting forth an ear-splitting scream.

Zêru clasped Hadlay's hand. "Wave to the people!"

And so she waved as the chariot rose, soaring up, up, circling over the crowd, then darted off toward the Tower.

MIXED FEELINGS

As soon as the chariot landed in the Tower courtyard, the emperor turned and gave Hadlay a fond smile. "Thank you, little one, for delivering your people to me." Without waiting for a reply, he vanished, leaving swirling winds behind.

"You were wonderful!" Zêru exclaimed. "Father said the Igigi would tell us what to say—it was the strangest thing, wasn't it?"

Hadlay still gripped the side of the chariot, trying to comprehend what had just happened. She had agreed—before all of Turris—to marry Zêru! What if her parents objected? Why had she not asked to consult them first? Surely the emperor would have understood.

Zêru was still rambling. He swept a hand toward the beasts that had brought them here. "By the way, do you like my newest mixes? I've been experimenting for a while on mixing more than two kinds of creatures, but it never came out quite right before. These are lion, eagle, and man."

A horn sounded from the pinnacle of the Tower. Zêru grinned at her. "Father wants me!" He caught Hadlay's hands. "Thank you for agreeing to be my bride. We are going to have such fun together!" He vanished.

Hadlay numbly stepped down from the chariot as nervous stable boys came to take charge. She shuffled to the stairway that led up to the Tower's giant doors and sat down hard, staring at nothing as her mind reeled through the day's events.

She had not even had the chance to kiss her parents goodbye. And the Oresed—they were furious. Recalling their murderous expressions as the chariot had taken flight, she feared that their rage would turn itself even more strongly against the Ramash. What if they sought to harm her parents?

What could she do? "*Igigi, hitnâshunûti!*" she whispered, summoning the powers to protect the ones she loved. Of course she had no way to know if it would work.

⚬

Some time later, the first of the carriages arrived, bringing the initiates back from the public square. Nomish jumped out, carrying the two golden platters. He held one of them out to her. "You forgot this." His voice was expressionless.

Hadlay looked up at him, studying his face. His eyes were red, his mouth tight. She could see his jaw clenching. "Nomish, I didn't know—"

He waved off further explanation without looking at her. "Mother tells me that she had spoken with Fa'an's parents shortly before we were chosen. She says they would be open to a match. I like Fa'an well enough." He turned away, walking up the stairs without a backward look.

"Nomish—" Hadlay watched him go.

Did this end their friendship, then? She tried to imagine life in the Tower without Nomish. She couldn't envision herself enjoying a meal if Nomish was not there beside her. He had always been her friend, as long as she could remember. His family had been hers as well. Now, Alila barely spoke to her—and it seemed his mother had been seeking a way to match him with another even before they had come to the Tower. Why? Had they ever truly cared for her at all?

She studied her reflection in the platter. What was it about her that everyone seemed to hate so much?

"Hadlay! Congratulations on your betrothal!" Ma'at sat down on the stairs beside her. Kayshti hurried on after Nomish, casting Hadlay a sour look. "My parents were so excited," Ma'at said. "A Ramash marrying the emperor's son! They could hardly wait to ask your parents to sup with them!"

"Did you see my parents?" Hadlay brushed away her tears with a finger.

"Oh, yes! Their friends all crowded around them, shaking their hands, hugging them! They had a grand escort back home, I tell you!" She leaned in. "For a moment, I was a little afraid of the Oresed, but Asinus called them all to the platform so our families could safely leave."

Hadlay doubted very much that Asinus cared for their safety, but it reassured her to know that her parents had gotten home all right.

"But there is something else." Ma'at moved a little closer, glancing over her shoulder. "Rezen's parents visited us last eve. They asked why she had not returned home with us. I told them about Sfika summoning her in the middle of the night, and they looked most distraught. They said they hadn't seen her since she left to serve in the Tower." She paused. "What do you think happened to her?"

"Well, we know she was sent home," Hadlay said. "If she never got there, then someone must have prevented it." She thought a moment longer. "Alila told me that there are Oresed marauders who are robbing and killing Ramash. They must have gotten her."

Ma'at frowned. "Perhaps. But the man that accosted Asinus this morning—I asked, and learned he was Tahat's father."

"Tahat—is that the Oresed girl who was also dismissed from Tower service?"

"Or so we were told."

"But if both have gone missing . . ." Hadlay didn't want to say what she was thinking.

"Do you suppose they were sent to the dungeon?"

Hadlay shrugged. "Perhaps." But she didn't believe that was it. After all, when Ma'at, Nomish, and Kayshti had been sent there, it was no secret. No, she hated to even think it, but another possibility seemed more likely.

That white elephant—the one she had seen when she went flying with Zêru. Its face had looked nearly human, and its tusks were crooked like a boar's. That had bothered her, and she realized now that those tusks had reminded her of Tahat's crooked teeth. And that same day, Zêru had spoken of a new mix in the moat. "She has lovely, long hair," he'd said, "and sings beautifully!" She recalled Rezen's beautiful voice.

It had not occurred to her before to wonder where Zêru obtained the humans he was mixing. Shuddering, she rose and climbed the steps to the Tower.

As she made her way up to the doors, it felt very like the first time she had entered the Tower. The doors opened, and she saw servants going about their daily duties. One was filling Bonobos's lamps with wine. Another was walking Zêru's nuppy.

But when they saw her, everything stopped. After a moment's hesitation, everyone fell to the floor. Even the nuppy slumped a bit.

It took a moment for Hadlay to realize that they were prostrating themselves for her. Ma'at, a step behind her, froze, then realization dawned on her face, and she too dropped to her knees, touching her forehead to the floor.

Hadlay stared at them. What was she supposed to do? "Please—please, get up, everyone! Go on about your business."

As the servants got up and resumed their work, Sfika flew into the main hall. "There you are!" She buzzed up to Hadlay. Snapping her fingers, she summoned a cluster of maids. "We must get you up to your chambers and dressed—you're expected at the emperor's table for midday meal, dear!"

Hadlay shook her head. Almost nothing the woman had just said made any sense at all. And had she just called Hadlay *dear*?

Sfika grasped her arm and propelled her toward the corridors. "Come along, now. You mustn't keep His Majesty and Prince Zêru waiting!"

Hadlay turned back and waved at Ma'at as Sfika steered her round a corner. "Where are we going?"

"Your new chambers have been prepared for you." Sfika picked up her pace, so that Hadlay had to trot to keep up. The maids flocked behind.

"But . . . my tunics . . . my things are all in the dormitory!"

Sfika kept going. "You have no need for those old gray tunics, dear. There are much finer things in your new chambers. As soon as word of your betrothal reached us, the wardrobe master began creating clothing for you."

Hadlay stopped short. "My picture!" She cared little for the tunics, but the picture let her see her parents' faces now and then.

Sfika gave her a tight smile. "You can retrieve it later. But we have artists who are capable of far better likenesses if you want a picture." Her grip on Hadlay's arm tightened. "Now, come along, dear. We must hurry!"

Their journey ended at a chamber that was just below Zêru's, guarded by two menacing scorpion guards. Sfika stopped just out of range of their tails and waited for the doors to open. Hadlay realized that she must know about the stingers.

"Here we are!" Sfika eased between the guards and drew Hadlay inside.

To Hadlay's eyes, the room seemed nearly as large and grand as Zêru's suite. She stood, staring open-mouthed at walls three men high, with gem-colored tiles inlaid in intricate patterns. A large window dominated the far wall, filling the room with brilliant light. To one side, a huge bed sat high up off the floor on a wooden frame. It was covered with a blazing red sheet of silk, and bronze and gold pillows rested at its head.

The maids scattered, one rushing off to another room where Hadlay heard water running. Two more went to a huge wooden wardrobe, which opened to reveal an array of clothing that made Hadlay gasp.

A large, inlaid table sat in the corner opposite the bed, set with a dozen gold platters like the ones Zêru had given Hadlay. One of the maids took the platter Hadlay held and added it to the group. She wanted to protest—she had intended to take that platter straight to Magira—but she decided it was best if Sfika not know of it.

Sfika clucked her tongue. "I did say you must hurry, dear. Go take your bath and allow the maids to help you dress. You will have plenty of opportunity to admire your new chambers when you return."

The maids hustled Hadlay off to the privy, where again Hadlay stopped cold. The room gleamed with ivory tiles inlaid with blue and gold designs so intricate Hadlay could have spent the day gazing at them. The fixtures here were gold too, from the stool to the bath to the small basin for washing hands and face.

For a moment she was too caught up staring at it all to notice that the maids had divested her of her new cloak. They were now tugging at her tunic, trying to pull it off. She crossed her arms in alarm.

"Now, dear, this is no time for modesty. We must get you cleaned up and clothed and out the door. No more dawdling, if you please!" While the phrasing made it a request, Sfika spoke in loud, crisp tones that brooked no refusal.

Hadlay shyly raised her arms and allowed the maids to take her clothes.

A moment later, she was immersed to her neck in warm, scented water. One of the maids massaged her tired muscles, while another worked scented lather through her hair. It was awkward to have such things done for her.

Then one of them dumped a bucket of warm water over her head, rinsing off the lather. Hadlay sputtered, reaching blindly for a cloth to dry her eyes.

Sfika clapped twice, and the maids hurried to help Hadlay out of the basin.

"Just stand still!" Sfika struck a pose, with her arms stretched out to the sides, and Hadlay imitated her while the maids flocked around her. Two dried her off and applied oils to her skin while a third worked a comb through her tangled curls. Another team of maids presented several expanses of different colored fabric, each one draping a section of cloth over an arm, so Hadlay could see how it hung.

Hadlay looked at Sfika, wondering what was expected.

"Choose, dear! Which do you want to wear this eve?" At Hadlay's dumbfounded look, Sfika exhaled a sharp breath. "Never mind. I think the ivory will do nicely."

The ivory turned out to be a length of pale, creamy silk with gold and green threads embroidered around the edges. Two maids wrapped the cloth around Hadlay's body, fastening it over one shoulder. This left some extra length at the rear, which could be brought up to cover the other shoulder in a cloak or left to trail behind. Hadlay kept running her hand over the fabric. It almost felt like liquid.

The other maids hurried off with the rejected selections and returned with several large boxes, each one filled with jewelry. The first held rings and chains made of silver and gold, some inlaid with precious stones.

Was she supposed to choose again? As she hesitated, Sfika took charge, and, in a moment, the maids had fastened a golden chain at Hadlay's ankle and a pendant around her neck.

It was all too much. Hadlay looked at Sfika. "These are for me?"

Sfika nodded. "The jewelry once belonged to the empress. Prince Zêru wanted you to have them now."

"The empress . . ." Hadlay remembered wondering about Zêru's mother. "What happened to her?"

"It is a very sad story. I will leave it to Prince Zêru to tell you one day."

The next box contained a selection of headdresses. Hadlay goggled at the largest: a mat of gold leaves meant to be draped over an elaborate hairstyle. The leaves would lie across the top, dangling down around her face. And above them, several delicate gold flowers bloomed, each set with radiant gemstones rising up on sturdy wires to form a crown.

"Not that one—it's much too heavy." Sfika selected a much plainer one—a simple gold band, shaped as a vine with dangling leaves that would hang across Hadlay's forehead. A maid slipped it on, anchored it with combs, and arranged Hadlay's magically dried curls around it.

From yet another box, Sfika chose a large gold band and slipped it onto Hadlay's bare right arm just above the elbow. She had picked out a ring, as well, but a lovely, flashing red stone caught Hadlay's eye.

"I like this one!" Hadlay said, picking it up and holding it to the light. It glowed so red that she was reminded of ripe cherries.

"Very well, then." Sfika returned the other ring to the box. "Let's be off!"

Two maids eased silk slippers onto Hadlay's feet. The others were busy drying the tile floors where she had stepped out of the bath.

"Tomorrow, you will choose your own attendants," Sfika said. "I imagine you'd like one or two of your young friends to serve you."

Her own servants! Hadlay's mind was swimming with all the changes that had come on her in the last day. This morning she had awakened in a stable, and this evening she would sleep in a silken bed larger than the whole of her old home! She, the daughter of a slave, would have her own servants!

Who would she choose? Ma'at, of course. And Nomish.

Hadlay swallowed hard. No. Not Nomish. Nomish wanted to work with Bonobos. He would not be happy serving her.

"I suggest you select both Oresed and Ramash attendants—it will help to smooth things in the city," Sfika said.

The idea was not pleasing. With Oresed serving her, she would never feel entirely safe. And she especially would not want Ba'ar lurking about.

Perhaps Citna wouldn't be too bad. But wait! Hadlay *would* request Ba'ar. She had been wondering what she could do to keep Ba'ar from becoming Asinus's apprentice, and here was her opportunity. And she could always give Ba'ar things to do that would keep her out of the way. Like clean up after Filch when he got into food that loosed his bowels. Hadlay giggled.

"Come, dear!" Sfika started toward the doors, which opened before them.

As she left the room, Hadlay glanced back and caught a sullen look from one of the maids. It was enough to remind her that she was still Ramash. In a strange way, the thought was comforting.

The long walk to the emperor's chambers proved more difficult than Hadlay had expected. Unaccustomed to the weight and length of her new gown, she kept tripping over the fabric.

After the first stumble, Sfika took a firm hold of her arm to keep her from falling. "Kick out the hem as you go, dear, like this!" She showed Hadlay a funny, goose-stepping walk that did keep the hem from underfoot, but it felt awkward and Sfika's pace was so rapid Hadlay could not maintain it. The leaves on her headdress jingled when she stumbled, as if they were laughing at her clumsiness.

She wondered if she would ever truly become accustomed to all this.

The Royal Treatment

The doors to the emperor's dining hall swung open.

Hadlay had expected to dine with Zêru and the emperor alone, as she had done previously, and she'd hoped to ask about Rezen and Tahat. She was surprised to see the long table covered with platters. The emperor was seated at one end of the table and Zêru at the other, with a space beside him that Hadlay guessed was meant for her. The guests seated nearest the emperor were mostly Nafal. Those closer to Zêru were Nafalin, mixes of human and Nafal. Hadlay glanced at their platters, noting the reddish tinge on their food, and suppressed a shudder.

"Hadlay!" Zêru rose and came to greet her. "We were just served a moment ago. We would have waited, but we were unsure how long you would be." Taking her hand, he led her to the seat beside his own.

"Gentlemen." The emperor raised his glass, and all the guests came to their feet. "Here is the girl I have spoken of who has been such a help to us. May I present Hadlay Mivana."

Each of the men at the table bowed. Uncertain how to respond, Hadlay bowed in return.

"Hadlay, may I present Gader'el, Pinim'e, Kasadya, Asb'el, Yeqon, and Azazel." Hadlay recognized these as the names of the Nafal princes the emperor had placed over the Lands Beyond.

At the mention of their names, each of the Nafal giants nodded and took his seat.

"And these are their firstborn sons: Anak, Gibor, Emah, Ziz, Arba, and Og," Zêru gestured to the Nafalin seated near him.

Zêru waited for Hadlay to sit, then took his place at the end of the table. Ayom appeared beside her, filling her platter with broiled fowl, fresh greens, and Magira's special fluffy rolls.

The meat dripped with juice and sliced as smoothly as warm butter. Hadlay remembered the tough pigeon stew she'd had last eve. It did not seem right to eat like this when her family was likely going without, having used up their best for the meals given Hadlay and Nomish.

"Is something amiss, Hadlay?" Zêru asked her.

She glanced at the others to assure they were not listening, then turned to Zêru. "I was merely thinking of my family."

"They are not well?"

"They are well enough, though much poorer than when I first came here." She watched his face. "I tried to take those gold platters to them, but they tell me that they cannot trade them. Worse, the Oresed have formed parties of marauders who raid Ramash homes for things of value. I fear I have put them in danger."

Zêru smiled. "You need not worry, Hadlay. Father has placed protective powers around all the Ramash. The Oresed will trouble them no further. And your parents will soon be quite wealthy."

Hadlay felt some of her tension drain. "Thank you, Zêru."

"Well, we cannot have our people come to harm, can we? Their service will be most important to us." Zêru smiled and turned his attention to his guests.

Hadlay tried to interest herself in her meal, but in truth, she was too disoriented by the day's changes to be very hungry. She took nibbling bites, much distracted by the jewelry she wore. The ring felt clumsy, and the dangling leaves of the headdress kept catching the edge of her vision, making her feel she should duck some flying creature. Between nibbles, she sneaked quick glances at the strangers at the table.

Gader'el was dressed as a warrior, with silver breastplate and sword. Azazel's robes were trimmed with gold. Hadlay noticed an odd symbol on his collar, and recognized it from Bonobos's lessons in alchemy. Kasadya frightened Hadlay—or perhaps it was the snake that writhed around his neck and down his arm. And then there were Asb'el and Yeqon. Their hair was loose to their ears, then woven almost like a garment to the shoulders, with gold beads along the ends, and they wore close-cropped beards.

The Nafalin, like Zêru, were smaller, though still almost twice Hadlay's height. Only Og and Arba were old enough to have sparse beards. The rest wore their dark hair back, braided in various ways. They watched her with unnerving intensity as they ate. Hadlay dropped her gaze to her platter and tried to focus on her meal.

The emperor spoke quietly to his guests in a language Hadlay did not know. Occasionally, she would hear a word that sounded familiar—*kakku* meant "weapons," *qulâ* she knew well, meant "burn," and *mêlulti passî* meant "game of pawns." She realized that they were speaking the language of the powers.

Zêru noticed her attention. "I am sorry you do not understand the discussion, Hadlay." He gestured to the men at the table. "Father was just explaining our plans for the conquest of the first of the Lands Beyond."

"Conquest?" The emperor had mentioned conquering before, but she had not given it much thought.

"Father and his ambassadors have spent these last many years preparing strongholds in all the lands. Now that we have the means to build our army, we will soon be ready to go out and conquer, until all the lands are ours, just as Turris is."

"Does this trouble you, human?" Ziz, one of the Nafalin asked. He watched her with piggy eyes as he ate, and he did not swallow before he spoke. Hadlay decided she did not much like him.

"*Does* it trouble you, Hadlay?" Zêru asked.

Hadlay gave a noncommittal shrug. "I only wonder why you must conquer them. Do the peoples of these other lands not wish to be ruled by your father?"

Zêru did not seem offended. "Most of them would accept him. But we do have enemies. A rival Lord has found allegiance among many in these lands. We must defeat him if we are to rule absolutely." He took a bite of his meat and spoke again once he had swallowed. "Now that we can build our army, we will soon be ready."

"Yes, thanks to you and your people." Anak grinned at Hadlay.

Hadlay returned his gaze blankly.

Ziz laughed. "She still does not realize, does she?"

Hadlay looked at Zêru. "What are they saying?"

Zêru shrugged. "You remember I told you that Father wanted to build an army of mixes, like the scorpion guards and horsemen and lion warriors?"

A chill entered the room. "Yes?"

"Well, in order to make these mixes, we need willing men to mix with the beasts. And we need others willing to feed them once they are mixed. Now, thanks to your words in the square, many Ramash have already sought out the collectors, asking to make their pledges of obedience. It will not be long before we have many scores of thousands ready to help us in our cause."

Hadlay stared at him in stunned silence for a moment. "You're going to take my people and . . ." She pushed back from the table, fearing she might vomit. She watched Zêru's face, thinking surely he would break into a grin at any moment. But if this was a joke, it wasn't very funny.

Zêru gave her a quizzical look. "You look troubled, Hadlay. If they agree, where is the harm?"

Hadlay wanted to shout at him, but she kept her voice even. "But they have not agreed to *this*, Zêru. They believe that they are agreeing to help you build barracks and work the farms to supply your army, even to become soldiers. But they have no idea that you plan to make beasts of them—to make food of them!"

Zêru shrugged, still looking confused. "Those who are mixed will not be harmed. They will be made better. They will be stronger laborers, faster messengers, more deadly and fearsome warriors on the battlefield. And those who feed them will not die, at least not so long as those feeding are careful not to take more than they should. Surely your people would be only too happy to give some blood in order to raise up a new N'de!" Hadlay stared at him. Perhaps Zêru, being accustomed to taking blood from a willing source, truly did not understand the offense of all this. She struggled to find a way to reason with him. "Zêru, you say they must be willing. But in order to truly be willing, they must understand what they're agreeing to. Let us tell them, at least. Then if they agree, you will truly have willing subjects to mix and to feed the mixes."

Zêru waved a hand. "They will take a pledge to obey us in all things—and they will give it willingly. That is all we need."

Hadlay rose to her feet. "They are agreeing to obey willingly because

I assured them that you have their best interests at heart! These are my people, Zêru! I thought you and your father cared for them—that you meant to make them equal!"

"She isn't very intelligent, is she?" Gibor spoke with a smirk on his face.

Ziz snorted. "None of them are. Even with the Refa muddling their minds, surely they had to see that all your changes did nothing but bring them harm."

"They blamed the Oresed for that," the emperor said. "That's why I raised up overlords and authorities like Asinus and his minions. Their hatred for the Ramash made certain that the Ramash would be made to pay dearly for every kindness we extended. But the people would think it was done against my will. In their increasing desperation, they will cling to me as their savior."

"Brilliant!" Pinim'e said.

Kasadya nodded. "Never underestimate the power of human emotion. Fear, hatred, hope—all these things can be molded to our purpose."

Hadlay stared at the emperor. "I spoke in your favor today—before all the people! You used me!"

Yeqon chuckled. "Ah, yes, pride—my favorite. Did you really think, little human, that you were anything but a tool in the emperor's hand to be used as he chose?"

Hadlay ignored him. "Please, Your Majesty. I love my people! Please do not do this terrible thing to them!"

"Even love is a fine tool," the emperor said, stroking his silky beard, "when directed properly." He rose and crooked a finger toward Hadlay. She felt herself being lifted, carried across the room, and set down at his feet. He placed his hand on her head, and she could feel the surge of power prickling through her body.

"Little one, you have a choice to make. You willingly pledged your unwavering obedience. The question now is how you will serve. If you continue in the course I have set for you, you will become princess of Turris. You will rule at Zêru's side. You will speak for me among your people and continue to deliver them to me and to my son. In exchange, your family will be preserved. I will give your parents a bride price—two thousand talents in gold. That is enough to purchase half of Turris. Your father will be made an overlord. And neither your parents nor any of your friends will be mixed or fed upon."

Hadlay glared at him. "All the Ramash are my friends."

The emperor chuckled. "I have always enjoyed your spirit. Even when Asinus had you pulled, when your friends were trembling and seeking escape, you threw up your arms to receive the chains with hatred in your eyes. I thought even then that you might be the one who would serve us best." His expression was almost sympathetic. "You cannot save all your people, Hadlay. But if you continue to obey me, I will spare those you love most dearly."

Hadlay lifted her chin in defiance. "I will never do your bidding again! You are wrong—you are *evil!*"

The emperor's eyes flamed. He made a fist, and Hadlay felt something cold encircle her neck, tightening slowly until she choked. It lifted her from the floor. Hadlay clawed at the hands that gripped her throat, but she could find nothing to take hold of, nothing to pry away.

"If you resist me, Hadlay, things will go very badly for you and those you love." He clapped his hands, and a messenger appeared. "Go and find Hadlay's young friend, Ma'at. Ask her if she would be willing to help feed the emperor's guests. When she agrees, tell her that Hadlay wishes her to come."

"No . . . please!" Hadlay whispered.

The emperor seemed not to hear her. "One by one, each of your friends will be brought here until you agree to do as I say. It is your choice, Hadlay."

Hadlay closed her eyes. How could she allow her friends to suffer again because of her? But if she chose to spare them, all their people would suffer! She kicked her feet, struggling to break free of the emperor's magical stranglehold.

The emperor made a fist again, and the grip tightened, shutting off all breath. "Let us talk about your family. Have you ever seen a camel spider? I will have Zêru mix your father with one." As he spoke, an image appeared before Hadlay of a tan spider as large as a child's head. Its tail was raised like a scorpion's, and its legs were covered in light hair. Its mandibles, huge and sharply pointed, promised a painful bite. Then it jumped at her. Hadlay jerked, trying to turn her face away as the image disintegrated. The emperor smiled. "Do you think your mother will enjoy feeding him her blood, once he's mixed?"

Everything was growing dim. But just as Hadlay was certain she would pass out, the grip on her throat released, and she fell to the floor, ragged breaths searing her lungs.

The emperor watched her struggle for air, his expression almost kind. "Well, little one? What have you to say?"

Hadlay rubbed her throat and coughed, using the wall to brace herself as she got back to her feet. Tears stung her eyes as she glared at the emperor. "I thought you were good," she rasped through her bruised throat. "I thought you were Meshah!"

A deafening snarl ripped through the room, like the sound of a thousand voices shrieking. Hadlay covered her ears. The Nafal and Nafalin had leaped to their feet. Those who had daggers drew them.

"Do not speak that name!" The emperor swept his hand across the table, and everything on it flew at Hadlay, striking her and covering her with blood-soaked food. She was flung against the wall with such force that her head cracked a tile. She hung there, pinned by hard, invisible hands.

Zêru stepped up before her, a look of annoyed frustration on his face. "You should not defy my father like this, Hadlay. It's a very stupid thing to do. We are the saviors of your people. They would perish under the Oresed oppression if not for this alliance you've helped us make."

"You will destroy my people with this so-called alliance!" she retorted. "You and your father are worse than monsters!"

For a moment, he actually looked hurt, but then he saw his friends laughing, and his eyes darkened. He advanced toward her, so close that she could feel his breath on her face as he spoke. "I would prefer that you cooperate with us, Hadlay," he said, his voice soft. "You are my friend, and I enjoy our fun together." Then he drew the curved knife at his belt. "But I will not object if you choose the other way. I have always wondered what your blood would taste like."

Hadlay struggled, but the hands that pinned her to the wall held fast.

Grinning, he put his knife to her neck, trailing the cold, sharp tip along her vein. She barely felt it at first, thought perhaps he was just threatening.

But hot blood pulsed from the wound, gushing down the front of her gown. The Nafalin hissed, watching like hungry dogs.

Hadlay grunted, straining against the growing pain. "No! I refuse to feed you!"

Zêru's eyes were black, terrible as the dungeon. "Do you think you can deny me? You pledged yourself to me this very day!" He dipped his finger in her blood and brought it to his tongue. "What did you think you were agreeing to, Hadlay?" He leaned in, his mouth closing over the open wound. Hadlay tried to wrench away, but the invisible hands kept her still.

She felt her strength drain quickly, flowing out of her with the blood. A terrible darkness closed in, dimming her sight. She shut her eyes, welcoming it. At least death would come quickly.

"*Simmasha tibbâ!*" Zêru whispered.

A new kind of pain consumed her, as if a thousand small needles pierced her skin, sewing the wound at her vein with a jagged stitch.

A hand caught her chin, and Zêru's eyes burned into hers. "Did you think you would find escape in death, Hadlay? Would you give yourself to the Refa so easily?"

"Better them than you!" She spat.

The Nafalin boys burst into raucous laughter.

"Does she really not know, Zêru?" Ziz asked. "By our fathers, she is an idiot!"

Zêru cocked his head, seeming bemused by her response. "What do you think the Refa are? What do you think I am?" The blackness of his eyes grew, expanding so that there was no light at all. "The Refa are what Nafalin become when we die, Hadlay. And I am their prince. You will never escape me, my princess. I will feed on your blood while you live, and I will feast on your soul when you die." His voice echoed all around her, battering her like a thousand fists.

A moment later, the messenger reappeared. He gave the emperor a deep bow. "The girl is outside, Your Majesty."

Hadlay opened her mouth to scream a warning, but the emperor made a fist again, and the hands were back at her throat, this time gripping so hard she thought they might wrench her head from her shoulders.

The emperor nodded, and the messenger flung the doors open.

As Ma'at entered, her eyes were focused on the emperor and his regal guests, and her face glowed with anticipation. Then she glanced around the room and saw Hadlay, and her cheeks went white. Hadlay mouthed the word "Run." The girl turned to bolt, but the doors slammed behind her. Ma'at screamed with terror as the Nafalin boys moved in on her.

Hadlay writhed and twisted, fighting the grip on her throat, desperately trying to break free. She saw a knife flash, opening a bloody gash at Ma'at's throat, and the Nafalin fell upon her. Ma'at screamed again, and Hadlay shuddered at the inhuman growling sounds the Nafalin made as they fed.

And then the emperor stood before her, blocking her view. "Shall I send for your friend Nomish next?"

Hadlay sobbed. It took all her strength to shake her head. The grip on her throat loosened, and she gasped, choking on the air that surged into her throat. She retched, then coughed, struggling to fill her lungs.

"You accept my terms, then?"

Broken, Hadlay nodded.

"Leave her, Zêru." The emperor grasped his son's shoulder. "Your mother's blood is enough for now."

Zêru retreated, wiping blood from his mouth with a sleeve. He grinned at Hadlay with red-stained teeth. "I'm glad you chose to obey, Hadlay. Think of the fun we'll have!" The unseen hands released her, and she collapsed to the floor.

"Well done, Emperor!" Azazel lifted his glass in a toast. "As you say. Love is a powerful tool."

Hadlay's eyes sought Ma'at. The Nafalin still crowded round her. There was blood on the walls and floor—too much blood—and the girl's feet hung limply. "Let Ma'at go. Please." The words rasped in her throat, and Hadlay coughed again.

"It is too late for her. She has gone to the Refa." As the emperor spoke, the Nafalin slowly drew away. Ma'at's body crumpled to the floor like a bloody rag.

"*No!*" Hadlay tried to rush to her friend, but she could not move.

"Let her death serve to remind you, Hadlay, of what will come to all those you love if you fail to keep your word." Shungallu gazed down at her with an eerie calm. "By now, you may have guessed that the powers—the

Igigi you summon to work magic in this Tower—are also called Refa. What you may not realize is that, when they agree to do your bidding, you place yourself in their debt. You give them the right to feed upon your living soul.

"You have worked a lot of magic here, Hadlay. Even now there are hundreds of Refa fixed to you like leeches. Nothing you do is secret. They are with you everywhere, and they hear and see everything. And while they may obey your commands for now, their allegiance is to me." He leaned down, speaking softly. "If you speak one word to anyone—if you try to warn someone or tell what happened here—the Refa will kill whomever you tell. And then they will report to me. And I will know you did not keep your part of our bargain. Do you understand?"

Hadlay could not look at him. But she nodded.

The emperor gripped her shoulder. "Enjoy becoming a princess, Hadlay. Enjoy seeing your family and your remaining friends thrive. Be the obedient bride of my son, and you and your loved ones will lack for nothing."

He flicked his hand at the doors, which hurled themselves open. "Good rest, child."

THE GUIDING TILES

Hadlay stumbled from the chamber, staggering past the scorpion guards and down the corridor until she rounded a turn that took her out of sight of the huge doors. Then she fell against the wall, her breath coming hard and fast. The image of Ma'at's lifeless body loomed in her mind, and she doubled over, heaving with such violence that her knees gave way.

When she was finally finished, she crawled to a corner and pulled herself into a tight ball, hugging her knees to stop the shaking. She felt numb, stunned like a beast in the slaughterhouse when the mallets failed to land a killing blow.

"Mistress?" The servant seemed to have appeared from nowhere. "Are you unwell?" The girl stepped delicately around the puddle of vomit, bending over Hadlay. "Shall I call for a physician?"

Hadlay pushed herself up. "No. I just . . ." She rubbed her eyes. "Ate too much . . ." The thought of the banquet made her stomach lurch again.

The girl watched her uncertainly. "Should I fetch attendants to carry you to your chamber?"

Her chamber. It seemed a lifetime ago that she had gaped in awe at the opulence, looked forward to sleeping in that massive bed. But how could she bathe and sleep in luxury, knowing what she had done? She could not go to the dormitories either. She could never face her friends, knowing what had happened to Ma'at, knowing what was in store for their families, not being able to warn them.

She dragged the gold headdress from her hair and threw it, heard the little dangling leaves jingle as they scattered across the floor. Still laughing. Still mocking her. It would have been better if Zêru had killed her. Without a word to the servant, she stumbled off. She did not know or care where she was going.

She had betrayed everyone she knew, everyone she loved. Ma'at was dead! Scores of her people had already pledged themselves to the emperor. When they learned the bargain she had made for their lives, even her parents would call her a traitor.

Where could she turn for help? The emperor was the most powerful person in all the lands—who could oppose him? Who would care enough for her people to even try? Who could ever make right all that she had done wrong?

A soft light began to glow, casting an eerie radiance. Hadlay hunched into the shadows, expecting to see someone coming up the corridor with a lamp. She did not want to speak to anyone. There was nothing she could say that could make a difference.

It took a long moment to realize that no one was coming. The light emanated from the guiding tiles. Their soft glow led away from her, down the long, dark corridor. Hadn't everyone said that the tiles did not work in the corridors near the royal chambers? She stared at them, wondering where they led. She had not thought of going anywhere, had she?

Perhaps she had. She wanted nothing more this moment than to find a place where no one would trouble her. Where she could have peace. Firming that thought in her mind, she followed the tiles.

They seemed to go on forever, winding round and round the Tower. Judging from the thick dust on the floor, which barely allowed the tile light through, she had entered a part of the Tower no one visited. She thought of stopping here but the tiles brightened and continued on, as if to tell her there was an even better place ahead. Hadlay followed.

Around the next corner, the tiles led straight up to an ancient wall. Unlike the rest of the Tower, this wall was made of stone, not brick. The guiding tiles disappeared beneath it. Hadlay stopped.

It should be dark here, since there were no lamps or torches, but it was not. The rocks themselves seemed to give a little light, so that Hadlay could see. The tiles lit again, coursing up to the wall and under it.

Hadlay stepped forward, wondering what she was meant to do. She could not go on, clearly. The wall was solid stone—or was it? On the far wall, some of the stones were framed by wood, as if there was a doorway there, perhaps concealed magically. She reached out and touched the stones within this frame.

The walls lit more brightly.

"Do you have the key?" The stones called out the question in ringing, musical tones, and the beams of the woodwork shivered.

Hadlay jumped away, startled. Then she glared at the stones. "I have had enough of magic, Refa! Leave me alone!"

"There are no Refa here," they answered. "Except the ones with you, and they are blind and deaf here."

What sort of trick was this? She turned to leave. But the hallway she had come down was no longer there. She turned all the way around, but the wall completely encircled her. She bent to examine the floor, looking for the trail she had left through the thick dust. It led to a wall and under it.

She rapped that wall with her fist.

The stones in the frame brightened again. "Do you have the key?"

Hadlay stilled. This was the room of her dreams—that strange, doorless room! And in each of her dreams, the Being had told her to seek a key. Shame gripped her as she remembered his rebukes. She had never made much of an effort.

Then again, why would she want to? She had come to believe in recent days that the dreams had been leading her to the emperor, and to Zêru. If that was so, why would she want to find their stupid key? If there were any way to make things worse, that would probably do it.

Hadlay sat on the floor. "If you are not going to let me leave, I may as well be comfortable. I wanted to be alone, anyway." It seemed odd to talk to a wall. But then, it had talked to her first.

She sat silent for some time, too numb to think clearly. It was strange to be sitting here in this room that she had seen in her dreams. This was real. And if this doorless room was real, then perhaps everything else she had seen in her dreams was real. Perhaps the Being was real!

The thought made her heart beat faster. She was still half-afraid that this was another trick of the emperor's, but she wanted to see this Being.

Because in her dreams, gazing at him had brought her greater joy than she had ever known. If the Being was real, something inside her said that he could not possibly be evil. If he was real, she wanted more than anything to know him.

The one thing that was missing in this room that she had seen in her dream was the mirror, and that was where the Being had appeared. The framed stones seemed to be about where the mirror should be. She reached out and touched the wall once more.

"Do you have the key?"

"I'm sorry, I don't," she replied. "Could you tell me where to look for it?"

The stones glimmered. "If it is to be found, you will find it within."

"Within what?" Hadlay looked around. "Within this room?" All she could see in this room were the stone walls and floor. She ran her hand over the dust, but it was not so thick it could conceal anything like a key.

"Seek within yourself," the wall said.

Frowning, she wrapped her arms around her legs, perching her chin on her knee. What had the Being said to her? If she could remember his messages, maybe they would tell her how to find the key.

The dreams began replaying in her mind, as clear as if she had just awakened. The first one's message said, *On this day, your laughter will give way to dread. When this takes place, you will begin to grasp the key.* Had she seen a key that day, when Asinus had caught her and her friends laughing at Ba'ar? She did not remember one.

She sighed, turning her thoughts to the second dream: *On this day you will hear words you long to hear, a promise as good as the one who makes it.* Well, that had proven true. The emperor was not good, and neither was his promise!

What else had the Being said? *What you fear most this morning will seem trifling by midday; you will face a trial you did not expect. Recall my words and you will not see its end. By this you will begin to grasp the key.* Had she seen a key then, when the purgation they had feared had turned into an Oresed riot that had nearly killed them? Nowhere in her memory of that day did she recall a key!

What of the third, then? In this dream, the Being had begun giving warnings. *Seek the key, little love, for if you refuse it, you will know only destruction*. Well, the course she had taken certainly ended in destruction! But how had she refused the key?

With growing urgency, she concentrated on remembering the rest of the message: *On this day, you will fail in the task that you set yourself to accomplish. When you see that my words are true, you will begin to grasp the key.* he had believed at first that this prediction had proven false. After all, she had been given a task by the emperor, and she had passed. But then she'd realized that by the end of the emperor's test, she had meant to disqualify herself. And in that, she had indeed failed.

The night she had made that realization, the Being had told her that she had come close to rejecting the key, but now she had returned. What had changed? How had she nearly rejected the key? How had she returned? She tried to remember all the events of that day, but she could not recall seeing a key, let alone rejecting it. Frustrated, she rapped her knuckles against her forehead. "Think!"

She wished Nomish were here to help her solve the puzzle. He was so much wiser than she was. But Nomish was no longer her friend. None of the Rakams were friends anymore. No one would be, when they realized what she had done. A tear slid down her cheek. If everyone she loved hated her, did it matter if she was bound for destruction? Maybe she should just stay here in this doorless room until she starved.

If only it were just her! But her people would be destroyed as well—and it would be her fault. Even if they all hated her, how could she bear to let them suffer?

She sniffled. "I'm sorry . . . so very sorry." The words seemed useless. "Sorry" could not begin to repair the harm she had done.

The stones flickered. "Remorse is not the key."

Hadlay turned her mind back to the problem. In the next of her dreams, the Being had said, *A choice is coming, two ways to help your people. One will seem a blessing but be a curse. And one will seem to bring great danger, but there is no loss you could suffer that could surpass the reward.*

Well, she had certainly found the first way—and it had seemed a blessing but had turned out to be a curse. So what was the other choice, the other way to help her people? Did this mean that, if she found the key, she could not only save herself, but her people too?

She pushed herself to her feet and began to pace. If the key was a solution, she needed to find it. "Help me, wall! What is this key?"

"You nearly know," the stones replied.

Hadlay wished she could slap them without hurting herself. "What do I nearly know?" All these accursed puzzles!

There was no reply. Scowling, she turned her thoughts to the last of her dreams.

Choose me, as I have chosen you. Choose the path back to N'de . . .

She had thought that the emperor had brought that path. He had spoken of making Turris rival N'de. But the Being had said she should choose the path *back* to N'de. Not to a rival N'de, but the first. Was the key a way for her people to escape Turris and its evil emperor, a way for them to go to N'de? She paced some more, repeating the dreams again in her mind, testing every word. But there were no clues that would lead her to any kind of key.

She flopped down on the floor again, stirring up a cloud of dust that made her throat itch. It was no use. All she knew was that everything the Being had said to her was true. She could trust that, couldn't she? Even if she trusted nothing else?

The stones in the frame began to change. They grew brighter and smoother, until soon they were so smooth and clear they looked like still water. In a moment, they became a mirror.

Hadlay gasped at the sight of herself. A dried brownish crust of blood smeared down her face, and her lovely ivory gown was a filthy rag, blood-stained and mottled with dirt. A terrible, jagged wound snaked down her neck, which was encircled by darkening bruises. Worse, there were horrible, black *things* crawling all over her, like monstrous insects. Only they had faces. Faces very like Zêru's. She sobbed as she clawed at them, trying to pry them away, but her hands passed right through them, and her fingernails left red welts on her arms.

Then her image dissolved, and in its place, a majestic white horse appeared in the mirror—only he was not a horse. His body was luminous, traced with every color she had ever seen. His mane was silken, and every fine strand seemed to glow with its own light. Where other horses' eyes were dark, his were bright as the sun, and lined with the whitest lashes.

He had wings of pure flame, blazing, glorious gold light. His hooves were silver, and she could hear their crisp click against the stones on his side of the mirror. And on his forehead, three gold rings intertwined.

A silvery tear traced down his face as he looked at her, as if he could see the pain she was in, the pain she had caused, and his heart was broken.

Hadlay was filled with a burning sense of awe—and dismay. She flung herself to the floor, covering her head with her arms. "Please do not look at me! I cannot bear it!"

The sound of his hooves drew nearer, causing her to tremble. "You are still my beloved." The Being brought his nose down near her face and nudged the mirror. The surface rippled like water. He stretched out his wings and fanned her gently.

Hadlay could not stop crying. The sobs that racked her body seemed to pour out all her pain and grief as the warm wind from his wings enfolded her like the arms of a loving father. A sense of peace filled her, and with it a joy unlike anything she had ever known.

"Remain here with me, beloved. Rest."

THE CHOICE

She did not know how long she slept, but when she woke again, she was stretched out upon the floor. Though she had rested on stones, she felt more refreshed than if she had slept upon the softest bed.

She looked up to find the Being still standing before her in the mirror. His colors brightened as she met his gaze. "Have you had enough of doing things your way, little love?" he asked in a whispery voice. "Will you let me guide you?"

She brushed the dampness from her lashes, pushing herself up to stand before him. "What would you have me do?"

"You must renounce the emperor and his son."

Hadlay bowed her head, remembering the Refa that were attached to her and the emperor's warning. "I cannot speak of this with you. If I do, the Refa will kill you—and the emperor and Zêru will destroy my family!"

The Being's gaze was steady. "They will destroy you and your family either way, Hadlay. You know this."

Once again, the Being spoke the truth. She could turn away, be princess of Turris. She could take her revenge on the Oresed and wear those fine gowns and jewels. She could see her father become an overlord, her mother dressed in fine jewels. But though they would live in luxury, they would suffer. They would watch in horror as their people entered living death. They would become infested, just as she was, with these Refa, who would drain their souls and devour them when they died. And she knew, too, that even if Zêru abstained from taking her blood again for a time, he would not do so forever. There was no escape from him—not even in death.

271

She shuddered. "Can you save my family—my people?"

The Being's voice was grave. "Those who receive the key will be saved. But they must choose. I cannot make the choice for them. Or for you. You have begun to grasp the key, but you have not received it fully. And without it, you will only know what you have seen."

"What of the emperor? He will know soon—if he does not know already—that I am with you!"

His colors intensified. "He will know. But at this moment what matters is that you make your choice. Will you renounce the emperor and follow me?" His glowing eyes fixed her with a gaze that seemed to penetrate the deepest part of her soul. "I have chosen you, Hadlay. I loved you before you were conceived. But now you must choose me—or turn away. Which will you do?"

Hadlay hesitated. She had certainly been fooled before, trusted unwisely. But how could she reject him? Whatever he was, she loved him—she felt she had been born loving him. Even when she had sought favor with the emperor and Zêru, in her heart she had hoped that she was following this Being. And that was her answer. Even though she was terrified of the price, even though she was certain that the emperor would pour out his wrath upon her and all she loved, she knew she could never turn away from this Being. She could never wound him in that way.

No matter the cost, she had to follow him.

But how could he want her? She remembered the image she had seen in the mirror, how hideous she had looked, filthy and covered with blood—and Refa. She shuddered. "Please, let me go and cleanse myself first, and I will return and give you my allegiance."

The Being's eyes pierced the depths of her soul. "Do you think you could wash away all that offends me in a scented basin?"

Tears sprang to her eyes as his meaning struck her. The purest water could not wash away the fact that she had chosen—out of hatred, bitterness, and lust for power; out of her own selfish concerns—to deliver her people to the emperor.

His colors warmed. "You have helped to mislead them, Hadlay, but they make their own choices. Some will choose the emperor's way, hoping for riches and power and ease. But you must choose now, for yourself. If you will let me guide you, I will show you how to reveal the truth to those who are willing to see it."

A delicate seedling of hope sprang up in Hadlay's heart. She knew now what she must do. She bowed her head. "Wherever you lead, I will follow. I am yours."

He fanned his wings. "You will suffer, Hadlay. You will pay a price for choosing me."

A price? What more could she possibly lose? The answers—her parents and others she loved—nearly made her turn away. But she could not bear to do so. Hadlay stretched out her hand, touching the surface of the mirror where his nose had been. "I would suffer more if I turned away from you. You have chosen me. Now I choose you."

The stone walls glowed again, even brighter than before. His voice was warm and rich when he spoke again. "I have longed to hear you speak those words."

He touched the mirror where her hand rested, and Hadlay gasped as she felt the pressure of his nose through the surface. His nose emerged, then his head. As she watched, he stepped all the way through the mirror and stood before her, silvery and shining.

The mirror itself was now only an empty frame. The Being spread his flaming wings, and the heat of them filled the room with a golden glow. Hadlay fell to her knees. For a long moment, she could do nothing but gaze at him in awe.

He nudged her, and she felt his breath against her cheek. A soft, tingling warmth enveloped her, like being drenched in a desert rain. Tears coursed down her cheeks, though she was laughing like a child. She saw a terrible, bleeding cut appear on his neck, ringed with vivid bruises. The wounds dissolved before her eyes.

After a moment, the Being stepped back. "Now, see yourself." He held up a wing, and it smoothed to reflect her image.

Hadlay drew in a sharp breath. The cut on her neck was gone, as were the bruises. Her gown, where it had been soiled and scarlet with blood, was now white as snow. Even her hair was clean and shining like polished gold. The Refa—all of them—were gone! She gazed at him in wonder. "And N'de—it is real?"

He bobbed his head. "More real than Turris."

"Are you . . ." She hesitated to speak the name.

"Meshah?" At the sound of the name, the wall began to hum the most beautiful song Hadlay had ever heard.

He pranced, his silver hooves flashing in the light. "I am not, yet we are one. I am the Atheling. He has sent me to call his people home to N'de. Those who will come."

"Will you tell me your name?"

The Being stepped forward, drawing her against his chest and enfolding her in his wings. Even in her own father's arms, Hadlay had never felt so loved, so safe.

"I am Sirach."

SIRACH

Sirach.

Hadlay felt as though she had known the name all her life, as though it was the first name she had ever heard. "Will you tell me about N'de?"

Sirach lay on the floor, with Hadlay sitting curled against his shoulder. They had been many hours like this, resting and speaking freely to each other.

"I will show you one thing. Behold." Sirach blew out his breath, and the room around them dissolved. They were in a garden, surrounded by beautiful trees and flowers of every kind. They were very like the flowers she knew, but their colors were so clear and pure they almost seemed to be made of crystal. A breeze tickled their petals, and the sound was like delicate bells chiming. The breeze was laden with a fragrance sweeter than any fruit or flower Hadlay had ever known. She knew she would remember this scent for as long as she lived.

"They gleam so brightly—like jewels!" Hadlay held up the ring she had chosen, the one with the brilliant red stone. By comparison to the crystal flowers, it was dull and dark. She cast the ring aside. It was the finest thing she had ever touched, but she no longer wanted anything that came from Zêru or the emperor.

The garden vanished, replaced again by the stone walls in the Tower.

Hadlay turned to Sirach. "Is there more? I want to see it all!"

Sirach shook his head. "There is more to N'de—things more wondrous than you could imagine. But if I showed you now, you would long for them."

"I already do. Can't we go there now?"

"Would you leave all those you care for in the emperor's grasp?"

She bit her lip. She was being selfish again. "No."

"You have answered well, little love. There is much yet for us to do here. Are you ready to begin?"

Hadlay hesitated. The idea of leaving this place and going out again into the Tower frightened her. She had no idea how long she had been here, nor did she know what had happened to the Refa that had infested her. Had they gone to the emperor, warned him, so that he would be waiting for her when the walls opened?

Sirach shook his mane. "Do not fear the emperor or his powers, Hadlay. They have only the authority you give them. You will come to understand as you are tested."

Hadlay did not like the sound of that. "Tested?"

"Your grasp upon the key cannot become firm unless it is tested. But do not fear. You will not be given more than you can bear. Cling to what you have now, and all will be well."

"I do not understand. What am I to cling to?"

"What did you have when the portal opened for you?"

Hadlay's teeth gritted. Why did he force her to deal in puzzles?

The Being's whickering laughter danced around her. "It would be a riddle even if I told you plainly, child. You will never understand until you understand. Now, what did you have when you entered this room?"

It seemed wrong to be irritated with him, but Hadlay could not help it. "I don't know! All I knew at that moment was that I believed what you said."

His colors shifted to the shades of a sunrise. "That is the key! It is all you need. Are you willing to begin?"

She was still confused, but she took a deep breath and nodded.

"Then your work begins in the gong farm."

Hadlay studied him. Did Sirach mean for her to labor in that terrible filth?

Sirach's gaze seemed to pierce her thoughts. "I do mean for you to work there, but not in the way you expect. You will find a problem there—one that not even the emperor could solve. Bring it to me."

A part of the wall began to shimmer, and Hadlay saw a portal open. She got to her feet.

Sirach rose as well, moving to stand before her. "You will be tested as soon as you leave this room. But cling to what you have, beloved, and all will be well."

THE MAZE

Hadlay made her way down the darkened corridors, following the guiding tiles. How long had she been with Sirach? It seemed as though she had remained with him for many hours. But it was still dark, still night. Or had she been with him a full day and this was another night?

Had the emperor missed her? What if he'd assumed that she had run away? Had he summoned her parents and harmed them while she rested with Sirach in that doorless room?

She stopped short. What if she had only dreamed it all? Was Sirach real? What if she had been driven mad by the terror of last evening's events?

Blinking back tears, Hadlay forced herself onward, though each step grew heavier. Weariness overtook her, dragging her down, so that she wanted nothing more than to just stop and rest.

Why was she doing this? It had all seemed real to her just moments ago, but now, in the long corridors of the Tower, she was not so certain. Her dreams had always seemed real. And then she would wake, and everything in Turris would be the same.

The tiles wound endlessly through the Tower until Hadlay began to believe that they were leading her in circles. What if the tiles could no longer be trusted?

Still, Hadlay pressed on. She had to follow the tiles, she realized, because without them she would be hopelessly lost. Likewise, she decided to continue to trust Sirach, because without him there was no hope for her or her people.

As she thought these things, the tiles grew brighter.

Hadlay stopped. The darkness that had seemed to surround her—the fear and confusion she had been feeling—she knew those things. She had felt them in the dungeon, and again last evening in Zêru's presence. These things came from the Refa! Were they trying to cling to her once more?

Well, she would not listen to them—never again!

With renewed determination, she pressed on, following the tiles. She would go wherever they led, turning this way, then that, no matter how long it took. They had never let her down before. Neither had Sirach. She refused to doubt them now.

Sirach had told her that she would be tested. Was this what he was warning her about? He had told her to cling to what she had, and all she had was her belief in him.

As she rounded yet another bend, and was greeted with another long, dark, winding hall, a new thought struck her. If N'de was real—if Meshah was real—then the maze must be real as well! And if she had found the Mirror in these corridors, then the Tower itself must be the maze!

She had to smile. All these generations, her people had told their children this legend—this *fable*—not believing that it was real. So many ages ago, the emperor had brought the Oresed to conquer this land, take the maze, and build upon it, making it more and more confusing, hoping to bury its secrets. But he could not keep the tiles from guiding her to Sirach. He could not keep Meshah's promise from being fulfilled. The riddle was real—its solution was the key, and she had found it! She trusted in Sirach!

Catching up her skirt, she began to run.

THE GONG FARM

It was your fault!"

"No, it wasn't!"

The argument reached Hadlay before she passed through the doorway into the great foyer at the entry to the Tower. Nomish was there, along with Rasab. They were arguing with three Oresed boys.

One Oresed boy jabbed a finger at Rasab. "You threw the first punch!"

"You pushed me!"

Nomish stepped between them. "It's bad enough that Sfika has ordered us to work in the gong farm before morning meal every day this week. She'll do worse if we fight again."

"You should not have stepped on my toe!" the Oresed boy said.

"I did not know you were standing behind me!" Nomish stilled and took a deep breath. "Let's just get to work."

One of the Oresed boys saw Hadlay as she crossed through the large entrance hall. He broke off and bowed, though his eyes glittered with resentment. Seeing her, the others went silent and bowed as well. Nomish avoided her eyes as he did so, his jaw tight as if he were gritting his teeth.

Hadlay stepped up to them. "What is the trouble?"

No one spoke at first. The Oresed boys glowered as though they expected her to take sides with the Ramash, and Nomish stared at the floor, his lips set in a severe line.

Finally, Rasab stepped forward. "It is unimportant, Mistress Hadlay. Do not concern yourself."

"That *remesh*—" One of the Oresed boys blurted the word, then checked himself, casting an anxious look at Hadlay. "That thug Kayshti struck me!"

"He was worried about his sister," Rasab said, turning to Hadlay. "Ma'at did not return to the dormitories last evening. She was summoned to the royal chambers—they said you wished for her to come. Do you know where she is?"

Hadlay felt the color draining from her face as the memory of Ma'at's last moments returned vividly to her mind. She rubbed her throat, feeling the grip around her neck again. "K-Kayshti . . ." the name slipped out in a whisper. "Where is he?"

"He went ahead to the gong farm, mistress."

This must be the problem Sirach had sent her to deal with. Hadlay spun and hurried toward the doors. She had no idea what she would say to Kayshti. She knew it was not safe to tell him everything, but she had to get to him, persuade him to follow her back to the hidden room. To Sirach.

Rasab scrambled to open the doors for her. "Where are you going, Hadlay?"

"To the gong farm!"

"The gong farm?" His brow puckered. "If you need something—er—if you want something—uh—if there is something I can do for you there, mistress, I would be happy to. You should not go yourself!"

Hadlay ignored him, continuing down the long stairway. A moment later, she heard the clatter of sandals as Rasab hurried after her. She glanced back and saw Nomish following some distance behind. The Oresed boys remained where she'd left them.

She hiked up the skirt of her gown and raced across the courtyard, then down, through the dark entry and into the stinking depths beneath the Tower.

"At least let me precede you, mistress. I can try to cleanse your path." Rasab rushed ahead of her, kicking away debris that had splashed up onto the catwalk.

Hadlay had not gone far when she found Kayshti, and she realized she would not have to tell him anything. He was on his knees in the sludge, sobbing over something half covered in rotting vegetables. The only thing visible through the waste was a face, with lifeless eyes that stared at Hadlay in accusation.

Hadlay stumbled, throwing a hand over her mouth to hold back the wave of sickness that threatened to overcome her.

When the Nafalin had finished, they had dumped Ma'at's body into the chute with the garbage.

THE MESSAGE

Nomish and Rasab launched themselves off the catwalk and waded to Kayshti. Nomish cleared the debris from Ma'at's upper body, feeling for her pulse. He stopped when he saw the gaping, bloody slash across her throat.

Recovering from her shock, Hadlay climbed down from the catwalk and made her way over, dropping to her knees in the muck beside the body.

Ma'at's eyes stared vacantly into the air, her mouth open as if to scream. Hadlay remembered the horrible noises she had heard as the Nafalin had attacked, and she shuddered. Now her friend looked like a broken doll. She reached out to smooth the girl's hair back from her face.

Nomish snatched Hadlay's hand away. He glared into her eyes. "You summoned her! You must know what happened to her!"

The rage and accusation in his voice shook Hadlay, reminding her of her guilt. But she remembered Sirach's instruction. *You will find a problem there—one not even the emperor could solve. Bring it to me.*

She tugged on Nomish's hand. "Come with me—all of you! Bring Ma'at!" Somehow, she sensed that she should not explain further. Sirach had dispensed with the Refa that had infested her, but her friends had worked their share of magic too. No doubt more Refa clung to them and would do them harm if she said too much. She had to get her friends to come, but without saying why.

Nomish pulled his hand away. "I am not going anywhere with you." He turned back to the body. "And Ma'at is staying with us. We need to bury her."

"No!" Hadlay sloshed around to face him again. "Please—this is more important than you can imagine."

Nomish would not look at her, so Hadlay turned to Kayshti. "Please, Kayshti. I can't explain, but Ma'at needs to come and so do you."

Rasab gripped Kayshti's shoulder. "I know you are suffering, but Hadlay is our friend, and she has done much for our people. We should do as she says. I will carry Ma'at." Rasab was not a large boy, but he lifted Ma'at's slight body without strain. Ma'at had been lying there long enough that her body barely sagged as he held her. He turned to Hadlay. "You lead. I will follow."

The Oresed boys had arrived and were standing above them on the catwalk, sniggering at the sight of Hadlay in a mound of dung. They went silent when they saw Ma'at's body, and they stepped back from the ladder to allow Hadlay to climb up. Kayshti followed, his eyes vacant. Hadlay helped him lift Ma'at's body so Rasab could climb up.

But Nomish hung back, staying in the muck where the body had been. Hadlay wanted to shrink from the fury in his gaze.

"Come on, Nomish!" Kayshti called.

He shook his head, turning away. "I have work to do. Call me when you are ready to bury your sister."

"Please, Nomish!" Hadlay stared after him. But he continued walking deeper into the trenches.

Rasab touched her arm. "Hadlay, he was very hurt when you accepted the prince's proposal. I think he understands you had no choice. But he is still in pain."

"You can command him to come," one of the Oresed suggested. "You are an authority now that you are betrothed to His Highness."

Hadlay was tempted. But she did not want to use that power—or any power conferred by the emperor—even for good.

Nomish sent her one last, scathing look before taking up a shovel and setting to work.

She gestured to Kayshti and Rasab. "Follow me."

A small group of servants were clustered in the main hall, gaping at the sight of the prince's betrothed entering the Tower soaked in muck. Then they saw Ma'at's body and gasped with shock.

"We must hurry," Hadlay whispered to her friends. "Word of this will spread quickly, and someone might try to interfere."

The boys fell in behind her, walking abreast with their arms beneath Ma'at's body.

The journey was not as difficult as Hadlay expected. They rounded only a few bends, and then they were there, just as the morning horn sounded. It was as if the tiles understood the need for hurry and found a shortcut.

"Do you hold the key?" The walls resounded with the question. Kayshti and Rasab went pale. They were probably not used to hearing a wall speak.

"I trust in Sirach," Hadlay said with confidence. The wall opened, revealing the doorless room.

The boys stood frozen, their jaws agape, as they beheld Sirach in all his glory.

"What— Who—" Kayshti looked as though he might drop his sister, so Hadlay hurried over to help her friends put the girl down. Sirach stepped closer, dropping his nose to Ma'at's stiff body.

The boys pulled back, their faces white.

Hadlay remained kneeling beside the body. She touched Sirach's neck. "Is this what you wanted me to do?"

His colors warmed as he looked at her. "It is, beloved." Turning his attention back to Ma'at's body, he nudged her shoulder. "Wake, little one."

"She's not sleeping, sir," Rasab said. "She's—" His eyes widened as a glow transferred from Sirach's nose to Ma'at's shoulder, spreading over her until she was fully clothed in light. Her body rose from the floor and floated.

"Wake, dear Ma'at," Sirach commanded again.

Hadlay's breath caught as Ma'at's hands, once clenched in death, loosened, and her stiffened body relaxed. Her eyes had closed, and she seemed now to be sleeping, just as Sirach had suggested. The wound at her neck appeared on Sirach, and vanished just as quickly. Then Ma'at blinked and tried to sit up. She drifted, still glowing, to the floor and rested gently.

A loud grunt came from Kayshti. "She's . . ."

"Come and see," Sirach said.

The boys moved closer, then Kayshti fell to his knees beside his sister, weeping.

Ma'at's eyes fixed on Hadlay. "Was I dreaming? Those boys, they—" Her face paled at the memory.

Hadlay pressed in near to her friend, stroking her hair. "It was real, Ma'at. But you are safe now. Sirach has brought you back."

Ma'at's eyes drifted to the magnificent Being who still stood over her. "You! I dreamed of you when I was a child!"

Sirach nodded. "I dreamed of you as well, sweet girl."

With a glad cry, Ma'at flung her arms around his neck.

THE HARD TRUTHS

At Sirach's urging, Hadlay told the others about the emperor's intentions for their people.

Rasab paled. "My father gave his pledge right away—before we even left the square! How can we stop this?"

Tears slipped from Sirach's eyes.

"It is too late," Rasab whispered. "He has already been mixed, hasn't he?"

Sirach bobbed his head.

"No!" Hadlay put a hand on Rasab's arm. "There must be something we can do. If we brought him here . . ."

"He rejected the key. I cannot help him."

"But he did not have all the information!" Rasab protested. "He was deceived!"

Sirach gazed at the boy. "He had many opportunities to receive the key, just as you've had. But he rejected me when he made his covenant with the emperor. He knew in his heart that he was doing so."

"But . . ." Hadlay hesitated. "I made a covenant with Shungallu too—a far worse one than Rasab's father did. Why am I here with you, if he cannot be?"

Sirach's eyes glowed. "You never stopped seeking me, Hadlay, even when you tried to deny your dreams, and even when you bound yourself to the emperor and his son. You always hoped that the things you did would lead you to me."

Watching Rasab cry, Hadlay was overcome with guilt. "This is my fault. I led my people to this evil."

Sirach folded her under his wing. "No one will be lost who did not knowingly reject me, dearest."

"The emperor deceived us all, Hadlay." Kayshti sat with his arm around Ma'at, leaning against Sirach's flank. "I told my family I thought he might be Meshah!"

Ma'at's eyes grew round. "He must be Lelyeh! The Khalam that hated Mada!" She turned to Sirach. "He is, isn't he?"

Sirach nickered. "Now you see."

"I should have known it." Hadlay shuddered, remembering the violent reaction both times she had mentioned Meshah's name.

"The Refa blinded you," Sirach said.

A new concern occurred to Hadlay. "Where did the Refa go when you removed them from us? Have they warned the emperor you are here?"

"They will not trouble anyone again. But very soon the emperor will know that I am here. He will come here to destroy me."

She sprang to her feet. "Then we must leave this place! We must find a way to hide you before he comes!"

Sirach did not move. "I will face him. This chamber is the place between Turris and N'de, between time and infinity. This world belongs to the emperor, and I cannot enter it unless he himself releases me." He stretched out his neck and pulled Rasab in. The boy fell against his chest, still crying. Sirach's eyes gleamed with unshed tears.

"The emperor will never let you enter Turris—not if he knows that you are sent by Meshah." Hadlay paced, anxious. "He will come here and kill you. Or worse—turn you into one of his creatures."

"He will try to do those things."

"What is your plan?" Kayshti asked. "Do you have an army prepared for war?"

"I came alone. I am sufficient."

"But how can you defeat him if he can keep you in this room?"

"He will defeat himself. He has already begun by bringing you to the Tower."

Sirach seemed so certain that Hadlay smiled. "Then what must we do before he comes?"

"Go to the kitchen and eat. You will see some of your friends. Bring them here, but speak with care."

Kayshti rose and helped his sister to her feet. Then he held out a hand for Rasab. "Are you ready?"

Sirach nickered. "Let him remain with me."

Rasab pulled away from Sirach. "No. I will go."

Tears traced down Sirach's face. "It is your choice."

Rasab, still sniffling, accepted Kayshti's hand and rose.

THE WALLS HAVE EARS

Rasab broke down crying again, and ran off shortly after they left Sirach. Hadlay and the others decided to let him go. He probably needed to be alone.

Just inside the kitchen, Kayshti stopped short. Hadlay and Ma'at, walking behind, ran into him.

"How long were we with Sirach?" Kayshti whispered.

"Many hours," Ma'at said.

"Then why are the others just leaving the morning meal?"

Hadlay looked beyond him. Most of the initiates had apparently gone on to their day's business, but a few were still clearing the tables, sending platters and knives off to the scullery. From the look of it, the meal had been fresh fruit and bread.

"It seems time is different with Sirach," Hadlay said. *Between time and infinity,* he had said. She did not understand it, but it seemed that hours spent in the chamber were only moments in the Tower.

"Come in, you three!" Magira called from the ovens. "I just pulled out a fresh loaf." She carried it over to the counter, then turned to Hadlay. "I had planned to bring something up to your chamber, but if you prefer to eat with your friends, sit down."

The initiates who had been clearing stopped their work and bowed.

"Don't—I don't want you to bow," Hadlay stammered. "Go back to your business."

Magira gave Hadlay an approving wink. "I knew you would never stand on ceremony. No more than your betrothed."

"He's not—"

Kayshti elbowed Hadlay, silencing her protest. "Those loaves smell wonderful, Magira! Let me fill a platter for you, Hadlay."

A sharp gasp came from the direction of the scullery, followed by the sound of platters dropping to the floor. Hadlay whirled to find an Oresed boy standing in the doorway, staring at Ma'at. Hadlay recognized him as one of the boys who had been in the gong farm.

Ba'ar came in from the scullery and glared at him. "Clumsy oaf! Now look what you've done!"

"That girl— I saw her dead this very morn! Her throat was slashed to the bone!"

"Yet here she stands." Ba'ar gave the boy a scornful look.

The boy glared at Ba'ar. "I know what I saw! She's a shade, then! Look how bright her tunic is."

Indeed, Ma'at's tunic, once stained with blood and rot from the gong farm, now shone white as snow. Apparently, this had happened when they were with Sirach.

"Enlil's earwax! She's no shade." Magira walked over and gave Ma'at's arm a squeeze. "You see? She's as real as I am."

Red-faced, the Oresed boy bent to clear the mess he'd made. Ba'ar scoffed once more, then made her way back to the Oresed table to collect more platters.

Hadlay crossed to the Ramash table where Fa'an and Aa'mash directed damp cloths to wipe down the wood surface. She shuddered, thinking of the dark and hideous things that did this work, and kept her distance from them. "Where's Nomish?"

"He said he wasn't hungry." Fa'an paused. "I hope you don't mind that our parents have made a match for us. Since you accepted the prince."

Hadlay did mind, but she was not upset with Fa'an. Mostly, at this moment, she was concerned that Nomish come to meet with Sirach. But she doubted he would agree to anything she asked.

"I will find him after we eat." Kayshti filled three platters with fruit. "He'll come if I have to drag him."

"Come where?" Fa'an asked, suspicion dawning on her face.

Hadlay hastened to allay her concerns. "We want you to come as well."

"There's no need to carry all that, boy," Magira said to Kayshti, who was headed for the table, balancing the platters on his arms. "Just summon the powers!"

Kayshti blanched, then managed an apologetic smile as he hurried to the table, still carrying the platters. "I . . . I keep forgetting . . ." "The word you need is *bil!*" Magira told him. "Let's hear you say it."

Kayshti hurriedly stuffed his mouth with bread, then gave Magira a foolish grin, pointing to his puffed-out cheeks. "Deliciouf!" Magira smiled and returned to her labors.

Hadlay's stomach rumbled. It felt as though she had not eaten for days. She took a bite of bread, then turned back to Fa'an and Aa'mash. "When we finish our meal, Ma'at and I would like to show you something." She wanted to invite Magira as well, but something told her that the emperor would be alerted if she did so.

The girls nodded, returning to their work. The cloths continued wiping, moving to the Oresed table where Ba'ar was stacking the last of the platters. Fa'an directed one of the cloths to go after a stain on the wall.

"That was close," Ma'at whispered to her brother. "What if Magira had demanded that you command the powers?"

He glanced over his shoulder to make sure Magira was still at the counter. "Now that I know what they are, I want nothing more to do with them."

Hadlay tapped the table and nodded toward one of the cleaning cloths that had stopped its work and now drifted toward them. As they looked, it went back to its work, scrubbing hard at the stain on the wall. Finished, it drifted off to the scullery. Hadlay glanced back to see where the other cloth was working, and found Ba'ar watching them.

Hadlay turned back to her food, exchanging a stealthy glance with her friends. They would have to be much more careful.

NONE SO BLIND

What do you mean, 'He's right here'?" Fa'an stood in the center of the hidden room, staring past Sirach as if he were not there. "There's no one here besides us!"

Hadlay exchanged a glance with Ma'at, who looked as confused as she felt.

"She will only see me if she wishes to," Sirach explained.

"What can we do to persuade her?" Ma'at asked.

"Who are you speaking to?" Fa'an scowled, impatient. "I swear you have all lost your minds!"

Sirach struck the floor with a silver hoof. "Tell her that when she visited her home, she used the powers to make her brother spill the kettle so that she would not have to eat rat stew."

Hadlay repeated what Sirach had said.

Fa'an paled as she stared at Hadlay. "Nobody knew that was my doing! Are you like the emperor now? Do you know what we say and do?"

"I'm nothing like the emperor!" Hadlay said indignantly. "And neither is Sirach!"

"Tell Aa'mash that it is my voice she sometimes hears whispering in her dreams," Sirach said.

Hadlay did as she was told, then turned to Sirach. "I see you have been visiting the dreams of many of my people. I thought I was specially chosen."

Sirach brushed her cheek with his nose. "Don't be jealous. Everyone has dreamed of me, and I of them, though not all dreamed of the riddle. I would that everyone would heed my call. But no one could replace you in my heart."

"Did he just say you were jealous?" Aa'mash asked.

"Do you hear him now?" Ma'at asked.

"You are beginning to grasp the key, dear one." Sirach spoke to Aa'mash directly.

"I see him! Oh! He is so beautiful!" She reached out and touched his neck, then burst into tears.

Fa'an studied her friend with a perplexed frown. "Are you drugged? What has come over you?"

A scuffle outside caught their attention.

"Don't push me!" Nomish stumbled through the portal, with Kayshti close behind, twisting his arm.

"Let him go," Sirach said. "You cannot force your friends to know me. This one will come to me in his own time, if he wishes."

Kayshti released Nomish. "I'm sorry, Sirach. I did not understand."

"Who are you talking to?" Nomish glared at Kayshti. Then he saw Fa'an. "Why are you here with *her*?" He jerked his head at Hadlay.

Fa'an scowled at him. "Was I supposed to refuse the prince's betrothed?"

"Well, if *Her Highness* commands," Nomish gave Hadlay a mocking bow, "then I suppose we must obey."

"Please, Nomish." Hadlay's eyes stung with tears. "You have every reason to hate me—even more than you know. But if you won't listen to me, *please* listen to Kayshti—he's still your friend. And Aa'mash, and—"

Nomish cut her off with a scathing look. "They'll believe anything you tell them, *Princess*. I'll tell you that I believe too, if it pleases you." He turned to look at an open space beside Hadlay. "Why, he's a fine looking fellow, this Sirach. Now, by your leave, some of us have duties to attend to." He turned to go, shoving Kayshti out of his way. The portal to the room opened.

"Nomish Rakam!" Ma'at rushed to the portal and blocked his exit. "Even if you won't believe Hadlay, who has been your best friend all your stupid life, are you such a stubborn donkey that you won't believe me?"

Nomish evidently had not noticed Ma'at before, because now his face went white. "Ma'at! But you were . . ."

"Dead. Kayshti said that you were there in the gong farm. You saw what those horrible creatures did to me. But here I stand. Because of Sirach."

He reached out, tilting her head back so that he could see her neck. "How . . . how did . . ."

"Sirach brought me back to life. Before the eyes of Rasab and my brother—and Hadlay."

Nomish swayed, and Kayshti rushed forward to hold him up.

"The em-emperor . . ." Nomish stammered. "He must have healed you the way he h-healed me . . ."

Sirach snorted.

Nomish whirled, then went even more pale as his eyes beheld Sirach.

"The emperor cannot heal, boy; he can only fool your mind. How many nights have you lain awake when the pains in your leg would not let you sleep? How many times have you heard your own stutter when your concentration failed you?" Sirach's hoof struck the floor, marking a spot. "Come to me."

Nomish pulled away from Kayshti and lurched forward, dropping to his knees before Sirach.

Sirach touched him, and as with Ma'at, Hadlay saw his body begin to glow. He rose slightly from the floor, then settled down again.

"Now, stand."

Nomish rose gingerly, testing his leg. Then he began to move, tentatively at first, then dancing wildly, laughing aloud. "The pain! It's truly gone!"

Sirach whinnied and cavorted through the room, dancing with him. Hadlay laughed too, delighted with the joyous celebration.

"Stop it!" Fa'an's angry voice shattered the merriment. The dancing stopped. "You have all gone mad! Seeing things? Floating? Dancing for no reason?"

"How can you not see him?" Aa'mash asked. "He's as real as anyone here!"

"I suppose you believe in Refa too!" Fa'an jeered.

Kayshti stepped forward. "Fa'an, my sister was dead. I found her body in the gong farm this morn. Her throat was slashed to the bone!"

"You heard the Oresed boy say this," Hadlay said. "He saw her too!"

"So you say. *I* did not see her dead. I can only believe it was a trick—one that has deceived you all." She glared at Hadlay. "You are confusing people with wicked magic!" She turned to Nomish. "And I cannot believe, after all she has done to you, that *you* would be deceived!" She whirled and fled the chamber.

"Let her go," Sirach said, when Nomish and Kayshti moved to follow. "She has been blinded by the Refa and by her own jealousy. She will not see me. It is her choice." It hurt Hadlay to see the sorrow in his eyes.

Kayshti still stared at the portal. "She'll go to one of the overlords. She'll tell them you are here!"

Sirach shook his head. "She is too angry to think of it just now. But time is growing short."

Kayshti turned back to Sirach. "Say, where is Rasab?"

"He is about his business." Sirach tossed his head, then nodded at the portal. "Two more servants will perfect your number. And they wait outside this chamber. They followed you when you brought Nomish. Bring them in now."

Kayshti hurried out the portal. He returned almost instantly—alone. He stared at Sirach. "I must have misunderstood you. Did you say bring those two in here?"

"I did."

"But they're—"

"Do you think I am unaware?" Sirach's voice was soft but firm.

Kayshti bowed his head, but his jaw had a stubborn set.

Sirach turned to Hadlay. "You go."

Glancing at Kayshti, Hadlay passed through the portal. As she reached the other side, she nearly stumbled over Ba'ar, who was bent double, inspecting the foot trail through the thick dust.

Behind her, Citna stood, gaping at the wall. "Did you just walk through . . ."

Hadlay froze. These two? Did Sirach mean for her to bring *them* into the hidden chamber?

Ba'ar straightened with an important air. "Prince Zêru has been summoning you all morning—why have you not obeyed?"

Hadlay frowned. The thought of bringing these two into Sirach's presence galled her. But if she did not, no doubt Ba'ar would run to Zêru and tell him where she was.

"What is behind that wall?" Ba'ar rapped the stones.

They lit. "Do you have the key?"

Ba'ar jumped away, nearly toppling Citna as she did so.

Hadlay grimaced. Sirach said he wanted them to enter. He must have his reasons. She turned to the portal with a sigh. "I trust in Sirach."

AND ALSO TO THE ORESED

The reaction inside the chamber was even more intense than Hadlay's had been. Aa'mash hissed and rushed to stand between the Oresed girls and Sirach. Nomish joined arms with her to form a shield.

"Not these two, surely!" Ma'at exclaimed.

But what was even more surprising was Citna's reaction. The moment she entered the chamber, she went pale as a shade. "You!"

Hadlay followed her gaze. She was speaking to Sirach.

Sirach nudged his way between Nomish and Aa'mash and stood before her. "Yes." He brought his wings forward, touching them to her shoulders. "I have long awaited this moment, dear one."

Citna took a shuddering breath, then burst into joyful laughter, though her eyes were bright with tears. "I thought you were just a childish dream!"

Nomish gaped at Sirach. "But she is Oresed! There are no dreamers among them!"

"Who told you there were not? They too are children of Mada and Avakh. Their ancestors did not remain with the maze as yours did. But they returned, in time."

"Yes, to conquer and oppress us!" Aa'mash nearly shouted. "They are our enemies!"

Sirach tossed his head. "In N'de, there are no enemies."

Hadlay's mouth gaped open. Ba'ar—her hated adversary—in N'de? The thought horrified her.

Ba'ar scowled at her with equal distaste. Hadlay wondered if she even saw Sirach. A small hope glimmered—perhaps she was like Fa'an. Really,

Hadlay could probably tolerate Citna—she had softened toward the girl after her time in the dungeon. But Ba'ar? Sirach might as well welcome Asinus himself!

"Would you turn from me because of Ba'ar, Hadlay?" Sirach asked.

"How could I turn from you? But I was nearly killed because of Ba'ar. And she would have loved to see me die! I hate her!"

His eyes remained steady on Hadlay's face. "This girl—Citna—was nearly killed because of you. And many more—your own people—will die. Are you so much better than Ba'ar?"

The point struck Hadlay like the sting of a whip. Tears blurred her vision as she hung her head.

Sirach came to her, tipping up her chin with a wingtip. "You are forgiven for all you've done, my love. Can you not forgive this girl?"

Hadlay wiped the dampness from her cheeks. She did not want to, but if Sirach said she must, she would try.

He drew her in, his wings enfolding her with warmth. "And the rest of you?"

Hadlay heard murmurs of assent, though the voices did not sound pleased.

Sirach turned to Ba'ar. "I know your heart, Ba'ar. It will be difficult for you to receive me, knowing I came first to the Ramash. But though you have spent your whole life feeling unloved and unvalued, I have treasured you since the hour you were conceived. I will carry you on my back to N'de when your time comes, if only you receive me now."

To Hadlay's great surprise, Ba'ar gave forth a wrenching sob, throwing her arms around Sirach's neck. Despite herself, Hadlay smiled a little.

After a long moment, Sirach stepped away and gave a whinny that sounded at once anguished and triumphant. "My hour has come."

THE BARGAIN

Hadlay's blood froze as the portal opened.

"Here he is!" Rasab stepped aside to admit the emperor and Zêru.

"Rasab!" Ma'at cried. "How could you?"

The boy glanced at her and flushed, then turned back to the emperor. "I have done my part. When will you unmix my father?"

"This is where you've been?" Zêru demanded, seeing Hadlay beside Sirach. "I have been summoning you all morning!"

As his black eyes touched her, memories of last night rushed back. Hadlay could almost feel his Refa clawing at her, trying to attach themselves. She wanted to scream and never stop screaming. All thought of standing to defend Sirach fled her, and she scrambled away, seeking to hide herself among the others.

As the emperor and Zêru came forward, Asinus, Sfika, Bonobos, Buthotos, and Aurum, accompanied by a large number of guards, filed into the chamber until there was no more room. With no way to leave, the frightened initiates huddled against the far wall.

The emperor assessed Sirach with a cold eye. "I have been expecting this day. I assume *he* sent you."

Sirach said nothing.

"What do you want?" The emperor strode forward until he loomed over Sirach like the Tower over Turris. Sirach looked so small! Hadlay wondered how she had ever believed he could triumph.

"I have come to the children of Avakh and Mada to deliver a message from Meshah."

A roar began to echo through the chamber at the sound of Meshah's name. But it was quickly drowned by the singing of the stones. The overlords and guards threw up their hands, covering their ears as though the singing caused them great pain. Even Zêru snarled and held his ears. The sight gave Hadlay more confidence. Perhaps Sirach did have power to defeat his enemies.

At a gesture from the emperor, the roar silenced. When the singing stopped as well, he grimaced. "The people of Turris are his subjects no longer. They have given themselves to me."

"You deceived them."

The emperor gave a harsh laugh. "They were willingly deceived. Your King abandoned them, and they languished for want of a ruler." He stroked his beard, staring at Sirach. "If you have come to invade, where is your army?"

"I am alone."

Shungallu bent so that his face was a few inches from Sirach's. "If you came alone, you are under my dominion. I have spent these long ages building a legion of Refa numbering in the millions. I will destroy you!" He raised a hand, uttering the words to call forth all the Refa under his command.

Sirach stood silent, gazing at his adversary.

The emperor froze in mid-gesture, and a shrewd look came upon his face. "Or if I destroy you, will your King send others in your place?"

"He will send no one else."

"Why would he send you alone to face all my powers? What is your mission?"

"I told you. I have been sent to speak to the people of this world. Those who receive me will return to N'de."

The emperor frowned. "If that is your goal, why are you hiding in this chamber? You have wings—why have you not already flown from this Tower?"

"I can only enter your domain if you release me."

The overlords smirked.

"You may be certain I will never do so. You will die here in this chamber."

Sirach tossed his head. "If I must."

"But first, since you are so full of information, I will learn as much as you will tell me." He turned away from Sirach, gazing around the room.

His eyes found the frame where the mirror had been, and he strode to it. The initiates, who had been huddled nearby, scattered to avoid him. He bent to inspect it, then glanced at Sirach. "Where is the mirror that was the portal to N'de?"

Sirach shook his mane. "I am the portal. No one enters N'de except through me."

The emperor stroked his beard. "Through you?" He reached out to touch Sirach. A loud zap caused everyone to start, and he withdrew his hand quickly.

"You will never return, Lelyeh, for you renounced the key long ago," Sirach said, his voice mild. "N'de remains uncorrupted. Its light would strip your bones."

"Are you suggesting that the emperor is undeserving?" Asinus scathed Sirach with one of his withering glares. "His Majesty is a great and good ruler, more than worthy to enter any place he pleases!"

Sirach gazed at Asinus. "Even if what you said were true, goodness and worthiness are not the key."

Nomish sidled nearer to Hadlay. "How is it Asinus and the emperor can see Sirach, when Fa'an could not?"

Sirach turned to him. "These servants of Lelyeh know me, as he does. But they have put their trust in him."

"How dare you deny His Majesty?" Sfika strode up to Sirach. "The emperor commands everyone and everything in this world. You will hand over the key this instant." She held out a hand. "*Namzaqa bilâni!*"

Sirach snorted. "Power and authority are not the key."

Nonplussed, Sfika shrank back.

Bonobos stepped up with confidence, gesturing with his hook. "The emperor has mastered all the sciences. If he wants to enter this alleged N'de, he'll discover a way."

"Knowledge is not the key." Sirach nodded in the direction of the initiates. "Weak and foolish though these children are, they will live in N'de."

"They will not enter N'de!" The emperor's fierce snarl chilled Hadlay. "They are my subjects, and I forbid them!"

Sirach tossed his head. "You have the power to forbid them anything in Turris. But N'de is mine to bestow, and I have given it to them."

Without warning, the emperor flung out a hand, making a gripping motion and pulling it toward himself. Hadlay was yanked into the air and carried toward the emperor. "This one not only pledged herself to me, but she betrothed herself to my son. Do you deny that she has given us the right to use her as we will?"

Sirach shook his head. "I do not deny it."

Hadlay struggled against the invisible hands that grasped her, sending Sirach a disbelieving look. Had he not promised to set her free? What was happening?

With a sweeping gesture, the emperor sent her flying against the wall. The other initiates were launched from their places as well and slammed against the wall beside her. There they hung, pinned, unable to move. The grip on Hadlay's throat tightened, choking her. With effort, she turned her head and saw with alarm that Nomish's lips were turning blue, and Ma'at—dear heaven—Ma'at hung limp and still, as if she had died once more. Hadlay would have screamed if she could draw breath. Why was Sirach doing nothing?

The emperor turned to Sirach. "Well, since they have rebelled and proven themselves untrustworthy, I have no further use for them. I shall feed their blood to my warriors, and their souls shall feed the Refa." As he spoke, some of the guards, those with the tails of scorpions, moved in, and Hadlay saw the hunger in their eyes.

Sirach rested his gaze on each initiate in turn. "Cling to the key." Then he faced the emperor. "I am the only portal to N'de, and I will offer my life in their place. Spare them, and you may do as you will with me."

Hadlay saw the evil, calculating look that entered the emperor's eyes. She wanted to warn Sirach that Shungallu would never keep his bargain, but even as she opened her mouth to try, a hard hand clapped over it.

"Do not interfere, my princess." Zêru waved his curved knife before her eyes. "I will slash your throat here and now, and gorge myself on your blood."

Hadlay pried her eyes away from the knife, focusing on Sirach, silently begging him to help. When would he fight to save them?

"It hardly seems fair," the emperor murmured. "Your one, puny life for so many?" He seemed to debate the question, but the eagerness in his eyes betrayed him. "Still, I agree to your terms."

"So be it." Sirach lowered his head.

The emperor jerked his hand, and Hadlay felt the hold on her release. She and the others dropped to the floor. She dragged in a searing breath, and gagged on it. She nearly wept with relief as Ma'at began to cough.

The room darkened, as if a thundercloud had entered. The storm thickened, moved, closing in on Sirach. Weapons, taken from the guards, drifted toward him. Surely, this was the moment when Sirach's powers would be revealed!

The emperor raised his hand. "Dûkâshu!"

A sword slashed at Sirach, and it ran through one of his wings. There was a sound like breaking glass, and the tip of his wing crashed to the floor. Hadlay stared at the jagged pieces, shocked. This could not be happening! Surely now Sirach would rear up and fight back.

Sirach grunted as an iron spear thrust with brutal force, piercing his side, sending more bits of glass flying. Two more weapons, an axe and a club, smashed at his legs. Chips scattered through the room like sprays of blood.

"No!" Hadlay rushed forward, but Zêru's hand entangled in her hair and yanked her back. She twisted, trying to break free, but Zêru's hold did not relax.

With an agonized cry, Sirach fell and shattered.

"Sirach!" Ma'at's scream echoed through the room. Her wrenching sobs tore at Hadlay's heart as the girl struggled with the guard who held her down.

Hadlay stared at the broken pieces of Sirach—an ear, a leg, one of his beautiful eyes. She fought Zêru's grasp on her hair, feeling some of it rip from her scalp. She did not care. She only wanted to go to Sirach, to touch him again.

The weapons continued chipping away until there was nothing left but a pile of glittering splinters. Then darkness settled on the shards, leaching them of light.

Finally, the clubs and swords withdrew. Zêru released her hair, and Hadlay collapsed onto the pile. She felt a sharp sting as one large fragment dug into her hand. Sobbing, she rocked over the lifeless chips, scooping them together, trying to give them form. How could she bear to live without Sirach?

The emperor gestured toward her friends. "Seize them!"

"But you said—" Rasab protested.

The emperor's slap snapped Rasab's head back, and he slumped to the floor.

"Do you expect me to let traitors roam free in my city? I agreed to spare their lives." He smirked. "I did not say how they would live out their time upon this earth." He bent a finger, causing Rasab to be drawn up to his feet. "But rest assured, boy, you will see your father released by day's end."

Casting a guilty look at his friends, Rasab bowed his head. "Thank you, Your Majesty." At the emperor's dismissive gesture, he hastened from the chamber.

The emperor kicked at the splintered pieces of Sirach, scattering them from the pile Hadlay had formed and crushing the pieces beneath his feet. "Seal up the corridor to this room, and see that all this debris is deposited where it belongs—in the gong farm. And take these traitors to the dungeon." He turned his attention to Hadlay. "You chose the wrong side, little one. I have not forgotten our bargain. Your parents will join you soon."

Hadlay gasped as one of the guards prodded her with a spear. She stared at its sharpened iron point. All she had to do was throw herself against it, and all her pain and guilt would end.

The guard sneered, then caught her by her hair and dragged her to her feet. "I'll kill you when the emperor says to kill you—not before." He shoved her toward her friends, and they caught her before she could fall. With the guards goading them along with swords and spears, they filed from the chamber.

As they made their way down the long, winding corridors, they came upon a servant, supervising a broom as it swept up shards of glass from the floor. Hadlay looked and noticed several more piles of glass ahead of them.

"What happened here?" Zêru demanded, halting the procession to query the servant.

The servant looked at him and gulped at his ferocious expression, then peered at the fearsome guards who still held their prisoners at spearpoint.

"The—the mirrors, Your Highness. They shattered—all of them, throughout the Tower—a little while ago. No one knows why."

Zêru frowned at this. "It may mean something. Has anyone told my father?"

"No, Your Highness. He and all the overlords were busy, we were told."

Zêru turned back to the guards.

"Take my betrothed to the bestiary. Lock her in one of the cages." He bent down so that his face was near enough that Hadlay could feel his breath on her ear. It smelled like something rotten. Hadlay turned her face away. "I will be hungry soon."

DEFEATED

Hadlay sat in a corner of her cage and hugged her knees against her chest. The cage was large enough to stand in, a cube perhaps as tall as Nomish. How soon would Zêru come for her? She cast her eyes around for something sharp, some way to end her own life before he could feed on her again. But even that would be useless—she would merely be giving herself over to the Refa. She wondered if that could possibly be worse.

A honk startled her, and she looked up to find Filch at the door of the cage looking at her with his head cocked. He raised a webbed foot, begging for some food. When he realized Hadlay had none to give him, he trotted off.

Hadlay had never felt so alone. "Oh, Sirach. I wish you were with me."

"I am."

She blinked. She thought she'd glimpsed a sparkle of light between her fingers. Her eyes were playing tricks, seeing phantoms.

But there it was again.

Hadlay turned up her hand, stunned to see a bright light emanating from her palm. She remembered the pain she'd felt as one of the fragments from Sirach's shattered body had dug into her hand. It was still there, embedded in her palm, glowing. A piece of Sirach's mirror, a little bigger than her thumb.

She picked at it with her fingernail, but she could not pry it free. And it didn't hurt as she would expect a shard of that size to do. She sighed, touching it with her finger, stroking its almost liquid surface. She did not want to remove it anyway. At least a part of Sirach was still with her. The thought gave her some small comfort as she thought of what lay ahead.

The surface shimmered, then a shape began to form in its reflection. She saw a hoof, a flaming wing, and then a face, with its marking, like three gold rings intertwined.

"Sirach!"

He tossed his head, giving a soft nicker. "When will you learn to cling to the key?" She felt his nudge against her palm. "Did I not say that the emperor would release me from the chamber?"

A laugh burst from Hadlay's throat, and she brought her palm to her chest, over her heart. "I thought I had lost you forever!"

Sirach gave a whinny, clarion and triumphant, and the creatures in the bestiary stilled to hear it.

Hadlay could not stop crying—or laughing. She pressed her lips to the mirror and felt his soft nose brush them. "I am so glad you are alive! I can face anything, knowing you are still with me!" Then she paused. "I am sorry, Sirach, that I ran from your side when the emperor arrived."

He shook his mane. "You were not the one who had to face him then. But your time will come."

"But I'm such a coward!"

Sirach chortled. "Did you not just say you could face anything with me?" He brushed her palm again. "Do not fear, little one. Keep hold of the key, and together we will set your people free." He paused as if he was sniffing the air. "The prince is on his way." When Hadlay trembled, he nudged her palm again. "Stand firm, and you will begin to see what the emperor has released into your world."

Hadlay scrambled to a corner of the cage as she heard Zêru enter. She rested her forehead against her knees, not wanting to meet his eyes. She hoped against all hope that, if she seemed to be sleeping, he would simply feed his animals and go.

But Zêru walked straight to her cage and kicked the door. "When I have had enough of your blood, I think I will mix you with a dung beetle and send you to the gong farm for your meals!" Hadlay flinched, but did not raise her head. He kicked again. "Look at me when I speak to you!" he thundered, and a thousand voices echoed him.

Hadlay raised her head, closing her fist against his invading eyes. She didn't want him to learn that Sirach still lived.

"Why did you betray me?" the prince asked, and Hadlay was surprised to hear sorrow in his voice. "I thought you were my friend."

"You betrayed me first," Hadlay whispered. "You lied to me. Used me to destroy my people. And even if all that were not so, I would still love Sirach, because he loves me, and he came from Meshah."

Once again, at the mention of the name, a thousand horrid voices screamed in rage. But this time, Hadlay did not cringe. She rose to her feet, surprised at how calm she felt. The elation at finding Sirach alive buoyed her.

Zêru flung a finger at her. "*Qulâ!*"

Hadlay flinched, remembering the terrible, burning pain that word had brought her once before. But this time, there was no pain.

Zêru frowned. "*Hadlay qulâ!*"

Still there was no pain. Hadlay looked around the cage, wondering why his curses were not working. Had he become as impotent as Asinus?

Red-faced with fury, Zêru laid a hand upon the bars of the cage. "*Siddâ!*" At his word, the bars began to glow a fiery orange-red. All around her, the straw that littered the cage floor smoked, then small flames flared up like little torches. Hadlay looked down, surprised to see that the floor she stood upon was red as well. But even through her thin silk slippers, she felt no heat at all.

"*Shisâ!*" Zêru made a summoning motion. Hadlay felt no magical pull, though the cage itself quivered and slid toward him.

A strange expression mixed of rage and apprehension dawned on Zêru's face. "*Bêl galli deki!*"

In a moment, the emperor appeared beside him.

"Something is wrong, Father. The Refa will not touch Hadlay."

The emperor flicked his hand, and Hadlay expected to feel a hard slap. But nothing happened. He closed his fist in a tight grip, but Hadlay felt no hands around her throat. She grinned.

The emperor pursed his lips, his fingers touching the tip of his beard. When he spoke, his voice was quiet, but the seething menace in his whisper made Hadlay shudder. "Where is he?"

Hadlay knew what he was asking. She did not reply.

"*Quttâ!*"

The cage that contained Hadlay exploded around her. Hadlay flinched as bars rained down on all sides. The air filled with straw and feathers.

A pucker appeared between the emperor's brows. "Summon the guards!"

Zêru did as he was told, and several scorpion guards rushed through the door, arms at the ready. At the emperor's gesture, the guards rushed forward, pressing sharp swords to Hadlay's ribs.

"What will we do with her, Father?"

The emperor paced, stroking his beard. Then he turned to Zêru. "Feed on her—take her blood until she is dead. Do it now!"

Zêru grinned, moving in on Hadlay. She wanted to turn and run, but the swords at her sides barred her escape. The feel of Sirach's steady breath against her palm reassured her.

"Stand firm. I am here," she heard him whisper in her mind. Had he become part of her now?

She stilled, even tilting up her head to expose her throat. If Zêru killed her, at least she would die knowing Sirach was with her.

Zêru drew his knife from his belt and brought it to her throat. She heard a loud *zap*, as when the emperor had tried to touch Sirach. Zêru leaped back, shaking his hand as if it burned.

Hadlay giggled. "Oh, Sirach! You are *wonderful!*"

The emperor regarded her with narrow, cunning eyes. His voice was soft, almost too quiet to be heard above the noises of the bestiary. "Take her to the dungeon."

"But Father—" Zêru stumbled back a pace when he saw the fierce look in the emperor's eyes. He nodded to the guards, and they herded her from the bestiary.

LIGHT IN THE DARKNESS

The dungeon was as black and horrid-smelling as Hadlay remembered, but somehow the darkness was not as fearsome. As the guards closed the door, Hadlay heard the sound of small feet scurrying toward her. She lifted her palm, seeking comfort in the glow of Sirach's mirror, and the light that gleamed from her hand illuminated the space around her.

Shrieks and squeals echoed through the dank chambers as the creatures slipped back into the shadows.

Her friends were here somewhere. The emperor had commanded that they be taken here while she had been sent to the bestiary. It seemed likely, given her previous experience in this place, that they would be found in Ummi Ekleti's cell. She had no idea which way to go, but with Sirach's light, she was able to make out some of her surroundings.

She saw now that the dungeon was one great chamber littered with crates and straw, with darkened doorways along the outer walls. Some of these doorways were open, while others were shut and barred. From the closed cells, Hadlay heard terrible growls and snarls. She wondered if the creatures of this place had locked those cells because the beasts inside were even more fearsome than they were.

She saw a dim light coming from one of the cells. She remembered that Ummi Ekleti had candles in her cell, so she walked toward the glow.

She found her friends clinging together just inside the door, while Ummi Ekleti busied herself near the far wall making some of her strong-smelling tea. A candle flickered beside her. Ba'ar and Citna sat on the bed. Nomish, Aa'mash, Kayshti, and Ma'at sat together on the floor.

"Hadlay!" Nomish peeled himself away and came to her side. "I had given you up for dead! The emperor and Prince Zêru were so angry!"

Ummi Ekleti hurried over to Hadlay, catching her face in firm hands. "Did you find the key?" She seized Hadlay's hand, and her eyes widened when she saw the mirror. She burst into cackles, dancing about the cell, dragging Hadlay's hand—and the rest of her—along.

Then she stopped and stared at Hadlay's palm again. "Come to save us, have you? What are you doing in this child's hand?" She whirled and rushed from the cell, giggling wildly. "He's here! He's here! He's finally here!" The noise was greeted with shrieks and snarls from the denizens of the dungeon.

"What set her off?" Nomish asked.

Hadlay shook her hand, which ached from Ummi Ekleti's tight grip. She felt something drop between her fingers. When she looked, she saw the piece of mirror on the floor. Dismayed, she bent to pick it up, hoping she could press it back into her palm, but when she lifted her hand, the original piece was still there.

Sirach tossed his head. "Share."

Hadlay took Nomish's hand and pressed the new piece into his palm.

Nomish's eyes went wide as a camel's yawn. "Sirach!"

Hadlay felt another piece drop, and she caught it in her fingers. This one she gave to Ma'at. Soon Nomish, Ma'at, Kayshti, and Aa'mash were staring at their palms, crying and talking to Sirach.

Hadlay turned to find Citna watching her. Two more pieces dropped into her fingers. Sirach gazed at her with firm resolution.

"All right," Hadlay said. Taking Citna's hand, she gave her a piece.

Hadlay looked at Ba'ar in the shimmering light of the mirrors and held out the final piece. "If you will take this from me, it is yours."

Ba'ar glared at Hadlay for a long moment, then she snatched the mirror and stalked away.

Sirach spoke from Hadlay's mirror. "Now your number is complete. Go out among the people and speak openly of me. Do not fear the emperor or his powers."

"But we're in the dungeon!" Kayshti protested. "How are we to do this?"

"There! There he is!" Ummi Ekleti rushed into the cell, trailed by several filthy prisoners, some Ramash, some Oresed. All of them had gaping wounds covering their bodies, and most entered the cell with fearful eyes darting around the room.

"Where is he?" one of them ventured, his voice a dry rasp.

Ummi Ekleti hurried over to Hadlay and caught hold of her arm. "Here—right here in this child's palm!"

The others exchanged pained glances.

"Her mind has finally departed her." The smallest one, barely recognizable as a woman, shook her head. "It is a wonder this did not happen long ago."

"Now she has drawn us out of our hiding places!" a man said, terror trembling in his voice. "The creatures will lie in wait for us."

"He is here—right here! Show them!" Ummi Ekleti pushed Hadlay toward them.

Hadlay glanced at Sirach. Should she comply? He had said that their number was complete. But he nodded, so she raised her hand. The strangers covered their faces, unaccustomed to any kind of light.

Then, one of the Ramash prisoners saw Sirach, and he took hold of Hadlay's hand, drawing it closer. The glow from the mirror grew brighter, lighting the cell so that even Hadlay had to close her eyes. When she looked again, the newcomers stood before her whole—not a single wound remained upon their bodies. The Ramash man looked at the others, then at Hadlay, his mouth dropping open as if to speak. But then he simply shook his head.

"Hadlay?" Zêru's voice sounded through the chamber. "Hadlay Mivana!"

Outside the cell, Hadlay heard creatures fleeing in the darkness.

"He's coming!" one of the strangers whispered. She caught Ma'at's arm. "Come, we must hide quickly!"

The others slipped from the cell, taking with them all of Hadlay's friends. Ummi Ekleti took Hadlay by the hand and led her to a tiny cupboard that sat empty beside her bed. "You are small enough to fit—hurry!"

"No. I must face him." Hadlay wondered how she could be so certain, but she seemed to feel an assurance from Sirach.

"So be it, then." Ummi Ekleti settled on a stool beside her bed, looking resigned.

Zêru strode into the room and stalked up to Hadlay, glaring at her as if his eyes alone could kill.

"Let her be, my son!" Ummi Ekleti caught his arm. "She is special."

Hadlay gaped at Ummi Ekleti. "You're his mother?" The instant the question formed on her lips she realized she already knew the answer. So this was Shungallu's wife, Zêru's mother! And she had tried to kill Zêru—her own son! And he was the darkness that fed on her! Suddenly it all made sense.

Zêru flicked his hand, and Ummi Ekleti slumped to her bed as if he'd struck her. "Leave us, Mother. This concerns me and my betrothed."

Ummi Ekleti pushed to her feet and edged around them, fleeing from the chamber. Zêru watched until she was gone, then his burning glare returned to Hadlay.

"Do not fear," Sirach whispered.

"Is *he* with you now? The *thing* that came through the mirror?"

"His name is Sirach."

Zêru's nose wrinkled as if he smelled something vile. "We should have known never to trust *remesh* in the Tower, but Father thought—"

"He thought if he could win our trust, he could destroy us. And he nearly did."

"We will still destroy your people. You are here in this prison. You and that creature. You cannot save anyone from here."

Hadlay smiled. "I have a feeling we will not remain here long."

Zêru studied her with narrow eyes. "Perhaps not. Father wishes to strike a bargain."

"Sirach needs nothing more from your father." Hadlay had no idea how she knew this, but she did.

"He does not wish to deal with *him*." Hadlay distrusted Zêru's smile. "Father believes that if you will still consent to wed me, we can negotiate a treaty with N'de—"

Hadlay snorted. "Do you really think Sirach—or I—would bind ourselves to you?"

"If you do not agree, you will languish in this dungeon forever!"

"I would rather be in this dungeon with Sirach than in the royal chambers with you."

Zêru's fists tightened. "Father will send for your family—and that boy you like, his family as well. One by one, you will both watch them suffer all the agonies we can devise, until you change your mind."

"Stand firm," Sirach whispered. "Cling to the key."

Hadlay did not reply. After all she had been through, she still faced the same horrible dilemma the emperor had given her last evening—had it really been just one day? Some part of her wanted to bargain. Perhaps she could even demand that, in exchange for her acceptance, he would spare the Ramash and find another way to raise his army.

But then, how could she trust any promise he gave? In the end, he and his Refa would still possess her and everyone she cared about. And what of N'de? It would forever be lost to her and her people. Would Shungallu be able to raise a force powerful enough to conquer Meshah?

"Stand firm," Sirach said again. "Trust in me."

Hadlay lifted her head, addressing Zêru. "You will not change my mind."

She felt a sudden blow between her shoulder blades and a searing pain that radiated outward, numbing her limbs. She staggered, and as she turned she saw that someone had slipped up behind her in the shadows. Rasab! His knife now dripped with her blood. The room spun, and Hadlay's legs gave way.

Zêru laughed, triumphant. "We have her! We have them both!"

FURMITES

Her back hurt. And something hard ground into her belly. Hadlay forced her eyes to open.

Rasab had her over his shoulder and was carrying her through the dungeon.

"Straight ahead!" She heard Zêru's voice behind them. "Asinus will meet us in the torture chamber."

Hadlay raised her head. Asinus? *Torture chamber?*

Zêru grinned. "Now that we know that humans can harm you, Father wants us to hand you over to Asinus and his torturers. They will break you soon enough."

Hadlay turned her palm upward, seeking Sirach's face. He gave her a calming nod. "Stand firm. You will not suffer more than you can bear."

Hadlay didn't think she could bear very much. The pain in her back was already making her sick.

Zêru bent, staring at her hand. "Is this where *he* has joined with you?" He tried to grasp her wrist, then hissed as if it burned him. "Well, straight-away I will have Asinus cut off your arm. Perhaps that is all it will take to finish this Sirach."

Rasab jolted Hadlay, shifting her hard upon his shoulder for balance. She grunted as she felt fresh blood seep over her shoulders, wetting her clothing. The room began to spin again, and lights like fireflies circled around her.

Rasab stopped walking so suddenly that Hadlay nearly slipped off his shoulder.

"Put her down." A woman's voice came from beyond the lights.

"*Sikpâshunûti!*" Zêru commanded the powers to push the lights aside. The lights did not move.

"Sirach is with all of us now." The voice was Ummi Ekleti's, though she sounded somehow changed. "Your Refa cannot touch us."

Hadlay blinked dizzily. The lights seemed to be real. She squinted and saw the shapes of people—many people—closing in.

"Mother?" Zêru's mouth gaped open. "You would come against your own son?"

A man's sharp laugh came from the dim glow. "What do you know of being a son, spawn of Shungallu?"

The lights grew brighter and increased in number. The chamber filled with horrible shrieking, as if many awful creatures were in pain, and the darkness slowly dispersed like storm clouds in the desert heat.

Zêru flinched back from the brightness, raising a hand to shield his eyes. Hadlay grunted as Rasab let her fall to the ground and backed away.

Then Nomish was beside her, cradling her against his body. A pathway opened up between the lights.

"Get out!" Nomish's voice crackled with command.

Rasab shifted, sliding off between the lights, heading for the door.

"Come back here!" Zêru shouted. "Coward! Your father will die for this!"

Rasab hesitated, then turned back, resignation on his face.

"He is already dead, is he not, son?" Ummi Ekleti said. "That is what your father meant when he promised this boy he would see his father released."

"How did you know?" Zêru blurted.

Rasab's mouth dropped. "You . . . you lied to me?"

"Why are you surprised, boy?" one of the prisoners asked. "Did you not see that the emperor and his son are deceivers?"

Rasab turned to him, opening his mouth as if to speak. Then, with a sob, he spun and raced away. The doors of the dungeon slammed behind him.

As the lights closed in even tighter around Zêru, he began to shake, just a little at first, and then with increasing violence.

"Enough! I cannot bear it!" He vanished, leaving the room with a swirling wind.

A gentle hand touched the wound in Hadlay's back. She winced, then sighed as a healing warmth radiated from the touch. Soon it no longer hurt to move.

"Can you stand?" Nomish asked.

She took a deep breath to gird against the pain she expected, but when she moved, it didn't hurt. She let him help her up.

"We should go."

"Where?"

Nomish shrugged. "Didn't Sirach say that we should go out among our people? Let's try the door."

As Hadlay had expected, the dungeon's door was locked.

Nomish scratched his chin. "How are we to go out when we're locked inside a prison?"

"Perhaps when they come to feed us . . ." Kayshti suggested.

Nomish shook his head. "The emperor knows by now that Sirach is with us and that his powers cannot touch us. His only advantage is that we are trapped here. He will try to destroy us by starving us."

"*I* will not starve!" a snarling voice came from the shadows that lingered near the edges of the dungeon. "Not so long as you require sleep." A figure emerged from the shadow, and Hadlay recognized the lion-man who had attacked her before. His cat's eyes glimmered in the half-light. One of the prisoners held up his hand, shining his mirror toward the beast, who hissed and slunk away.

Hadlay shuddered, and Nomish's arm came around her shoulder. She glanced up at his face, and her eyes blurred with tears. He had forgiven her. She folded herself against his side.

A woman stepped forward, and it took a long moment for Hadlay to realize it was Ummi Ekleti. No more was she wild-eyed and half-crazed. Her smile was calm and confident, and her gaze had clarity, and Hadlay saw the mirror glowing in her palm. It seemed Sirach had healed this woman's mind, just as he had healed Hadlay's wounds, and those of her friends.

Ummi Ekleti looked at Nomish, then Hadlay, and she spoke one word, her voice strong with assurance. "Furmites."

Furmites? Hadlay and Nomish exchanged a confused glance. Perhaps the woman was still a bit off her saddle after all.

One of the prisoners touched Ummi Ekleti's arm. "Do you mean the furry things in the iron box?"

Ummi Ekleti nodded. "They were some of Zêru's mixes. Something with termite, I think. I heard that, when the pests started drilling holes all over the Tower, Shungallu demanded that they be exterminated. Zêru could not bear to kill them, so he boxed them up and brought them here. He feeds them chunks of brick and old shoes when he visits." She pointed to one of the darkened doorways. "He keeps them in that cell."

Several of the prisoners hurried off, and Hadlay heard the sound of hinges groaning. A shout came from the cell, followed by an awful buzzing noise. Soon chips of stone were flying through the doorway.

"We can only hope that they won't burrow their way to the moat and drown us all!" Nomish spoke quietly.

"We may as well be comfortable while we wait." Ummi Ekleti took Hadlay's hand and guided her back toward her cell. "Thank you, child, for choosing rightly. If only I had done the same."

ENHEDUANA

In the hours that followed, the initiates rested and listened to Ummi Ekleti tell her story. She had once been a poet living in a place called Sumer in one of the seven Lands Beyond. Her father was king there, and when he had made his allegiance to Shungallu, he had given his daughter in marriage. By the time she had realized what her husband really was, she had been pregnant with his son—Zêru.

"When he was born, and I saw what he would be, I thought the world would be a better place if he were dead." She hung her head. "It is a terrible thing for a mother to try to kill her son. But was I wrong?"

"I think you had great courage, Ummi Ekleti," Hadlay said.

"Call me Enheduana, child, for that is my true name. You think I had courage? Not enough." Enheduana smiled sadly. "When the moment came, I hesitated. But Shungallu realized my intention, so he had me caged. I have been a prisoner since the first week of Zêru's life."

As the story continued, Hadlay felt a nudge against her palm. She turned her hand up and gazed into Sirach's glowing eyes. "It's not over, is it? The emperor will hunt me. My family will be in danger too."

"They are already in danger. The emperor will send for them very soon."

A thrill of fear shot through her. She reached for Nomish, thinking to bring him into the discussion, but Sirach shook his head. "Cling to the key, and all will be as Meshah wills it."

She wasn't sure she liked the sound of that. It wasn't a promise that all would be well.

Sirach breathed against her palm, and she felt the warmth of his breath spread through her, even in the dank cold of the dungeon. "You will know great loss, Hadlay, and much danger. You will suffer much for my sake, but do not fear. We are joined now, you and I, and nothing can ever separate us. I will do great things through you until your hour comes to return to N'de. And when that day comes, beloved, I will carry you home myself and there will be great joy, a celebration unlike any ever known in all the worlds."

As if she were there already, Hadlay felt the welling of bliss, greater than she had ever felt, within her heart. She could smell the sweet scent of the flowers of N'de as if she wore them as a wreath, and for a moment, she saw herself clothed in glowing light, like the finest gown. Her eyes filled with tears of happiness, and oh, how she longed to put her arms around Sirach's neck and kiss the three twined rings on his forehead.

Again she felt his nudge against her palm, as if he too longed to hold her. He sighed. "But now, beloved, there is work to be done."

She smiled. "I'm ready, Sirach. I will not fail my people again—or you."

Sirach shook his gleaming mane, and all the colors of the rainbow rippled through it. "Of course you will fail, for you are only human. But you can never disappoint me, for I knew you, knew everything that you would ever do, long before you breathed. Always know, always trust, that I love you and that nothing can separate you from me, no matter how far your journey takes you."

She frowned. "Journey? But I must remain in Turris to help my people."

"The emperor will not permit it. You will not have a safe place to rest your head in Turris."

"How, then, will I warn the Ramash about the emperor and his plans?" She wanted to spread the truth quickly, before more of them could give their pledge.

Sirach tossed his mane. "You must trust me—cling to the key—for it is *my* work to reach your people. For you, I have another task."

Another task? But hadn't he promised that if she trusted him, he would help her free her people? "I want to help the Ramash, Sirach. It's my fault they believe him, my fault that so many are deceived."

"Some of them will be lost, even some you love—there is no help for it. I can reach only those who wish to be reached."

"But if I speak to them—"

"That is not your work. Will you do as I ask you?"

She started to protest again, but stopped when she heard the sound of Sirach's hoof striking stone.

"When will you learn that you must cling to the key? Without it, you'll do no one any good."

"I do trust you! It's just—"

There was a stern expression in his gaze. "You want your own way, even though you've seen where that will lead you."

Hadlay sighed. Why could he not see how responsible she felt? If she didn't at least try to help her people, she would bear the weight of every soul that was lost to the emperor's deception.

"Do you know best, beloved?" He asked the question gently, but the point of it was sharp. Hadlay chewed her lip. She still wanted to argue.

Sirach nickered, and it sounded a little like laughter. "Do not be stubborn, little love. Now, go and seek your family, for your work begins with them."

A man appeared in the cell's doorway. "The furmites have broken through. It appears they bored out through the Tower enclosure as well. We'll be with our families by evening's fall."

Nomish got to his feet. "We should go quickly before the passage is discovered." He gave a hand to Hadlay, pulling her up beside him.

Enheduana smiled, brushing a finger across Hadlay's cheek. "Farewell, friend of Sirach. With another son, I would have been glad to call you daughter."

"Are you not coming with us?"

"Sirach tells me I am needed here. Think how many enemies of Shungallu are sent to this place and how many may be won for N'de!"

"But Zêru—"

Enheduana laughed. "Even if Sirach would allow it, I am changed, and my blood would be poison to one such as he." Pausing, she quirked an eyebrow. "Perhaps it would be worth it to permit one final cut."

"Are you certain you wish to stay?" Nomish asked.

She nodded. "I have brought evil into the worlds, and I will gladly do what I can to defeat it."

Hadlay pulled her into a hug. "Be well, Enheduana!"

"And you, friend of Sirach."

Citna came and hugged the woman as well. "Thank you for all that you did for me when I was—" She looked at Hadlay and hesitated.

Hadlay touched her hand. "I am sorry for what I did to you, Citna. You did wrong me, but you did nothing to deserve what you endured in this place."

Citna shuffled. "All the time I was here . . . I found myself thinking about the things I did to you—more than you know. I was in the crowd at that purgation. I threw the stone that cut your cheek. I was raised all my life to hate Ramash. I believed you deserved to suffer, even though I didn't know what you had ever done wrong." She caught Hadlay's hand. "I am sorry as well."

Before Hadlay knew what was happening, the two of them were hugging. She could not quite overcome the strangeness of it, embracing an Oresed, but somehow it seemed right. She smiled. "You are my sister now."

A sniff called her attention to Ba'ar, whose face was red with restrained outrage.

Hadlay grinned at her. "You as well, Ba'ar. In Sirach, we are all family."

Ba'ar huffed, then started to retort. At the last moment, she thought better of it and turned and stalked away.

Nomish watched her leave, an amused twinkle in his eyes. Then he kissed Enheduana's cheek. "We should go now."

One by one, the initiates crawled through the newly bored tunnel. As they neared its end, they could see the sky above them blooming with the colors of the dawn. They were truly free.

ACKNOWLEDGMENTS

A great many people made it possible for me to write this book, which for various reasons took nearly a decade from first concept to the final draft. I fear that I may have forgotten someone who contributed over these many years; if I have, please know that it was not intentional.

First, always, I thank my Lord for his unending and much-needed grace, and the opportunity, again, to see a dream come true.

Many thanks to Chuck Missler, founder of Koinonia House, whose wonderful Bible studies at www.khouse.org introduced me to some of the wild ideas that went into this story. Also John Granger, whose books about the Harry Potter series started me thinking about Christian allegory.

I owe a debt of gratitude to all the people who've read this along the way and given invaluable feedback: my good friends Mariam Mazooji, Carolyn Chaw, Christi Hill, Pat Scholes, Larry Baden, Lucie Ulrich, Laurie A. Green, Ardyth DeBruyn, and all the wonderful critters at critiquecircle .com.

Olivier Lauffenburger and Lance B. Allred were invaluable in helping me with ancient Mesopotamian customs and the Akkadian language. Efrat Aviv helped me with some of the Hebrew.

Thanks to Dennis Hillman, Steve Barclift, Cat Hoort, Janyre Tromp, Jeff Gerke, Esther Sharpe, Dawn Anderson, Ryan Hill, Nick Richardson, Leah Mastee, and all the folks at Kregel for their help, support, and prayers.

And, finally, I thank my wonderful mother and the rest of my family and friends for their love, patience, and long-suffering support.

GLOSSARY OF AKKADIAN TERMS

Akkadian is the earliest attested semitic language, spoken in Babylon, Ur, and Chaldea, and extinct long before the first speakers of Latin or Pictish walked the earth. This fascinating language was rediscovered in 1767, and through diligent study, though no one has heard a native speaker, scholars have been able to discern how the words were pronounced. There are treasure troves of Akkadian tablets, containing everything from the Enûma Eliš to a student's lament about his boring day in school to a good recipe for T'rru bird stew. I include the terms and their literal translations here for those who might be curious.

Amâtîsha kinnâni – Confirm her words to me

Ana bît kîli shukshissi – Take her to the prison

Ana bît nuhatimmi shûlîshi – Take her up to the kitchen

Ana hurshi shûrissunûti – Bring them down to the kitchen storeroom

Ana urush malki shûlânni – Bring me up to the prince's room

Bêl galli deki – Call up the lord of demons

Bil – Carry

Bu'ish – Stir

Butuq – Slice

Dûkâshu – Kill him

Elish bilshunuti – Carry them up

Espâ – Gather

Ibrîsha mushsherâ – Set them free

Igigi, bilâshi – Igigi, carry her

Igigi! Ibrî Hadlay hitnâ – (to one) Igigi! Protect the friends of Hadlay

Igigi, Hadlay hitnâ – (to one) Igigi, protect Hadlay

Igigi, hitnâshunûti – (to many) Igigi, protect them

Kizrassa shuddâ – Pull her braid

Kubussu leqâ – Take his hat

Kussânni – Cool me

Lêssa mahsâ – Slap her

Lêt kalîshunu mahsâ – Slap them all

Misâ – Clean

Mušâtsiat – She who delivers

Nâmara idna – Give me the mirror

Namzaqa bilâni – Bring me the key

Naparki – Stop

Naptî – Open yourself

Nikkassî epush – Balance accounts

Pu'is – Smite

Qanna sha kaspi ana talbultîsha litukkapû – Let a silver fringe be sewn to her
     garment

Qâssa qulâ – Burn her hand

Qulu! Qulânni – Burn! Burn me

Quttâ – Destroy

Sha itbû kullimâniâti – Show us what happened

Shisâ – Summon

Shutur – Write

Siddâ – Melt down

Sikpâshu – (to one) Push him away

Sikpâshunûti – (to many) Push them away

Simmasha tibbâ – Treat her wound

Tabalshû-ma rihis – Go off and be rinsed

Tûra – Come back

Turrershu – Shake him